TREE OF LIBERTY

TRILOGY

Lawrence L. Allen

DEDICATION

This book is dedicated to my parents, Louis and Kaleope Allen, whose 1980 trip to China inspired me to find my career path, and whose love and devotion to their children is the foundation of all that is good and meaningful in my life.

CONTENTS

BOOK I: LABYRINTH

BOOK II: ASCENSION

BOOK III: REVOLUTION

ABOUT THE AUTHOR

Doolittle Raid

In memory of the quarter million Chinese civilians murdered by the Imperial Japanese Army in retaliation for China's participation in the Doolittle Raid on Japan—including providing aid, protection, and safe passage to the American air crews.

Flying Tigers

Blood chit issued to the American Volunteer Group Flying Tigers by the Chinese Nationalist Government Commission for Aeronautical Affairs, circa 1942.

"This foreign person has come to China to help in the war effort. Soldiers and civilians, one and all, should rescue, protect, and provide him with medical care."—Blood Chit Translation

BOOK I: LABYRINTH

CHAPTER 1

The aromatic brew of eggs, sausage, and coffee rolling through the airplane cabin brought Curtiss to, like smelling salts. He gasped his way to consciousness, only to recoil, groaning, from it.

The severity of the ringing in his ears and throbbing pain in his head bespake the achievement of a new low with this hangover.

He eased open his eyes. Finding the cabin mercifully darkened, he reached from beneath the blanket that had been placed over him at some point during the flight and, with great care, raised the window shade. The fading, orange and yellow light of the setting sun was bearable, and he found himself able to appreciate how strikingly it backlit the dark volcanic mountain on the horizon.

"A lady's breast as she is lying on her back."

These words were intoned to his back in a smooth, Southern American drawl.

"They say Mt. Fuji there looks like a woman's breast as she is laying on her back."

Curtiss gently swiveled to the middle-aged man sitting next to him, smiling a knowing smile his way.

"Do you see it?" the man asked.

Encased in the surrealism of the moment, Curtiss stared, dumbstruck, at the man. Was he dreaming this? Should he answer?

"Will Saunderson," the man said, extending his hand. "I fly this route about five or six times a year."

"Curtiss Bradley," he replied in what was left of his voice, swallowing hard and then clearing his throat as he shook Saunderson's hand.

"Damn, boy!" Saunderson said, reeling from him. "Did you drain the whole liquor store last night?"

Curtiss struggled to sit up straight in his seat. "It sure feels like I did."

"Well, you may be a young man, but you can't keep drinking and survive these trips, Curt, I'll tell you that. Believe me. I've been doing it for nearly five years now: day and a half in Seoul, day and a half in Taipei, day and a half in Manila, day and a half in Hong Kong, and a quick stop in Tokyo on the way back. Room service and in bed no earlier or later than 10:00 pm, no matter what time zone you're in. And above all, no drinking. That's how you get through."

The cabin lit up and Curtiss winced at the glare. The flight attendants began their breakfast routine, periodically emerging and retreating behind the galley curtain. Curtiss and Saunderson each took a steaming hot towel when presented to them with plastic tongs by the flight attendant.

The road-warrior businessman gazed thoughtfully at Curtiss. "I'm in auto parts. What line of business brings you to Asia?"

Curtiss placed the hot towel over his face and laid back heavily into his seat. He could bear the light, but why should he? "I'm not . . . I mean, I'm not on a business trip."

"Well this is a fine way to start a vacation, I suppose."

Curtiss sorted through his jumbled, piecemeal recollection of the past twenty-four hours and placed it into order. Staggering to a taxi in Midtown Manhattan at dawn. Withdrawing cash from an ATM on an empty city street. Buying a round-trip ticket from New York City to Taipei, Taiwan at the airport ticket counter. Boarding the flight and boosting his waning buzz with a parade of tiny bottles of booze.

"I'm not on a vacation, either."

"Well there's got to be a good reason you'd voluntarily get on a twelve-and-a-half-hour flight, son. You don't look like a soldier to me. Are you a student? An English teacher?"

"I'm a bond trader with Drexel Burnham Lambert," Curtiss exhaled, enjoying slowly melting under the warmth of the hot towel. Now if he could just not talk. But, though he was becoming irked by Saunderson's questions, his rural Pennsylvanian upbringing mandated that he remain polite. "I'm looking for someone."

"Well now . . . " Saunderson sounded satisfied to have extracted information that he could use to prolong their conversation. "That'd be a girl, I'd bet."

Further annoyed that he'd been pegged so easily, Curtiss didn't respond. And then a flight attendant bailed him out by appearing to ask if they would like the Western or Korean breakfast.

"Korean," said Saunderson. "So, are you staying in Seoul or going further, Curt?"

Curtiss reluctantly removed the towel from his face and sat up. "I'll have the Western breakfast, thank you." To Saunderson's question, he answered, "Taiwan."

"Taipei, Taiwan: the city is a mess, but the food is good. Real friendly people, too."

Curtiss cautiously took the half-full cup of lukewarm instant coffee from the flight attendant and struggled to find a place for it on his crowded food tray, while Saunderson peeled back the foil covering on his main course and contemplated his prefabricated meal.

Just when Curtiss was thinking they'd moved on, his fellow traveler resumed his third degree. "So, your girl is from Taipei, I take it?"

Curtiss paused, uncomfortable with himself for not knowing such a simple fact about a woman important enough to him to have entirely upended his life for. "She's from Taiwan. I don't know where exactly."

Saunderson grinned at him. "Well, there are only twenty million people in Taiwan, but I'm sure you'll find her. Love conquers all, right?" Saunderson propped himself up in his seat and Curtiss braced himself for the lecture that he sensed was at hand. "You know, it's none of my business but you need to be careful, son. Things are different out here. Especially when it comes to our 'Romeo and Juliet' notions about romance. Folks out here approach life different than you and me. You know, east is east and west is west, and all that. There's a reason we say Asians are inscrutable. It is hard for us to get a reading on what people out here are thinking. And they aren't so open about sharing it, either."

Despite his weariness with the man, Curtiss couldn't help but recall how utterly poleaxed he'd been when Jacqueline, his girlfriend of six months and the presumed love of his life, had picked up without warning and left New York for Taiwan less than two weeks earlier.

"Most of the folks that you're likely to meet out here are the survivors, Curt. And family always comes first. They'll make sacrifices for the good of the family that you and I just wouldn't be willing to make. Or at least would never have to, not in our privileged world."

Was that what this was? Jacqueline left him for . . . cultural reasons? Just like that, Curtiss's fevered, single-minded (and, yes, drunken) plan to find her and convince her of his worthiness was thrown askew. Damn, doubt. Why did Saunderson have to raise that doubt?

"I've seen a lot of east-west marriages, and I supposed most of them probably work out, but it can't be easy. You marry a girl out here, Curt, you might as well adopt her whole family, because you'll be bringing half of them back to America sooner or later. And you'll never know if she really loves you, or she just needed you for what you could do for her and her family."

"That's awfully cynical."

"Maybe, but in my experience that's just the way it is." Saunderson leveled his eyes at Curtiss. "You take those GIs overseas: young, dumb and full of . . . " He made a rolling hand gesture to indicate that his Southern gentlemanliness was checking his use of profanity. "You know what I mean. And these girls know it, too. Hell, most of those boys, all they know is kissing their high school sweethearts under the bleachers. All those girls have on their minds is managing their reputations, not looking out for their entire families."

Curtiss wondered if euthanasia for its namesake would mean he wouldn't be arrested in Asia for the mercy killing of Saunderson— merciful for Curtiss, since it would end his own suffering. Was there enough overhead storage remaining to conceal this man's corpse?

"But these streetwise bar girls out here are on the prowl for some gullible young ticket to America—"

"She's no bar girl," Curtiss said tersely. "She's a grad student at NYU. And apparently her father's loaded."

"And I'm sure that's true," Saunderson said quickly, as though sensing that he had gone too far. "Look, Curt, this is 1988, and I'm no racist. And this is about more than just money and opportunity. It's about culture and upbringing. These are old cultures out here, with traditions that stretch back thousands of years. It's just tough to

4

beat that, son. That's all I'm saying."

"I'll do fine," Curtiss said, turning his shoulder to him. Against all odds, Saunderson appeared to take the hint.

As Curtiss watched the airplane's wing slice through the fuchsia sky, his mind drifted back seven years and settled in under the Milton Hershey High School bleachers with luscious, writhing Debbie Carey. "Hershey is a small town, Curt," she said, pushing him away in half-hearted protest. "I've got my reputation to think about," were her very words.

Bastard, Saunderson.

Curtiss took stock of where he was and what he had with him. His tie was nowhere to be found; his passport was in the breast pocket of his suit jacket, which was also stuffed with a wad of cash.

It was at this point that he realized he honestly couldn't recall whether he had a bag with him or not.

He waited until all the other passengers had disembarked before he checked the overhead bins for a bag that he could recognize. All the bins were empty, except for his lone overcoat that was hanging halfway out of a bin. Curtiss slipped it on as he walked off the plane.

* * *

Kimpo Airport in Seoul Korea had all the style of a state driver's license office. His connecting boarding pass showed flight NW021 departing SEL at 18:15 and arriving TPE at 20:30. It was only 4:30 pm in Seoul.

Realizing that he had a wait on his hands, Curtiss followed signs to the transit waiting area, where he bought a cup of instant coffee and made himself as comfortable as possible in a row of orange plastic chairs among the dozen or so fellow travelers dispersed throughout the room. He set his watch to the local time, flipped through the unmarked pages in his passport, glanced occasionally at the unfamiliar images of Korea on the television at the far end of the room, but mostly watched the steady in-flow of passengers who joined him in his traveler's purgatory.

Curtiss made eye contact with a young Asian woman who gave him a broad savvy smile. He reflexively averted his eyes then looked back when he saw an American soldier saunter up to her and put his arms around her. The soldier was easily a quarter taller than her and bent over to give her a kiss that she requited from the tips of her toes, her thin, dark arms wrapped around his thick, white neck. While still in his embrace she caught Curtiss watching and shot him an impish grin that caused him to nervously look away again and, against his will, think about what Saunderson had said earlier.

An hour later, easily a third of the transit area was filled with young Asian ladies and their GI boy-toys in tow, all apparently oblivious to everything except the prospect of the next time they were alone together in a hotel room with their attentive new brides.

When Curtiss's flight was called he walked to the gate, which he found mobbed with passengers in no discernable line or order. He decided to wait until the crush of impatient people subsided and only the last trickle of the more patient passengers remained. He had a ticket, didn't he? His seat would surely be there for him.

Shortly after the plane touched down at the Taipei Airport, the impatient passengers sprang back into action, unbuckling their seat belts and some even standing up and removing their bags from the overhead bins while the airplane was still slowing to taxiing speed before heading to the gate. Though Curtiss was content to wait until the plane had stopped at the gate and the fasten seat belt sign was turned off, the passenger beside him wasn't. He sidestepped between Curtiss's knees and the seat in front of him to join the fray unfolding in the aisles, stepping on Curtiss's feet in the process.

In the immigration hall, under the scrutiny of armed soldiers positioned at the four corners of the room, both the patient *and* impatient passengers waited in well-formed lines leading to each open counter. The hall was nearly empty when he reached the counter. He handed his passport to the immigration officer, who flipped through the pages, first from front to back, then back to front. He looked up from his passport and announced: "You have no visa."

"Uh, I didn't know that I needed one."

"All visitors to the Republic of China are required to have a visa."

Queasiness seized the pit of his stomach as he contemplated the words "Republic of China." Had he boarded the wrong flight in Seoul? Was he in China?

Frozen in place, heart jumping in his chest, he was imagining he was going to be hauled off to some communist gulag for his infraction when he glanced first at the badge of the immigration officer that read "The Republic of China," then up at the large, mosaic-tile tourist map of the island of Taiwan on the wall behind him. It was then that he recalled a conversation he'd had with Jacqueline months earlier, when she explained how her father fled Mainland China with the Nationalist Army of the *Republic of China* to Taiwan when the communist armies of the *People's* Republic of China won the Chinese Civil War in the years just after the end of World War II.

Curtiss collected himself. "I'm sorry, nobody told me that I needed a visa. Not at JFK, not in Seoul."

The immigration officer raised his hand like a schoolboy requesting permission to speak, attracting a more senior-looking officer to the immigration counter. The two officers began speaking in Chinese in hushed voices.

Finally the senior officer lowered his head, closed his eyes for a moment, took a deep breath, then looked at Curtiss. "You shouldn't have been allowed to board the flight in Seoul without a visa," he calmly explained in English. "You will have to go back to Seoul." Glancing at his watch, he sighed. "The last flight for Seoul left an hour ago."

"I'm here now, so can't I just get a visa here?" Receiving no response from the immigration officers, he volunteered: "Maybe I can go to the U.S. Embassy tomorrow morning and they can help me get a visa?" Both immigration officers stared blankly at Curtiss.

"There is no U.S. Embassy in Taiwan, I'm afraid."

Curtiss turned to see a mature Western lady smiling at him from her place before the immigration counter marked "Diplomatic Channel." She went on in her Russian-accented voice: "The United States hasn't had an embassy here in Taiwan since it recognized Red China on the Mainland in 1979, and dropped formal diplomatic relations with the Republic of China. It's a sensitive issue here," she added.

She was a lovely, serene woman with pure white hair pulled into a bun held in place with a pair of black-lacquered chopsticks. Her regal bearing and dress—she wore a black, almost Victorian-style dress, its high lace collar clasped together with a white, oval scrimshaw pendent—brought to mind nineteenth-century portraits of European aristocrats that Curtiss had seen hanging in museums.

Under the influence of her calm, steady smile, Curtiss felt his frazzled nerves being soothed. When she said, "Why don't you come over here, dear, and we'll see what we can do for you?" He practically floated to her side. Though it was in Curtiss's nature to be embarrassed to require the aid of little old ladies, this wasn't just any little old lady—and he was in way over his head.

Curtiss's noble guardian angel spoke in Chinese to the immigration officers, several of whom had now gathered behind the counter. The senior officer nodded to his colleagues and turned a stern look upon Curtiss. "We will give you a temporary permit."

"Hsieh Hsieh," the Victorian lady said, thanking the immigration officers.

"You must go to the Taipei Central Police Station first thing tomorrow morning," the senior officer said as he handed him his passport. "Apply for an emergency visitor's visa and register a temporary place of residence."

Curtiss assured him he would, and then thanked the woman for rescuing him. "I don't know what I would have done without you," he added. "I'm Curtiss Bradley."

"That's all right, dear. I'm Sonya." One moment her warm, knowing eyes were scanning his face and the next Curtiss was taken aback by the sudden, inexplicably penetrating burst of intensity beaming from them. And then she turned it off, like switching off a heat lamp. "You'd better do exactly what the officer told you to do and go to the police station tomorrow morning. They are serious about that kind of thing here, as you can see."

They walked together toward the baggage claim, Curtiss wondering what could have explained that sudden blaze of interest in his face. It was as though she'd recognized him, but he was quite certain he'd never seen her before now.

"Is there anything that I can do to help you?" he asked. "Do you have any luggage?"

"Well, I do have just a couple of checked bags, dear . . ."

Curtiss was pleased he could in some small way return the favor. The baggage carousel was turning round, but was still empty. He excused himself and made his way over to the currency exchange counter to change a few hundred dollars—enough, he felt, to tide him over for a while. The small bookstore next to the currency exchange window was closing and Curtiss noticed a pocket Wade-Giles Chinese-English translation dictionary on the wire-rack display that the shop attendant was pulling from the threshold into the store.

He bought a copy, stuffed it into his pocket, and walked back to Sonya.

"So, what do your bags look like?"

"They are a matched set, dark brown with a pink ribbon tied to the handle of each."

While waiting for her bags to appear Curtiss pulled the Taiwan currency from his pocket and noticed a pleasantly smiling man on the front of a five hundred New Taiwan Dollar bill. "Who was he?"

"Oh, he was Chiang Kai-shek, dear: The president of the Republic of China. Madame Chiang, his wife, is a lovely lady. She is from a prominent family in China, the Song family. She has exquisite taste, is a patron of the arts, and quite an accomplished painter herself, as a matter of fact." She paused, contemplating her next comment as a schoolteacher preparing a lesson, then went on to explain that Madam Chiang was a special friend of the United States and had appeared before the U.S. Congress on several occasions, the most famous time being when she asked for American assistance during the war. Sonya paused once again to measure her commentary and concluded: "She lives in New York City now. Pity we don't see her back here very often anymore."

Curtiss was convinced that Sonya did not mean her last comment figuratively. By the way she spoke about Chiang Kai-shek and Madame Chiang, it was clear to him that she knew them both personally, but he was too polite to ask.

There were five suitcases in all within Sonya's matched set, which Curtiss stacked in a near-perfect pyramid shape on the luggage cart atop the largest one: a steamer trunk.

"Don't you have any luggage, Curtiss?" Sonya asked with some degree of surprise.

Curtiss only replied that he didn't. It would take too long to explain why he had left a Midtown Manhattan restaurant at 5:30 the previous morning, gone to JFK airport, and bought a round-trip ticket for the next flight leaving for Taiwan. Maybe he couldn't explain it at all, beyond simply saying that he loved a girl and couldn't bear the thought of giving her up. He could almost imagine confessing such a thing to someone like Sonya . . . but he didn't.

They passed unimpeded through customs, the officers there reflexively nodding Sonya through as if they'd done so dozens of times before. As they made their way toward the arrival area, Sonya explained that there was an airport shuttle bus that dropped off at several points throughout the city. She recommended he get off at the "Jen Ai" road stop, owing to its proximity to the national police station, and choose from any number of small hotels there.

Through the cacophony of Chinese-speaking voices in the crowded arrival area, Curtiss heard the urgently spoken English words, "Madam Sonya, my apologies, please." A thin middle-aged man dressed in a black suit, white shirt, and thin black tie shuffled excitedly over to them, his Adam's apple rising and falling as he spoke, unimpeded by the size-thirteen collar of the shirt that hung loosely around his scrawny, size-nine neck. "The traffic was very bad and I couldn't find commander Wen in time to let me through security to meet you at the gate." He then shoved Curtiss out of the way and took over the luggage cart without even looking at him.

"That's all right, Mr. Kao," Sonya said with her calming smile. "This young man here helped me with my bags."

Curtiss turned and smiled at Kao, but Kao seemed to remain unaware of his presence. With Kao leading the way, the three of them walked out of the terminal to the passenger pick-up area outside, where Kao opened the rear passenger door to a late-seventies Cadillac.

"Don't forget to go to the police station," Sonya said as she slid into the car. "First thing tomorrow morning, now." Though her comments made him feel like a child being reminded to wash behind his ears, he was saddened to say goodbye to Sonya. Not only was she a genuinely fascinating person, she knew the local language and her way around, which would be a great help in finding Jacqueline.

Nonetheless, Curtiss's ego had taken a bit of drubbing under her charge. As he watched her car pull away, he found himself looking to being an independent man on his own again.

He rubbed the stubble that had emerged on his chin, pulled his hair back, and took a deep breath of Taipei, Taiwan evening air. The thick humidity blunted his mind even as it poured like sludge into his lungs. Though the temperature was on the cool side, he began to sweat, as if his body was struggling to find a way to cope with a climate so dramatically different from the dry airplane air and crisp, early spring New York weather. He felt as if he were treading another planet, not just another continent.

* * *

Curtiss boarded the Airport-City shuttle bus, which immediately plunged into near-total darkness when it exited the terminal for the expressway. At first the darkness was broken only by the occasional street lamp, orange flame from a refinery, or passing car. They were evidently well outside the city. Curtiss saw a lighted road sign with universal symbols that indicated the services available at the next exit: a wrench, a pay phone, a gas pump, and a rice bowl with a pair of chopsticks standing beside it.

As the bus approached the outskirts of Taipei, lights began to appear with ever-increasing frequency and variety. Before long the bus was awash in lights of all kinds: car and scooter lights, street and traffic lights, spotlights on billboards and decorative lights on bridge overpasses, office building lights and on the taller ones flashing red aircraft beacons. And, of course, thousands of neon signs bent into the complex shapes of Chinese characters for as far as the eye could see. Either low-hanging clouds or smog served as a palate upon which Taipei's kaleidoscope of light painted rippling multicolored bands that stretched across the night sky.

The bus made its first stop at the Brother Hotel then continued to lurch and weave its way through the Taipei city traffic until it approached its third stop and a recorded voice announced: "Hsia I Chan Shih Jen Ai Lu, the next stop is Jen Ai Road." Curtiss helped a mother and her young daughter take their heavy suitcase from the bus's in-cabin luggage rack and placed it on the street.

"Hsieh Hsieh," the little girl said, smiling shyly at Curtiss. Her mother smiled too and nodded her head in gratitude.

"You're welcome." Curtiss recognized the little girl's words of thanks from Sonya's conversation with the immigration officers.

As the bus drove away, Curtiss licked his lips, detecting not only the flavor of the bus's swirling diesel exhaust, but the fumes emitted by the World War II army surplus two-stroke outboard boat motors at his middle-school summer camp. Like that, even though he imagined he couldn't be further away from them on the planet, he was transported to the rolling, lake-studded hills of Central Pennsylvania, where he had learned to repair outboard motors as part of his vocational training at the Milton Hershey School's summer camp. The odor had to be coming from the countless two-stroke scooters buzzing up and down Jen Ai Road and darting in and out of the many small, capillary-like alleyways feeding that major artery.

With no hotel in sight, Curtiss picked a direction and began walking under the thick, mature trees that lined the broad, multi-lane boulevard. Most of the alleys were choked with cars parked halfway up on their narrow sidewalks. Tangled bunches of wires and cables were strung along the sides of the buildings and across the alleyways like popcorn strings on a Christmas tree.

In one alley he saw a sign in English: "George's Palace – Motel." It amused him that someone would name an establishment stuck down a disheveled alleyway a palace, or for that matter a motel, since his image of a motel was a one-story building located on a lonely highway. He decided to have a look and stepped around the overflowing garbage cans and dodged streams of dripping water as he made his way to the front door.

An artificial whistling-bird sound started up when Curtiss opened the door, then stopped when the door shut behind him. He found himself in a painted concrete corridor that had been converted into the motel's reception area. Weirdly, it smelled of the Greek Orthodox Church near Detroit's Greektown to which his University of Michigan classmate, Jimmy Yamandakos, had once taken him to attend a wedding.

But this smell came from burning incense on a small, red-lit religious altar mounted at shoulder height on the wall behind the reception desk. In front of a red-faced, ancient warrior-style idol on the altar sat a bowl containing a neat mound of rice with a couple of pieces of yellow-skinned chicken perched on top. It was accompanied by a plate of some kind of cut fruit that was shaped like a starfish, and a bottle of clear alcohol with a half-full stemmed shot glass standing next to it.

A slender man emerged into the corridor from a doorway beneath the concrete stairs that led to the second floor. He was wearing a hairnet, a silk shirt unbuttoned to reveal gold chains around his neck, bellbottom jeans, and platform shoes. His sideburns traveled down his sunken cheeks to his bony jawline. A thin moustache dipped at both ends as it extended past his thin lips, from which hung a burning cigarette.

"You need room?"

"Are you George?"

"You bet. And this is my palace. You're American, right?"

Curtiss nodded cautiously.

"I lived in America for a few years," George said proudly. "Saw KC and the Sunshine Band at Studio 54. Fantastic!" He then turned serious. "You people don't like Chinese." He wagged his finger at Curtiss. "You live in nice houses in the suburbs and you crowd us Chinese into Chinatown in New York and San Francisco." Laughing a chain-smoker's leathery laugh, he revealed the full extent of his red-stained teeth. "Okay . . . " George said, slipping behind the reception counter. "You a student?"

"No."

"You a teacher?"

"Nope."

"And you don't look like no senior citizen to me. So, no discount for you. But, for my American friend, you get my number-one room: the Presidential Suite. NT Dollar five hundred."

Curtiss quickly did the math and figured twenty bucks American was a fair price for a presidential suite. He handed George one of his 500 NT Dollar bills.

"Okay, let's go." George grinned as he took a key off the key rack and Curtiss turned to follow him up the stairs. Though he had low expectations for what he would find upstairs, Curtiss was so tired that he didn't care where he laid his head that night.

"We get a lot of foreign students here. English teachers, too. Businessmen all stay at the Lai Lai Sheraton. And you've got no luggage, so I don't want to know what you are doing here."

Curtiss stumbled several times on the way up the stairs. Was he still drunk, or just exhausted? By the fourth floor landing, he was seriously winded. "How many floors is this building?"

"Four. But I added a fifth one last year. So your room is brand new." The final flight of stairs was steep and narrow and made of diamond plate sheet metal. "Be careful when you come down these stairs, especially at night," George cautioned.

They stepped up into a corridor made from prefabricated insulated white plastic panels held together with aluminum strips and screws, and lit with hanging fluorescent lights. Doors, numbered one through seven, lined one side of the corridor and George thrust the key into the lock on the door marked "1." Inside, George flipped the light switch and an overhead fluorescent light blinked to life revealing a Spartan, but clean, room.

"If you need hot water for tea there is a water heater at the end of the hall. If you need ice, go to Alaska. Checkout is at twelve." George handed Curtiss the key. "My number-one room," he laughed, as he closed the door behind him.

Curtiss fell backward onto the bed fully clothed, closed his eyes, and within a minute was sound asleep.

At 10:30 pm he was awakened by a knock at the door. He opened the door to find squat man at his threshold babbling at him.

"Wait a minute, wait a minute." Curtiss reached into his pocket for his translation dictionary and gestured for the man to repeat himself, slowly. "Yao Bu, what now?"

As though talking to a child, the man said, "Ni...Yao Pu Yao...Hsiao Chieh?"

Curtiss thumbed through the dictionary: Ni...you, Yao...want, Pu Yao...don't want, Hsiao Chieh...young lady.

Seeing from Curtiss's face that he understood, the man smiled eagerly and began rocking up onto the balls of his feet, then back onto his heels, while swinging his stubby arms back and forth.

"Not unless you can find the one I am looking for," Curtiss said as he closed the door in the man's face.

* * *

The next morning Curtiss found himself still unsteady on the stairs and looked to find that they were unusually narrow for his size-twelve feet, and somewhat shallow as well, which accounted for his stumbling on them the night before. He landed on the first floor to find George tending the reception counter with his mound of jet black hair, now liberated from its hairnet, combed straight back without a single hair out of place.

"Disco George, the little man who lives under the stairs." Curtiss scowled at George. "Last night some guy came knocking on my door asking me if I wanted . . . company." He cracked a sardonic smile. "I was sleeping, George."

"Hey, a guy comes to a motel with no suitcase. I thought you might need a little . . . company."

"What I needed was sleep."

Following the immigration officer's instruction to register a temporary place of residence, he asked George for a business card. Even if he didn't stay there another night, at least he'd have an address for the paperwork.

As he took the card from George's hand, he detected a slight hint of a foul odor—sewage?

"How do I get to the Taipei Central Police Station? Can I walk it?"

"In trouble with the cops, eh?" George looked sideways at him. "Yeah, you can walk there. I'll show you."

As he followed George to the front door, the foul odor grew in intensity. When George opened the door, they found a man with what looked like a rolling stainless steel hotdog stand set up just outside. From it, a column of steam billowed from a boiling pot of red-colored liquid with square chunks of something floating inside. He'd found the source of the odor.

"Go to Jen Ai Road and make a right," George said. "Then two blocks down, make a left. It will be on your right." George dramatically gestured each turn of his verbal directions with his hand.

Unable to stand it any longer, Curtiss pinched his nostrils. "Ugh, what is that stuff?"

"Ch'ou Tou Fu. Stinky tofu. It is delicious."

"You mean people actually eat that?"

"Hey, don't knock it until you tried it, man. That's what we think of your stinky cheese. Tastes much better than it smells, right?" George grinned. "Really, it's good. You should try it."

"Sorry." Curtiss smiled skeptically. "Sayonara, George."

"What? That's Japanese, not Chinese. Do I look Japanese to you?" George laughed as Curtiss began walking away down the alley. When he reached Jen Ai Road he turned back to see the stinky tofu vendor handing George a blue plastic bag that sagged under the weight of its contents, and George turn and reenter his Palace.

What a character, Curtiss thought, then panned up to the fifth floor and saw that he had spent the previous night in a prefab, spare garage-like structure perched atop the four-story walk-up. Only for as long as it takes to find one lady on an island of twenty million people.

As he walked, a 7-Eleven store appeared before him and he walked in. On the counter he saw shriveled hot dogs rolling on an automated warmer—just like home—but the large Crockpot next to it with eggs boiling in an inky black liquid was something he'd never seen in a 7-Eleven, or anywhere else for that matter. There was no coffee dispenser in sight. "Coffee?" he asked the cashier. The cashier pointed to a clear plastic warming stand on the counter, which contained several shelves stocked with tomato paste-sized cans labeled "Mr. Brown's Coffee." Curtiss took one from the warmer, paid the cashier, stood just outside the 7-Eleven, and slowly sipped at the can of coffee. It was pretty terrible, but coffee nonetheless.

Taipei looked quite different by day. Though the city was remarkably green, the air pollution was palpable, the result no doubt of the traffic maelstrom that was playing out before him, in particular the scooters swarming the streets. Dozens of them weaved and flowed forward between the cars and busses queued in long lines at intersections like balls falling through the obstacle-studded face of a pachinko machine. One scooter had an entire family aboard: a father, a toddler standing on the footplate between the father's legs, and a preteen on the seat sandwiched between her father and mother, who appeared to be well into her third trimester with another child. To Curtiss's untrained eye there wasn't even organized chaos on the streets, but it seemed to work fine for the people of Taipei.

Emerging from the police station with a one-month visitor's visa in his passport Curtiss found that a light rain had descended upon the city. As far as he could see, scooter riders wearing the same yellow plastic rain gear stitched brightly colored horizontal threads into the fluid, tartan-like fabric of Taipei's landscape.

Curtiss found George mopping up shoe prints from the floor of the entrance to his palace. "Hey Bradley, back so soon?"

"What can I say, you keep a clean place and you are conveniently located."

"Another satisfied customer!" George exclaimed as he took Curtiss's 500 NT Dollar bill.

"Do you know a good place to get a meal around here?" When George grinned in a way not unlike he did when he informed Curtiss that he would be staying in his presidential suite, Curtiss added: "And no stinky anything, okay, George?"

"Sure. You foreigners all seem to like the loud family restaurant. Down the alley one block, on the right."

A remarkably appetizing smell emanated from the restaurant as Curtiss stepped in onto a raft of jumbled cardboard boxes that had been broken and laid flat to prevent people from slipping on the wet floor. The busy restaurant's décor had all the warmth and comfort of a butcher shop. One entire wall was composed of a collection of fish tanks holding live fish and crustaceans, some Curtiss couldn't even recognize. Beside one of the tanks, a patron pointing to an albino trout was directing a waitress holding a net. The waitress quickly dipped the net into the tank, expertly netting the fish, then presented it, writhing and gaping, to the patron for his approval while droplets of water flew in every direction. He nodded and the waitress whisked the fish toward the back of the restaurant and disappeared into the kitchen.

Another waitress with menu in hand walked Curtiss to a round table that was covered with the detritus of a well-had Chinese meal: little piles of well-chewed bones and fragmented crab shells; used plates; bowls with chopsticks spanning their mouths; overflowing ashtrays; and bottle caps that were separated from their spent, green, malt liquor-sized beer bottles held in a wire carrier on the floor.

"Non-smoking, please?" Curtiss shouted as politely as possible to the waitress over the roar of voices that reverberated off the white-tiled walls of the restaurant. The waitress just smiled and shrugged.

A skinny boy wearing an apron scurried over with a bus tray, placed it on one of the orange-colored plastic stools that surrounded the table, and quickly swept everything into it. After he'd wiped the table with a wet, somewhat clean rag, Curtiss sat down and flipped through the grease-stained picture menu, which had no English, in search of something that looked familiar. He looked at the waitress, then pointed to a dish that looked like one of his favorite Szechwan dishes: Kung P'ao chicken.

"Kung P'ao Chi Ting!" the waitress screamed over the din of the restaurant.

"Kung P'ao Chi Ting!" echoed another waitress near the window to the kitchen.

"Kung P'ao Chi Ting!" repeated a muffled male voice from within the kitchen.

Curtiss was startled at first, then amused by this verbal relay race with his order. He then cautiously pointed to a spicy-looking tofu dish: "This isn't stinky . . . "

"Ma P'u Tou Fu!" screamed the waitress.

"Ma P'u Tou Fu!" echoed the waitress near the kitchen.

"Ma P'u Tou Fu!" repeated the voice from the kitchen.

It was at this point that he made a mental note to ask George if he called the restaurant the loud family restaurant because it was run by a family with the surname Loud, or if it was because the family that ran it was loud.

The waitress said something in Chinese, repeated it once, then smiled, flipped through the menu that he held in his hands, and pointed to a picture of white rice in a rice bowl. He nodded that he did want rice to the waitress and smiled back.

"It sure is loud in here, isn't it?" a voice said in perfect Midwestern-American English.

Curtiss turned to see a bespectacled, studious-looking Chinese youth sitting at the table behind him and agreed that yes, it certainly was.

"Very Chinese, you know. It is, like, there is a competition at each table to see who can be the loudest."

Though Curtiss doubted what the young man was telling him, he could see no evidence to the contrary. The young man then explained the science behind loud restaurants, citing studies conducted in America that have shown that loud restaurants draw in more people because people innately understand that busy places have good food, and that loud sound vibrations actually stimulate appetite and that people eat more and faster in loud restaurants.

"Of course the Chinese had that all figured out thousands of years ago, well before Western science," the young man said, smiling with pride. "I'm Marty Tung." He held out his hand and they shook. "What are you doing here? We don't see many foreigners in this part of Taipei; not ones wearing a suit, anyway."

"I'm looking for someone."

The waitress placed a steaming hot plate of diced chicken and a bowl of white rice in front of Curtiss. He pulled the disposable chopsticks apart, rubbed them together to scrape off any burrs and took a bite of the diced chicken. He had guessed right: it was Kung P'ao chicken, but better than he had ever tasted.

"My parents have been sending me back to Taiwan for Chinese language summer school ever since I was a little kid."

"You look a little old for that now," Curtiss said as he paused between wolfing down the diced chicken and rice.

"Hey man, I'm a junior at MIT," Marty said, laughing. "But my parents are a pain. They didn't want me wasting my spring break having fun in Florida with all my buddies. Nope, not Martin. They send me here now hoping that I will find a nice Chinese girl to marry."

The Ma P'u Tou Fu arrived and Curtiss spooned some into his rice bowl, picked up the bowl and shoveled the delectable contents into his mouth with his chopsticks—efficiently enough, though somewhat less skillfully than the other patrons.

"Meeting girls here is easy, man," Marty said, cracking a big smile. "Hey, all I've got to do is let my U.S. passport pop out of my breast pocket and I'll never be lonely in Taiwan, you know what I mean?"

Curtiss recalled his conversation with Saunderson on the airplane. "Aren't you worried about them wanting you only for what you can do for them and their family?"

"Are you talking about love? Hey, come on," Marty giggled, then stared up beyond the ceiling. "Right now I should be hanging out in Daytona Beach watching buxom blonds flashing the crowd." He frowned. "Instead, I'm back here . . . again. Meeting this family's daughter and that family's daughter. I mean, they are real sweet and everything, but hey, most of these girls don't even speak English. How am I going to bring them back to the States?"

Marty's buoyant personality evaporated in a wince of despair. Before Curtiss could think of something consoling to say to him, he bounced back with an eye-scrunching smile: "But hey, silicone blondes will just have to wait, right? Besides, they are a bit cliché . . . I guess. You know what the propensity for Asian men seeking out blond westerners is called, don't you? The 'Asian Man's Overbite,'" Marty said, laughing. He then repeated the word "overbite" while shaking his head, at once amused and offended. "Yeah, like we're all those buck-toothed Japanese soldiers in World War II propaganda posters."

Curtiss thought he'd better change the subject. "So where are you from?"

"Philly. Born and raised."

"Really? I grew up in Hershey PA."

"Nice town, Hershey. I toured the chocolate factory there once."

Curtiss took the check from the waitress, which was a plain sheet of mostly wet paper decorated with smears of Chinese scribbles and the number 189 written at the bottom. Curtiss handed the waitress

200 NT Dollars, then wiped his fingers on a thin tissue that he had pulled from a dispenser on his table. Marty noticed. "The dirtier the restaurant, the better tasting the food, we Chinese always say."

"No fortune cookies, though?" Curtiss joked.

"Fortunes cookies are an American thing. Some guy in San Francisco invented them, and for a Japanese restaurant, too." Seeing that Curtiss was preparing to leave, curiosity got the best of Marty's manners. "Come on, man, really, what are you doing here in Taiwan?"

"Same as you." Curtiss smiled out of the corner of his mouth, stood, and patted Marty on the shoulder. "To find my bride."

CHAPTER 2

The previous year, in the fall of 1987, Curtiss daydreamed through the rain-speckled window of a New York City taxicab careening downtown along empty avenues. The Rastafarian driver's music created a mobile cocoon of warmth and sunshine in an otherwise cold and drizzly Sunday morning.

Having just completed six months at his first post-college job as an entry-level bond trader at Drexel Burnham Lambert, Curtiss was thoroughly exhausted from the plebe overload that Wall Street firms were famous for. He looked forward to any time spent outside of the office, and none more than his regular Sunday morning meetups with Jimmy Yamandakos at a Chinatown restaurant.

Within a week of their meeting during their freshman year at college, Jimmy had become not only his friend and confidant but his *de facto* life mentor. The son of a Detroit Greektown restaurant owner who had kicked him out of the family restaurant business, insisting he do better than his father, Jimmy was the first in his family to go to college. He carried the burden of his father's expectations with ease. He graduated from the University of Michigan law school with honors, had three job offers in hand at graduation, and was now an attorney with a leading New York law firm. It was their mutual ambition to make it big in their respective fields that had drawn them together. That they both ended up living in Manhattan was serendipitous.

Looking up at Manhattan's towering skyline, Curtiss thought of a graduation ceremony that he had attended at the Hershey Founders Hall, and of the alumnus who'd returned to campus to speak at the

21

ceremony. The man was a towering figure, almost as bigger-than-life in Curtiss's mind as Milton Hershey himself. Orphaned like Curtiss, he had made himself into a New York City tycoon and one of the most prominent business figures of his time.

Listening to this man attribute his success to the Milton Hershey School's sacred values of honest hard work, integrity, positive spirit, commitment to mission, and mutual respect was a life-changing event for Curtiss. Replicating his success became a persistent fantasy that evolved into his personal manifest destiny. Everything he did since that day at Founders Hall, every sacrifice he made and difficulty he endured only strengthened his commitment to achieving his goal. And the harder he worked at DBL, and the more hours he put in, the closer he felt to achieving that dream. It was only a matter of time, he thought, before he would occupy the top floor of one of those buildings parading past his taxicab window.

It was a stroke of great luck that Curtiss had found himself working in Jake Belkin's department at the firm. Belkin was Wall Street's junk bond king. After his five-minute job interview, Curtiss hardly had anymore face time with him, but in those five minutes Belkin convinced him that he could have a very profitable career in junk bond financing at DBL, and told him that he could retire before he was thirty.

Curtiss had doubts it was going to be that easy, but was just excited to be on his way, on the leading edge—the bleeding edge—of his industry. It was his shot and, though his Hershey, Pennsylvanian programming for humility gave him partial immunity to pomposity, being a millionaire by the time he was thirty would have suited him just fine. He promised himself that once he'd made it, his penance would be to abstain from self-aggrandizement and the ostentatiousness of conspicuous consumption: the order of the day for yuppies of his generation.

At least fifteen minutes in the cab was still before him, so he pulled the financial section from the block of paper that was the Sunday *New York Times* sitting on the seat next to him—and there was a cover page article about DBL: an investigation into corruption and insider trading.

The article was really nothing more than a summary of the rumors Curtiss had been hearing for months—no concrete accusations, no proof of any wrongdoing—and Curtiss himself knew he'd done nothing illegal in his tangential capacity. But Hank Jarvis, a star junk-bond trader and fast-tracker who worked on special projects for Belkin, had confided in Curtiss that he was becoming concerned about some of the things that Belkin was asking him to do on behalf of preferred clients. At the time, Curtiss hadn't given it a lot of thought. Given Belkin's position within the firm and reputation in the industry, he felt the man deserved the benefit of the doubt. But now he found his pulse racing as he read the piece.

As Curtiss entered the restaurant, and breathed in the intoxicating aromas trailing the dim sum carts traveling its aisles, he found Jimmy sitting in their regular booth.

When Jimmy had first taken him to a place that served authentic Chinese cuisine after he arrived in Manhattan, Curtiss hadn't recognized any of the food. Jimmy told him: "This isn't like that hole in the wall we used to get greasy chop suey or chow mein from in Ann Arbor, Curt. This is the real deal. And once you get used to the authentic stuff, there is no going back to Americanized Chinese food."

They talked of things that young single men with a little money burning a hole in their pocket talk about: girls, cars, sports. And they also talked jazz, for which they shared a passion, though Jimmy didn't play. Curtiss himself hadn't picked up his trumpet in months, for that matter, but he did manage to hit the city's jazz clubs with Jimmy from time to time.

Curtiss had played an Ann Arbor jazz club three nights a week during his junior and senior years at U of M, in part to earn walking-around money, but also because playing provided an emotional charge he found nowhere else. He still had the trumpet given to him by the Milton Hershey School, and upon arrival in the city had found an amateur group that played impromptu jam sessions at clubs before opening hours. That had all come to an abrupt halt when he'd been thrown into DBL's meat grinder, and ever since, whenever he had time to take a breath, he realized how keenly he missed playing.

Curtiss and Jimmy stayed until well after the check was paid and their fortune-cookies' fortunes had been read, until the restaurant had emptied to just a few stray diners scattered among the tables. It was, therefore, easy for Curtiss's eye to lock onto the young Asian woman who was eating lunch with a stack of textbooks.

Her long, dark hair cascaded over her shoulders and down nearly the entire length of the gentle curvature of her back. Her features were extraordinarily delicate, and as she read through her large, black-framed glasses, her slender fingers twirled a pen, subconsciously spinning and flipping it in acrobatic feats heretofore unknown to Curtiss.

Everything *about* her was heretofore unknown to Curtiss.

* * *

Curtiss looked up from his desk in the firm's dealing room and saw Jake Belkin striding into the office's conference room with Hank Jarvis, two New York City policemen, and what Curtiss was sure was a federal agent in tow.

The dealing room somehow managed to be both as raucous as ever and seized by a preternatural quiet. No one in the place watched the conference room, but at some level no one was aware of anything else.

The conference room door remained closed for the better part of an hour before Jarvis did a perp walk out of the office, accompanied by a policeman at each elbow.

In another moment, Belkin's unusually tall and lanky figure filled the doorway. He shook hands with the federal agent, who was then escorted out of the office by one of Belkin's assistants. When the assistant returned, Belkin turned to the dealers in the room, raised his hands and said, "Can I have everyone's attention for a moment." He then proceeded to speak to the entire bond dealing team about what had just happened, starting off with a brief, one-bad-apple caveat, followed by a lecture about sloppiness and inappropriate behavior that culminated in a recitation of everybody's responsibilities to the company's shareholders.

The bond trader who sat beside Curtiss in the open-office dealing room leaned over and said in a hushed tone, "I would hope old Belkie would be a little more supportive if they ever came for me like that." The sheen was beginning to come off his idol, Belkin.

For the rest of the afternoon of the day of Jarvis's arrest, Curtiss focused intently on his work to block any creeping doubts about his established world view, and to avoid embarrassing himself with his own naive thoughts about the world that he now found himself in.

By 7:00 pm he decided to call it an early day and was headed for the elevators when a female voice stopped him in his tracks: "Curt!"

It was Antonia, the luscious Jamaican receptionist that every so-inclined male in the office found irresistible, frantically clicking her heels toward him with a manila envelope in her hands. She held the envelope out to Curtiss. "This is your passport application. It is company policy now for all executives to have a valid passport in case they need to travel for the firm."

The sudden and immediate proximity of Antonia's massive, Egyptian-queen eyes and mind-numbing figure set Curtiss's heart hammering in his chest. He counted himself lucky to keep his voice from cracking as he said, "Sure, Antonia. When do you need it?"

"By the end of the week?" she said, pirouetting and flashing a coquettish smile. Did she somehow sense the rush of hormone-driven adrenalin happening behind his nonchalant façade?

Only on the elevator ride down did he look at the envelope in his hand and process her words. *Need to travel for the firm?* To date, Curtiss hadn't been asked (or even encouraged) to leave the floor of the dealing room. It was new company policy, she'd said, but he'd heard no one else talking about it.

He decided this was a good thing. They were thinking of him, anyway. Someone was making plans for him.

*   *   *

"I hear that they are having a little trouble over there at DBL," Jimmy said the following Sunday, in clear violation of their no-talking-business-at-dim sum rule. His firm had taken on some legal work for the city for their case against the firm, he said.

Curtiss shrugged. "There's a thin line in our business," he said, paraphrasing Belkin's speech, "and the guy crossed it." This in spite of Curtiss suspecting by now that Hank Jarvis had just been carrying the bag for Belkin, and had been sacrificed for the sake of the firm—and Belkin.

Jimmy was watching him.

"Besides," Curtiss said, "everyone knows that Belkin's dealing room is a Permian swamp. Hey, if you can't stand the heat . . . " He took a hard swallow of tea so he wouldn't have to hear himself talk.

Jimmy's concerned look remained trained on him. "You've really got to watch yourself there at DBL, Curt. You're swimming with sharks."

Assuming a patient but fatigued tone, Curtiss assured him that he would. "Believe me, I don't trust anyone at work. The only real friend I have in New York is you," he announced in a mock sentimental tone.

Jimmy chuckled, and the two young men toasted their friendship with small white porcelain teacups.

As Curtiss drank his tea, he saw that the spectacular Asian girl he'd seen in the restaurant the previous week had reappeared, and was now looking up from her books and smiling at them. He returned her smile, and they held their gaze in a brief embrace before she looked away.

What was *that*?

Curtiss saw that she was unable to fully erase her smile, even after she returned to her books. He noted the title of one of the books that were stacked at her elbow—he had his opening line.

Without a second's stage fright, Curtiss got to his feet, winked, and smiled at Jimmy the way they did to each other when meeting girls in Ann Arbor bars, and confidently approached her table.

"*In Search of Excellence*," he said. "Tom Peters is one of my favorite authors, but I think he's an even better public speaker."

When the girl looked up from her book at Curtiss, she appeared to be holding back a much bigger smile than she was giving him. "I haven't started reading it yet," she said in near-perfect high British English. "It's good, though?" she added, taking off her reading glasses and letting loose the full smile she'd been restraining.

"Uh. Yeah," he managed. Good God, she was beautiful. "I mean yes, it is a very good book—business." His brain and mouth were now communicating on a five-second delay.

She laughed, but kindly. "Well, that's not such an enthusiastic endorsement, is it?" After an awkward moment of silence she glanced over at Curtiss's table and back. "Are you with a friend?"

"Who? That guy? I've never seen him before in my life."

Another laugh. "I assume you came over here expecting that I would invite you to sit down." She let Curtiss hang for a moment then showed him mercy. "Well, go ahead." She gestured to the seat directly across from her. "I'm Jacqueline," she said, keeping the initiative.

"Are you a student, or do you just like having lunch with a bunch of books?"

She explained that she was a student at New York University, while flicking the pen in her hand with optical illusion-like acrobatics.

"I noticed that," Curtiss said, nodding to her pen. "It is amazing what you can do with a pen."

"Oh, it is nothing." Conscious of it, she stopped flicking her pen. "Every schoolchild in Taiwan learns to do it."

"So you are from Taiwan?"

"Yes. I was born there. But I went to a U.K. boarding school when I was twelve."

Curtiss asked her what year she was in at NYU and she explained that she was working on her MBA master's thesis. "I graduate in six months."

"Do you plan to stay in New York after graduation? Or go back to Taiwan . . . or England?"

"I haven't thought that far ahead yet," she replied obliquely.

Curtiss only barely noticed Jimmy as he passed by their table on his way toward the door. "I love everything about dim sum except that you can't get a decent cup of coffee afterward," he said, teeing up his next line. "Little Italy is just a few minutes' walk from here. How about an espresso?"

Jacqueline leveled her eyes at Curtiss, doing her best to read him. "Sure. That sounds lovely right about now."

"Due caffè espresso e un Babà al rum," Jacqueline said to the portly middle-aged man who came from behind the counter at the Little Italy pastry shop.

"Lei parla italiano," he said.

"Sì," Jacqueline replied. "Ho imparato durante le mie vacanze estive sulla costa amalfitana."

"Hey!" the man patted his substantial midsection in delight, "La mia famiglia è da Napoli!"

"He says his family is from Naples, near where I used to spend my summers on the Amalfi Coast," Jacqueline translated for Curtiss. Then, to the shop owner, "Napoli è reale l'Italia."

This beautiful, English-accented, Italian-speaking woman from Taiwan now completely beguiled Curtiss. Luckily, he wasn't called upon to speak just yet.

"I'm Jacqueline," she said, burying her slender, well-manicured hand into the man's thick working hand.

"Just like Jackie Kennedy, eh?" he said in a thick New York City accent.

"Well, actually you are correct, my father did in fact name me after her. He says that she is everything that a lady should be."

"How about that. Your father is a smart man." He turned to Curtiss and pulled on a broad, mock Italian accent. "You-ah don't-ah let this one-ah get away, she is-ah something es-special," he said before walking over to the counter to prepare their pastry and coffee.

Curtiss could only nod in agreement, not taking his eyes off Jacqueline.

"So," Curtiss said, "you are from Taiwan and your father named you after Jacqueline Kennedy. Turns out my father named me after something too."

"And what would that be?"

"An airplane." Jacqueline giggled at the suggestion. "The C-46 Curtiss Commando, as a mater of fact. That's Curtiss, with two S's."

"Why on earth would he do that?"

Curtiss explained that his father had been a World War II airman and had flown one of the B-25 bombers launched from an aircraft carrier on the Doolittle Raid on Japan. He told of how they couldn't land their planes back on the ship and how they were supposed to land in China.

Jacqueline acknowledged that she'd read about it and asked what had happened to his father.

His father's plane made it to the China coast just before they ran out of gas and had to ditch. He was MIA in China for two months and later wrote letters home about how the Chinese people had helped him avoid the Japanese and escape to . . . Curtiss paused to take a shot at Chinese: "koo-mung?"

"Kun Ming," Jacqueline corrected.

"After recovering in Kunming, he got transferred to flying the C-46 Curtiss Commando, a cargo plane, over the Himalayas for the rest of the war. He loved that plane so much he named me after it."

The shop owner brought the coffee and pastries. "Gratzie," Curtiss eked out meekly, bravely risking embarrassment in the face of Jacqueline's fluency in three languages—that he knew of.

"So, Jacqueline Kennedy." Curtiss smiled. "Her story is pretty tragic, isn't it?"

Jacqueline tilted her head.

"What I can't figure out is how, after JFK, she could marry an old man like Aristotle Onassis."

Jacqueline shrugged. "Well, just look at her life, Curt. Even before she was married to Kennedy her world was all about power and money, and the attraction to power and money. Onassis wasn't about some physical fling, though she was certainly entitled to that from time to time. It was about being together in each other's world and sharing . . . " She took a moment to carefully consider her words. " . . . Surviving it together," she concluded. "Aside from his obvious wealth, I'm sure Onassis was a way for her to remain independent, but still within the cocoon of wealth, power, and privilege."

Curtiss wondered why Jacqueline would know so much about such things, but had the common sense not to ask.

"So you know some things about me," Jacqueline said, "but I don't know anything about you . . . except that your father was in the war."

Curtiss felt Jacqueline's comment to be somewhat strange since he still knew practically nothing about her. Nevertheless, he paused momentarily to prepare himself to talk about some things that he knew he would struggle to say. "I'm an only child and lost my dad when I was young."

He explained that his father was killed while serving as a military advisor in the Vietnam War. An image of his father in uniform getting into a green military car at the end of their driveway surfaced in Curtiss's consciousness. He was frustrated that he couldn't remember his father's face, aside from the black-and-white photos of him that he used to supplement his childhood memory.

The image of his mother's face, however, was vivid and her compassionate expression as she comforted his anxiety about his father leaving them alone again was as fresh in his mind as if it had happened yesterday.

"Not long after my father died my mother and I were in a severe car accident together." Curtiss drew a deep breath in anticipation of his breathing seizing up under the weight of his emotions. "She was killed instantly. I was asleep in the back seat of the car and survived without a scratch."

A small, sympathetic sound escaped Jacqueline, but Curtiss, not trusting his hold on his emotions, purposely didn't look at her. He went on to explain how he was supposed to go into a foster program, but one of his father's army buddies intervened and enrolled him in the Milton Hershey School. And, since students were taken care of by the school through college, he went on to university, courtesy of a Milton Hershey School scholarship.

It had been several years since Curtiss had spoken to anyone about his parents and he was surprised and a little pleased by how, now on his own in New York and independent of the school, it felt much more like he was talking about events in the past than about something that was continuing to happen to him.

Jacqueline listened intently as Curtiss told her about growing up in one of the student homes scattered across the rolling green fields surrounding the idyllic and pristine Americana of Hershey PA. He talked about the house parents, married couples from the area with child rearing experience, who volunteered to take care of a house full of a dozen students within each home. And he talked about life sharing a bedroom with another child, sometimes two, and how that made him never feel like an only child. He told her about the dairy farm chores after classes, explaining the history of the Amish community in the area, and described the scent of chocolate and flag-waving Memorial Day parades that rolled down Chocolate Avenue in town.

And, since Emily Post hailed from neighboring Wilkes-Barre, Pennsylvania, he told of how they were all required to carry a dog-eared copy of her book *Etiquette*, and of ballroom dancing lessons and formal balls. "Real Norman Rockwell stuff," Curtiss concluded, though he could see from the polite smile on Jacqueline's face that the reference to that artist was, understandably, lost on her.

"Seven months ago I landed a job as a bond trader at Drexel Burnham Lambert. And here I am, living my dream in the city, working for Jake Belkin, ready to make my mark on Wall Street."

Jacqueline regarded him for a long moment without saying anything, and Curtiss was encouraged by how unflustered he now was by this spectacular young woman's attention. "Your story is quite tragic as well," she said at last. "But you've done so well for yourself, all things considered. You must have a strong heart." She said this with an expression on her lovely face that combined genuine admiration and compassion.

Curtiss felt taking a risk was in order. "You know who you remind me of a little?" Jacqueline squirmed in her seat and eagerly shook her head like a schoolgirl waiting to hear a secret. "That character Holly in the movie 'Breakfast at Tiffany's.'"

Jacqueline squealed and clapped her hands. "That is my absolute favorite movie, Curt. However did you know?" She grabbed Curtiss's arm. "She was such a rebellious child, yet courageous at the same time. Defying the powers that be to win her freedom and independence. It was so sad that both the lead characters, Holly and Paul, were manipulated by the rich and powerful around them." Jacqueline took a breath from her excitement. "But in spite of all that, in the end, their love prevailed." Curtiss watched as an expression of sadness came over Jacqueline's face.

"You play the hand you are dealt, I guess," Curtiss said, slightly embarrassed that his comment might have come off as a little trite.

"Indeed we do."

CHAPTER 3

Staring through the rain-speckled window of the Taipei taxi, the rain droplets acted as a kaleidoscope backlit by the city lights. Through it, Curtiss watched a slide show in his mind's eye of his and Jacqueline's trip to Aruba. He could see her terrified face, accompanied by a scream of delight, as her parasail suddenly lifted her off the back of the speedboat; the bathing-suit tan lines on her luscious body as she showered off the salt that had accumulated on her skin from a day spent swimming in the ocean; her long black hair and darkening skin wrapped in the white sheets of their bed at the resort.

In his mind, Curtiss had made the journey back to New York and resumed his climb to the top of Wall Street, with Jacqueline by his side. But the harsh, nasal-guttural Taiwanese language monologue of the radio storyteller blaring in his ears and the sickly sweet smell of the Jade Orchid flower that hung from the Taipei taxi's rearview mirror reminded Curtiss that he was very far from Aruba, home— and, still, Jacqueline.

The alcohol in Curtiss's body enveloped him like a warm blanket and, having lost count of how many drinks he'd had that evening, and how much money he had spent, he only hoped that he had enough local currency in his pocket to pay the driver.

The taxi scurried along late night streets like a rat in a maze, mostly along the city's small tributaries, but occasionally spilling onto main-line roads with exotic names such as Hsin I Road, Chung Shan Pei Road, and Tong Hua Pei Road.

They eventually reached Jen Ai Road and the alley that harbored

33

George's Palace.

Now, having spent more than two weeks in Taipei, Curtiss faced up to the fact that his search for Jacqueline would take some time, and he'd decided to take George up on his offer of a weekly rate. In the late afternoons, through the window of his presidential suite, Curtiss thought of Jacqueline as he watched his neighbor across the alley release dozens of pigeons that he kept in rooftop coops, then signal instructions to them with a small flag tied to the end of a long, thin bamboo pole. The thick Taipei air pollution turned the setting sun into a bright red Chinese lantern that hung just over the horizon and, swirling between the city's scattered high-rise buildings, the birds would flash like white lightning each time they changed direction at the behest of their keeper. Some evenings the pigeons would return to their coops on cue, and sometimes they wouldn't, no matter how frantically their master signaled for them to come home before dark.

Curtiss wondered what signals he would use, once he found Jacqueline, to draw her back to his roost in New York City.

He fumbled with his cash, paid the driver, struggled to pull his size twelves out from between the front and back seats of the tiny cab, stumbled out of the taxi, and found the front door key that George had given him for just such a late-night occasion. Curtiss carefully walked upstairs, making it to his bed just in time for a round of alcohol-powered bed spins before sleep came to put him out of his misery.

After sleeping through the morning, Curtiss decided it was well past time to send Jimmy a letter. The guy was his best friend, after all. More than that: he was Curtiss's closest thing to family. Back in college, when the holidays had come around and students headed home to be with their families, it was to Jimmy's Greek-American family in Birmingham, Michigan, that he'd gone. They'd all but adopted him. Thanks to Jimmy, for Curtiss Thanksgiving was lamb cooked on a spit, rather than a turkey, and Christmas was scented with the aroma of baking spinach pie and stuffed grape leaves, a commercial-sized tray of golden-crusted pastatiso from their family's Greektown restaurant, and big, warm hugs from Greek-accented yayas.

Curtiss walked to the nearest post office, bought a stamp, envelope, and post office stationery, and stood at a little wall-mounted counter to write. But what to say? While his mission had proven more daunting than he'd imagined during the drunken flash of inspiration that had launched him across the globe in search of Jacqueline, he remained absolutely committed to it. Still, no matter how he imagined committing it to paper for his friend, it came out sounding sappy, stupid, or outright crazy. He finally opted for a bare-bones approach: "In Taiwan. (I know.) Will be back in a week or two."

Striking out on foot again he did his best to ignore the fact that his quest was not going well. He'd had only one even halfway promising brainstorm, but, knowing only Jacqueline's foreign-language name, an earlier visit to the Taipei city bureau of records had produced nothing but frustration. As on a dispiritingly large and growing number of days before this one, all that presented itself to him was another aimless stroll through the city in search of inspiration.

It was late afternoon and rush hour traffic was just beginning to build to its daily gridlock when an American flag hanging over a pub across the street caught Curtiss's eye, as did the name of the establishment: General Chennault Pub. He recognized Chennault's name from the research he had done on his father's military service in China during the Second World War. Curtiss cautiously jaywalked across the street and ambled in.

The bar was decorated with World War II memorabilia and Curtiss spent several minutes studying war-buddy photos taken in front of army tents, dented airplane propellers, flying goggles together with a leather helmet, an aerial photo of the USS Hornet aircraft carrier, and other artifacts that were hung on the wall, including a Flying Tigers blood chit in a glass-covered frame on proud display behind the bar.

His attention was next caught by a large, carved-wood and engraved-brass commemorative plaque listing the names of the flyers on the 1942 Doolittle Raid on targets in Tokyo and four other Japanese cities.

Curtiss's heart stopped as he came to a name on the plaque: William Jack Bradley.

His father.

Three days after his eighteenth birthday, Curtiss had returned from final exams to find a legal-sized envelope from the U.S. Military Intelligence Corps on the mail table at his Milton Hershey School student home. It was his eighteenth birthday present from the U.S. government: the official report about the circumstances surrounding his father's death. He'd never worked up the courage to open it and so it followed him in silence, stuffed in a plastic milk crate together with his other legal documents, ever since.

A female voice broke into Curtiss's consciousness. "You want a drink?" He followed the voice to a robust Asian lady with unusually large breasts who was standing behind the bar.

"This is my father," Curtiss said, pressing an unsteady fingertip to the inscribed name on the plaque.

"Really?" She moved from behind the bar to peer at the plaque with him. She was really spectacularly buxom, and heavily made up. She appeared to have strategically stuffed herself into an undersized bra and blouse for maximum effect. "For real?"

"William Bradley was my father," he assured her. "He was a pilot on the Doolittle Raid."

She responded with a broad smile that lasted all of two seconds. "So do you want a drink, or what?"

"Okay. What do you have on tap?"

With each stride on her way back behind the bar her undersized skirt strained to contain her Rubensesque hips. Even her shoes appeared to be too tight. She shook her head. "Trust me, you want bottled beer right now. We just opened and I haven't had a chance to flush the cockroaches out of the beer taps yet." She placed a large green bottle of Taiwan beer on the bar and Curtiss took a seat in front of it.

He thanked her and, out of courtesy, asked her name.

"Wendy," she answered, melodically but mechanically, as if asked her name by patrons dozens of times every evening.

"How long have you worked here?"

"My late husband left me his share in this pub—I'm half owner. He was a pilot in the war too, like your daddy. He died about five years ago." She was no longer smiling, but still seemed little fazed by the mention of her late husband. *Inscrutable Asians*, he thought.

Wendy appeared to be in her early forties, Curtiss judged, which meant her husband must have been about twenty years her elder for him to have been a pilot in the Second World War. Another young Asian woman seizing a GI husband as her meal ticket? Curtiss batted away the thought, and the unwelcome ghost of cynical Saunderson with it. He felt better concluding that it was eccentric love.

Wendy returned in kind Curtiss's standard bar-counter questions by asking him what he was doing in Taiwan.

"I'm looking for someone." Curtiss took a long draw from his bottle.

"Let me guess. A runaway girlfriend, right?"

Curtiss smiled and resigned himself to being absolutely predictable. "Yeah. My girlfriend. Jacqueline Kao. Hey, you wouldn't happen to know her, would you?" he asked, mockingly.

"I don't know, maybe I do. What does she look like?"

"Chinese; slim; thick, straight black hair; dark eyes; average height . . . " said Curtiss, making a trenchant return in their volley of sarcasm.

"Oh, *her*," Wendy said, but then got serious and shifted her weight to one leg. "What do you know about her?"

"She was a student at New York University. We dated for about half a year. Then she came back to Taiwan to get married in some kind of arranged marriage thing. That's about it."

"So, you are here to rescue her, is that it?"

"Pretty much." Curtiss took another long draw on his beer.

"Have you checked the wedding announcements in the newspaper?"

"The papers with wedding announcements are all in Chinese."

"Imagine that." She laughed. "What is her full name in Chinese?"

Curtiss shrugged.

"Really? You date a woman for half a year and don't know her full name?" Wendy shook her head. "Okay, she went to university in New York. What else do you know about her? The family name is Kao, right? How old is she?"

"About twenty-five." Curtiss then thought for a moment, trying to recall anything else about her that might be useful. "She went to boarding school in England, her father is some kind of influential businessman, or something. Anyway, he has a lot of money." He'd regretted his comment to Saunderson about Jacqueline's family being loaded. He wasn't comfortable acknowledging her family's wealth to others. The fact was, he wished they weren't as well off as they were. Then he could be sure his future success on Wall Street couldn't possibly be attributed to his wife's inherited wealth, leaving untarnished his manifest destiny to be a completely self-made man.

Wendy pulled a local newspaper from beneath the bar and scanned the wedding announcement page. "Nothing." Pointing a plump finger at Curtiss. "Okay. You come back here every day and I'll check the wedding announcements for you. But you've got to drink something. Okay?"

"That won't be a problem," Curtiss said, having just drained his bottle of beer.

"You know," Wendy said while popping the bottle cap off another bottle, "it is very romantic that you came halfway around the world for a woman." She'd tilted her head to one side and produced an animated, dreamy smile, but now snapped a serious expression into its place, startling Curtiss a little. "But, you should go home. If her family arranged her marriage, it is hopeless."

Before Curtiss could react, a familiar, Russian-accented voice came from behind a large wooden Chinese screen at the end of the bar: "You should take her advice."

When Curtiss slid off the bar stool and peered behind the screen, he found Sonya sitting at a table with a martini glass in one hand and an open book in the other. With her high-collared, full-length black dress and grandmotherly white hair, she looked as out of place in the pub as Whistler's mother would have in a speakeasy.

"Well, well," Curtiss said, smiling broadly. "Hello, Sonya."

"Come," Sonya said, gesturing with her martini glass for Curtiss to take a seat at her table. "Please, won't you join me?"

"I wouldn't have figured bumping into you in a place like this."

"Oh? Why is that?"

Curtiss bit his tongue, knowing he'd already stepped in it.

"Wendy's husband and I were old friends from the war years. I'm Wendy's partner in this bar. Half of the things on these walls were her husband's; the other half are mine and my late husband's."

"You just seem a little out of place here, that's all," he said, aware he was only digging himself in deeper. He could see Wendy shaking her head behind the bar. "I didn't mean to imply—"

Sonya stopped Curtiss before he could further embarrass himself. "The years that we collected all of this was an important and meaningful time, not only for us but for the rest of the world too. This is history, Curtiss, and we are proud to have been a part of it." After pausing to sip her drink, she said, "I apologize for eavesdropping, dear, but did I overhear correctly: did you say that your father was in the war?"

"Yes. William Bradley. He was a pilot and flew one of the planes in the Doolittle Raid on Tokyo. He flew cargo planes over the Himalayas for the rest of the war."

Sonya nodded, a newly pensive look on her face. "And where is he now?"

After a pause, Curtiss said, "He died when I was young."

"I am truly sorry to hear that, dear," Sonya said, in almost a whisper.

Curtiss worked up a smile and asked Sonya how a Russian had ended up settling in Taiwan.

"Russian-American," Sonya corrected. "I'm a White Russian, Curtiss. Do you know what that is? Besides the drink, I mean." Sonya explained to Curtiss that she had never actually been to Russia, but was born and spent her early years in Harbin, China, a city near the Russian border. Her family was part of the Russian aristocracy that fled to escape persecution from the Bolsheviks. "They were the Russian communist revolutionaries, dear."

She described Harbin as a modern city for its place and time, where many of the more cultured Russians settled after the revolution. As a little girl there, her grandmother would take her to the opera, the ballet, and Russian social clubs. "There were several Russian Orthodox churches there, too," she said while gesturing to a painting of an onion-shape domed Russian Orthodox Church hanging on the wall behind her.

"So you grew up in China. That's how you learned to speak Chinese."

"Yes. My nanny taught me," she said. "My mother had grown frail after I was born; she was traumatized by the experience of living as a refuge, poor dear. She was unable to raise me on her own, so my grandmother raised me, as a Russian."

Seeing what must have been a sympathetic look on Curtiss's face, she made a dismissive, that's-all-in-the-past gesture with her hand. She described her father as a gentle man, a former White Russian general who was completely devoted to his family. The Soviet-Japanese Neutrality Pact made it possible for her family to live in Japanese-occupied China. "They left us Russians alone. At least it kept us out of the labor camps. And it gave me the opportunity to secretly leave Harbin to do my part in the war." She had become a nurse and, through her father's connections with the American military, she went to Kunming, where General Chennault was setting up the American Volunteer Group (AVG) Flying Tigers.

"That's where I spent most of the war years," Sonya said, repositioning the aviator's watch that hung loosely around her wrist. "And that's where I met Frank, my husband." She pointed to a framed, eight-by-ten black-and-white photograph of a man in an American uniform that hung on the wall. She described him as a dashing young man with a rare zeal for life. Like the rest of the Flying Tiger pilots, he was barely out of his teens, and was brazen, and at times reckless and foolhardy. But, she explained, living on life's edge—facing life-and-death battles on an almost daily basis—will do that to a person. "When they weren't flying, they were always in some sort of trouble or another."

It dawned on Curtiss that his father was younger than he was now at the time of the Doolittle Raid. He wondered what might have been going through his father's mind when it was his turn to push the throttle forward on a land-based bomber that had no business taking off from the deck of an aircraft carrier almost 200 miles short of their designated launch point somewhere in the Western Pacific Ocean.

Sonya explained that men like his father were the tip of the spear while on the Doolittle Raid, taking the fight to the heart of Japan and winning one of the most important psychological victories of the war. That it was not so much a defeat for the Japanese, but a psychological victory for Americans: a victory over a defeatist attitude that had developed after having suffered more than four months of successive losses since the attack on Pearl Harbor.

Curtiss had had the opportunity to speak with people from his father's generation about the war, but Sonya had a way of animating the black-and-white images of his father's face that Curtiss kept in a handed-down photo album, and in his mind.

"Frank and I were engaged to be married when I returned to Harbin to rejoin my family." Her father had developed a personal friendship with a Japanese general who had arranged for their escape to Shanghai, just ahead of the Chinese communists at the end of the war. "We had no love for the Japanese army, mind you. But the Chinese communists would certainly not have tolerated aristocratic Russians within their new China. That Japanese general saved our lives."

Her family's attempt to rebuild their lives in Shanghai after the war was short-lived. Sonya's fiancé was temporarily assigned to Tokyo, so their wedding would have to wait. Her grandmother had cultivated Sonya's love of the stage, and it had been her childhood dream to become a theatrical set designer. "I studied it for a while, but war caught up with us again—that would be the Chinese Civil War, dear, the one between the Chinese Nationalists and the Communists." Her family moved to Switzerland to live with relatives. She and Frank were married in 1949, the same year they arrived in Taiwan. "We lived here, among the U.S. forces and Chinese exiles, until Frank passed away in 1969."

He asked why she hadn't joined her family in Switzerland or gone home to the U.S. after that.

"China has always been my home, Curtiss."

He paused momentarily to gather his thoughts. He wanted somehow to speak of the chasm that listening to Sonya's tales had opened up within him—the yawning disparity he felt between the weight of his "mission" and the life-and-death battles men like his father and Sonya's husband had waged when they were his age. But he could only fight the battles available to him, couldn't he? And he wouldn't belittle his love for Jacqueline, or his determination to find her and bring her back with him.

Instead, Sonya turned the conversation to an introductory lesson on Chinese culture. "Curtiss, you can't understand this culture by comparing it to what you know." Cultures are living things, she said, with their own DNA. "Greek Democracy, the Magna Carta, the Renaissance, the American Revolution, and government of the people were all part of your cultural DNA, not theirs." That Chinese cultural DNA is based on Confucian tradition, one of family hierarchy and the supremacy of the needs of the group over the individual. "For instance, whereas we say, 'Man does not live by bread alone,' the Chinese say, 'Min I Shih Wei T'ien,' or 'For people, food is heaven,' meaning that the essence of what is most important in life is a full belly."

"So you're saying they haven't evolved as much, culturally, as we have in the West?"

"Evolved *differently*, Curtiss," Sonya corrected. Modern republics and the Western form of democracy have only had a couple hundred years to demonstrate their sustainability, while China has been governing itself through successive dynasties and dictatorships for over five thousand years. There were a number of times throughout history where the West lagged far behind China in social development, and in science and the arts. "The last few hundred years, where the West has surpassed China, is what the Chinese call the 'Western Accident.' And that was due to mismanagement by a foreign dynasty, the Manchus, who took over from the Ming, which was a Han Chinese Dynasty."

Sonya must have noticed Curtiss's eyes beginning to glaze over. "In any event," she concluded, "China is an ancient country and it would be wise for one to keep an open mind."

Just then the door swung open and Kao, Sonya's driver, appeared and informed her that she was going to be late for a dinner appointment. To this point he'd ignored Curtiss as though he didn't exist, but now he looked daggers at this foreign stranger who had dared reenter his Madam Sonya's little realm. "Madam Sonya," he said, without looking away from Curtiss, "we really don't have time to *waste* here."

Sonya gave in to Kao as a mother does to a petulant child. She smiled at Curtiss as he rose to his feet along with her. "It has been wonderful chatting with you, dear. You must experience some of the local culture while you are here. I will arrange for tickets to the Chinese opera and we'll go together one evening."

"That would be lovely, Sonya," Curtiss said, grinning at Kao, whose eyes burned with disapproval.

* * *

Curtiss smiled with pride after having tied his bow tie into an acceptable form on only the third try. He then donned the jacket of the tuxedo that Sonya had made for him at the tailor's next to the jewelry shop in the lobby of the Lai Lai Sheraton hotel.

He had picked up the tux the day before. While waiting for the tailor to make some final alterations, he stood outside the Lai Lai jeweler's storefront window drinking a can of coffee and eating a bun stuffed with dried meat. This was Taipei's Tiffany's, so he slid easily into the memory of Jacqueline graciously accepting his gift of a Tiffany's necklace. Then as now, he'd thought of how ideal she was for the role of the woman to support him making it to the top. She'd drawn the attention of any room they entered: men wanted to be with her, and women wanted to be her, as a saying of the day went. While she didn't appear to relish that kind of attention, she didn't shrink from it, either.

Looking back on it now, it did worry him a bit that she might be a little too used to it, but that didn't in the least temper his ache for her.

Curtiss made his way down the stairs, careful not to brush up against the dusty railing or walls, and found George manning the reception counter. "Hey, Curtiss. Look at you! You find that girl that you're looking for?"

"Nope. This is another one." Curtiss smiled. "A lovely Russian lady, in fact."

"A Ruskie, eh? We don't get very many of those here in Taiwan." Grinning, he leaned in and spoke to Curtiss in a hushed tone: "She isn't a commie spy, is she?"

Curtiss leaned in in turn and said with a wink and a nod, "I certainly hope so, if you know what I mean."

Both men laughed a devious laugh together.

"Has she got a friend?" George asked. "Hey, we should double date one night. I'm MBA you know? Married But Available."

He completely ignored George's suggestion.

Curtiss felt somewhat a spectacle hailing a taxi on the streets of Taipei in a tuxedo, and his feeling was affirmed for him by the slack-jawed stares and smiles he drew from passersby on the street. The taxi dropped Curtiss at a large, classical Chinese-style gate, through which Curtiss emerged into a city park. He scanned the gathering crowd in front of a large, red-columned building with orange-tiled sloping roofs that cascaded into upward-sloping eves at the four corners and caught sight of Sonya's white hair among the entirely dark-haired crowd. She saw Curtiss at practically the same time and waved him over. Curtiss concluded that he must stand out from the crowd in Taipei as much as Sonya did.

"My, don't you look nice, all dressed up," Sonya said before placing motherly kisses on each of this cheeks.

"Thank you again for the tux. Such an extravagant gift!"

Sonya waved away the comment. "Every young man of culture needs a tuxedo, for goodness sake."

"Well, I never dreamed of owning a custom-tailored tux."

She took Curtiss's arm and they entered the National Theater. The reception area was floor-to-ceiling classic Chinese in design, with thick red columns that thrust into a complex latticework of multiple layers of interlocking beams that framed hand-painted dragon, phoenix, and other designs. Inside the theater, Curtiss was impressed by the wonderfully balanced blend of Chinese-style design and modern theater architecture.

"This was my dream, Curtiss," Sonya said as she gestured broadly toward the stage when they took their seats. "Theatrical sets are fleeting, like Indian sand paintings of the American Southwest: They only exist for the purpose and duration of the ceremony, then blow away into so much dust."

Curtiss wondered out loud what they would see behind the curtain that evening.

"Well, since this is Chinese theater, perhaps just another curtain," Sonya said with a smile, then explained that, unlike Western opera, Chinese opera sets are often little more than a curtain and a few tables and chairs; that the focus tends to be wholly on the actors and their singing and motions. But that sometimes they do experiment with more complex, multidimensional sets. "We shall see."

Witnessing Chinese opera for the first time—especially with someone who knew it and was patient enough to explain it—was a welcome respite from the frustration of his search for Jacqueline. It was so foreign, and such an exotic art form to him, that his mind struggled to comprehend it. Though it had singing actors, music, and dance, it wasn't comparable to any European opera, ballet, or 42nd Street musical that Curtiss had ever seen.

He took Sonya's advice to heart and tried not to understand it by the measures of his own experience, but to experience it for what it was. He allowed himself to be overwhelmed by the pageantry of colorful costumes and dramatic face paint; the whipping motion of the incredibly long peacock feathers and the actors' habitual flicking of their ridiculously long sleeves; the actors' melodramatic movements and the falsetto singing, that, like the falsetto-voiced dialogue, fluctuated continuously up and down the scale; all accompanied by whining stringed instruments. The entire performance was hyper-dramatized and segued scene to scene with bizarre sounds made by exotic instruments that pinged, clanged, and rattled in an arrhythmic percussive musical form that would have been unimaginable to him as music before that night.

* * *

Another week in Taipei had passed and, in spite of Wendy's daily assistance with the newspaper wedding announcements, still no Jacqueline.

"Nothing today, lover boy," Wendy would say in her melodic voice as she put a cold beer in front of Curtiss in a welcome, near-Pavlovian response to his daily arrival.

One day she startled Curtiss when she abruptly leaned forward, laid her sizable breasts on the bar, then sighed as if a weight had been lifted from her shoulders—which apparently it had been. "You don't know what it is like carrying these things around with you all day. My back is killing me."

"Interesting problem to have." Curtiss gave her an amused grin. "Maybe you ought to leave them there like that. It could be good for business."

Wendy looked at Curtiss with distain, then abruptly withdrew them from atop the bar, put her hands on her waist and stretched her back.

Today, Curtiss asked about Sonya and Wendy informed him that she was in Hong Kong, where she goes every month, and that she'd be back in a few days.

"Wendy, that watch she wears around her wrist. That's her husband's, right?"

"Yes, of course. Do you know she has worn black every day since her husband died? That's almost twenty years. After that, my husband and I were like her family. They wanted children, but couldn't have any themselves." Wendy looked off in space with an expression of pity for the unfortunate couple. When she went on, she described them as being like celebrities in Taiwan. Sonya's husband had served under General Chennault himself, and Sonya was very close to Chennault's second wife, Anna. "Sonya and her husband knew everybody here in Taiwan. And everybody knew her." Wendy nodded to the Russian church painting hanging on the wall. "She painted that herself, you know."

Curtiss looked over his shoulder at the painting. The painting was, of course, wonderful. *What an amazing woman.*

Wendy commenced every bartender's ritual of drying glasses and hanging them on the rack above the bar. "Bet you didn't know that one of her Chinese ink-brush paintings is hanging in the National Palace Museum. That's a big honor for a foreigner."

Curtiss turned back from the painting and contemplated Wendy for a moment. "It is like you are her daughter, isn't it? You run this pub for her, you look after her . . . "

Wendy quickly interrupted Curtiss. "Sonya can take care of herself. She is not some helpless, sweet old lady, believe me. But, yes. I love her almost like my own mother." Wendy quickly changed the subject back to Curtiss. "You really don't know what you are getting yourself into with this East-West romance, do you?"

"Love conquers all, Wendy." Curtiss crutched his self-confidence with a long sip of beer.

"Hey, don't forget, I was married to one of you American guys for twenty years. I know what I am talking about. Sure, there were a lot of nice things, like when we ate fish: I ate the head and the tail, and he ate the middle." Wendy paused to laugh at her own joke. "And, more holidays, right? We celebrated your Christmas and our Chinese New Year . . . " Her face then turned serious, as always, as if a switch were flipped. "But one day you will open your refrigerator and it will be full of smelly sauces and jars filled with strange things—some that even shock me!" she exclaimed within laughter.

"But the most difficult thing is communication. At first, it is fun, you know . . . figuring out how to say each other's body parts in each other's language." She smiled widely and winked one of her heavy false eyelashes at Curtiss. "But after you actually live together for a while, things change. It gets harder to be as patient with your differences.

"You guys want everything explained in such detail: questions, questions, questions. It used to drive me crazy! And I know I used to drive my husband crazy, too—he always said he couldn't get a straight answer from me. That's because you guys think the shortest distance between two points is a straight line. But, for Chinese, the smartest way is never so simple as a straight line. Sometimes in an East-West marriage there is just no place to meet in the middle."

"Sounds like just about any marriage to me," Curtiss said.

Wendy 'humphed' at Curtiss's comment, clearly miffed at his

dismissal of her hard-won lessons bridging Chinese and Western cultural DNA.

"I'm going to get a meal," Curtiss announced, as he stood and stretched. "Just put it on my tab."

"Ha! No tabs here, mister," Wendy said, holding out her palm. "200 NT Dollars." Her fingers twitched, indicating that payment was due immediately.

* * *

Only after leaving the pub did Curtiss realize how fed up and frustrated he was with the rut that he had gotten himself into: waking up at noon, drinking coffee out of a can, eating at the same noodle stands every day, and showing up at the General Chennault Pub only to have Wendy tell him "nothing today," then drinking himself into a stupor into the early morning hours. But he wasn't ready to consider that his search for Jacqueline might be coming to an unsuccessful conclusion.

This evening, he thought, at least his menu was going to be different: He went to the steakhouse at the Lai Lai Sheraton for a USDA prime beef steak-n-potatoes dinner.

The singularly satisfying taste of grilled American steak wheeled him back nearly two decades to American flags flying off porches of thrifty, '30s, Dover- and Columbia-style homes snug along Hershey PA's mature oak and ash tree-lined streets; rolling hot cobs of corn atop big blocks of butter from the local dairy farms and eating watermelon on the rind at backyard barbeques; reaching into an aluminum ice chest for a cold soda and opening it on the bottle opener attached to the side.

A quaint vestige of the Milton Hershey School's early twentieth-century rural agricultural roots was that students participate in daily farm chores, which in the day and age that Curtiss attended the school was more about building personal character than providing the children with practical, marketable trade skills. Still, Curtiss milked cows twice daily: before and after school.

So vivid were his culinary musings that evening at the Lai Lai Steakhouse they even raised in his mouth the flavor of the unpasteurized milk that the children would squirt at each other straight from the cow's udder when the farmers weren't looking—

their laughter still ringing in his ears.
Curtiss was homesick.

CHAPTER 4

Spring 1988 blessed New York City with exceptionally good weather, and Curtiss and Jacqueline spent as much time together outdoors as they could, taking driving trips into the Pocono Mountains in Pennsylvania and dining in street-side cafes in the city. They'd stayed as happily occupied together the previous winter, enjoying ski weekends in Vermont and the beaches of Aruba. In the evenings, no matter where they started out in the city, they always seemed to end up at one jazz club or another.

On one Sunday morning, Curtiss woke Jacqueline with a kiss. He looked out the window of his apartment and announced in a whisper: "It's another picture-perfect day."

Jacqueline stretched then put her arms around Curtiss's neck. "What shall we do with it?"

"Well, we could have coffee at that place off the park." Curtiss paused, a little apprehensive about the chance he was about to take. "And later . . . you can join me and Jimmy for Sunday dim sum."

"Thanks, but no. That's really a guy thing. Besides, I don't think Jimmy likes me very much."

Curtiss's first reaction was surprise, as he hadn't noticed any animosity between Jimmy and Jacqueline. Then again, blinded by the emotional vortex he entered whenever he was with her, he might not have picked it up if it had been there. Thinking about it now, he had to admit he couldn't recall any sign of them exactly warming to each other, either.

All the more reason to bring them together and get past it, he reasoned. And in any event, he was determined to not let anything spoil the surprise that he had for her that morning. He reached into the nightstand drawer next to his bed and pulled out a small white bag.

"*Tiffany's*," Jacqueline said, smiling broadly. Her favorite jeweler, he well knew. He watched her slide the long rectangular box from the bag. "Oh, a necklace," she said with pleasure before opening the box, and then freed the glistening thing and held it to the light. "Mmmmm." She held it out to him, and when he'd taken it sat up in bed, spun herself around and pulled her long black hair aside to allow Curtiss to place it around her neck.

As Curtiss obliged, he couldn't resist gently kissing the nape of her neck and, drawing a deep breath of her, felt an aching deep in his chest. It was at that very moment that he realized he was in love with her.

When she turned to Curtiss, he suspected that she mistook the emotion behind his kiss for sexual passion, since she reflexively pulled him closer in a way that implied that they were going to make love at least once before he left for dim sum that morning.

Some time later, Curtiss stirred out of his endorphin-induced stupor enough to check the clock. Only a half hour before he was supposed to show up for dim sum. He jumped out of bed. "I'm going to be late!"

As he dressed, he decided to put off his plan to strike an accord between his lover and his best friend. Jacqueline would take time to get ready, and besides—they'd had a perfect morning. She was more than amenable to his suggestion that they do their own things that day.

"I'll be out of town tomorrow," he informed her. He would be breaking in his new passport taking the company jet to the British Virgin Islands on some business he wasn't yet clear on. "Can we grab dinner tonight? I won't be back until late tomorrow night."

"Sorry," Jacqueline said, stretching in bed, "but I've got plans."

Plans?

During the cab ride to Chinatown and dim sum, the virulent pathogen of passionate love worked within Curtiss's mind. Even after six months, she was impossible to read. He could've just asked her what those "plans" were that would be robbing him of her at dinner tonight—but no, he really couldn't have, not without sounding like what he was: jealous of anything that took her away from him.

No, better to just marinate in his concern that her inscrutability might be concealing something that he should know about her. He knew she cared about him—passionately, he thought—but she still withheld herself from him, refused to open her heart to him. There was no way for Curtiss to know if she didn't want to, or wanted to, but for some reason couldn't. All he knew at that moment was that she was the one, and he had to do everything within his power to make her a permanent part of his life and American dream.

Jimmy had tickets to an auto show and after dim sum they spent the rest of the day ogling exotic cars. At the show, a debonair Italian Lamborghini executive approached Curtiss and Jimmy as they lusted after his Lamborghini Countach that was on display there. "She is gorgeous, yes?" he said with a smile. "The word countach is Piedmontese, the language of the Piedmont region of Italy. It is an expression of astonishment; what our Piedmont men say when they are pursuing an extremely beautiful lady." He smiled again, politely, before moving on to more financially promising showgoers.

"I'm in love with Jacqueline."

It had just tumbled out of him. Neither he nor Jimmy had looked away from the gorgeous car before them. After a long moment, Jimmy asked, "Does she feel the same way about you?"

Curtiss didn't answer. Couldn't.

Jimmy sighed. "Curt, I have to say it. I'm sorry to say . . . sometimes I can't help but get the feeling that she is just playing with you."

Curtiss could have gone on the defensive at this, but he didn't. What could he have said? That it wasn't possible? That the possibility hadn't ever crossed his mind? Jimmy didn't have to say anything more, because Curtiss knew exactly what Jimmy was thinking: that, like the exotic automotive thoroughbred now before them, Jacqueline was out of his league.

That evening back at his apartment, Curtiss yearned to be with Jacqueline and thought to call her, but decided not to. He couldn't risk being perceived as needy. Instead, he stuffed a rented videotape of *Scarface* into his VCR in a vain attempt to withdraw into Hollywood's fantasy take on the gangland drug world of South

Florida. But a line from the movie brought him right back to his plight: "In this country, you gotta make the money first. Then when you get the money, you get the power. Then when you get the power, then you get the women."

Soon, another line would remind him again of his own struggle to win the heart of a seemingly unattainable woman: "With the right woman, there's no stopping me. I could go right to the top." And Jacqueline was indeed the perfect woman for that role.

He switched off the television. Guiding his life according to Hollywood movie scripts and otherwise indulging childish impulses to romanticize life were not the Hershey PA way. The only way he was going to get to the top was through hard work and determination.

When Curtiss picked up a work-in-progress prospectus of a Detroit-based client from his nightstand—his homework for his trip to the British Virgin Islands—he noticed that Jacqueline had left her Tiffany's necklace on his nightstand after he'd left for dim sum that morning. He put it in the drawer for safekeeping, and fell asleep reading.

* * *

Curtiss noticed that small planes seemed to roll and pitch more than larger commercial planes as the DBL corporate jet made its final approach to Beef Island/Tortola Airport in the British Virgin Islands. The other two passengers on the plane, a tax attorney and a DBL client, quietly debated some federal tax regulation while Curtiss looked through the jet's large, round window that afforded a panoramic view of the lush green island paradise in its native habitat: floating in the cyan Caribbean. The sight of the tropics reminded Curtiss of Jacqueline and their time in Aruba. He burned for her.

When the plane had rolled to a stop and powered down beside two black four-door sedans in front of a small private hanger, Curtiss went to the aft luggage area to collect the heavy rectangular black pilot's flight bag that he had been given to deliver to the firm's BVI office. Early that morning at the White Plains airport a frantic senior DBL company officer, who had yet to shave or dress for work, had caught Curtiss just as he was about to leave the waiting area for the plane. He opened the case, stuffed one more brown manila envelope in among a dozen or so others just like it, and relocked the case. He then handed Curtiss a standard, letter-sized envelope and told him to give it to the BVI office managing partner who he would join for lunch, together with an important client at noon that day.

As they disembarked, the two other passengers continued their tax debate, ignoring the smiling pilot's offer of thanks and a handshake as they stepped through the forward doorway. Curtiss made a point to thank the man and shake his hand.

"Thank *you*. Hope you enjoyed the ride," the pilot said. "I'm bringing someone back at four o'clock. Is that you?"

Curtiss read the man's name, Whelan Michaels, off his pilot's license that hung in a frame attached to the cockpit door. "Yep. That must be me, Whelan."

He appeared pleased that not every DBL jet passenger regarded him as just another part of the plane's furnishings. "All that money and they are too cheap to put us up for one night, I guess."

When Curtiss stepped off the foldout stairs onto the tarmac, one of the sedans had already left with the lawyer and the client, and the uniformed driver of the other walked over. "You Curt Bradley?"

"That's right," Curtiss said. When the driver reached for his case, Curtiss pulled it back slightly. "That's all right, I can carry it."

The driver nodded, grinning. "Yeah, all you DBL guys are a little squirrelly about those cases."

The two men settled into their respective driver and passenger seats. "I'm Manny," he said into the rearview mirror. "You got me all day, Curt: first to the Road Town Office, then to lunch at the Hilton with Jerry Stein, the office managing partner, and Mr. Bartakamous, then back to the airport by 3:45. Bing, bang, boom. Not much of a vacation for you, huh?"

Curtiss was surprised at how small the one-story DBL BVI office building was. A man in a three-piece suit was standing at the main entrance door, checking his watch. "Bradley? Come on," the man said brusquely as he led Curtiss into a small conference room. "We've got to sign a release for the case." The man pushed two pieces of paper in front of Curtiss. He signed both documents where indicated; the man co-signed. "Keep this one." He handed Curtiss one copy. "Give it to Belkin's secretary when you get back to the New York office."

Curtiss rose to his feet when the man opened the conference

room door and left him alone in the room. It was only 10:30 am and, not knowing what else to do with himself, Curtiss took a seat.

At nearly eleven o'clock Curtiss overheard voices coming from the hallway: two men were having a conversation about how to best play one of the holes of the golf course on the neighboring island of St. Thomas. After bidding their good-byes in the reception area just down the hall, one of them, a tanned gray-haired man, stopped at the conference room door and looked in. "Are you Curt?"

Curtiss instinctively stood and reached out his hand. "Yes sir."

"Hi, I'm Jerry," he said shaking his hand with a smile. "We're having lunch together with a client today, is that right?"

"Yes. Mr. Bartakamous. I have a letter for you." Curtiss handed Jerry the envelope he had received that morning at the White Plains airport.

Jerry opened the envelope, put his glasses on and read the letter. He then closed the door and both men took a seat. "So, it looks like you are going to be our new courier, Curt." Jerry looked at him over his glasses. "But you know delivering the weekly black case is only part of the job."

Curtiss sat uncomfortably in the silence that Jerry let fill the room.

"What do you know about Bartakamous?" He didn't give Curtiss time to respond. "He is one of our most important preferred clients, and frankly a royal pain in the ass. Demanding as all hell."

Curtiss knew better than to attempt to respond.

"He's always looking for inside information from us, which is why we agree to only meet with him here at the BVI office. You're part of that Detroit-deal financing team, is that right? He'll want to talk with you about that today . . . in detail, if you know what I mean."

Jerry let another silence envelop them.

Curtiss did know what Jerry meant, at least on the face of it: He was being asked to pass along insider information to a man presumably paying top dollar for it. What Curtiss wasn't sure of were the implications of agreeing to perform this task. Was this simply part of paying your dues at a firm like DBL? Had Hank Jarvis, his perp-walked predecessor, not done his work well enough? Or, perhaps, somehow too well? Had he not been discreet enough?

Curtiss took a breath. Belkin, a top player at the firm and on Wall Street, was doing this, so how illegal could it be? Was he really so naive as to believe that his childhood hero, the Hershey School alumnus New York City tycoon, never did anything like this to get to where he got to? There was no doubt that Milton Hershey School virtues had served Curtiss well in Hershey PA, and even Ann Arbor, but could those virtues alone help him navigate a top New York firm? The real world was a complex place, and the meek wouldn't inherit anything within it. This was his opportunity to get out of the dealing room and onto the fast track at DBL; this was the gateway to money and power. And with Jacqueline at his side, there would be no stopping him.

"I understand."

"Good. Then we'll see you at the Hilton at 12:30." Jerry stood, shook Curtiss's hand and welcomed him to the club.

* * *

Curtiss got back to his apartment from the White Plains airport at 10:30 pm and thumbed through the dozen or so restaurant takeout menus that he had collected over his near year in the city, but nothing seemed appetizing to him. He wanted to call Jacqueline, but didn't. Too late, too needy.

The next day, he had an extremely full schedule that started before dawn, and included his first dinner with two of the firm's senior officers. That dinner concluded with after-dinner drinks with the men that stretched to 11:30 pm. Consequently, Curtiss reluctantly let that day, too, go by without speaking with Jacqueline.

Wednesday proved equally busy, but Curtiss made time midday to call Jacqueline during a short break in the action. She didn't answer; nor did her answering machine. *Frustrating.* He spent the rest of the day together with the Detroit-client team and didn't have a moment to himself until he returned to his apartment building at 8:30 pm.

Curtiss retrieved a bundle of mail from his mailbox, went up to his apartment, and immediately called Jacqueline. No answer, and still no answering machine. *Worrisome.* A creeping, twisting feeling had taken residence in his gut even before Jacqueline's handwriting on a plain white envelope among the stack of the day's mail caught his eye. Curtiss tore the envelope open and read the letter inside.

Jacqueline had left for Taiwan on the Monday-morning flight.

Her father had arranged her marriage back in Taiwan.

She made some attempt to describe the cultural reasons why she could not defy her father's will and thereby dishonor her family. She apologized for not having the courage to let Curtiss know that their romance was on borrowed time from the start, and closed by telling him (at last) that she loved him, and wished him a happy life.

* * *

Curtiss attempted to completely submerge himself in work during the two weeks following his return from the British Virgin Islands, which, he was told, thoroughly impressed his bosses at DBL.

Unable to sleep, he found himself frequently staying at his favorite jazz clubs till closing. Even a chance encounter with Herbie Hancock one evening—the man stepping up from the audience onto the stage and playing "Cantaloupe Island"—a song of his that Curtiss loved but had never managed to master on an emotional level—provided not even a full minute's relief. Jacqueline's absence was always with him. Would always *be* with him, he was sure of it.

Another night, a different club. Though Curtiss had earlier been able to hold his own with the other amateur players with whom he attempted to jam that evening, his distracted and pathetic performance at the club's pre-opening session this night earned him nothing but frustration and patronizing looks. After the club opened, he drank steadily the rest of the evening and by the end of it was barely able to carry on a coherent conversation. This he learned when he called Jimmy from another bar at 1:30 am to let him know where he was and that he needed his help.

Jimmy arrived some time later to find him slumped over at the bar.

"Good thing you got here when you did," he heard the bartender say to Jimmy. "We're just about to close and I would've had to call the cops."

Jimmy roused Curtiss, helped him walk to a nearby twenty-four-hour restaurant.

"I can't live without her, Jimmy," Curtiss said when they finally had their coffee cups before them, barely holding back tears.

Jimmy didn't bother to try to reason with him yet, just kept pouring coffee into him and steered the conversation to their college days and the things that were important to Curtiss before Jacqueline had entered his life. When he must have thought Curtiss had sobered up enough to hear it, though, Jimmy wasted no time making him face the reality of his situation. "You can't do this to yourself, Curt. She's gone. You've got to let her go."

Though Curtiss knew Jimmy was right, he didn't respond, so Jimmy hit him with the brutal truth he'd only hinted at before: "Face it, Curt. She was one pay grade above you . . . maybe two. She's out of your league, man."

The words cut Curtiss deeply. Because if he wasn't in her league, what other leagues was he not fit for? Losing Jacqueline meant losing everything he had believed he was destined to become. "I know I could make her happy," he feebly protested.

They continued talking until 5:30 that morning, when Jimmy finally said, "I have got to go, Curt. I've got to catch a 9:00 am flight to LA. Promise me you won't do anything crazy until I get back?"

Curtiss nodded, took a deep breath and released a calm sigh. "I'll be fine."

"I'll put you in a cab and send you home. I want you to go straight to bed and take the day off. You've been working too much."

It was dawn when the two men walked out of the restaurant. Jimmy hailed a cab, opened the door for Curtiss, and gave the driver his address. Away from the diner's bright lights and coffee, Curtiss found he was still well under the influence. Reeling as the cab took the first couple of turns, he asked the driver to pull over. "I'm going to get out for a second. Can you wait a few minutes?"

Curtiss stepped out of the cab, but didn't throw up. It was better, out in the cool dawn air. He filled his lungs, contemplated the empty city streets. He then walked over to a nearby ATM machine, withdrew from his checking and savings accounts all the machine would allow, and got back into the cab.

"JFK," he announced to the driver.

"You got it." The driver swung the cab into a U-turn.

CHAPTER 5

Curtiss woke in a panic as the presidential suite at George's Palace seemed to come crashing down on top of him. His still-adjusting eyes seemed to look up from the bottom of a pool filled with blood.

It was in fact a blaring, grinding noise that had so abruptly awakened him. It sounded as if someone were broadcasting the sound of fingernails scratching a chalkboard through a blown loudspeaker. He rose from bed and followed a pulsating red light to the window and looked down into the alley. The sun had just finished setting and a gathering of perhaps one hundred people had blocked off the entire alley. It looked to Curtiss as if a carnival had been set up just below his window.

It took a few moments for it all to register in Curtiss's mind. As he panned from one end of the alley to the other, he gradually began to discern individual images from the confused scene below. At one end he saw a small procession of people in traditional Chinese dress carrying what looked like a six-foot-long effigy of an automobile made of white paper stretched around a wire frame. They put it down on the street and set it ablaze; it went up in a bright flash of flame that lasted all of five seconds. Curtiss could see several more white paper effigies, one that he could make out to be a house, waiting their turn at the fire.

At the center of the alley scene were tents with people milling around and between them. At the other end, Curtiss identified the source of the incessant noise: a vehicle the size of a midsize moving van that had been converted into something like an old-style traveling circus's show wagon, complete with a stage at the back that had floor lights, a knee-high railing, and a curtain from behind which an entertainer or salesman would emerge. Beside the carnival van was a woman dressed in a white robe who was wailing into a microphone that was hooked up to the vehicle's bull horn-style loudspeakers. She was accompanied by a half-dozen other women, all dressed as she was, who were also crying and wailing in a melodramatic fashion.

Curtiss got dressed, headed down to the first floor and found George watching the street scene while leaning against the doorjamb of his motel entrance, calmly smoking a cigarette.

"What the hell is going on, George?"

"It's a funeral. Mr. Ma down the street passed away. This is his funeral."

"Right here? On the street?"

"Why not? This is where he lived."

Half-burned papers, some with still-glowing edges, blew in front of them and Curtiss picked one up that was nearly intact. It looked like some kind of money: the words "Hell Note" appeared in English across the top and its denomination was $10,000,000.

"Burning fake money?"

"Sure. You don't think you need money in the afterlife?"

"Okay, but why burn it? Why not just bury it with him in his coffin or something?"

"Burning transmits . . . " George paused to search for the right word, " . . . *transforms* it so it can be used in the spiritual world." He explained that Chinese ancestor worship is all about continuing our relationship with the dead. That to Taiwanese Chinese, ghosts are just loved ones who've passed, and who are still among us. And they can still influence our lives, for good and for bad. "So it is best to keep them happy, you see?"

"And burning the car and house effigies is a way to send him a car and house," Curtiss said, speaking aloud his Chinese cultural DNA epiphany.

"You got it." George took a long drag off his cigarette.

Curtiss felt uneasy with the prospect of continuing relationships with dead people. Or maybe guilty, for he certainly hadn't continued his relationships with either of his dead parents. He'd just ossified them in his memory; he pulled them out every so often with fondness and a kind of anesthetized longing, but that was it. Maybe there was something to this ancestor worship after all.

No. For Curtiss, the spectacle before him amounted to living for the dead, something his own cultural DNA told him was socially and emotionally unhealthy.

Still. Remembering Sonya's caution against judging other cultures by the assumptions of his own, he took a step back. This was a way of life that seemed to work for the more superstitious of the Chinese people in Taiwan, and it was clearly a big part of their way of life.

"Those wailers are pretty good," George said, pointing his cigarette butt toward the women. "Maybe I'll hire them to cry at my funeral."

The wailing abruptly stopped, the voices of the crowd hushed in unison, and silence rolled down the alley. The lights encircling the stage on the carnival van began flashing and tango-style music poured through the overloaded loudspeakers. Moments later the stage curtain was thrown open from behind by a woman dressed in something akin to a belly dancer's outfit. Her gyrations were interspersed with dramatic tango dance moves and the entire crowd watched in fascination.

"An exotic dancer at a funeral?"

"Hey, he loved it in life, so why deny him that in death?"

Curtiss grinned. "So are you going to hire her for your funeral, too?"

"No, my wife would kill me."

"So what? You'll already be dead anyway." The two men laughed together.

"Hey, Curt, look over there. You've got to see this. You Americans can't believe it." George grabbed Curtiss's arm and pulled him through the alley to one of the tents, where several men, bare to the waist, were meditating at the center of a circle of onlookers. One of the men pulled what looked like a long stainless steel barbeque skewer out of a bag and swabbed it with alcohol.

"Now watch this priest," George said with glee. "A spirit has taken over his body, so now he can feel no pain."

The priest raised both his elbows in the air, pointed the skewer at one of his cheeks, then gently thrust it in through one cheek and out through the other.

"Christ," Curtiss murmured. George giggled.

The priest was turning around in a slow circle to display his impalement to the crowd. Another priest picked up a baseball bat with nails sticking out, raised it over his head and began hitting himself on the back, drawing blood. A third approached a metal caldron filled with burning incense, dug his hands in, and rubbed the ashes in his face as if he were washing his face at a sink, spilling still-glowing cinders on the ground. His face now blackened from the ash, a lady came out of the crowd and dressed him in a robe and hat. When another woman gave him a drinking gourd, he began to dance humorously and randomly approach people in the crowd asking them: "Yao Pu Yao Ho Chiu?" *Do you want a drink of alcohol?*

"What. The. Hell."

George explained that the god of wine had entered his body. "This spirit loves to drink and get drunk," he said. "A Chiu Kuei . . . kind of like you, Curt."

The priest made his way around the crowd and approached Curtiss. "Ni Yao Pu Yao Ho Chiu?"

"Sorry, I'm driving," Curtiss replied in English, and the priest shrugged and moved on to the next bystander in the crowd.

"How late will this go tonight?"

George laughed. "Oh, this will probably go on for another three days."

"You've got to be kidding me."

"Why don't you get out of the city for a few days, Curt? It will do you some good. Come back after it is over."

The prospect of listening to professional wailers all night for three days did not appeal to Curtiss in the least, so he asked George for a suggestion of where to hide out until it was over.

George suggested Pei T'ou on Yang Ming Mountain. "There are hot springs there."

* * *

Curtiss returned from Pei T'ou relaxed and refreshed, and found that the only thing that remained from Mr. Ma's funeral were scorch marks on the alley's pavement.

The quiet and solitude of Bei T'ou had given Curtiss pause to think about what he was doing in Taiwan. After three days of rest and alcohol-free contemplation, he managed to reluctantly accept that his search for Jacqueline had come to its end and that he needed to return to New York, rebuild his life, and find a way to live without her. The funeral for Mr. Ma was over, but the mourning for the death of his dream of Jacqueline accompanying him to the top of Wall Street was just beginning. Though his heart was as scorched as the pavement in front of George's Palace, it was time to go home.

Curtiss went to the Chennault Pub to say thanks and goodbye to Sonya and Wendy.

"Where have you been?" Wendy exclaimed as Curtiss entered the pub.

"Out of town."

"You are more trouble than you are worth," Wendy said, sliding a three-day-old newspaper across the bar to Curtiss. "Kao Lung Ch'ing is your lover's name," she scolded.

Curtiss picked up the paper's wedding announcement section and saw a photo of Jacqueline in a wedding-photo pose. She looked even more beautiful to Curtiss than she had the first day he saw her in the Chinatown restaurant. "So she's married," he said under his breath.

"No. She is not married yet. That's just a wedding photo: Chinese also take wedding photos before the wedding." Wendy explained that the wedding banquet wasn't for another week, so the couple probably hadn't done their marriage registration yet.

"So there is still time."

"Oh, no. You stay away from that girl, Curt. Her father is Hei Shou Tang."

"Who is that?"

"*What* is that, you mean. The black hand . . . the Mafia," she said. "You forget about her now and go home. Or you will be in big trouble."

"The hell with that. I just survived a three-day funeral in my neighborhood, I can survive an angry father."

"You are going to have one of those funerals yourself if your stick your nose into this," Wendy cautioned.

"Yeah? Well it's my funeral."

Back at George's Palace, Curtiss called the phone number that appeared under Jacqueline's photo. A woman answered the phone. "Wei?"

"Is Jacqueline there?"

"Huh? Wei?"

"Jacqueline Kao?" Curtiss paused. "Kao Lung Ch'ing?"

"Teng I Sha," Curtiss heard the phone being placed down on a table and could hear voices in the background.

Another woman answered. "Hello? This is Spring-Fortune Weddings. Who is calling?"

Curtiss explained that he was from America, a friend of the bride, and that he was in Taipei, had lost his invitation, and needed Jacqueline's phone number.

After he hung up, Curtiss sat on his bed staring at the phone number he had just scribbled on the palm of his hand. He could wash his hands, get on an airplane, and resume his life back in New York City. But what if all he needed to do to claim a life with Jacqueline was make this one call? He picked up the phone and dialed the number.

"Wei?" The sound of Jacqueline's voice melted Curtiss from the inside.

"Jacqueline?"

There was a brief silence on the other end of the line.

"Curt?" Jacqueline said. He could swear she sounded as if she too had longed to hear his voice. "What are you doing calling me?"

"I'm here."

"Here? In Taipei? How did you find me?"

"I need to see you."

"I'm getting married. I thought I'd explained that in my letter."

"Yes. I know. But I need to speak with you."

"Curt . . . " She paused. "That's not a good idea."

"Please. No promises. Just see me so we can talk."

There was a long pause, and then Jacqueline said, "Meet me at the Cantonese restaurant at the Brother Hotel tomorrow at 11:30. We'll have dim sum."

* * *

It wasn't until the automatic plate-glass doors to the Brother Hotel parted for Curtiss that he became conscious of the fact that, mere moments away from succeeding in his quest to find Jacqueline, he had no idea what he would say to her.

He scanned the lobby without spotting her, so decided to wait just inside the hotel entrance. Mercedes Benzes, BMWs, and Cadillacs arrived one after another, offloading their precious cargo of Taiwan's who's who, one of which, eventually, was Jacqueline.

"Curt!" Jacqueline threw her arms around him. "I can't believe you are really here." Curtiss did not reply, content to simply savor their momentary embrace.

As they made their way up the immense white marble spiral staircase at the lobby's center, the tall, gold Ch'i P'ao-clad greeters posing on every other step melodically repeated in unison "Huan Ying, Kuang Ling"—*Warmly welcome your arrival.*

The second floor Cantonese restaurant was decorated in the ornate vein of the National Theater. The hostess recognized Jacqueline and led the couple to her family's private table located within a row of secluded coves along the windows.

"How long have you been in Taiwan?" she said with a broad smile once they were settled.

"Oh, about a month now." Curtiss forced a smile to patch over the hollow sense of foreboding growing within his gut.

"Well, what do you think of Taiwan?"

"It's different." Though eager to dispense with small talk, he knew this answer was inadequate. "The city is a bit of a mess, but the food is good. People are real friendly, too."

Where had he heard *that* before? Saunderson, the plane. Right on all three counts! The bastard even irked him in absentia.

"Where are you staying?" Jacqueline continued to bubble with enthusiasm as if they were reunited school chums, as if she were unaware of what might have motivated Curtiss to fly halfway around the world and spend a month in Taipei.

"Oh, it's a little place . . . a boutique hotel. You wouldn't know it." Curtiss hesitated. "Jacqueline—"

"Curt," Jacqueline interrupted. "I am really sorry for the way I left New York. I realize that it wasn't fair to you. And I am sorry for that. But you need to understand that I am Chinese and my family is very traditional. It's our culture."

"No. I understand that. It's an old culture with thousand-year-old traditions." Curtiss grimaced.

"And Curt, we just aren't going to beat that."

He couldn't bear it. "Jacqueline," he protested, "it just seems like arranged marriages are so . . . archaic, and you are so . . . modern, that's all. I thought we had a life back in New York. We were going somewhere, together."

Curtiss found himself rambling on, anything to keep her from speaking, from shooting him down. He laid bare all of his plans for them, all of his dreams. Explained that he was on a fast track with DBL and that it was only a matter of time before it all broke open for him. That he couldn't do it alone and needed her at his side. That it would be *their* success, not her father's. Something that they would achieve on their own.

Jacqueline slowly hung her head, draping her long black hair over her face like a curtain.

"*Jacqueline.* Think! 'Breakfast at Tiffany's' couldn't have ended with Holly going back to Texas with her husband." As much as he dreaded the answer, Curtiss forced himself to ask the question: "But the important thing is: Is this wedding what you really want?"

Jacqueline looked up at Curtiss and, from behind an ephemeral, melancholic expression, said, "It is what I really want to do."

"For yourself, or your family?"

"They're the same thing, Curt," she replied in a tone that pleaded for him to stop pressing her. After composing herself, she opened the menu. "Shall we order?"

As they dined together over the next hour, Curtiss was stunned by how different Jacqueline was from how she'd been in New York. At some points during their conversation, he felt as if he were with a complete stranger. The sophisticated, independent woman he'd fallen in love with in the city had somehow vanished, or been snuffed out. This Jacqueline prattled on about the social status of people she'd met recently, the latest bizarre behavior of an American pop music star, and the exoticness of the honeymoon destination that awaited her.

Curtiss felt as though he was losing her all over again. Finally he had to say it: "You are like a different person here, Jacqueline, I—"

As always, Jacqueline was one step ahead of him. "This is who I really am, Curt," she said, stiffening. "There is nothing to resolve here. New York was New York, London was London, Italy was Italy. They were all wonderful experiences. But this is who I am and this is where I belong."

While the sedans queued at the Brother Hotel's entrance to collect their masters, one by one, Jacqueline and Curtiss mouthed promises to stay in touch that they would not keep. As Jacqueline's beefy driver opened the door for her, Curtiss couldn't help himself. He swept her into his arms and she melted there as she always had, as though she, too, were straining to assimilate one final impression of him into her soul.

But then she slipped away from him into the car without another word, leaving him alone with the driver, whose cold and remorseless eyes had plenty to say to him: *Mind your own business.* He watched Jacqueline's car drift away from him as if a rope that had tethered their lives together had been severed.

Curtiss was cast adrift in Taipei.

CHAPTER 6

"So what happened?" Wendy sang when she saw Curtiss enter the pub. She popped the top off a bottle of beer and slid it across the bar. "Did you find her?"

Curtiss managed a nod.

"She said go home, right? I told you it was hopeless."

He needed to talk, not receive a lecture from Wendy. "Where's Sonya?"

"I don't know. Come on, Curtiss, what happened?"

"The Jacqueline I knew is dead." Curtiss washed his words down with a long swig from the bottle that Wendy had placed in front of him.

Tough little barmaid that she was, Wendy rallied. "You are lucky, you know that? You got off easy, fooling around with the mafia boss's daughter." She poured whiskey into two shot glasses. "This one is on the house," she said, handing him one of the glasses.

"There's my favorite enabler," Curtiss said, and together they downed the contents of their glasses.

Wendy paused for a moment to take pity on Curtiss, then moved down the bar and gave a warm welcome to two new patrons. Back in action. Curtiss flipped a hundred NT Dollar note on the bar and walked out the door into a sticky Taipei evening.

"Where do you want to go?" the Taipei taxi driver asked, in unusually good English.

"Anywhere I can get a drink."

Curtiss saw the driver glance at the bar he had just emerged from, then give a little shrug. "Back when the American military bases were here in Taiwan, I used to take all the GIs and even some officers to the Combat Zone."

"Sure. That sounds about right."

"You're American, right?" Neon washed over the spot Curtiss chose to fixate upon on the window next to him as they lurched and bumped across town. Seizing his chance to practice his English, the driver related wilder days when the GIs were in town. He had told war stories, all involving local women, alcohol, bar fights, and military police, by the time they reached their destination.

The driver was grinning over the front seat at him. "This is the President Hotel," he said, raising his eyebrow. Curtiss peered out at the aging structure. "At least when the bases were here, all you guys said you can get a decent meal at the Ploughman's Cottage. It is at the end of Shuang Cheng Road, the one right behind the hotel."

Curtiss thanked him, paid him and stepped out of his cab. A sweaty middle-aged foreign man and a scantily clad Chinese lady slid through the taxi door that Curtiss had left open for them, and through the large picture window of the hotel he could see a number of similar couples populating its lobby.

As Curtiss began walking down Shuang Cheng Road—a two-lane street narrowed to barely one lane by hundreds of scooters parked along both sides of the road—someone spoke to him. "Ni Yao Pu Yao Hsiu Hsi?" It was a woman, perched atop the back seat of one of the scooters nearby. Curtiss shrugged, understanding only that she was asking him if he wanted to take a rest, and he kept walking. A few steps on, he realized what she'd been offering. Did he want that? Curtiss was in unexplored emotional territory. Could he ever make love to another woman? Or had the experience with Jacqueline ruined him for life where women were concerned? All he wanted was another drink.

Shuang Cheng Road was a bar street, littered with lit, English-language signs with names like "Pig and Whistle," "Hsiao Lin Pub," and "Maggi's Place." It pulsated with an arrhythmic agglomeration of musical beats from the jukeboxes and bar bands deep within its caverns. When Curtiss's barhopping down Shuang Cheng Road landed him at the Ploughman's Cottage at about 10:30 pm, he didn't feel much like eating and waved off the offer of a menu. Receiving his umpteenth beer of the evening, he swiveled around on his bar stool and watched the band play through the end of their last set of the night. He'd spoken a total of maybe a dozen words that night, having fallen back down into himself, the music echoing sullenly within the hollow emptiness left inside him by the death of New York Jacqueline, and the end of his quest.

Where would he go from here?

When the lights came up, the bar was revealed as a grungy, smoke-grimed space littered with a bizarre collection of foreign castaways ensconced in Taipei's bar-street backwater: third-tier businessman, English teacher, and student alike. All of them caught, as though in the stop-action flash of a camera, frozen in indignation at the interruption of their self-indulgence and lechery. "Time to go," the bartender bellowed. "Finish your drinks and go home."

Curtiss stumbled on the stairs on the way out of the bar. "Damned Taiwan stairs," he cursed, then set himself staggering along Taipei's now darkened streets.

Down one narrow alleyway, he caught sight of a stark-white light cutting through the darkness at street level at some distance. Alone in the dark alley, Curtiss decided to follow the bright light that prevented his eyes from properly adjusting to the darkness around him, keeping him from clearly making out the squeaking shapes that seemed to be crawling around him in the alley. Whatever they were they couldn't be good, Curtiss thought, and picked up his pace.

The light led him to a night market: a food bazaar located at a convergence of alleyways lined with street stalls, each one lit by a single, bare, unfrosted light bulb. Over displays of raw meat, veined internal organs, and exotic sea creatures, a small electric motor hung from a wire, wobbling as it twirled a bent coat hanger that had a ragged strip of dirty cloth tied to one end to keep the flies at bay. Behind the displays, sweaty, tank top- and T-shirt-clad proprietors manned bubbling vats of oil and hot griddles, upon which they cooked food to order. Their patrons sat atop Taiwan's ubiquitous orange plastic stools around chipped and cigarette-burned folding tables that encroached well into the street—the men with their pant legs rolled up over their knees and shirts rolled up over their pot bellies.

The smell of cooking food raised Curtiss's appetite and he strolled the area in search of something he thought he'd have some hope of keeping down. Attracted by steam billowing from a Japanese-style noodle stand, Curtiss took a seat at its street-front counter and began slurping a bowl of noodles. Perhaps it was the food hitting his belly or the realization of just how far he had wandered off the path of his life that was sobering, but Curtiss snapped to.

What the hell was he doing here?

This was it. He would go to the airline office the very next morning and use his return ticket to book a seat on the next flight home. He imagined his bills piling up out of his mailbox at his New York City apartment and his possessions at his desk at the office boxed up and sitting in a closet somewhere, or worse, in a Dumpster. Would DBL even take him back? Curtiss could see the scowls on the faces of his supervisors as he asked for his job back. And how could he face Jimmy after his month-long departure from common sense?

Come what may, it was time to deal with it and get his life back on track. Jacqueline was gone for good. He had only his career to think about now. Junk bonds were Curtiss's ticket to the top, his big chance, and he was blowing it wasting his time alone, across the planet, sucking noodles on some hellish street in Taipei, Taiwan.

Curtiss paid the noodle vendor and set off along an adjacent alleyway in search of a main road where he could hail a taxi. Halfway down the alley he felt a hand tap him on the shoulder. Had he underpaid at the noodle vendor? He turned around to see three large, dark figures haloed by the lights of the night market behind them. Curtiss's diaphragm spasmed as one of the silhouettes jabbed his fist into his gut, and the other two silhouettes quickly stepped up and grabbed Curtiss's arms to keep him from folding to the ground. Another fist landed squarely on Curtiss's mouth, sending a sharp pain through his front teeth and jamming the hinge of his jaw into its socket. With his hands forced unnaturally high up his back, several more blows to his rib cage landed unopposed, and he could feel a rib or two crack from the impact. Unable to take a breath and dazed from another hammer-like blow to the side of his head, he was helpless to resist as the two men forced his knees to the ground and bent him over, each one putting one of his knees on his shoulder blades and raising his arms straight into the air. Curtiss was conscious of the blood streaming from his mouth, gathering in a black pool on the ground under his face. He could only see the shoes and hear the voices of the men who were so expertly beating him.

"Kao Lung Ch'ing no more," ordered one of the silhouettes in broken English. "You go now."

The last thing Curtiss saw before being knocked unconscious was a foot sweeping backwards from the knee, like a soccer player preparing to kick a soccer ball.

Curtiss woke to a stabbing pain from his fractured ribs as he struggled to draw a breath through his blood-encrusted nose. His face on the asphalt, he looked up into the dawn light to see the muzzle of a dog, half bald with mange, sniffing curiously at him—this human debris dumped near overflowing garbage cans. Curtiss swatted the dog away several times, but it repeatedly came back to lick the dried blood caked on his face and hands. He finally connected on the mutt's nose and it yelped and limped away on three legs, its fourth leg dangling and atrophied—no doubt the result of some misfortune that had occurred during its hardscrabble existence.

The only other time in his life that he had been knocked unconscious was when he was kicked by a horse while working an Amish farm one summer. But this felt nothing like that. It felt much worse. He feared that, like the Taipei alley mutt who had just finished snacking on his blood, he had received an irreparable injury that would leave him hobbled in some way for the rest of his life.

After Curtiss rocked himself into a sitting position, he realized that the dog was far from the vilest critter in the alley. Nearby garbage cans hosted rats, some that, from his ground-level perspective, appeared nearly as large as the dog.

He knew that he had to get up and get himself some help. The pain and stiffness throughout his body made the task of getting to his feet extremely difficult, made all the more challenging by a spinning sensation that continuously twisted him off his balance.

Using the wall for support, Curtiss felt his way back to the night market as a blind person would. All the shops were closed and, alone on the street, Curtiss staggered over to a polished stainless steel panel where he could look at his reflection. The swelling and dried blood on his face made him unrecognizable to himself. His nose appeared to be just bruised, not broken, but one of his front teeth was completely missing and the other merely a broken fragment of root dangling from its socket. No, this was not like getting kicked by a horse.

A nearby leaking water pipe served as Curtiss's faucet and his formerly white shirt—buttons missing and saturated with blood in front—became a washcloth that he used to clear away the dried blood from his face and wipe the filth from his wounds. Curtiss knew that he was in bad shape, but his eyes and ears were undamaged, as were his testicles, and he derived some degree of relief in that. Unlike the pathetic mutt, he would eventually heal.

Curtiss walked back to the scene of the crime to pick up his jacket and slip it over his battered upper body. His wallet and cash were still in the breast pocket; apparently Jacqueline's father's henchman were well disciplined and focused on the task at hand, which was to provide him an incentive for never interfering in Jacqueline's life again.

Walking had to become a deliberate act for Curtiss to make it to a main road. He embraced the cliché: one foot in front of the other. As the dizziness subsided, pain took its place and there was simply no way—walking or standing still—to avoid it. Taxi drivers first slowed, then sped off when they had a good look at this gruesome, blood-stained zombie staggering out of the alley. Half a dozen cabs passed him by before one took pity on him and stopped. "Hospital?" the driver asked in English as Curtiss collapsed into the back seat of the taxi.

"No." A new pain from the hinge of his jaw made its appearance as Curtiss tried to speak. He told the driver the location of George's Palace, whistling through the hole where his two front teeth used to be as he did so.

George was busy placing burning incense sticks into his alter when Curtiss appeared in the doorway. "Ai Ya!" he exclaimed. "What happened to *you*?" He rushed over to Curtiss and pulled one of his arms over his shoulder.

"Oh, you know . . . " Curtiss slumped, crutching himself on George. "I had a little disagreement with my girlfriend. I guess I lost the argument."

"She must be one tough chick." George helped Curtiss up the stairs to his room, resting frequently along the way. He turned the shower on for Curtiss, who thanked him but insisted that he could take care of things from there.

Sticking his head under the shower, he turned the faucet until the water ran cold, exacerbating his throbbing headache, but soothing his scrapes and bruises.

The water having washed away the rubble, Curtiss could properly survey the damage in the bathroom mirror. In spite of the severity of the blows to his face, he did not have any deep cuts, but was scraped and bruised badly in a number of places. He pulled back his fat lip to have another look at his bloodied mouth and the hanging fragment of tooth. It stung when it came in contact with the cooler air. Curtiss knew it had to go: he grabbed the tooth fragment with his fingertips, closed his eyes, and pulled.

Despite the pain from his injuries, Curtiss had managed to sleep through the entire day and the next morning. George was knocking on his door. "Curtiss. I have someone here to help you. Can I come in?"

"Yeah," Curtiss shouted lamely, having stiffened up to such a degree that he felt he was unable to get out of bed, even just to open the door.

Using his master key, George entered, together with an elderly man wearing a traditional Chinese overcoat and carrying a large leather bag. "This man is an herbalist. He's going to help you."

The herbalist repeatedly chirped his lips and exclaimed "Ai Ya," as he made clinical note of Curtiss's extensive injuries.

"He is going to try some remedies on you, Curt."

Curtiss nodded. The treatment began with the offering of a pill. "What is this?" Curtiss asked.

"Aspirin."

Curtiss laughed but quickly stopped, wincing at the pain. He wanted to ask George how aspirin could be considered a Chinese herbal remedy, but it was not worth the pain to ask. He downed the pill.

The herbalist had Curtiss roll over onto his stomach and used a pair of chopsticks to insert a small, flaming cotton ball into a thick glass cup to heat the air inside. Curtiss watched in the reflection of a blackened TV screen as the herbalist then pulled the cotton ball out and quickly placed the mouth of the cup onto Curtiss's bare back. This created a vacuum inside the glass, which stuck it to his skin. The herbalist repeated the process until Curtiss could feel his back covered with leeching glass cups. Later, in the mirror, he would see two neat rows of large circular hickeys down the entire length of his back.

"Pretty strange, eh?" George asked rhetorically. "The suction draws out the poisons in your body. Kind of like, another way of cleaning out a wound so it can heal properly. Except for the entire body." Curtiss nodded and wondered if it worked for drawing out the infection of love, purifying the heart and brain of the pathogen that makes people do stupid things in its name.

Curtiss paid the herbalist, who then handed George a few hand-made, folded paper sachets and left.

"You need to take this powder for the next few days. It smells bad . . ."

"But it is good, right?" Curtiss unfolded the sachet, revealing a white powder that smelled of moldy backwoods after a spate of rain. He brought it to a glass of water next to his nightstand to dissolve it.

"No." George stopped him. "You dump it in your mouth first, at the back of your throat, then quickly wash it down with water. If you try to make a solution out of it, you'll never be able to drink it all because it tastes so bad. Trust me."

Curtiss, trusting George's judgment when it came to eating bad-tasting things, gagged on the powder, but quickly washed it down as he had been instructed to.

George gave Curtiss a paper bag wrapped with twine. "Here, these are pajamas. You are going to need a lot of rest."

*   *   *

Curtiss's self-consciousness about visiting the neighboring courtyard in only pajamas and slippers faded quickly when he found it populated by elderly people meandering around in the same attire.

He took the opportunity over his near two-week convalescence among Taipei's seniors community to improve his spoken mandarin, learn a few basics about Chinese written characters while playing Mahjong, and, in the latter days, practice T'ai Chi. One lady began bringing Curtiss homemade lunch boxes filled with all kinds of delectable foods, and soon there were a half-dozen lunchboxes and doting little old ladies to greet Curtiss at the courtyard every morning competing for his taste buds.

By the beginning of the third week after his beating, his facial wounds had largely healed, save for some bruising and the white patches of virgin skin that replaced his scabs. He felt well enough to invite George and his family to a dinner at the Lai Lai Sheraton

Cantonese restaurant to thank them for their help. At the end of the dinner, Curtiss presented the family with a box of European chocolates and California red wine.

"George, if it wasn't for you and your family," Curtiss said, raising his glass to them, "I don't know what would have happened to me. You really saved my life."

"Na Li, Na Li," George said, waving his hand dismissively. "We didn't save your life. You were going to survive. We just took care of you a little, that's all. We did *not* save your life. Don't put that on us!"

Later, George elaborated. "It's a curse, Curt, for the one who saves the person's life. If the person you save turns out to be a bad guy, and steals or kills somebody, then you are responsible." Curtiss looked blankly at George, who rolled his eyes at Curtiss's thickness and tried again. "If you hadn't saved that person's life, they wouldn't have been around to do those terrible things." George then looked at him with a seriousness Curtiss had not seen in him before. "I don't want to be responsible for whatever you are going to do the rest of your life."

Curtiss considered asking George what atrocities he thought him likely to commit, but instead opted to add this concept of liability with two degrees of separation to his growing collection of stray bits of unresolved Chinese cultural DNA. He'd just go with the flow on this one. "That's pretty profound, George. Did Confucius say that?"

"No. Some Hollywood screenwriter made it up. So-called 'ancient Chinese wisdom' for some Charlie Chan movie back in the 1920s or 1930s. Still, it sounds pretty good, eh? If Confucius didn't say it, he should have."

* * *

The previous evening's red wine with George and his family ended the drinking hiatus he'd been on during his recovery. He walked into the Chennault Pub just after it opened.

"Curt?" Wendy was genuinely surprised to see him. "Where have you been?"

"Around." Curtiss took his usual seat at the bar.

Wendy studied his face, which still retained some patchy discoloration and swelling. "What happened to you?"

Curtiss revealed his two missing front teeth with a broad, cheesy smile. "I had a little disagreement . . . "

"Ai Ya!" Wendy exclaimed, stepping back with one hand locked on her hip and the other over her mouth. "I told you," she said, wagging her finger at him. "You're lucky you weren't chopped into Ma P'u Tou Fu-sized pieces and thrown into the Tan Shui!"

The cold beer braced his throat, soothing his craving. Alcohol flowed through him as his courtyard T'ai Chi instructor had explained Chi should flow, if unchecked.

He had kept the flow unchecked for two more rounds when light streamed into the darkened bar. He turned to find Kao holding the door open for Sonya.

"He's back," Wendy sang out, as she headed into the storage room behind the bar.

Curtiss rose to his feet and Sonya kissed him on the left, right, then left cheeks. She placed her hands on both sides of Curtiss's face and said, "I see that they found you."

"They did." Curtiss smiled.

"They did indeed," Sonya said, closely examining Curtiss's face. "Have you eaten?"

"Not yet. I was planning to—"

"Kao?" Sonya called, pulling a thousand NT Dollar note from her purse. "Be a dear and get us some takeout from the Lai Lai's Italian kitchen." She recited an order of two types of pasta and gnocchi with a marinara sauce to scowling Kao. "Wendy?"

"Hai!" Wendy's voice echoed from the back room.

"We'll have wine tonight. A nice bottle of red, please."

"Hai!" Wendy acknowledged.

"Shall we sit?" Sonya took Curtiss by the arm and escorted him to her table behind the screen.

Their private dinner of red wine and pasta was by far the most civilized experience Curtiss had had since his night at the opera with Sonya, and a welcome change from his steady diet of bone marrow, bitter vegetable, and tofu soup during his recovery (save the spoils of the courtyard culinary competition he'd enjoyed courtesy of Taipei's seniors).

Curtiss looked around the room at the war memorabilia. "You know," he said, "when my father was younger than I am now, he was already a Doolittle Raider, a Lieutenant in the U.S. Army Air Force with men under his command. And me? The sum total of my contribution to the world to date has been sitting at a desk peddling junk bonds."

Sonya smiled sympathetically. "Selling junk makes an important contribution to society too."

Selling junk. Curtiss was darkly amused by how succinctly Sonya's statement summed up how he now felt about his work at DBL.

She told Curtiss that he shouldn't compare his life to the war generation. That during the war, people around the world were killing each other wholesale, by the millions, and that made everyone dream for a better world. Her eyes seemed to focus in space as she appeared to reflect deeply on that phase of her life. "Those men, those *boys*, weren't perfect. Believe me, you learn a lot living with a bunch of mercenary pilots for a couple of years. They had their flaws and their lapses in judgment. And they made mistakes, some that even cost the lives of their fellow soldiers and airmen.

"A lot went on that you don't see in the newsreels. Fear, dread, and regret about the horrible things that happen in war and the things that war forced them to do." Sonya looked sternly at Curtiss. "The Japanese army executed a quarter million Chinese men, women, and children to intimidate China, and as reprisal for them helping Doolittle Raiders like your father escape." She paused, seemingly to let that fact sink in.

Men like his father were nonetheless remarkable, she went on to say. And what made them great was that, in spite of their faults, in spite of the horrors they had seen and been a part of, they aspired to build a better world when it was all over. "The world you grew up in, Curtiss, is the world that they fought for." Sonya smiled tenderly at him. "The world you've experienced, dear, was your father's gift to you."

But Sonya's words only added weight to Curtiss's self-imposed burden to pay tribute to his father's accomplishments, and made him feel even less sure about himself and what he had been doing with his life back in New York.

He wondered why Sonya had taken an interest in him the way she did. Was it because he was a fellow American abroad who needed a hand? Or was it pity because he was so pathetic?

"I'm going home now, dear," Sonya announced as she began rifling through her purse. "You'll need to get your mouth fixed." She handed Curtiss a business card. "This is the best dentist in Taiwan.

Dr. Chuang. His office is located in Snake Alley. He's done my dental work for years." Sonya smiled, showing off her perfect teeth. "I'll phone him and let him know to expect you."

* * *

"Hua Hsi Chieh," acknowledged the taxi driver as he handed the dentist's business card back to Curtiss.

Hua Hsi Alley was a pedestrian alley lined with small shops that were closed during the day. Hand-painted images of cobras and other snakes on small billboards above some of the shops confirmed that he was in the right place: Taipei's Snake Alley.

He followed the street numbers and walked up a flight of stairs to Dr. Chuang's second-floor dentist office. Dr. Chuang spoke near-perfect English and his diploma from UCLA medical school hung prominently on the wall. His office was stocked with the usual dental equipment and was orderly, clean, and well lit. The dentist made an impression of Curtiss's upper teeth and told him to return in a week for fitting his prosthetic teeth. When he asked about payment, Dr. Chuang explained that Sonya had told him that she would take care of it and that he was not to accept any money from him.

Though he'd accepted Sonya's largesse once with the tuxedo, having her pay his medical bills was another thing altogether. It would only further degrade his deteriorating self-image. Curtiss vowed to pay for his new teeth in the end.

With a week to kill until his teeth were ready, Curtiss immersed himself in the purgatory culture of misfits and runaways in Taipei's Combat Zone.

Bobbie, a petite, tight-bodied Taiwanese lady, dominated the pool table located in the basement of the Ploughman's Cottage, fleecing unsuspecting foreign businessmen who fell through the cracks into the Combat Zone for a night of slumming. Curtiss watched her admiringly as she plied her trade as a pool shark. She wore high-heeled shoes, hot pant-length jean cut-offs and a barely adequate tube top, and swung her long, black hair over her shoulder when making stretch shots as her signature distraction move. Marks who dared play around with her when it came time to pay up would get fair warning from Bobbie, who would raise her fist and say, "I'll give you a knuckle sandwich if you don't pay up." Twice during the week he'd seen her follow up this warning with a pop to the jaw.

Bobbie and Curtiss liked each other from the moment they saw each other and their desire to consummate this mutual attraction was irresistible—bringing to an end Curtiss's self-imposed celibacy. Bobbie was married to a pot-bellied Swede, but although both of them lived in the same house in Taipei's suburbs, they lived their own lives. Her husband, Bjorn, showed up at the bar one night with a twenty-something girl hanging on his arm while Bobbie was coaxing a double or nothing bet from a British businessman. Bjorn threw her the family car keys, letting her know that he was planning to stay in town with his girlfriend that night and that she should stay sober enough to drive the car home. Her husband smiled and raised his glass to Curtiss from across the bar, and Curtiss, ever polite, reflexively returned the salute. But was he really toasting the man whose wife he was sleeping with? Did people really live like this? Was there nothing that was off limits in the Combat Zone?

* * *

When Curtiss arrived at Dr. Chuang's office for his 6:30 pm appointment to receive his dental implants, Hua Hsi Alley's shop owners were busy rolling up street-front steel doors, rolling out storefront displays, and unfurling cloth awnings for the evening trade. Curtiss didn't give it a second thought that the street's shops were closed during the day and opened at night, dismissing Snake Alley as just another Taipei night market.

As Sonya promised, Dr. Chuang did excellent work. The prosthetic front teeth were well sized, shaped, and colored to match Curtiss's natural teeth. The fitting needed some finessing, but after repeated adjustments, they finally inserted perfectly in place.

As Curtiss descended the stairs toward the front door of the building, tonguing his new front teeth and savoring the feeling of having something there again, he became aware of a din coming from behind the exit door. He opened it, revealing what struck Curtiss as a vision of hell on earth: Quiet and subdued by day, Hua Hsi Alley had transformed at night into a festering wound of iniquity cut deep into the heart of the city.

The street was packed with people from end to end. Curtiss wondered if it was his imagination or the bad lighting, but this crowd somehow looked inexplicably different from any other he'd encountered in the city—abused and downtrodden in the way they carried themselves, physically twisted and broken, both pitifully hopeful and hopeless.

Something solid and wet smacked the brick wall near his head, sending a shiver up Curtiss's spine and leaving one side of his shirt speckled with moist bits of red and green. Picking the colored bits from his shirt, Curtiss moved across the street to where a vendor was standing on a platform at the front of one of the shops. Like a carnival barker he was working the crowd that he had drawn. After shouldering his way to the front, Curtiss could see that the shop was packed with cages filled with live snakes and turtles. Several disemboweled, skinless snake bodies hung next to a bloody chopping block. In a glass display case, among jars preserving snakes and scorpions, he saw what looked like a stick of beef jerky with fur on the tip at one end and a bone on the other. The price on the display card in front of the item read NT$ 7,500, and the English translation: deer penis. Displayed on the wall were several poster-sized animations of a cut-away view of the lower human male torso, complete with Chinese characters labeling arrows pointing to various parts of the reproductive organs.

It occurred to Curtiss that he was standing before a kind of organic male virility shop.

An orangutan, its foot chained to a wall inside the shop, perched upon a trapeze with a dispassionate expression on its face. Narrating each of his actions, the showman went to work, starting by skillfully milking venom from a snake into a shot glass. He then plucked a different kind of snake from one of the cages by the tail and swung it in a vicious circle, violently bouncing its head off of a stainless steel table. Clasping the thoroughly stunned snake's head in a large metal paperclip that hung from the ceiling on a wire, the man pulled the snake's body taut by its tail and, using a pair of rusty, blood-stained scissors, slit the snake open from anus to jaw. The showman moved quickly to capture the blood dripping from the snake's body with the shot glass with one hand and, with the other, pulled out what Curtiss was later told was most likely the snake's gall bladder. Though disemboweled, the snake writhed when the man let loose and proceeded to squeeze a green liquid from the snake's gall bladder into the bloody shot glass, along with a few snippings of the gall bladder itself. Finally, he placed the shot glass onto a silver tray, laid a pill next to it and offered it to the crowd. An average-looking man wearing a suit stepped forward and placed three thousand NT Dollar notes on the tray, put the pill in his mouth, and downed the contents of the shot glass in one go, as casually as if he were finishing off a rum and coke in a bar.

The reek of the amalgam of high-potency preserving alcohol, animal blood, and excrement provided olfactory competition for the grotesque horrors assaulting Curtiss's visual cortex in a race to separate him from his last meal.

The orangutan, bored with the proceedings, bided its time by fidgeting with several turtles in a tub that were awaiting their time at the chopping block. When he picked one up and placed it on top of his head, the turtle, in a defensive action, clamped down on the hair there. It wasn't until the orangutan attempted to remove the turtle that it discovered that a sizable wad of its hair was locked in the turtle's mouth. With a remarkably human expression of horror on its face, the orangutan hooted in panic as it pulled wildly on the turtle until it came away, together with a mouthful of orange hair. Annoyed at the audacity of this lower life form, the orangutan flung the turtle, gangling simian-style, over the heads of the crowd, missing Curtiss by mere inches, shattering it on the wall across the street.

Curtiss staggered back into the center of the alley, realizing now what had earlier decorated his shirt green and red. A bizarre thought leapt to mind: What if it had flown only five inches or so lower and hit him in the eye? And if he lost his eye, how would he ever explain what had happened? What could he say—"An orangutan hit me in the eye with a turtle"? Would anyone believe him? He longed for the bright street lights and flowing traffic of an intersecting thoroughfare at the end of the alley: the promise of a return to normalcy.

Passing a dozen or so similar slaughterhouses along the way, he stopped momentarily to peer down a narrow, well-traveled side alley lit red with hanging lanterns. Down the length of the alley, prostitutes leaned from narrow doorways, reaching out melodramatically as if attempting to snare potential customers who strayed too close to the entrance of their lairs. Curtiss got it: Here was where the snake blood and venom merchants' customers went to put their purchases to the test.

One door down from the alley, Curtiss saw a sandwich board

standing in front of a shop that had a Caduceus medical symbol on its door displaying graphic photographs of various advanced-stage skin diseases on and around male genitalia. Repulsed, Curtiss still had to marvel at the efficiency with which the Chinese anticipated their customers' needs. Snake Alley was not just another Taipei night market.

* * *

When Curtiss landed on the floor it took him a beat to realize it was the floor of an apartment and that he was in a bedroom. He was wondering what he might have done to his bedmate—*Nina? Or was it Tina?*—to justify her pushing him out of her bed when she screamed in terror from the bed above him and the floor beneath him began moving in a way that floors should not move.

At last it dawned on him that he had been thrown out of bed by an earthquake. On the eighteenth floor of a twenty-story building, it felt as if a giant hand was repeatedly pushing the side of the building, sliding him and everything in the room to and fro across the floor. There was one final, violent shove, after which the building seemed to hang for a moment as it leaned precariously to one side. Curtiss could feel it straining, as if deciding if it might want to snap in half. In that split second Curtiss saw himself, quite clearly, crashing down to the ground inside the top floors of the building.

But the building snapped back instead, rocking back and forth several times before settling back on its foundation.

"Ai Ya!" the young woman exclaimed.

"Ai Ya is right," Curtiss said, rejoining her on the bed just as she pulled the sheet over her warm, naked body. Sliding a palm over that silky sheet and the luscious warmth beneath it, he discovered that the fear engendered by his near-death experience had not only flooded his system with adrenalin, but proven itself a male enhancer surely as efficacious as any deer penis jerky or snake blood, venom, and gall bladder juice cocktail.

"Ni, Hao Ma?" he asked.

Though clearly shaken by the quake, she hadn't forgotten why she had invited Curtiss to come home with her the night before, and raised the sheet for Curtiss to slide in under.

Curtiss and his lady friend had worked up an appetite and, with her snugly under his arm, they sauntered to the Combat Zone for a British-style breakfast of blood sausage, eggs, and baked beans at the Ploughman's Cottage.

It was Sunday morning, and with his first Bloody Mary of the day in hand, he scanned the scene. A good portion of the bar crowd from the night before—the usual suspects of expats and stray businessmen—were in the Ploughman's basement nursing hangovers with one hair-of-the-dog remedy or another.

Before their breakfast had arrived, a fortyish American man stepped up onto the stage where the regular Ploughman's band played in the evenings. He turned on one of the amplifiers, pulled an electric guitar from a guitar case leaning against it, and stepped up to the microphone. "This is a little known Chinese song," he announced. "It's called 'T'u Ning.'" And then began tuning the guitar, accompanied by moans from the audience at his pun.

It wasn't long before another middle-aged man joined him on stage and took a seat at the band's drum set, thumping the bass drum as he rejigged the other drums and cymbals into his preferred configuration, and another man loosened his fingers doing scales on the keyboards.

Curtiss stepped to the stage. He pulled a trumpet free from its stand at the same time a long-haired, twenty-something Taiwanese man finished slipping the bass guitar strap over his head and began slapping the strings with one hand, while frantically fingering the fret board like a lead guitarist doing a solo with the other.

The keyboardist then played the legendary riff from Herbie Hancock's "Cantaloupe Island," spontaneously drawing the other instruments together like a 78 RPM record coming up to speed on a gramophone, and the impromptu band fell into sync.

Curtiss played.

The membrane of restraint that had always held Curtiss in as a player, that allowed him to be a careful, responsive session member but never take off, burst open that morning. The music flowed through him and from him, like unblocked Chi. The spirit of jazz spontaneity and genuine improvisation was upon him in that grungy basement bar for the first time in his life. He reached for the notes and they were, effortlessly, there: the right notes at precisely the right time.

The other players and the audience did their parts—the players played, the audience applauded and cried out—but they all did so with a new restraint of their own, all of them hanging back as if to give space to what all of them might have sensed was the most astounding, authentic performance of Curtiss's life, when his body seemed to fade away and his raw emotions became one and the same with his instrument, manifesting in music all his sadness and joy, his pain and lust, fear and triumph, and rhapsodizing the attainment of his complete emancipation.

Curtiss was free.

* * *

Curtiss asked George to show him where the Northwest Airlines office was on his frayed Taipei city map, walked there, and cashed in his return ticket. He inserted enough cash to cover his dental work into an envelope, wrote Sonya's name on the front, stuffed the rest into his front pocket and left for the General Chennault Pub.

"Sonya's not here," sang Wendy as he entered the pub door.

"I'm not staying," Curtiss said, raising his hand to stop Wendy from popping the cap off a frosty bottle of Taiwan Beer. He gave Wendy the envelope and asked her to pass it on to Sonya.

"Sure." Wendy squinted at Curtiss. "Going somewhere?"

"Nope." He then leaned over the bar, pulled Wendy over, and gave her a sincere kiss on the lips. "Looks like I'm going to be around for a while."

CHAPTER 7

Curtiss had become the only true regular at the Ploughman's Sunday morning jam sessions. The band called itself The Usual Suspects, which was ironic since, given the rate of churn among the pool of expats from which they drew, each jam session would invariably begin with a call for a bass player or a keyboardist, or drummer, or a singer.

But since he never knew where he'd end up the night before, Curtiss's trumpet was always waiting for him in its case behind the stage, where the management was kind enough to allow him to stow it.

This latest Sunday morning's jam session was by far the worst performance of The Usual Suspects to date. The chemistry for synchrony and improvisation just wasn't there for that day's crew of second- and third-timers, and new volunteers that Curtiss had called up to the stage that morning. The thrill of that one, magic impromptu session was long gone.

It was the height of the steamy-hot Taipei summer—nearly four months since his arrival—and the thrill for the parade of faceless Taiwanese female playmates through his life had also faded. Sitting among the usual suspects in the audience at the Ploughman's that morning while downing his Bloody Mary, he watched with disgust as a man in his late fifties harried a Taiwanese girl, who was doing her level best to conceal her discomfort. Where would his own recent life of debauchery and hedonism lead him, after all? Was there ever an end to it? When he looked at the degenerate across from him, was he looking at his own future?

It was then that it dawned on Curtiss that he was the only remaining member of the original Usual Suspects. All the others had gone. Everyone was going somewhere, except him. It was at that very moment that he decided that he needed to head back to New York. Whether with DBL or another firm, or out of the industry altogether, he needed to rebuild his life there. It was time to go home.

The first step: he had to rebuild his cash reserves, and fast. He needed enough to buy a one-way air ticket back home and to support him long enough to find a job there. He figured he needed a stake that would support him for at least six, maybe nine months, in order to get back on his feet. He'd no doubt been evicted from his apartment, but could probably count on the building's superintendent to have collected and stored his unsalable possessions, including the milk crate containing his personal records and his father's U.S. Military Intelligence KIA report, in the building's storage room in the basement. So he'd likely need to repurchase home furnishings and a wardrobe. Taking into account security deposits, monthly rent, and other expenses, the figure he needed to amass surprised and depressed him.

* * *

The phone rang in Curtiss's presidential suite. "Wei," he said into the receiver.

"Hello, is this Curtiss?" a husky, Chinese-accented female voice asked.

"This is Curt." He did not recognize the voice and so asked who it was.

"I know you from the Ploughman's, but you probably won't remember me."

Faces flashed through Curtiss's mind, but none separated itself from the jumbled agglomeration of his alcoholic-hazed memories from the Ploughman's. He couldn't recognize her voice. "Well, are you going to tell me who you are?"

"I'd rather not. Can we just talk for a while?"

Curtiss's curiosity got the best of him. "Sure. What do you want to talk about?"

"Let's talk about you. I like you, Curtiss."

"I'm sure I would like you, too, if I knew who you were."

"Oh, we could never meet again. But we can talk."

Now officially intrigued with this mystery caller, Curtiss made himself comfortable on his bed and spent the next half hour talking with her. She was highly skillful at getting him talking and persuaded him to discuss his journey to Taiwan with relative ease. Curtiss was a believer in the wisdom of the adage 'always know who is buying your lunch,' but the conversation with this stranger was so cathartic for him that he enjoyed it immensely and set caution aside. "Are you sure you don't want to meet somewhere?"

"No. That is not possible. I'll call you again sometime." She hung up the phone.

Over the next week Mystery Caller began calling with greater frequency and their conversations became increasingly like those one would have with a true confidant, or even a psychiatrist.

When the phone rang one night at 7:00 pm, their 'appointed time,' Curtiss knew it was her. "An educated foreigner like you can make a lot of money in Taiwan, you know." She explained that she worked for the *big brother* of the Taiwan-China import-export business who might take him on for a few months. It was very lucrative. "Who knows, you might make a career out of it. Why don't you at least meet him and see? Meet Ta Ko."

"I don't know . . . " Curtiss hesitated, his detached and carefree lifestyle of late having left him wary of even the slightest burden of responsibility.

"Well, you do know that this path that you have been on—drinking every night, womanizing—is all an act of emotional self-immolation."

A little stunned by the harshness of this critique, Curtiss didn't respond.

"Curtiss, Jacqueline will never be a part of your life again."

Jacqueline suddenly appeared there in the room with him, conjured up by his skillful anonymous analyst. But rather than the usual hollowness that had always expanded within his chest whenever he thought of her, as he still did from time to time, this time his mind and heart were a blank slate for Mystery Caller to write upon.

"The best way to get past something like that is to go in a positive direction, not one of self-destruction. Otherwise, this obsession with her will never end, and will continue to rule your life."

Curtiss knew she was right. His obsession for Jacqueline over the past six months had led him right to where he was. And being completely honest with himself, not returning to New York was as much about lack of money as it was his reluctance to return to a life there without her.

* * *

Taipei's ubiquitous tile-clad suburban apartment blocks yielded to gated entrances to private driveways as Curtiss's taxi wound up the lichen-stained Yang Ming Mountain road, deeply embedded among a thick canopy of overhanging sub-tropical trees. The driver dropped Curtiss in front of one of the gates.

"Ni Shih Shei?" the guard asked from behind the gate.

"Curt Bradley. I'm here to see Ta Ko," he said in Mandarin.

The security guard spoke into his walkie-talkie, mangling the pronunciation of Curtiss's name, but received permission to let him through nevertheless. The guard gestured to follow the driveway that snaked through lush flora to a large house with a moss-covered red tiled roof supported by white stucco walls.

The large wooden front door he approached, ornately carved with a dragon and phoenix, was opened by a man in a black suit who indicated to Curtiss that he should remove his shoes and don slippers. The man then led him to a Japanese-style tatami room with floor-to-ceiling picture windows on three sides, a tatami mat floor, and a two-foot-high table with pillows for seating at its center.

Curtiss took a moment to take in his surroundings. Out one window was a well-tended Japanese dry-garden; thick jungle was framed in another; and a third afforded what must have been a spectacular view of the Taipei city lights on a clear night. A woman dressed in a Chinese Ch'i P'ao entered the room carrying a tray that held a clay and porcelain tea set. She smiled politely at him as she knelt beside the table. Watching her carry out an elaborate tea preparation ritual, Curtiss embraced how the serenity and sense of balance of the world in which he now found himself soothed his muddled emotional state. He breathed deeply the blend of the soft rush and rice straw of the tatami mats with the tea as she dumped the first steeping into a bowl.

"The first infusion opens up the dried leaves and rinses them. You start drinking from the second infusion," said a deep male voice from the room's entrance.

Curtiss turned to see a tall, broad shouldered man in his late forties entering the room. He was well groomed, with slicked-back hair, and was dressed in a Chinese T'ang Chuang jacket and baggy black pants. He held out his hand. "You must be Curtiss."

"Yes. Curt Bradley," he said shaking his stout hand. "And you are Ta Ko?"

"Call me Lu. Ta Ko means 'big brother.' It is an informal title of . . . respect," Lu said with a warm smile. "Please, we'll have some tea." Lu gestured him to the tea table. "Taiwan produces some of the best tea in the world, you know. And there is a market for it in Mainland China." The men sat down together and Lu spent the next quarter hour educating him on the merits of Taiwan tea, and the art and practicalities of Chinese tea preparation. He then asked Curtiss about his possible interest in his import and export business.

"Yes. Our mutual friend mentioned that you could use someone with my background."

Lu smiled and studied Curtiss for a moment. "What do you know about Taiwan and Mainland China?"

Curtiss revealed that he knew that they were technically still at war and that Taiwan has a Three-Noes Policy towards the communists: no contact, no compromise, no negotiation. Lessons learned from his earlier conversations with Sonya.

"Yes, that's true. But Mainland China has its Three-Linkages Policy: opening up postal, transportation, and trade links between China and Taiwan. And China has been winning the three-policy cold war lately. Things are changing, Curtiss. And where there is change, there are gray areas. And where there are gray areas, there is money to be made."

Lu explained that Taiwanese travel to and trade with Mainland China was one such gray area. And to sweeten the pot, China had invited first-time visitors from Taiwan to bring Japanese motorcycles, cameras, and TVs, American cars, and other consumer goods into Mainland China duty-free. His travel agency provided the Taiwan tourists to China, his Hong Kong partner provided the goods, and their partner in Mainland China extracted the revenue for all of them.

Lu smiled and looked at Curtiss in such a way that Curtiss thought he might be seeking some affirmation of his understanding.

"So you run a travel agency?"

Lu acknowledged that he did, but told him that that is not where the money is being made.

"Sorry, but I don't quite follow. How do you make money when these tourists bring goods into China duty free?"

Lu elaborated. His tour guides give each Taiwanese traveler 500 Hong Kong dollars to carry waybills—shipping invoices—across the China border, where Chinese Customs *chops* them—stamps them with an official seal—approving them for duty-free importation. His tour guides then bring the waybills back to his Hong Kong partner, who has matching containers of goods ready to ship from the Hong Kong port into China. And they use the waybills to deliver the goods into China duty free.

"Okay, so the tourists don't actually own the goods, your partners do. So, it is an import and export business."

"Yes, but that's where the 'gray' part comes in." Lu went on to explain that after the goods are received by his partner on the China side duty free, he resells them at duty-paid full price in China and that all the partners share in the proceeds. They not only make a profit on the sale of the goods, they in effect pocket the duty on them as well. And China's import duty rates can be as high as 100% on some categories of goods. "The duty-free angle alone is worth tens of millions of dollars a year," Lu said with a broad smile.

Curtiss took a moment to absorb the arrangement, recalling Wendy's line from one of her East vs. West coaching sessions: The smartest distance between two points is never so simple as a straight line.

"In China you need to always look beyond the apparent to see where the real value is being transacted," Lu said as he refreshed his teacup, then explained that, especially when it came to gray areas, things are rarely what they seem. That as China transforms itself— reopened itself to the world—nothing is black and white.

"Okay. So how can I be of use to you?"

Lu made it clear that gray-market businesses depend on trust. And trust only went so far in their business. Having a westerner like Curtiss involved—a so-called "legitimate foreign businessman"— would help him keep things in check. His buffer against corruptibility. "I can insert you as a professional manager who is going to help us professionalize the management and operation on the Hong Kong side. At the same time you can keep an eye on things for me."

"It all sounds illegal to me."

"Let's just say it is not illegal . . . for now. That is, there is no specific law against it." Lu patiently explained the pragmatism of China's application of law, that they were indeed exploiting a policy with a loophole that allowed them to do what they were doing. And that it is that way by design. For one thing, politically, China wants to encourage travel and trade with Taiwan. Also, China wants to encourage overseas Chinese to get vested into China trade, so that later when they impose and enforce rules, and taxation, investors will be in too deep to back out. "The loophole will close someday, when it best suits China's needs. But in the meantime, there is a lot of money to be made."

Curtiss paused for a moment to ponder Lu's last statement. "How much money?"

"We are running an average of twenty busloads of tourists per week across the border. I can pay you ten thousand American dollars a month. Cash."

Curtiss silently sipped his tea, did some quick math in his head related to rebuilding his stake, but also cautioned himself to slow down. Could this, like his first meeting with Jerry Stein at DBL's British Virgin Island office, be another defining moment in his life? Wasn't it likely that those engaged in this business—like those at DBL, who also made their livings on the margins of the law—would inevitably succumb to the temptation to cross the line?

But did all that matter out here in the wild east? His sensible rural Pennsylvanian values said it did. But he wasn't planning to build a career with these guys, after all. And everything in this part of the world was in flux, so pulling thirty or forty grand out and leaving it all behind in a few months' time might be worth the risk.

"Take some time to think about it, Curtiss. I'm flying to Hong Kong tomorrow at 6:00 pm to meet with my partners. I'll have an airline ticket waiting for you at the China Airlines ticket counter at the airport. If you are interested, I'll see you there at 5:00."

*   *   *

It was the first time Curtiss had been back to the Chiang Kai-shek Airport since his arrival in Taiwan a half-year earlier. Lu, now dressed in a designer western business suit, was standing by the ticket counter and smiled when he saw Curtiss. "Very good." Lu handed Curtiss his ticket.

"You seem pretty confident that I would accept your offer," Curtiss said with a wary smile.

"Well, from what I understand, you weren't doing much of anything important anyway."

Curtiss discovered that first-class service on Asian commercial airlines was on par with that of the DBL private jet and he enjoyed the break from his Spartan life of late. Lu shared stories about the perilous times during his youth growing up in Mainland China, which Lu described as "Chi Ku," or eating bitter. In his twenties, Lu had been a soldier in the People's Liberation Army and was stationed in southern China, where he manned electronic listening posts that monitored U.S. Air Force and Navy communications as they made bombing runs into North Vietnam. It was also when he learned English.

Even for a soldier he had been destitute, so much so that he and his fellow soldiers would sometimes come down off their mountaintop listening post to steal chickens from the local villagers in order to get a decent meal.

Lu loved his country and, like Curtiss with his American Wall Street dream, with every sacrifice he made and difficulty he endured, Lu's commitment to the communist revolution grew stronger. But at the height of the frenzy and chaos of the Cultural Revolution, Lu's parents, who were educators, were arrested for expressing politically incorrect thought then brutally murdered by a renegade band of Red Guards as police stood by, not daring to challenge Chairman Mao's vicious and barbaric rabble. Heartsick by the death of his parents and brutally disillusioned with the new China under Mao and the communist revolution as a whole, he made a desperate escape from the country by holding on to a basketball and floating down the Pearl River. Hong Kong fishermen picked him up floating in the South China Sea, still clinging to his basketball.

Lu's story sparked Curtiss's private reflections upon his own incubating disillusionment with his ability to achieve his dream to become a Wall Street tycoon. How serious a setback had his half-year sidetrack in Taiwan been? Hong Kong was even farther from New York than Taiwan, so why was he heading away from his dream?

Would he ever find his way back? Living with chronic self-doubt was an unfamiliar condition for Curtiss, and it seemed ever-present now. He had to fight through it. Like Lu, he was now clinging to whatever kept him afloat as he now drifted to Hong Kong in the South China Sea.

Lu told of his year at Hong Kong's Rennie's Mill after his rescue, living amongst remnants of the defeated Nationalist army, Kuomintang political exiles and refugees that the Hong Kong colonial government had resettled there starting in the 1950s. The fact that Rennie's Mill had at one time been called Tiu Keng Leng, which translates to "Hanging Neck Ridge," was not lost on Lu. He had refused to accept the futile limbo that was Rennie's Mill and defected to the Nationalist army in Taiwan.

Once China reopened its doors in 1978, Lu used his cross-border connections to do specialty trading with China, with permission from Taiwan's government. He began by exporting Taiwan-grown tea to China and importing herbal medicines that are only available from Mainland China. His duty-free trading business had developed from there.

Curtiss was surprised that Lu had opened up to him the way he did and sensed that Lu had taken a liking to him. When Lu offered to take him under his wing and teach him the business, if Curtiss was interested, he agreed to seriously consider it.

As they made their descent into Hong Kong, the city's oasis of lights contrasted starkly with the abysmal blackness unique to flying over the ocean on a moonless night. But instead of continuing to the outskirts of the city, where most airports are, they flew straight into the heart of the city, as though their plane were landing in New York's Central Park.

Their final approach to Kai Tak Airport required the plane to pitch sharply while rolling to the right in order to line up with the runway that jutted into Hong Kong's Harbor. Skimming the tops of buildings at that angle, Curtiss was able to see into the windows of Kowloon's low-rise buildings off the starboard side, and he grinned at the sight of a bather toweling off through his apartment window.

The airport, like Hong Kong itself, was a miracle of efficiency. Though relatively small in size, it digested planeload after planeload of passengers, mostly from Boeing 747s, through its narrow corridors. Lu explained that Kai Tak was the busiest single-runway airport in the world and that the terminal was operating at four times its design capacity—a testament to Hong Kong's efficiency.

While waiting to pass through immigration, Curtiss observed that he was surrounded by the most eclectic crowd of humanity that he had ever encountered: Chinese and Japanese, Africans and Indians, Filipinos and Europeans, and even the occasional Russian. The airport hummed with a dozen languages and hosted a veritable fashion show of the world's dress: Indian saree and Saudi thobe, Cameroonian QuatrePoches and Philippine Barong Tagalog, and Armani suits and backpacker's torn blue jeans. As Curtiss would later discover, people from every part of the world came to Hong Kong to buy and sell goods. And whatever their national politics, they didn't bring them to Hong Kong: Pakistani traded with Indian, Jew with Arab, and communist China with the capitalist world. Hong Kong was all about business.

As Curtiss and Lu queued for a taxi, airplanes roared no more than two hundred or so feet overhead and the kerosene smell of jet fuel hung in the thick damp air. The blips and bleeps and unfamiliar Cantonese chatter blaring over the taxi's dispatch radio, compounded by the dizzying speed with which the driver twisted and turned the cab along the left side of Hong Kong's narrow streets from the right side of the car, was disorienting to Curtiss. It was all he could do to hold on so as not to slide across the cab's back seat into Lu.

When they rolled up to their hotel entrance, Lu informed Curtiss that he always stayed at the Peninsula Hotel, since it was the best hotel in Hong Kong. A large Sikh man opened the taxi door for Curtiss. When he stepped out, he beheld ranks of green Rolls Royce cars lined up on either side of the entrance.

Lu smiled at Curtiss's starstruck reaction to the vehicles. "They are the hotel's fleet cars. It is a Peninsula tradition."

The steak dinner at the Hong Kong Peninsula Hotel supplanted the steak dinner he'd had at the Taipei Lai Lai Sheraton as the best Curtiss had had while in Asia. After dinner, Lu insisted on a cigar and cognac in the hotel's club lounge, where he told Curtiss that he would be meeting his partners later that night at their nightclub.

Lighting his cigar, Lu said, "You've been to a Chinese nightclub before, right?" He smiled teasingly at Curtiss.

"Yeah, I know how it works." Curtiss did his best to remain inscrutable so as not to reveal his naiveté.

"You'll love this place. It is called Club Mercedes and the ladies are top quality. Anything you want: Thai, Filipino, Chinese, Korean. We even have a couple of Russians working there now." Lu smiled at Curtiss's surprise that Russian women should be working in a Hong Kong nightclub, and shrugged. "Glasnost."

When they arrived at Club Mercedes, the hostess immediately recognized Lu, withdrew his half drunk bottle of cognac from a glass cabinet and escorted them to a VIP room, where Lu's Hong Kong and China business partners were entertaining themselves.

At the center of the room, facing a projector big-screen TV, were three sofas assembled around a coffee table, surrounded in turn by artificial potted trees strung with Christmas lights and several sets of overstuffed chairs for two along the walls—presumably for privacy. A bartender tended the in-room bar.

Lu introduced Curtiss to the two Hong Kong partners first. Neither of them was friendly toward Curtiss, particularly Ng, the more senior one of the two, who weakly shook Curtiss's hand, produced a clearly phony smile and immediately confronted him: "So what do you know about Hong Kong-China trading?" He didn't allow Curtiss time to respond. "What do you know about Hong Kong or China, for that matter? What do you know about anything?" Ng said, laughing.

Lu interrupted and appeared to speak crossly to Ng, though Curtiss couldn't be sure since they spoke Cantonese and given his unfamiliarity with the language it could have gone either way. Whatever Lu had said, it caused Ng to make a dismissive gesture, turn his back and sit down to sulk.

One of the two China partners wore a suit with the brand label still sewn on the cuff for all to see. The other, Officer Zhang, wore a Chinese customs officer's uniform. Both spoke only mandarin Chinese, seemed genuinely curious about Curtiss and politely complimented him on his use of Mandarin—albeit still limited to light chitchat. Their red faces, the reek of Chinese Gao Liang wine on their breath and their cheerful attitudes all indicated that they were already well on their way toward inebriation.

The mama-san entered with eight young ladies, each dressed differently: one dressed in a Japanese schoolgirl uniform, one in punk garb, one in a business suit, one in a Thai Siwalai dress, one in a gymnastics outfit complete with headband and legwarmers, and one in a Chinese military uniform from the waist up and fishnet stockings and high heels from the waist down. "Whatever your fantasy, Curtiss," Lu said, wrapping his arm around Curtiss's shoulder.

The man wearing the customs uniform immediately had words with the mama-san then scolded the young lady about the inappropriateness of combining a Chinese military uniform with fishnet stockings. The mama-san ordered the offending young lady to leave the room, undid the custom's officer's tie, poured him and herself a drink, and they clinked their glasses and downed their contents together in one go.

"Officer Zhang is a little sensitive about any mockery of China," Lu said, patting Curtiss on his shoulder. "But mama-san Maggie knows how to keep her customers happy."

Ng grabbed the hand of the young lady wearing the Japanese schoolgirl outfit, tugged her over to one of the overstuffed chairs along the wall, pulled her on to his lap and groped her, egged on by her melodramatic mock-rape protests. The others made their selections in turn, with Lu choosing to spend most of his time that evening chatting and drinking with mama-san Maggie. The young lady in the Thai dress gave Curtiss a warm and inviting smile and Lu asked her to join Curtiss on his behalf.

Later, while walking back to their VIP room from the restroom, Curtiss found the corridor blocked by two men having a heated argument beside a cabinet full of unopened cognac bottles. One swung the cabinet's door open and grabbed a bottle by the neck. Curtiss cringed, convinced that argument was about to become violent bar fight, but the man dramatically smashed the bottle to the ground instead. The other man then took hold of another bottle and smashed it to the ground. After staring with indignation at each other for a moment, both men attempted to elbow each other out of the way to grab another bottle when security guards grabbed the two men before they could escalate their unusual bar fight. An elderly man edged past Curtiss with a broom and dustpan and calmly began cleaning up the mess.

Back in the VIP room, Curtiss explained what he had just seen to Lu. "Those guys were just showing off, Curtiss. To show how rich they are." Lu shook his head. "Petty criminals now flush with cash, most likely. You encounter more and more of these uncouth brutes these days."

Having suffered through mostly bad karaoke all evening, Curtiss enjoyed the breath of fresh air that was Lu's singing of early twentieth-century Chinese songs. Strangely, Lu never faced the audience when he sang and Curtiss later asked him about it. Lu explained that some types of old Shanghainese songs were very difficult to sing and required extreme contortions of the face in order to produce the sounds correctly. "People found out a long time ago that the singer's face becomes quite ugly in the process. So to protect the audience's enjoyment of the beauty of the music, the singer must turn his ugly face away."

The stages of the evening's debauchery could be measured by the deteriorating state of Officer Zhang's uniform, now reduced to a jacket draped over his shoulders as a cape, his shirt unbuttoned to mid-chest, revealing all of three chest hairs, and one out-hanging shirttail.

The evening came to its crescendo when Officer Zhang passed out in mid song and fell to the floor. This brought a roar of laughter from everyone the room, which was cut short when Officer Zhang came to only long enough to vomit into one of the fake potted trees in the room, shorting out the electric Christmas lights strung on the tree. This event marked the end to the evening's festivities, and Curtiss and Lu stayed behind to settle the bill. Lu's partners bade them good night as they carried the drunk customs officer away, with Ng cussing in Cantonese all the way, no doubt about the burden of being his brother's keeper. The little old man with the broom and the dustpan arrived to start cleaning up the mess.

That night, Curtiss and Lu began to bond, as men do when they drink together while in the company of beautiful women whom they don't need to impress. "You know, Lu . . . " Curtiss paused to down another swig of cognac together with Lu. "You Chinese have got an obsession with virility."

Lu looked at Curtiss with mock resentment.

"I mean, I was at Snake Alley in Taipei and the stuff people were drinking to get a hard-on was disgusting. And who would believe that deer penis and snake blood is going to make you into a stud anyway?"

"Curtiss . . . " Lu said, putting his arm around his shoulder. "Believe me, if male virility came in a pill, in a prescription bottle, and was produced by some big-name American pharmaceutical company,

American men would take it as eagerly as Chinese do their traditional remedies."

Curtiss and Lu halted in mid-conversation to watch the young lady dressed as a Thai bend in a feminine way to accommodate the confines of her Siwalai dress, while stooping to turn off the karaoke machine and collect the microphones.

Curtiss looked at Lu and smiled. "You haven't got any spare deer penis on you, have you, Lu?"

* * *

"Curtiss," Lu waved him over to his breakfast table in the elegant Victorian white and gold-leafed Peninsula Hotel lobby restaurant. "They make the world's best eggs Benedict here. You must try it."

Curtiss nodded to the attending waitress, affirming that he would have the eggs Benedict. "Wow. That was some night last night."

"Now you see what I have to contend with."

Over breakfast that morning the two men discussed the various aspects of Lu's operation that Curtiss would look after for him, from verifying the customs chop on the waybills to ensuring the manifest matched the contents of containers on the docks at all hours—day or night. "This isn't the kind of business taught at Harvard Business School, Curtiss." Cash businesses are built on trust, he reminded, and trust is hard to come by in his business. So, in addition to the mundane and routine aspects of his job, he needed Curtiss to also look after his interests for him. Specifically, he wanted Curtiss to report back on what he saw, and what his people and their counterparts in Ng and Zhang's crew were doing. "Just keep an eye out for anything that looks out of the ordinary. What you Americans are now calling: 'Management by Exception.'"

Lu also expressed his concern about the black market smugglers who operated at the same border ports, and were involved with anything from smuggling Afghan opium through China to corrupt generals selling arms to criminal gangs or even rogue states. "You give those guys a wide berth," Lu warned. "They are very dangerous. Keep an eye on them, let me know what you can, but keep your distance." Gray market, black market. What had he gotten himself into? But for some reason, he trusted Lu.

By the end of Curtiss's first month in the business, he'd managed to get a handle on the way things worked. He kept a detailed log of daily activities and a brief dossier on each of the three crews that were on Lu, Ng and Zhang's payrolls: their jobs, their affiliations and their competencies. During their weekly breakfast meetings at the Peninsula Hotel, Lu complimented Curtiss on his work, especially his reports, which Lu said were well written, insightful and thorough.

Curtiss was surprised by how openly the black market smugglers and criminal gangs operated, whether it was conspicuously spending money in Hong Kong or driving stolen, right-hand-drive Mercedes on China's right-side drive roads. Curtiss knew for a fact that some of the vehicles were stolen, since late one evening on the Hong Kong docks he saw one being loaded onto a modified powerboat that sped off into the night without running lights. Considering the boat's compact size and limited range, there was only one destination for them: Mainland China. Lu later told him that car-theft gangs worked both sides of the border, photographing target cars in the office parking garages and apartment block car-parks of Hong Kong's well-to-do and putting together an album to show potential buyers in China, who would select the cars of their choice to be stolen and delivered in China—often within twenty-four hours. Once in China, many of them bore Chinese military license plates, which helped explain the thieves' brazenness. That kind of protection is a double-edged sword, Lu explained, as it could be fatally fickle. Lu said the thieves *and* their customers would be wise to consider a Chinese saying: *Ren Pa Chu Ming, Zhu Pa Zhuang.* "People should fear fame the way pigs should fear getting fat,'" he translated, looking at Curtiss with utmost seriousness. "Someone is going to come along one fine day and slaughter you if you get too big."

After Curtiss's second month in the business, he had developed an appreciation for the sophistication of Lu's operation. Ivy League professors could learn a thing or two from the management efficiency with which it was executed.

Curtiss had taken the opportunity to return to Taiwan to thank George and his family for helping him through his difficult time there, and to say goodbye. George had accepted tins of some of Mainland China's finest teas as a gift, but refused the two months' rent Curtiss owed him. "You are a friend," George explained. "It was my pleasure having you as a guest." The men hugged as they parted, imparting upon Curtiss with the smell of Brylcreem that was noticed by some of his drinking buddies at the Ploughman's Cottage later that evening.

That gang was nearly all there. Bobbie, pool-hustling some sucker out of his travel expense money, winked at Curtiss as he entered. After less than an hour of catching up and carousing, Curtiss left quietly, not wanting to get entangled in long goodbyes. He preferred to remember everyone at the Ploughman's for whom he knew them to be: wayward travelers indulging their impulses in anonymity, if only for a while.

Curtiss also needed to get to the Chennault Pub before Wendy closed up for the night. Wendy tilted her head and smiled when he swept in with a bouquet of roses he'd picked up from the flower-seller on Shuang Cheng Street. "Curtiss, that is so sweet. You know, if you weren't such a jerk and so screwed up, things might have been different between us."

Curtiss just smiled politely.

Before his flight back to Hong Kong the next morning, Curtiss met Sonya for breakfast as appointed. He told her that he was now living in Hong Kong and working in import-export, choosing not to mention the marginal nature of the duty-free aspect of the business. She held his face with both hands, switched on her penetrating gaze, and said, "Now *that* is the way a young man with education and smarts should be."

Before they parted, Sonya asked Curtiss if he was still planning to work his way back to New York City and junk bond trading. Though he told her that was still the plan, in the taxi to the airport Curtiss searched his soul for the true answer to that question. The only thing that he was certain of was that DBL, Belkin, the British Virgin Islands, the black pilot's flight bag all seemed very distant from him now.

He didn't know where he belonged anymore.

The sharpness of that realization was blunted by his abiding preoccupation with doing his current job well, and the satisfaction that he derived from it. He would focus on hitting his financial goal with Lu, then figure out where to go from there.

* * *

Three months in, the business had become routine, though Lu

was increasingly concerned about getting stuck with counterfeit U.S. Dollars. North Korea had been flooding Asia's cash-business economy with counterfeit hundred dollar bills, which were eventually laundered through Macau's casinos. The copies were so good that even specialists were unable to detect them with the naked eye and they weren't being detected until they reached the banks. Lu asked Curtiss to keep an eye out for this and to see what he could find out about it.

Curtiss had settled into the Lee Garden Hotel on Hong Kong Island. Though clean and well maintained, while leaving the hotel late one afternoon to attend a meeting in Shenzhen China—the city just across the border from Hong Kong—he found the staff in the lobby abuzz about a nine-foot python found living off rats in the hotel. Having already eaten snake several times while in Taiwan and Hong Kong, Curtiss was more concerned by the presence of rats in the hotel than the snake that was living off them.

The fastest way across the harbor was by subway, then the Kowloon-Canton Railway, which took him through the New Territories to the end of the line: Lo Wu Station at the China border. After disembarking from the train he queued up at Hong Kong immigration before crossing the bridge into China.

Curtiss was glad that this evening's meeting would be held at the newly opened Kai Li Hotel, since it was one of the few places in Shenzhen that served brewed instead of instant coffee in their lobby café. Officer Zhang arrived wearing a windbreaker, yellow polo shirt, slacks, and brown loafers. Their entire conversation was in Mandarin, since they conversed mostly about numbers, though the fact was that Curtiss was rapidly progressing with the language.

It was approaching nine o'clock when they concluded their business, and Zhang invited Curtiss to dinner. Curtiss politely refused. He needed to meet Lu early the next morning for breakfast at the Peninsula Hotel, and dinners with Zhang always involved downing multiple glasses of Gao Liang wine. Officer Zhang arranged for his customs and immigration vehicle and driver to take Curtiss back to Lo Wu Station and Curtiss thanked him for his kindness.

At the station, Curtiss found a large crowd queued up for China Immigration at the border and took his place at the end of the most promising-looking line. He pulled a dog-eared novel out of his satchel and began to read.

Curtiss felt a tug at his elbow. It was one of Ng's Hong Kong crew, a man Curtiss had worked with before, but didn't know very well. The man told Curtiss that there was a midnight delivery at the old Shenzhen port and that there was no one of sufficient authority assigned to receive the container.

Curtiss had put a system in place to take care of this kind of contingency weeks earlier and made a mental note to have another talk with the dispatcher. The immigration officer waved Curtiss forward, holding his hand out for his passport. Curtiss reluctantly turned around and walked out of the immigration hall.

Curtiss and Ng's crewman slipped into a waiting taxi. Knowing that the old Shenzhen Port was several kilometers up the mouth of the river from the new main port, and that it was nearly impossible to get a taxi there, Curtiss told the driver that he would give him the fare on the meter plus five-hundred Hong Kong dollars to wait for him there at the port.

Ng's crewman explained to Curtiss that he had to make a document pick-up in the city and that Curtiss and the taxi driver should first drop him at the Ki Li Hotel, then pick him up on the way back to Lo Wu Station to return to Hong Kong.

Shenzhen's main streets were still under construction and after dropping Ng's crewman the taxi driver was forced to take several bypasses on the way out of the city center, which even at that late hour was abuzz with activity. Construction went on twenty-four hours a day in this newly-created city. Klieg lights atop cranes lit construction sites along the way, their intense white light punctuated by bluish, strobe-like flashes from welding torches to create a surreal night scene bearing some ghostly resemblance to an opening night at Los Angeles's Grauman's Chinese Theater. Within a half hour they were winding along unlit single-lane country roads, from which Curtiss could see the lights of the new port off in the distance.

When they arrived at the old port's main gate they found it unlit, and when the taxi driver jumped out of the taxi to swing open the chain-link fence gate, Curtiss observed that it, too, was unmanned.

The taxi driver pulled up to a dilapidated dockside corrugated steel warehouse and Curtiss stepped out. The container barge hadn't arrived yet. The driver made a three-point turn—repositioning the car, Curtiss presumed, before settling in to wait to take him back to the city. But instead the taxi drove away, leaving Curtiss cursing the driver under his breath.

He was relieved when he saw one of the container barges plying the river turn toward the pier; at least he would not have to wait long for the shipment to arrive.

When it arrived, he watched its crew jump to the dock to tie off the barge and searched the workers for the one holding the waybill copy, but found no one he recognized. When Curtiss asked who was in charge, the workers just ignored him and sat on the dock, talking among themselves and smoking cigarettes.

Car lights approached from the gate. The taxi driver had just gone to get a meal, or to fill up with gas, and was coming back to pick him up. Either that, or Ng's crewmember had come to meet him, which would be very helpful with sorting out the container receiving. In any case he was grateful to have a ride back to Lo Wu Station.

But as the car drew near, he saw that it was a right-hand-drive Mercedes with military license plates. The barge workers appeared to notice this at the same time, for they threw their cigarettes to the ground and jumped to attention.

The docks fell silent and motionless, and Curtiss, squinting into the vehicle's blinding headlights, felt an intense queasiness in the pit of his stomach.

The rear door of the Mercedes swung open and a tall man in an officer's military uniform with stark white hair cropped to a flattop emerged. He looked directly at Curtiss, still caught in the Mercedes' headlights like a deer on a country road, and stared at him for a moment. He then shouted orders—"Ta Shi Jian Dai, Zhua Shu Ta!"—and a half-dozen of the barge workers ran toward Curtiss and stopped within a few yards of him.

Curtiss's heart hammered in his chest. Time slowed. The barge workers were wearing threadbare and ill-fitting military uniforms.

He was in serious trouble.

The standoff lasted only a second before two of the soldier/barge workers moved toward Curtiss, and his fight-or-flight instinct took over: he dropped his satchel, turned, and made for the river at a full run.

Aware of each stride, Curtiss strained against his slow-motion perception of the moment. In real time, he deftly escaped the grasp of the soldier/barge workers who were within reach of him and broke through the line of the others, who were still standing at attention. When he leapt at full speed into the blackness of the river, he could hear the white-haired officer shouting over the report of a firearm.

As he swam past the end of the container barge, he could hear it ring like a bell as bullets ricocheted off its hollow steel hull. Curtiss knew better than to look back and kept swimming as fast as he could manage while fully clothed.

He ran out of steam midway across the river, began treading water and looked around to get his bearings. The Mercedes' lights on the pier were at some distance now and Curtiss was confident that they could no longer see him from there. The nearest thing to him was a Chinese junk that was bobbing a hundred yards down river and he swam with the current towards it.

When he reached the junk, he grabbed a rope that was hanging off the bow and pulled himself up to where he could peer over deck. The motor was running, but the boat must have been in neutral, since it was also drifting downriver. Across the deck, at the aft of the ship, Curtiss could see the junk's crew with their heads ducked beneath the engine hatch, completely distracted by some kind of repair operation. He pulled himself aboard.

He had just come within a fraction of an inch of dying and now, hidden in relative safety among crates bundled in cargo nets on the littered deck, his subconscious shouted back its displeasure to his consciousness with dramatic physiological distress signals. His hands began to shake, his knees weakened, and it was all he could do not to vomit.

That had been no beating: those people on the dock were seriously intent on killing him. Yet still, he thought, as his stomach and nerves steadied: in the midst of engaging the threat, he'd remained calm and focused.

Curtiss prayed that the boat was headed downriver, out of China, toward the South China Sea, and ultimately to either the Hong Kong or Macau colonies. Moments later he felt a thump as the clutch engaged the drive shaft and turned the boat's propeller. They were underway.

Upriver.

The chugging of the diesel engine and the darkness of night cloaked Curtiss's presence on deck. He knew that if he rode the junk all the way to wherever it was going, he would likely be discovered.

As he passed riverside villages on the way upriver that night, he considered jumping ship and swimming to shore. But a foreigner arriving soaking wet in a small village would surely stand out like a sore thumb, and there probably wouldn't be a telephone he could use to call Lu for help. The junk was most likely going to the city of Guangzhou, where 'foreign guests' like himself were relatively common, and he decided that he would jump ship just before the junk put into port there.

Though the sun hadn't yet risen, he could smell the crew's breakfast cooking and knew that dawn would not be far away. As the junk rounded a bend, he could see the lights of a city in the distance. Judging by the size of the city, as well as by the junk's speed and the distance he guessed they'd covered overnight, this was most likely Guangzhou.

It was just before sunrise when the junk reached the outskirts of the city and he overheard the sailors in the galley mention Guangzhou several times. That was enough for Curtiss. He stepped over the ship's rail and quietly dropped himself into the river undetected. He remained motionless in the water until the junk got some distance away, and then swam to shore.

He found an empty warehouse where he could wring out his clothes and take stock of what he had on him. His passport and money were soaked, but at least they were with him, and his pocket address book was wet but still legible. He dried these out the best he could, then spent the better part of the morning walking to the city center, drawing curious stares from the street vendors and pedestrians along the way.

He knew the White Swan Hotel from his last visit to Guangzhou, and he got his bearings and navigated to the hotel. After checking in, he bought a new set of clothes, then headed up to his room for a shower.

When Curtiss called Lu at the Peninsula and explained what had happened, Lu told him to stay where he was and that he would be there as quickly as he could—which, traveling by train from Hong Kong to Guangzhou, meant about five hours.

Exhausted from his overnight ordeal, Curtiss was asleep in five minutes.

* * *

"What the hell. Are you okay?" Lu looked Curtiss over from head to toe in the hotel room doorway. "Did they really shoot at you?"

"Yeah, they did. I guess they couldn't shoot very well." Lu came inside and Curtiss locked the door after him. "Do you want some tea? Sorry, it's only the hotel room tea bag, but that's all I've got."

"Do you have any idea who it was? Tell me everything you saw."

In his usual detailed and thorough fashion, Curtiss reported what had happened to him the night before. Lu concluded that Ng had set him up and that it had been the White General, as he was called in the underworld, who was in the Mercedes. "The White General is a particularly nasty character. It could have been arms stolen from a military base or even Afghan opium hidden in that container." Lu pulled at his lower lip, deep in thought.

"Well, he got a damned good look at me," Curtiss said, while pouring boiled water from an ancient cork-topped insulated flask into two teacups.

"Is there any way that he could know who you are?"

Curtiss thought for a moment. "I dropped my satchel before I jumped in the river. It had ledgers in it and some other papers."

"Damn. Now it is only a matter of time. I have to get you out of here, fast." He told Curtiss that he still had family in his hometown, a tiny farming village in the mountains in Guizhou, about 400 kilometers from Guangzhou. "You could lay low there for a while."

"Wait. You want me to hide *in* China? Isn't the White General Chinese military?"

"He's gone rogue. He's in deep with the Triads and uses the soldiers under his command like his own personal mafia. He is very well connected. He probably already alerted border security and immigration to start looking for you," Lu mulled aloud. "That is precisely why you can't attempt a border crossing right now. The military controls the border. It is just too risky to try to get you across to Hong Kong. Disappearing into a tiny village well off their radar screen is the better bet. And if I can get you to another province, all the better."

"What about Ng?"

"Don't worry about Ng. I'll take care of that son of a bitch."

At breakfast early the next morning, Lu said he'd been up half the night on the phone and had arranged Curtiss's disappearance. He briefed him on who would meet him where, and when, and what he needed to do. He would leave Guangzhou by motorized pedicab immediately, which would take him sixty kilometers out of the city to a town one of Lu's nephews was visiting. The nephew would take him by motorcycle on an overnight ride to Lu's village. "In two days you'll be having dinner in the house that I grew up in," Lu said with a smile.

After absorbing all that had just been laid out for him, Curtiss asked Lu about the twenty or so western couples—each with a stroller containing a Chinese baby—that had been filling up the restaurant during his briefing. Lu explained that Guangzhou is the designated city to process foreign adoptions, and that adoptive couples were organized into groups when they came to China.

It was the first time in nine months that Curtiss had been in the company of so many westerners at one time, and since they all seemed to be Americans, one part of him wanted to somehow integrate himself into the group and sneak back to America together with them. But Curtiss envisioned himself pleading with these couples holding their newly adopted children: "Please, I need your help! I am wanted by the Chinese authorities and need to hide within your group so I can escape." A crazy thought, born of desperation. Even if his ego allowed him to ask for help, he couldn't in good conscience endanger these budding families. His life back in the comfort and safety of Hong Kong—and New York City—would have to wait.

After breakfast, they met a waiting pedicab at the back of the hotel. Curtiss trusted Lu, and his judgment, but still his voice broke as he asked, "How long am I going to be there, Lu?"

"I don't know. A couple of months, maybe less. I'm going to have to find out how much damage has been done and get a sense for how far they are going to pursue this. Don't worry, I'll be checking on you all the time." Lu stuffed two cartons of Marlboro cigarettes under Curtiss's arm and handing him a couple bottles of Gao Liang wine.

The driver flipped open the canvas flap of the pedicab's cabin for Curtiss and he stepped inside. "Thanks Lu."

"You're already half Chinese now. Just blend in."

CHAPTER 8

As the only foreigner in sight, Lu's nephew easily identified Curtiss when he arrived at the center of the rural town. After a quick breakfast of Chinese-style donuts and hot soybean soup, they hopped aboard the motorcycle and began the first day of their journey. Stopping only long enough to slurp down a bowl of noodles at a roadside stand at midday, they rode until sunset.

Lu's nephew parked in front of a one-story building in an alley of a small town: their hotel for the night. They pushed aside the heavy green padded canvas blanket that served as the front door and walked in.

When they approached a large wooden desk that served as the hotel's check-in counter, they stepped over an open trough running with water that had been crudely cut into the concrete floor the length of the reception area and down the center of an adjacent hallway.

After some negotiation with the hotel manager, Lu's nephew announced that the price for each of their rooms was only five RMB, and smiled as only the utterly frugal do when they get a good deal.

They followed the hotel manager along the trough to the end of the hallway, where it ran under a door: Curtiss's room. The manager opened the door, revealing nothing more than a large, yellow-stained mattress and a green canvas blanket that hung from ceiling to floor over the far wall. The trough continued through Curtiss's room, under the canvas blanket, and presumably under the wall behind to the street. Lu's nephew joked that running water was good Fung Shui and bid Curtiss goodnight.

Street noises came through the canvas blanket, which waved slightly as if being pushed by a breeze through an open window. Curtiss pulled the blanket aside only to discover that not only was there no window, there was no wall. Except for the hanging blanket, his room was open to the street. Lu's nephew would later explain that the wall had collapsed in an earthquake and that the hotel was awaiting a supply of bricks to rebuild it. The day-long motorcycle ride had exhausted Curtiss and he wanted nothing more than to sleep. He pulled the hood of his jacket over his head, crossed his arms, lay down on the bed, and closed his eyes.

At some point during the night a subtle and intermittent shaking of the bed woke Curtiss up. In complete darkness, he wondered if it were a mild earthquake or Lu's nephew trying to wake him up. He let one hand fall to his side and felt a furry lump under his hand. When it moved, Curtiss realized that a large rat had joined him in bed and he slapped it away hard enough to send it flying off the bed.

In the morning, before departing on the next leg of their journey, Lu's nephew advised Curtiss to purchase a heavy overcoat, since it would be cold at the altitude of Lu's village that time of year. Curtiss selected from a dry-goods store a Chinese army overcoat, green with gold-colored buttons and chocolate brown, faux wool collar. All the better to blend in, he thought.

As Curtiss wearily rode on the back of the motorcycle, collar worn high, doing his best to conceal his identity as a foreigner, he reflected on his father's letters home about his two-month evasion of the Japanese army as he made his way from costal China to Kunming after the Doolittle Raid. His journey must have been one of darkness, filled with terror at the thought of capture, torture and death at the hands of Japanese soldiers. Did he fear being turned in by Chinese peasants who wanted to avoid having their entire village being slaughtered by Japanese soldiers—known to compete in beheading contests to win an R&R back in Japan on such occasions—as punishment for aiding the downed American pilots? Curtiss wondered what he himself would have done if the situation were reversed: given the choice between aiding downed Chinese pilots during the war or risking the Japanese Army conducting summary executions of every man, woman and child in Hershey PA. And what if someone felt it was their patriotic duty to turn Curtiss in now? A reasonable enough choice as, to their knowledge, they'd be turning in a foreign spy on the run from the Chinese army.

As Lu had promised, they arrived at his ancestral village in time for dinner and Curtiss was warmly greeted by Lu's extended family, who lived on a hillside in a simple brick and thatch-roofed home lit by kerosene lantern. They had slaughtered a duck for the occasion and laid out a spread of Chinese cuisine wholly unfamiliar to him, but marvelous in its unpretentiousness presentation and bold, natural flavors.

Throughout the feast Curtiss was surrounded by smiles and nervous laughter from people of all generations. Very few if any of the villagers had ever seen a foreigner in person, and the most likely images that any of them had ever seen were government propaganda-poster animations of demon-faced American soldiers and pot-bellied capitalists doing horrible things to Chinese peasants. Curtiss's sandy brown hair was of particular interest, and many took the opportunity to touch it. The children would giggle with joy after petting the foreign primate's head and hairy arms, and scream and giggle when Curtiss obliged by acting like a gorilla for them.

At the end of the meal, Curtiss placed the bottles of Gao Liang wine and cartons of cigarettes on the table and announced that they were gifts from Lu. As one, the men dumped the tea from their mini glass tumblers to the packed earth floor and smiled in anticipation. The women reacted in unison as well, grimly reciting "Ai Ya" in chorus, shaking their heads and going about cleaning up after the supper and shepherding children into a bedroom to sleep. It was time for the men to drink and smoke.

The bottle had just been uncorked, and the room had just begun to fog over with the smoke from a half-dozen lit cigarettes, when the village elder arrived. As if summoned by the gasoline-vinegar smell of the Chinese high-potency brew, he stepped carefully over the threshold, shuffled directly to the table, and took a seat beside Curtiss. He was a skinny man in his mid-to-late sixties, dressed in a Mao suit. Half his teeth were gone and the ones that remained hung tenuously in his mouth, fluttering slightly whenever he spoke. He allowed the dozen or so hairs that sprouted from a large mole just under the right edge of his chin to dangle to a length of about six inches, and used his calloused and twisted hand to habitually stroke the cluster of coarse, wavy hairs.

The village elder's odd accent rendered useless whatever Mandarin language skills Curtiss had acquired up to that point and left them to communicate via a combination of Mandarin-to-Mandarin translation facilitated by Lu's nephew, fragments of English, and sign language— a combination which seemed to become more effective the more they drank.

When it had been established that Curtiss was American, the elder sent one of the young men on an errand. He returned with a burlap bag that hung heavy with something inside about the size and weight of a portable typewriter. The elder gestured to have it put on the table, smiled broadly at Curtiss and, through the rough translation, led Curtiss to understand that it was some kind of World War II relic pulled from the wreckage of a plane that had crashed in the nearby mountains during the war. Curtiss peeled back the bag, revealing a mechanical instrument that he recognized from a school visit to the Washington D.C. National Air and Space Museum as a Norden bombsight, which were used on U.S. long-range bombers. When Curtiss asked if they would be willing to take him to the wreckage, he was informed that the plane had been salvaged for scrap metal decades before. All that remained were the bombsite and the unmarked graves in which the bodies of six airmen had been buried just after the crash. Curtiss wrote down the instrument's serial number on a scrap of paper and slid it into his wallet.

The village elder spoke at length about his friendship with the Flying Tigers as a teenager in Baoshan, and later Kunming, in neighboring Yunnan province. He was spellbound by the grandeur of both the American planes and the men who flew them, and dreamed of one day becoming a pilot himself. He had everything going for him: he was educated and his family had the means, but it was not to be.

In Mao's China, he explained, everyone was classified and society was turned upside down: if your family was dirt poor before the revolution, you were given automatic party membership and— educated or not—a job in the government. If you were middle class, or owned some land, it was seized and you were discriminated against and denied opportunities such as joining the military, and in those days, one needed to have been in the military to get good government jobs. And as for families such as the village elder's, former landlords: they were stripped of all property, denied employment, and shunned by society. All in the name of equality, fairness and economic justice. The adults were forced to sweep the streets from day to night without pay, and entire families lived off rations of ten kilos of flour a year, with only sweet potatoes comprising their main diet. Even though their children may not have even been born before the communist revolution, because of their family's pre-revolution status, they too were downcast and humiliated, and denied education and opportunities of any kind.

As former landlords, the elder's family became one of China's untouchables, a subculture where suicide was not uncommon, since it offered the only escape from the pain of institutionalized injustice and the unspeakable cruelty that had become a part of their daily lives. It wasn't until the last ten years that things changed and the classification system was dropped. But no matter: his life was over and the course of his son's life set. All hope now rested on his sole grandchild, who would live in a different China from the one he had suffered through. The village elder's face contorted in pain as he told his story, and he stared at the horrors of his past through the prism created by the tears welling up in his eyes.

Once the Gao Liang wine was finished, the men switched to the village's home brew, a local white lightning that put the Gao Liang wine to shame in terms of potency and repugnancy. Nevertheless, the men smoked and drank and talked until they'd had their fill and Curtiss stumbled to a guest room, together with several other men, to sleep it off. They slept side-by-side atop a waist-high platform that was covered with straw mats and blankets and ran the length of the room. There was a pile of coal in one corner of the room, and before turning in, one of the men leveled a shovel of coal and judiciously distributed even amounts into the four, hearth-like openings spread out along the base of the platform. Curtiss appreciated the ingenuity of the coal-heated bed as he fell asleep amidst the smell of coal dust and bad breath, and the sounds of belching and snoring.

He woke the next morning to the curious faces of the children who had come to the bedroom to check on their new pet gorilla, and they giggled, scattering, as Curtiss slowly rose from the bed. The taste of the Gao Liang wine and the home brew hung heavy in his mouth and, as he would later discover, would flavor his breath for days.

He bid good morning to his hosts, who were going through their slow-paced winter-season routines, and stepped out of the house to take in his new environment for the next couple of months, maybe less. The scenery was a replica of the black-and-white Chinese brush paintings that he had seen during his visit to the National Palace Museum in Taiwan—only it was in color. From the pinnacle of the mountaintops, misty white clouds cascaded down sheer black cliff faces and dispersed after splashing onto steep green hillsides at their base. Lu's ancestral home was high up on a hillside, nestled among terraced farm plots that were golden brown with the stubble of stalks that remained after the fall harvest. Further down, where the hillside leveled out to meet the river, aquaculture plots served as a pale blue and white borderline between the green slopes and the muddy brown river.

The beauty of the scenery inspired Curtiss to take a morning stroll. He meandered down the hillside, walking along the edges of the earthen barriers that separated the farm plots, before reclining atop an embankment high above the river. Several sampans were plying the river that morning and he watched them slowly drift past the occasional water buffalo grazing on water plants and the bamboo fish corrals that jutted into the shallows of the river from the shoreline. One of the riverside aquaculture ponds was awash with white ducks, and Curtiss pondered the simplicity of the life of the duck farmer who was tossing handfuls of grain to them.

Though Curtiss now found himself deep in the Chinese countryside it wasn't too far from the world of rural Pennsylvania—especially the Amish communities—and he was at peace for the first time in a long time. He spent the better part of the morning savoring the experience.

Curtiss drifted off to sleep embedded within the tall grass that waved up and down the hillside, encouraged by the morning's gentle breezes. He dreamed of his youth in Hershey PA, found himself walking along the town's main drag, which was lined with Hershey's Kisses-shaped street lamps and laced with the omnipresent smell of chocolate from the nearby factory. He heard footsteps, then stopped in his tracks: the White General, flanked by a squad of determined-looking soldiers, had emerged from an alley to face him there on Chocolate Avenue. He stared at Curtiss as he did that night on the Shenzhen dock, then shouted "Ba Ta La Chu Qu, Chan Bi!"—*Take him out and shoot him!*—to his soldiers.

Curtiss woke with start, frightening the child who had found him there in the grass to tell him that lunch was ready.

* * *

Within three weeks' time, Curtiss had helped repair a roof, rebuilt a rotting hog enclosure, replaced a rusting iron water pipeline that brought water to the house from an up-hill reservoir with new PVC pipe, and laid a fieldstone path between the house and the outhouse.

His latest project was helping Lu's nephew rebuild the engine of an iron ox: China's ubiquitous two-wheeled workhorse, which were put to every conceivable use across China's countryside and rural towns, from pulling plows through the deepest muddy rice paddies to hauling trailers filled with the harvest to market. It was a simple arrangement of engine, atop two deep-treaded tires, with handlebars, that could crawl up the steepest hills in low gear and hit close to twenty miles an hour on a straightway in the highest gear. Having worked on ancient boat motors and 1950s-era farm equipment in his youth, Curtiss understood the basics of its mechanical design, though he marveled at the crudeness of the parts' fabrication and the slackness of the tolerances of the oil-spitting, chugging beast. He would later come to appreciate, though, that besides making the machine cheaper to produce, the looseness of its parts helped ensure that it could keep running through the coldest winter in Harbin and the hottest summer Yunnan, at altitude and at sea-level; run on just about any kind of fuel if it had to; and be repaired in the field with only basic tools and a limited knowledge of mechanics. It was therefore perfectly suited to China's needs.

On this particular day, after washing up for dinner, Curtiss took his seat at the table. The fresh vegetables had run out and they would only have preserved vegetables, mostly cabbage, until the spring. Dried meat now garnished the soups and plates of preserved vegetables. Curtiss had learned to push the dried meat to the bottom of his rice bowl first, to allow the heat and moisture to soften it before chewing.

One of the teenagers read aloud a letter from Lu to the family, the third since Curtiss's arrival, but there was still no message from Lu that it was time for Curtiss to return to Hong Kong.

The table talk that evening focused on the coming Lunar New Year, which Curtiss determined, with a little help from Lu's family in converting from the Chinese lunar to the Gregorian calendar, would fall on February 6, 1989. It was explained to Curtiss that it would be the Year of the Snake and an Earth year, as opposed to one of the other five elements: water, fire, metal, or wood. Curtiss nodded and smiled politely, not having the slightest idea what that implied. He decided to simply furrow his brow at the addition to his consciousness of this newest unresolved snippet of Chinese cultural DNA—Sonya's words about the perils of trying to understand the Chinese culture by the measure of his own experience echoing in his ears.

The sound of Lu's nephew's motorcycle arriving outside the front door interrupted a debate between the men and women about how much to spend on fireworks for the coming Lunar New Year's celebration. Lu's sister-in-law laid down her chopsticks, sprang to her feet, and bolted for the door. Curtiss was informed that her daughter, Xiao Lu, was returning home from university for New Year's holiday. Lu's nephew had picked her up at the train station.

The door opened and a young woman carrying a backpack and toting a small suitcase entered. Dropping her things, she cried "Ma!" and threw her arms around her mother.

Lu's brother, Xiao Lu's father, smiled broadly and gestured for her to take a seat next to him at the table. "Lai, Lai, Lai, Chi Fan," come and eat, her father said. An aunt set her place at the table with a bowl of rice, chopsticks and a cup of steaming hot tea. Xiao Lu hugged her father around his neck, while he weakly protested her display of affection and encouraged her again to sit and eat.

The homecoming was a Chinese-style Norman Rockwellian moment for Curtiss. It deeply touched him and dislodged a homecoming memory of one of his father's R&Rs from Vietnam. For that moment, he could *feel* his parents' affections—hugs and kisses so uniquely theirs that they were imprinted on his soul. He felt them now as he imagined amputees felt their phantom sensations.

Lu's nephew high-fived Curtiss as he took his seat at the table, which drew Xiao Lu's attention to Curtiss. Her surprised expression at finding this foreign stranger at the family dinner table—and Lu's nephew's devious smile—indicated that she had not been informed about her family's new houseguest.

It may have been the long cold ride on the back of Lu's nephew's motorcycle, but Xiao Lu's cheeks were as flushed as any of the animated images Curtiss had seen of China's Cultural Revolution Red Guard Poster girls. And like those meant-to-inspire propaganda images, her hair was tamed into thick braids that hung on either side of her head, and everything about her projected youth, vigor, and pride. She stared at Curtiss with a completely expressionless face, slowly chewing a mouthful of food, evidently at a loss as to what might have led to her family adopting a fully grown foreigner.

Her father explained that Curtiss was a friend of her Uncle Lu's from Taiwan, that he would be staying with them for a while—they didn't know how long—and that she was not to discuss it with anyone outside of the immediate family. She blinked at the mysteriousness of her father's explanation, and the guarded expression she'd turned to Curtiss changed to one of beguiled curiosity.

Curtiss asked Xiao Lu what university she was attending. Slightly taken aback that Curtiss spoke Mandarin, she explained that she had just completed her final classes at Shanghai's Jiaotong University, was working on her dissertation and would graduate in the summer.

Xiao Lu's father proudly explained that his daughter was the future of the family. She had placed at the top of her class in the local high school and scored in the top tenth percentile in the province on the national university entrance examination. When he further explained that Lu was funding his niece's education, Xiao Lu's father choked up. His wife stroked his shoulder and changed the subject, asking Xiao Lu her opinion about whether they should spend as much on fireworks this year as last.

Now knowing how her father's generation was denied education during the Cultural Revolution, Curtiss appreciated the importance of Xiao Lu's achievements to the family's efforts to rehabilitate itself from the damage done by decades of institutionalized persecution in the name of equality, fairness and economic justice. Throughout the rest of the evening meal, Xiao Lu was barraged by her family with questions, not only about her academic studies, but also what life was like in Shanghai. Curtiss sat quietly, absorbing what he could through his improving Mandarin Chinese.

After dinner, Xiao Lu's mother encouraged her to sit with Curtiss and to speak English with him, smiling proudly while Xiao Lu shyly warned him that her English was not so good.

"No, you are doing very well. Please, don't stop." It was the first time Curtiss had heard English spoken in nearly a month, and it was music to his ears. "What is your major at University?"

"I studied international business, but English was my minor," she said, while pouring them both a cup of tea.

"What is your dissertation about?"

A case study about Beijing Jeep, American Motors' investment in China, she explained.

"I've actually done a bit of reading about that. I could help you if you'd like," Curtiss offered. When Xiao Lu looked down bashfully and didn't respond, he asked about her plans after graduation.

"I hope to get a job at an international company, in Shanghai or Beijing, but it is very competitive."

"I'd be happy to write a letter of recommendation for you, too, if that would help."

"That would very be nice, thank you," Xiao Lu said, at last looking up and smiling.

* * *

The morning of Lunar New Year's Eve, Curtiss woke to the sound of firecrackers. Lu's family spent the entire morning preparing for their trip to a nearby town, where they would celebrate the New Year with dinner at a famous "healthy food restaurant." About 3:00 pm, Lu's nephew appeared, grinning with pride as he hung off the side of an ancient flatbed truck with wooden rails that trailed a thick cloud of black diesel smoke as it groaned up the steep hillside to the house. This was to be their evening's transportation.

Curtiss helped Lu's family climb aboard the truck's flatbed, and distributed the army blankets that they would huddle under during the open-air journey to town. They would pick up the village elder and his family on the way. It was an honor to Lu's household to have the village elder, a widower, and his son, daughter-in-law and grandson join their family for the Lunar New Year dinner. The village elder and his family were packed into the truck's cab.

The truck stopped near the center of town, when it could go no further owing to the encroachment of street stalls onto the main road. General confusion had broken out on the street as trucks, bicycles, three-wheeled pedicarts, and iron oxen towing trailers filled with passengers all competed with the pedestrians crossing the street in every direction.

Lu's brother gave the order for everyone to jump off the truck and walk the remaining half-kilometer or so to the restaurant, then flagged down a three-wheeled pedicart to take the village elder and his family the rest of the way.

The brisk walk and the anticipation of eating something other than pickled cabbage, simple soups, dried meat, and steamed rice roused Curtiss's appetite. Fireworks periodically exploded from alleyways as the group made their way up the street; some alleys had already accumulated a layer of firework paper shreds an inch deep.

There was a crowd at the entrance to the restaurant and Lu's brother took a number written on a scrap of paper from one of the restaurant's hostesses. They would have to wait for a table.

The restaurant's entrance was flanked by stacks of chicken-wire cages that were filled with all manner of animals: dogs, bats, squirrels, turtles and even monkeys. Curtiss feared the worst for what would be served inside.

When he was informed that their table was ready he paused to watch the village elder point out one of the monkeys in the chicken-wire cages to the restaurant's hostess: this was going to be an interesting evening.

The village elder, Lu's brother, and another male relative entered the VIP room next to the large circular banquet table where Curtiss, Xiao Lu and the rest of the family sat.

"I thought this is supposed to be a health food restaurant," Curtiss asked Xiao Lu as they pulled their chairs up to their table.

"Yes, it is all very healthy food. You eat for what you need to improve your health." Curtiss felt he knew where this was going, and wasn't thrilled about it. "If your body is cold, you eat dog meat, which will bring heat into your body and bring it back into balance. And eating certain kinds of eyes are good for your eyesight. You see?"

"But I guess snake is off the menu this year, right?"

"Yes, that's right," Xiao Lu said. "That would be bad luck in the Year of the Snake. Now you've got it."

Curtiss nodded, but remained profoundly dubious as he scanned the restaurant's picture menu. Xiao Lu saw him pondering a picture of a football-sized white glutinous lump on a plate.

"Oh, that's moose nose. It comes all the way from inner Mongolia." Xiao Lu leaned over to Curtiss. "It is too expensive," she whispered from behind her hand.

Thank God for small favors, Curtiss thought. "But I suppose it helps you smell better, right?"

"Of course not, silly," Xiao Lu giggled at Curtiss's suggestion as if it were preposterous.

Swing and a miss on that bit of Chinese cultural DNA, Curtiss thought. But he really didn't see why the same logic wouldn't apply for eating a nose as it did for eating eyes and was about to challenge Xiao Lu on her dismissal of his suggestion when Lu's nephew put his hand on Curtiss's shoulder and whispered in his ear that he had been invited to the VIP room.

The village elder smiled and waved Curtiss over to the seat next to him at another round dining table, this one only large enough to accommodate four people. A domed steel wok lid was located at the table's center, and a waitress was busy placing individual dishes of various kinds of dipping sauces and small silver spoons in front of everyone.

When the village elder toasted Curtiss and the other men with a glass of Gao Liang wine, Curtiss noticed with a sinking feeling Lu's nephew looking at him with a big, you're-in-for-it-now grin on his face.

The village elder asked Curtiss if he knew how a man of the elder's age could still have a mind as sharp as his own. After Xiao Lu's fuzzy lesson in healthy Chinese eating, Curtiss imperiled his self-confidence with another swing at it and guessed by eating brains. The village elder roared with approval at Curtiss's answer, at which

Curtiss heard a startling, high-pitched squeal and felt something pull on his pant leg. Leaping back in his chair, Curtiss looked under the table. The torso and writhing legs of what was obviously a live monkey was suspended below its center.

Against his will, Curtiss lifted his eyes above the tabletop. As he did so, the waitress lifted the steel wok lid to reveal the top of the monkey's head, which protruded through the center of the table, and was held in place with a circular clamp at tabletop height.

Curtiss steeled himself, or tried to. This was going to happen, whatever, in its grisly details, "this" turned out to be. He wouldn't turn away.

His resolve was immediately tested as the waitress took a teapot filled with boiling water and poured it over the crown of the monkey's head, sending it into screaming fits. She then used the dull side of a knife blade to scrape the hair off the monkey's blanched scalp, cut an "X" into its scalp with the sharp edge, and peel back the skin, revealing the animal's bare white skull.

Curtiss gritted his teeth as she took a small brass ball-peen hammer from her pocket and used it to fracture the monkey's skull into several pieces, then employed a pair of pliers to pull away the pieces, revealing its pink, living brain.

"Dig in!" she then announced in Chinese before collecting her tools and leaving the room.

The village elder and the other two dug out small spoonfuls of the monkey's brain, sending it into screaming convulsions below the table. Curtiss summoned his will and forced himself to maintain a clinical attitude. Small amounts of blood squirted from within the rapidly vacating skull cavity, indicating that the monkey still had a fair amount of blood pressure and was possibly still conscious while parts of its brain were dipped into sauces and consumed.

Curtiss did not pick up his spoon, and no one at the table made a fuss about it.

After the brains were consumed, the monkey removed, and a fresh tablecloth laid over the table the men polished off the bottle of Gao Liang wine together in their smoke-filled chamber of horrors before joining the rest of the family at the banquet table in the main dining room outside. Everyone was in a cheerful mood and the dinner went on into the late evening. Their group was among the last in the restaurant, and as they were preparing to leave, Curtiss felt a sharp pinch in his mid-gut. It was going to be a long ride back and he had no intention of stopping to do his business somewhere beside the road, and so he walked dizzily to the bathroom.

The facility offered only squatters, no sitters, and Curtiss found it difficult to balance himself while assuming the position. At first he figured that he was just drunk, then thought it through and realized he had not had all that much to drink. When his gut violently let loose, he realized something was seriously wrong. Curtiss did his best to clean up as the pain in his gut, his muscles' stiffness, lack of coordination and mental disorientation intensified. When he stumbled out of the bathroom the room began spinning in circles, he lost his balance and collapsed on the restaurant floor.

"What do we do with him?" he heard Lu's nephew ask his father as they carried Curtiss out of the restaurant. "Should we take him to the hospital?"

Curtiss felt completely helpless as they discussed his fate. In his delusional state he found himself recalling the hospital room in which he'd been placed under observation after his and his mother's traffic accident. In his mind's eye, he saw again the pitying expressions on the faces of the nurses and doctors as they entered and retreated from his hospital room—trying not to discuss his case in front of him. And the moment Curtiss himself discovered he was an orphan when a State social worker, a plump, damp-faced woman, sat on his bed one morning and told him that his mother had been killed in their car crash.

"No. The hospital is too dangerous. We should take him to the Lao Wai," Lu's brother suggested. "His house is only about half an hour from here. He'll know how to take care of him."

Lu's nephew flagged down a motorized three-wheeled cart, loaded Curtiss in the back, and took off out of the city.

Curtiss writhed in a kind of pain that felt as if someone were twisting his small intestines with a pipe wrench. Though the journey took just over half an hour, it seemed like forever to Curtiss, who was physically exhausted from dry vomiting and bouncing upon the cold steel floor of the vehicle over the only partially paved roads.

When they finally arrived at a traditional Chinese-style family compound, Lu's nephew leapt off the cart, slung Curtiss over his shoulder, hauled him to the front door and knocked. Curtiss opened his eyes momentarily to see a hefty shadow filling the open doorway of the house. After Lu's nephew explained the situation, the man in the doorway said in English: "Bring him in, man. Bring him in."

* * *

Curtiss woke, feverish, shivering, and in the grip of severe pain, to the warmth of sunshine on his face and early Motown music playing on a portable record player sitting atop a nearby table.

He found himself stretched out on a rattan and bamboo recliner at the center of a small courtyard, whose walls were plastered with weathered posters of Chinese communist heroes striking action figure poses: solider, farmer, factory worker. Disoriented, he caught a brief glimpse of a young Chinese woman passing by one of the doorways leading into the courtyard. He wanted to shout out to her, but he'd lost his voice. Curtiss thought he smelled the distinct odor of burning marijuana before passing out.

He woke again at sunset as a young woman was giving him a sponge bath. He felt much better after the additional rest, and from the pleasantness of receiving a sponge bath. The sharp, intense pain in his gut had subsided to a dull, blunt, full-body ache.

When Curtiss's bather noticed that he had regained consciousness, she smiled, covered him up, put the sponge in her bucket of warm water and left him alone in the courtyard.

Again he smelled burning marijuana.

"You got to get the bug sooner or later," said a voice from behind Curtiss, in American English. "And you got it good, too. You've been out for two days."

Struggling to force his muscles to comply, Curtiss slowly turned to see a crew-cut western man in his mid-forties, wearing sandals, Mao-suit pants, and a Hawaiian shirt.

"You want a hit?" the man said, holding a smoking hand-rolled cigarette out to Curtiss. "It might settle your stomach."

Curtiss couldn't hold his awkward position for long and let gravity roll him onto his back.

"On second thought," the man said, "maybe you ought to take it easy for a little while longer. Give your immune system time to cover it." The man repositioned his rattan and bamboo lounge chair beside Curtiss. "I'm Gabriel. You are in my home."

The young woman who had given him the sponge bath earlier walked into the courtyard with a bowl of soup on a tray, then propped Curtiss up with pillows and left. Gabriel picked up the soupspoon and proceeded to slowly feed Curtiss. "It's bone marrow, bitter vegetables, and tofu soup."

"Yeah, I know," Curtiss croaked. "I've had something like it before."

"What's your name, soldier?"

"Curt. Thanks for taking me in."

"Hey, we're fellow Americans, right? What am I going to do, let you die of dysentery in some alley in China?"

"Is that what I have? Dysentery?"

"I don't know. Probably." Gabriel shrugged. "Where you from?"

"Pennsylvania," Curtiss said, feeling the warm soup transfuse life into his shattered digestive system.

"I'm from upstate New York. Schenectady. But I haven't been back there in a while." Gabriel laughed. "Literally, like in twenty years, you know?" He dabbed Curtiss's mouth with a tissue. "That's enough soup for today. Easy does it. You got to work on the herbal remedy now." Gabriel handed Curtiss a porcelain cup with a matching lid that contained green tea, twigs, a chunk of some kind of fungi, and another thing that looked like a shriveled cherry.

"Where is this place?"

"We're about a half hour from the town you came from, and an hour and a half from the family that brought you here. What the hell are you doing living with the Lu family all the way out there?"

"Cultural exchange." Curtiss propped himself up further until he was sitting nearly vertical. He began drinking the tea and herbal remedy in earnest. "I could ask you the same thing, Gabriel."

"Who, me? I've been living in China for over twenty years, man. This is my home. I belong here. You don't."

"Funny, coming from a guy from Schenectady."

"I came to China to join up with Chairman Mao's Cultural Revolution. Yep, I was here for the whole shebang, starting with the '66 rallies in Beijing's Tiananmen Square. I saw Mao waving to us from the top of the South Gate of the Forbidden City." Gabriel took a long drag off his joint. "You'll never know what it's like to stand in the middle of a million crazed people with their blood up like that. The energy was off the charts. People were chanting, crying, waving his little red book in the air. I mean, people were worshiping this guy. Woodstock had nothing on those rallies. And it was permanent revolution, too. I was hooked."

"You look pretty clean-cut for a `60s radical," Curtiss said.

"Yeah, well, until last month my ponytail was down to my beltline and I had a pretty groovy beard, too. People here said I even looked like old Karl Marx himself! But I had to shave it all off."

"Yeah? Why's that?"

"Well, first, you know that older Chinese men dye their hair, right? I mean, that's why you almost never see gray-haired Chinese men. Think about it."

Curtiss recalled the White General, but realized that, other than him, he couldn't recall seeing any other gray-haired Chinese men.

"So, when my gray was getting out of hand—and not just on my head but my beard, my chest, back, everywhere—I decided to join them. I used the same cheap local hair dye on all of it. And it worked great until I sat in a hot tub at the new, star-rated hotel that opened in that town you came from. The dye reacted with the chlorine and turned my hair purple and frizzy like steel wool. And brittle, too. So I had to shave it all off: hair, beard and chest hair."

Curtiss smiled in lieu of laugh, which most certainly would have hurt. "Well, now you look fit for the draft board."

"I left the U.S. before the army managed to serve me my draft notice, so technically I guess that means I'm not a draft dodger, right?" Gabriel laughed. "Hell, I wish I was young enough for the draft board to be interested in me." He then became serious. "Actually, this is the second time I've been shaved like this in China. The other time was when I was sent to prison. I was accused of being a counterrevolutionary and a spy. Spent six years in a Chinese lockup."

"Six years. You've got to be kidding. Couldn't the embassy help you?"

"What embassy? We didn't even recognize China back then. I mean, Nixon came over during my time in prison, but I wasn't going to ask for *his* help. *Nixon?* Come on."

"So while all your buddies were back in America going to college and enjoying the sexual revolution, you were in prison for the cultural revolution."

"Yeah. But there are things that I learned that they'll never know." Gabriel paused, rubbing his wrists. "Like when you're left unattended in a cell for days and your handcuffs are put on too tight . . . " Gabriel pulled his sleeves back to show Curtiss the scars around his wrists, and then demonstrated flexing exercises. "See? You've got to constantly flex your fingers, hands, and wrists like this to keep the blood going. Otherwise, your hands die and you'll get gangrene."

Curtiss didn't know what to say.

"Hey, look. I'm lucky. If I'd been in a prison in northern China, my hands probably would have frozen off in the first week."

"So . . . were you a spy?"

"Hell no. But there was this one Red Guard bitch that had it in for me. I'd made a pass at her and she got all freaky and accused me of being a spy. And in those days all you needed was someone to accuse you of being a counterrevolutionary, or a spy, and that was it. Bang, into prison you go." Gabriel took another long drag on his joint.

"Wow. Talk about getting shot down for making a pass. So why didn't you leave China the minute you got out of prison?"

"Hey, I still believe in the revolution. When I was released, I found a friend from the '66 rallies who had become the party head of this village. He registered me as being from China's Xinjiang Region—you know, because people there look more like us—and I was allowed to stay and live here. So this lovely little village took me in and I've been here ever since."

"Didn't you want to go back to the States at all?"

"Like I said, the revolution needed me."

A belch erupted from Curtiss, who then coughed and clutched his still-aching stomach.

"Whoa. You don't look so good." Gabriel waved over Curtiss's nursemaid and another young woman who had been patiently waiting in the courtyard and asked them to assist Curtiss to the bathroom and back. When he'd managed that ordeal, they covered him with a blanket against his shivering.

"Get some more rest," Gabriel said. The two ladies sidled up under his arms and each in turn gave him a significant kiss on the lips. "And for your information, there is free love here in China, too." Gabriel smiled and winked at him, then left, taking the two ladies into an adjoining room with him.

* * *

Though she had to ride her bicycle two hours each way to and from Gabriel's compound, Xiao Lu took charge of Curtiss's daily care. He tried insisting that she stop, and focus on her dissertation and being with her family, but Xiao Lu came anyway.

He asked her to speak only Mandarin with him, and to begin teaching him how to read and write Chinese. For each new Chinese character she would provide him a context: an anecdote from Chinese history and folklore. And as she did Curtiss could feel some of the random fragments of unresolved Chinese cultural DNA that had rankled in his subconscious begin to order themselves into understanding. Was she fusing Chinese cultural DNA with his own? Catalyzing a kind of cultural meiosis?

As his recovery progressed and the arrival of warmer weather had Xiao Lu wearing lighter clothing, he couldn't help but take notice of her as a woman. She was lovely, but she was Lu's niece and a member of the family he trusted, without reservation, with his life. And besides, her youth and innocence inspired in him protective, brotherly feelings, not romantic ones.

When Curtiss felt up to it during the early mornings before Xiao Lu's arrival, he would sometimes join Gabriel in his Tai Ji exercises.

"So what do you do for a living, anyway?" Curtiss asked one morning while mimicking Gabriel's motions.

"Well, you know how in the movie *The Graduate* the old guy takes the student aside at the pool-side party and says: 'I want to say one word to you: plastics'? Well, here in China that one word is: feathers. Goose and duck feathers, to be exact."

One of Gabriel's fellow American revolutionaries in New York had sold out and became a capitalist, making and selling down coats. "He knew I was in China, so he sent me a letter asking me if I had any sources for goose and duck feathers over here. Well, as you can see, there are geese and ducks all over the place here, so I started to supply him with goose and duck down. We buy feathers from the villagers, and I'm a shareholder in the business."

"Why, that's mighty capitalist of you," Curtiss joked. "So what's your share in the business?"

"We're fifty-fifty partners. Himalaya Sportswear, have you heard of it?"

Curtiss gaped at him. "That's a four, maybe five hundred million dollar company!"

"Yeah, something like that. Listen, before you start to lecture me about going back and living in some penthouse apartment in Manhattan, I only take what I need in this life, you got it? The business helps the people of this village. It creates cash-paying jobs, and my share of the profits has paid for surgeries, built schools and clinics that help keep qualified teachers and doctors here, and it has sent a whole bunch of kids to university." He shrugged. "Better than the IRS taking all of it."

At the end of their Tai Ji routine, the men bowed in the requisite manner and sat down together in the courtyard. "Education is what the future is all about here, Curt. Things got pretty messed up during the Cultural Revolution, when they closed schools and universities and persecuted professors and teachers."

"Yeah, I heard about that."

"Even before the Cultural Revolution," Gabriel went on, starting just after the communist victory in 1949, the educated and the literate were persecuted and brought low. One of China's strengths was that it has always been a meritocracy: anyone, including a poor farmer's child, could sit for civil exams and the best and the brightest could rise up to virtually any level of the government, short of the royal family. During the Chinese communist revolution, though, illiterate peasants were put in charge of everything from virtually day one. Of paramount importance was their political correctness and loyalty to the Chinese Communist Party. They were the government officials that ran all of China's bureaucracies, even at the central government level. Russia at least had technocrats to run its massive, central-planning bureaucracies, but not China, and this caused serious problems for rebuilding after the revolution, leading to mismanagement of the country and death by privation for tens of millions of people. Gabriel stared into the distance. Curtiss knew enough to know he was referring to the Great Chinese Famine of

1958-1962.

"Finding anything comparable to it in western history would mean...like, combining the reign of terror in France with the Black Death in Europe. Central planning mismanagement and corruption was so bad that entire villages starved to death next to unplanted farm fields. They even made peasants into surgeons, with no training of any kind, if you can imagine that," Gabriel sighed. "There are millions of these kinds of horror stories in China, Curt." Waxing poetic: "No one was untouched by the madness of a society turned upside-down and against itself."

"So why do you stay with this thing if it's so screwed up? Besides, I thought you were on the peasants' side."

"I am on the peasants' side, Curt. I still believe in the fundamental ideas behind the revolution. But the problem is that people twisted the whole thing: they turned equality, fairness, and social justice into weapons of social warfare."

"But Gabriel, communism? Come on."

"Anyway, it looks like that whole idea is about to run its course anyway, even here in China." He switched gears. "Hey, I have to go into town to pick up some stuff. Do you feel up to a long walk?"

Curtiss nodded that he did, smiling. "By the way, that guy in *The Graduate* was right about plastics. If you'd invested in the industry in the States in the 1970s, you'd be a multi-millionaire by now."

"I'm already a millionaire." Gabriel smiled.

*   *   *

When they arrived at the edge of town, the rumbling in Curtiss's lower gut put him on notice that he should keep an eye out for a bathroom. Along the tree-lined lane toward the village's central square, Curtiss saw a plain, rectangular brick building with no roof, and two openings on either side marked with Chinese characters: "Nu," for woman and "Nan," for man, spray-painted on its façade. "I need to use the bathroom," Curtiss announced.

Gabriel laughed, slapped Curtiss on the shoulder: "Good luck."

Curtiss stepped in through the entrance to find a half-dozen men with their pants down around their ankles, squatting over a trough of flowing water that ran along the back wall. The men, lined up shoulder to shoulder like birds on a wire, were reading various sections of the People's Daily newspaper. As a pair of them exchanged the front page for the sports section, they looked up and laughed at the expression on Curtiss's face.

The rank smell only exacerbated Curtiss's sense of urgency. Repulsive as the place was, he needed it. He was considering his options for wedging himself into the line when two men kindly crab-walked in opposite directions to make room for him.

When he emerged from the bathroom Gabriel, was overcome with laughter. "Welcome to the real China, Curt."

Curtiss smiled calmly at Gabriel. "The only disappointment was, with this thing I've got going in my stomach, I didn't have time to finish the crossword puzzle."

Gabriel's first stop was at the post office, where he dropped several letters and checked his mailbox. He then picked up his weekly provisions at a dry goods store, which included a bag of perhaps a hundred toothbrushes labeled "Hilton," each in its own individual plastic bag paired with a small tube of toothpaste.

"They make these in a factory near here for the Hilton chain," Gabriel explained. "Here, look, they're factory rejects," he said, pointing to the misshapen letter "n" in the word Hilton.

Gabriel laughed at the look Curtiss was giving him. "They're not for me. They're for the kids in the village. Hygiene habits are pretty bad out here, especially oral hygiene."

When they returned to the village, Curtiss watched Gabriel ham it up with the gang of children that swarmed him, digging their hands into his pockets to find out what he'd brought them from town. They didn't seem at all disappointed by the toothbrushes, instantly setting to the raucous business of trading brushes for the colors they wanted. The children were happy, and the look on Gabriel's face was one of utter joy.

Well on the road to recovery, Curtiss decided to make himself useful around Gabriel's house by doing some repairs. While looking for tools in a storeroom, he stumbled across a motorcycle with a sidecar residing under a green tarp. That evening at supper, Gabriel explained that it had been broken down for nearly as long as he could remember. Last time he'd looked, mice were nesting in the carburetor. He told Curtiss that if he could get it running, it was his.

Over the next week, Curtiss completely disassembled the vehicle, thoroughly cleaned the salvageable parts, scrounged replacements for the unsalvageable ones in town, and reassembled it. One of Gabriel's girlfriends was thoughtful enough to recover the rotten seat covers using donkey hair, straw and canvas.

Once Curtiss managed to get the engine running, he quickly became acquainted with its personality—the right fuel and air mixture to keep it breathing at all RPMs, which gear was sticky and which tended to pop out during hard acceleration, just how fast to release the clutch and how much gas to pour on for smooth takeoff.

"We're neighbors," Gabriel said to Curtiss as he stood astride the motorcycle on the day he finally felt ready to return to Lu's family home. "You've got wheels now, so don't be a stranger."

"You know, Gabriel, they say that if you save a person's life they become your responsibility forever."

Gabriel just grinned. "Good thing about being a communist: none of the old superstitions apply to you."

* * *

When Curtiss arrived at Lu's family's house, everyone came out to marvel at his restored vintage motorcycle, as well as his restored health. Lu's nephew showed a particular interest in the machine and Curtiss introduced him to all of its idiosyncrasies. "I will leave China soon," he told him. "And when I do, it is yours." But instead of the joyful reaction that Curtiss expected, the young man just looked down at his feet.

At supper that evening, Lu's family enjoyed the delicacies and Chinese spirits that Curtiss had brought from town. The mood at the table was somber, however, since the village elder had fallen gravely ill and was felt to be on his deathbed. He had asked for Curtiss during his absence, they told him, and suggested he visit him.

The next day, at the village elder's home, his son, daughter-in-law and grandson were standing vigil beside his bed. The village elder smiled when he saw Curtiss and gestured for his grandson to fetch something from the closet in the room. He returned with an American Army Air Force leather flight jacket. It was covered with emblem patches, and on the back was a rectangular blood chit identical to the one he'd seen hanging behind the bar at the Chennault Pub in Taipei.

Through his son, the elder explained that an American air force pilot, a Flying Tiger, had given him the jacket forty-five years ago, and that he wanted Curtiss to have it.

"But this is part of your family's heritage," Curtiss protested. "It should go to your son and grandson."

The elder shook his head and spoke to his son, who translated: "My father asks: what do you think the chances are that you, an American, would show up forty-five years later in our village, out of the tens of thousands of villages in China?" The elder believed that it was destiny that it go back to an American. His keeping it all these years, cherishing it and the memories that came with it, and Curtiss arriving at precisely the time when his life was coming to an end, meant that it must go back with him.

The village elder's family nodded with approval. "It is my father's wish that you have it," the village elder's son said to Curtiss. "Chinese people believe that it is important to return to your birthplace at the end of your life. So it will bring my father some satisfaction that it is going back to its origins at the end of his. Please take it."

The elder then raised his hand, made a circle of his thumb and forefinger, and spoke the only English words that he would ever speak to Curtiss: "A-okay."

Lu had sent a letter making an appointment for a phone call with Curtiss at 8:00 pm on April eighteenth, only days away, when Lu would next be at the Hong Kong Peninsula Hotel. The only place where Curtiss could receive Lu's international call was the star-rated hotel in town. Some of Xiao Lu's university classmates were returning home and she was planning to meet them in town around the same time. Curtiss offered to take her into town with him and pay for a separate hotel room for a couple of days where she and her friends could stay.

Early on the appointed day, Curtiss loaded his motorcycle's sidecar with duffel bags, Xiao Lu perched upon the jump seat behind him, and they took off for town. It was the height of spring and they rode past farmers and oxen plowing fields, flowering trees in full bloom, a profusion of bird life, and carp gobbling flies from the surface of the aquaculture ponds that mirrored the region's rugged mountains.

The scenery inspired Curtiss to reflect again on his father's two-month escape during the war. Had he had time to consider the beauty of the landscape on his trek? Had the locals treated him as warmly as Curtiss had been treated over the past few months? Curtiss felt a pang of longing for his father's company stronger than any he'd felt since his adolescence. As the old bike bounced along the road, he found himself wishing he could sit with his father beside the slow-moving river below him and listen to him describe his war years' experiences.

But what would his father think of him—also on the run in China, not from a wartime enemy but from stumbling into criminal activity?

Curtiss and Xiao Lu stopped only once on the way to town, to have a drink and stretch their legs beside a waterfall that Xiao Lu knew of. Here, away from her family, she relaxed and spoke at length, over the waterfall's quiet, ceaseless hiss, about her youth. The two of them traded stories of their small town upbringings and shared their love of the natural world.

After remounting the motorcycle, Xiao Lu reached around Curtiss's Flying Tigers jacket, held him tightly around his waist and laid her head on his back the rest of the way to town. He couldn't pretend he didn't enjoy the contact, but the fact was he'd adopted her as his little sister and could think of her in no other way. He suspected she already knew this, judging by the pouts that she would sometimes give him when he treated her that way.

There were two new buildings worth speaking of in town: the hospital and the star-rated hotel they would be staying in—known to Curtiss as the one where Gabriel had lost his hair to the unfortunate chemical reaction between Chinese hair dye and chlorine. Xiao Lu first directed Curtiss to the hospital and had him pull up to the main entrance, which featured a large bronze plaque bearing embossed Chinese characters, save two English words: Gabriel Zuckerman. Well, almost those words, as they were unintentionally printed backward, in mirror opposite, as not too infrequently happened with English words in China.

"Your friend is very well known as a philanthropist," Xiao Lu told

Curtiss. "He donated enough money to add an entire wing to the hospital: a pediatric ward." His name could be found on similar commemorative plaques on a number of schools, a small museum, and even a restored temple that had been badly vandalized during the Cultural Revolution.

After Curtiss and Xiao Lu checked in at the hotel and took a half hour in their respective rooms to clean up, Xiao Lu arrived at Curtiss's door. He would need to receive the international call in the business center on the third floor, she told him, and she would accompany him there to assist with the arrangements. "We've got some time. Uncle Lu won't call until eight o'clock, right?" she asked, hovering with an expectant smile at his open door.

There was no denying she was a lovely girl, but there was nothing for it but to say, "Might as well get there early," grab a notepad and pencil from the hotel room desk, and step into the corridor with her. "Thanks so much, Xiao Lu."

Her smile faded. "It is fine," she murmured.

"How do you like my hometown?" Lu asked with a laugh over the phone.

"I love it. I hate to even think about leaving it . . . but I am."

"Things are looking better for that," Lu said. "There is something brewing on college campuses that has everybody busy. Our friend is now occupied with official business and is keeping a low profile with his side business, too."

"So . . . when are you thinking?"

"Best time would be at the end of the May first holiday, among all the confusion of people returning to Hong Kong."

"Works for me."

Lu explained that a relative of his would soon arrive carrying a letter for Curtiss that would explain the routing and the people he would meet who would accompany him to the border.

"See you in a few weeks," Lu said with absolute confidence.

The next day Curtiss and Xiao Lu went to the town's central park, where Xiao Lu's friends began arriving at a designated time and place. When she informed them about the hotel room that Curtiss had arranged for them, they all became excited at the prospect of hanging out together in a star-rated hotel.

136

Curtiss was of course a source of great curiosity and interest for the girls. Judging by the smiles and glances between them, it was apparent that they suspected that Curtiss and Xiao Lu were an item—in spite of her pouts indicating to the contrary.

But the topic that was on everybody's mind was what was happening with the growing democracy movement on university campuses in Beijing and elsewhere. Curtiss listened with interest, and some concern, as they spoke of a great rally planned for May and June in Beijing's Tiananmen Square and Xiao Lu became deeply engaged in the conversation and engrossed in the topic. It would be practically all she spoke about during the weeks that followed.

The callowness of her idealistic bent concerning the student democracy movement was glaringly apparent; she saw only the upside potential in both the movement and the people involved in it. He was alarmed by her unshakable conviction that China was at an historic precipice from which there was no turning back. "My parents' generation had the Great Proletariat Cultural Revolution. My generation will have a great democratic revolution," she proclaimed. "It is my destiny to be there in Tiananmen Square where it is all happening! To be part of my country's transformation."

Knowing the risks inherent in mass rallies in China, Xiao Lu's parents were naturally against her going to Beijing for the democracy rally. But she more than matched her parents' determination that she not go. During a heated discussion over supper one evening, Curtiss found himself settling the argument by offering to accompany her in Beijing, even though it would mean that he would have to postpone his departure from China by nearly a month. On the plus side, going to Beijing with Xiao Lu would afford him the opportunity to leave China by air from there, rather than attempting a Hong Kong border crossing at Shenzhen.

It was agreed: Curtiss would chaperone Xiao Lu in Beijing, put her on a train back home after the rally was over, then fly to Hong Kong.

*   *   *

The day before Curtiss and Xiao Lu's departure to Beijing, Curtiss stopped by the village elder's home and found a posting of Chinese calligraphy on a white rectangular strip of rice paper on the front door indicting that the elder had passed away. His grandson was playing in the front yard and Curtiss called the boy over to his motorcycle and gestured for him to sit in the sidecar seat, where the Flying Tigers jacket was laying. The boy happily donned the jacket and jumped into the sidecar.

"The American pilot who gave this to your grandfather wanted it to go to a Chinese boy with big dreams," Curtiss said to the village elder's grandson. "Dream big dreams, like your grandfather, and it belongs to you."

The boy's father emerged from the front door of the house in a cloud of incense smoke. Curtiss waved to him, then started his motorcycle and gestured for the boy to hop out. The boy's father watched from the doorway, adjusting the black armband signaling his mourning, and nodded his thanks as Curtiss waved again and rode away.

That evening Curtiss and Lu's family said their goodbyes over a special supper, and before dawn the next day Lu's nephew drove Curtiss and Xiao Lu to the train station on Curtiss's motorcycle. When they alighted at the station, Curtiss braced Lu's nephew's shoulders and told him how much he appreciated everything that he had done for him over the past months. The young man looked up from his feet and smiled at him, firmly shook his hand and said, in English, "Thank you, my good friend, Curt." He gave Curtiss a thumbs up as he remounted the motorcycle, then rode away from the train station.

CHAPTER 9

Curtiss and Xiao Lu survived on bottled water and snacks prepared for them by Lu's family for their two-day train journey. After arriving at Beijing's central rail station at dawn on June second, they walked out into the large, open square in front of the station, where Curtiss's presence drew stares from some of the more curious faces that drifted by, none of them returning his smile.

There was a grayness to the entire scene: in people's clothing, in the coal-dust-stained buildings and sky, and in the expressions upon people's faces. Beijing felt completely different than southern China, where reform had brought a colorful energy and the return of a passion for life. Curtiss felt a shiver up his spine, witnessing what appeared to him a dystopian manifestation akin to George Orwell's Oceania, featured in his book *Nineteen Eighty-Four*.

He was surprised to see derelicts lying on the pavement around the capital city's train station, one even who had wet himself and exhibited signs of dementia as he rocked back and forth upon his knees and elbows. Xiao Lu explained that many of the people who were severely abused and persecuted during the Cultural Revolution had been psychologically damaged for life, and that the government did not have the resources to take care of all of them.

The vast majority of the crowd were either in their twenties or over fifty. Few if any of China's lost generation—the generation that included Chairman Mao's Red Guards—were to be seen. Having served Mao's purpose of reinstating him to supreme authority through their brief reign of terror, Mao's subsequent Down-To-The-

Countryside campaign dispersed his youthful servants in the Red Guard by the tens of millions across China's remote hinterlands, scattering them like hot coals from a fire so they would burn out individually, and harmlessly. Relatively few would ever manage to return to the cities, most spending the rest of their years in ignorance, isolation, and extreme rural poverty.

Nor were there many young children to be seen, thanks to China's One-Child-Per-Family policy. What children there were appeared as occasional, brightly dressed spots in the crowd. The excessive brightness of their clothing was overcompensation, Xiao Lu explained, by parents and grandparents who themselves had had no choice during their lives but to live in Mao's drab green and blue-gray world.

Curtiss and Xiao Lu walked several kilometers from the train station before they arrived at a hotel where they could get a taxi. They found cabs parked at the front of the hotel, but no drivers in sight. A security guard gestured for them to go to the back of the hotel. There they found the taxis' drivers drinking tea from screw-top jars, smoking cigarettes and playing cards. After Curtiss asked if any of the drivers would be willing to take them to the HuaQiao Hotel, one threw his cards on the card table, stood and adjusted his pants around his seemingly non-existent waist, and announced: "Zou Ba," *Let's go*, in heavily Beijing-accented Mandarin.

The doors of the driver's ancient Russian Lada taxi opened only with a forceful tug and Curtiss had to slam the door shut twice before the latch caught. The entire surface of the ugly little car was, if not either dented or scratched, rusted through. Its quarter panels shook and rattled as they went down the road, its body parts dangling precariously off its sides.

The driver appeared as much abused and neglected as his pathetic taxi. His scarred face winced involuntarily and the hand-rolled cigarette hanging from his mouth twitched each time he shifted gears, turned the wheel, or applied the brake or clutch. When he pulled the rattletrap vehicle onto Beijing's Second Ring Road, he didn't bother to look for a clearing in traffic, but rather swung directly into the flow, drawing a chorus of blaring car horns that he seemed oblivious to. Xiao Lu squeezed Curtiss's hand tightly as if to brace herself from an impending accident. All Curtiss could do was steel himself with her, and speculate in his mind about the driver's behavior, which far exceeded the commonly reckless driving he'd witnessed in cabbies elsewhere. Had they just had the bad luck of drawing a natural lunatic, or was he a victim of the psychological damage as Xiao Lu had described, or perhaps some kind of neurological damage? Was he merely an aberration, or the outcome of some unspeakable injustice, perhaps suffered at the hands of roaming Red Guard gangs during the Cultural Revolution? If so, what had been his crime? Was he accused of being a counterrevolutionary like Gabriel was, or had he just been on the losing side of a battle between rival Red Guard factions? Perhaps it was none of these, and simply an unfortunate encounter with farm machinery.

The HuaQiao Hotel was little better appointed than George's Palace, though George won higher marks for general cleanliness. Xiao Lu ran to hug and greet her classmates, who were congregated in the lobby. After planning the day's strategy, they all crowded into a single elevator and went up together to drop their bags in their rooms and freshen up from their long journeys before heading to Tiananmen Square.

Each time the elevator stopped to let people off at their designated floors, Curtiss noticed a security guard sitting at a desk near the elevators. Xiao Lu later explained that it was routine at big city hotels for a security guard to be present on each floor. When Curtiss got off, the security guard on his floor reached out and asked for his passport and room key. After making a note in his logbook, he handed Curtiss back his possessions and waved him down the hall to his room.

Curtiss cleaned up and put on a fresh set of clothes before heading back to the elevator to go down to meet Xiao Lu and her classmates in the lobby. As the doors to the elevator closed after him, he saw the guard make another note in his logbook. "Oceania," Curtiss muttered under his breath. While riding the elevator down he worried about whether conditions in China were really ready for the degree of freedom that students were now shouting for in Tiananmen Square.

Curtiss offered to pay for taxis to Tiananmen Square. They would have to split up. After arriving they would all meet under Chairman Mao's portrait that hung at the South Gate entrance to the Forbidden

141

City, overlooking Tiananmen Square. The masses in and around the square prevented them from going all the way by taxi: police stopped them eight blocks away and told them they would need to walk from there.

On the way they were stopped again, by a group of students and a four-vehicle military troop convoy that were blocking an intersection. Students were locked arm-in-arm across the intersection, deliberately preventing the convoy from passing through, while others had surrounded the truck and were shouting up to the soldiers in the back, pleading with them to turn around and leave the city. Though the students did their best to explain that they were doing the right thing, that they were peaceful and that the soldiers should not confront them, the soldiers—sons of peasant farmers rather than the privileged few who had the influence within the government and the financial means to send their children to university—appeared unimpressed. They were focused on following their orders and did not respond to or seemingly acknowledge the students in any way. Only the convoy commander had stepped down from the cab of the lead truck to speak with the students.

Xiao Lu tapped one of the students on the shoulder and asked him what was going on. He explained that rumors were that martial law had been declared for parts of Beijing on May eighteenth, including Tiananmen Square, and that troops had been trying to deploy in and around the city ever since. With a broad smile, he proudly told of how the students had largely prevented the army's complete deployment in the city through street actions like these.

Butterflies were fluttering in Curtiss's gut. He couldn't imagine any army, let alone the PLA, allowing itself to be stopped in such a way for very long. The expressions on the faces of the convoy commander and his troops clearly suggested to him that the army's patience with the students was wearing thin.

"We'd better go," he told Xiao Lu. "This is none of our business." Curtiss grabbed Xiao Lu's hand and pulled her away, bypassing the intersection, and they continued on to Tiananmen Square.

Xiao Lu's group of friends were not the only ones who'd thought to use Mao's portrait as a meeting place that day. There was a tightly packed school of what looked like maybe two hundred congregated under the mole on his chin. All were about twenty years old, black-haired and carrying plastic shopping bags, and it was therefore quite a task to identify Xiao Lu's friends. Once they had reunited, they walked together over one of the five white stone bridges there, then through one of the underground walkways beneath Chang An Avenue, emerging at the edge of Tiananmen Square.

Weeks earlier, during one of Curtiss's Chinese language lessons, Xiao Lu had taught him the Chinese phrase: "Ren Shan, Ren Hai," its direct translation being *people mountain, people sea*. She explained that it was an expression used to describe very large gatherings of people. Curtiss did not truly understand the idiom until he stepped out from the underground walkway into Tiananmen Square. Within the square's expansive area—from his perspective at ground level—there were people for as far as the eye could see. From his vantage point the immense crowd could very well have stretched to the mountains, and as far as the sea.

The hum of tens of thousands of voices required Curtiss, Xiao Lu, and her friends to have to shout to be heard. Passing by the ceremonial flagpole used for official daily flag-raisings, they were drawn toward the even thicker masses of people nearer the center of the square.

As they struggled through the crowd, Curtiss could see flashes of a large white figure contrasted against the sea of black hair in front of him. Getting closer, the figure revealed itself to be a makeshift statue of a woman holding a torch with both hands: off to one side and high above her head.

Xiao Lu clapped her hands over her mouth and jumped up and down, excited to see what she had earlier heard called the Goddess of Democracy. "Look, Curt!" she said, pointing at the statue. "It is just like your Statue of Liberty in America." Though there was some physical resemblance, the intended symbolic meaning was more apparent. And the symbolism of this and all that was happening in Tiananmen Square under the watchful gaze of Chairman Mao's massive portrait was not lost on Curtiss, either.

As they moved through the square toward the epicenter of the student demonstrations the near-unintelligible blaring of students' speeches through megaphones and loudspeakers dominated. They pressed on, fighting the crowds past the towering south gate, ending up within eyeshot of the Kentucky Fried Chicken restaurant off the southwest edge of the square. Having walked the entire length of Tiananmen Square, they thought to get a drink and a bite to eat there, and collect their thoughts. Night had fallen by the time they arrived and found the front doors to the restaurant closed with a bicycle cable lock and a handwritten sign posted on the inside of the door: "Closed. Out of food and drink."

One of Xiao Lu's friends had family in Beijing, an aunt who lived in a Hu Tong—a tightly packed cluster of old, single-story homes—not far from where they were standing. She offered everyone the option of staying there for the night. After first deliberating, then taking a vote, the small band of nascent democrats agreed that making the trek to the hotel, only to make the reverse trek back early the next morning, would be a waste of time. They would stay at the aunt's house.

As the group trickled down from the large buildings and wide streets surrounding Tiananmen Square into the narrow streets of the neighboring Hu Tongs, they were plunged into near total darkness, with only the light from curtained windows and the occasional kerosene lantern or low-watt light bulb to light their way.

Ai Yi, or Auntie, as they called her, warmly welcomed the group into her home, making sure everyone had a cup of tea, something to eat, and a comfortable place to sleep for the night.

At dawn on the morning of June third, Xiao Lu woke Curtiss as a child wakes her parents on Christmas morning. "Come on, Curt," she said as the smell of a Northern Chinese breakfast reached Curtiss's nostrils. "I don't want to miss a minute of this."

Auntie would not permit anyone to leave her house until after they had had breakfast. The group slurped congee from chipped blue and white porcelain bowls and chewed on steamed buns as they listened to Auntie wax nostalgic about being an activist in her youth; about some of the famous demonstrations that she had participated in during the Cultural Revolution, and how she spent months living off the hospitality of the people and the Army as she traveled around the country on trains free of charge.

Everyone thanked Auntie for taking such good care of them and each hugged her in turn as they prepared to leave. She bid them all a happy time at the demonstration.

On their way back to Tiananmen Square, the group was stopped in their tracks by a detachment of soldiers that had set up camp overnight in a small park along the way. Two armed soldiers blocked the road and signaled for them to turn around, away from the city center. Running, skipping, and giggling as if it were some kind of game—leaving Curtiss behind before he could stop her—Xiao Lu led the group through nearby alleys, bypassing the soldiers, back to Tiananmen Square.

The population occupying the square had dropped substantially overnight. Small tricycle carts and pedicabs bearing university insignias delivered bottles of water and food to those students who had camped overnight. City workers were pumping out the portable toilets that they'd placed there earlier.

By midday the crowds had returned and they spent the entire day walking around the square and its perimeter. As early evening arrived, the group agreed to split up for a while.

As Curtiss and Xiao Lu slowly walked out of the northeastern edge of the square, they were attracted to a commotion in front of a two-story government building. Through a tall iron fence they could see a couple hundred students chanting and pumping their fists in the air, facing off with six very nervous security guards protecting the building's entrance. The guards bore only electric-shock battens.

After a half-dozen low-pitched thuds, Curtiss saw a cascade of smoke trails arc up over the crowd's heads. Teargas canisters.

Heart pounding in his chest, Curtiss said, "Time to go," to Xiao Lu who, having never seen teargas canisters used either in real life or in any form of media, wasn't quite able to grasp what was going on.

As they walked east along Chang An Avenue, Curtiss saw that someone had thrown a bottle of black ink or paint, deliberately defacing the portrait of Mao that hung at the Forbidden City's entrance. He would later hear rumors that, after learning about the demonstrations in Beijing, a man came all the way from Southern China with the sole purpose to deface Mao's portrait.

"That's not good," he choked out over the lump that had taken residence in his throat. "We're leaving. Now. And, you are on a train home tomorrow. This is getting out of hand, Xiao Lu."

Xiao Lu yanked her arm out of Curtiss's hand, placed her hands on her hips and stood her ground there on the street. "Bei Gong She Ying!" she shouted at him. Xiao Lu had quoted a Chinese idiom that she had taught him during his recovery at Gabriel's house. The literal translation was that he was mistaking the reflection of a bow in a cup as being a snake: *she was accusing him of being paranoid.*

"Why would the government be setting up portable toilets for the students if there was any danger, huh? The Universities are bringing water and food to their students. The government is taking care of us, Curt. They *want* us here." She'd become terse with him for the first time. "Besides, foreign TV crews are everywhere. Everyone is talking about freedom now. They wouldn't dare do anything to embarrass the country."

She turned away, then spun around again with a woman-scorned look in her eyes. "This isn't about any real danger. This is about you treating me like a baby! Who do you think you are? This is *my* country, and I know exactly what I am doing!" Light flashed in her eyes. "And by the way, I'm not a little girl that you can just order around. I'm a woman. Why do you refuse to recognize that?"

And then she began to sob like a little girl.

Now she chose to confront this tension between them? Curtiss had to find a way to get them off the street—and fast. Without conscious thought, he reached out for her arm, pulled her to him and gave her a wholehearted and fervid kiss. As he'd known she would, Xiao Lu melted in his arms. When they separated, she looked dazedly into his eyes and produced a sleepy smile. Her infatuation had been realized.

Curtiss led a suddenly manageable Xiao Lu east along Chang An Avenue until they stopped to eat at a hotel coffee shop about a kilometer away from the square. Their kiss lingered between them, and Curtiss spent their quiet supper politely requiting coquettish glances from Xiao Lu while devising their extraction plan. He would worry about extricating himself from the romantic fantasy he'd allowed to bloom within Xiao Lu later.

After Curtiss had returned them to Chang An Avenue to begin the long walk back to the hotel, they heard popping sounds and saw flashes coming from the direction of Tiananmen Square.

"Fireworks," Xiao Lu announced excitedly. "We are going to miss the fireworks!"

"Don't worry," Curtiss said, keeping his grip on her elbow. "There'll always be plenty more fireworks in China." He turned them away from Tiananmen Square and headed toward the Second Ring Road and their hotel.

Only another block on, Curtiss and Xiao Lu heard loud voices and footsteps behind them and turned to see a trickle of students running toward them at a distance, breaking the stillness of the night like the first gust of wind that precedes a storm.

When he pulled her over beside a tree, she smiled and prepared herself to receive another kiss. "Stay right here," Curtiss instructed, much to her dismay. "I'm going up to see what the hell is going on." He climbed up the tree, but could only see that people were running toward them down the poorly lit street. He hopped down just before a pedicab rode by them with three bloody bodies stacked inside, one atop another.

"They are killing us!" shouted the pedicab driver. And the storm was upon them: a rush of frantic people—some running at full tilt, some injured and limping, and all panicked—engulfed Curtiss and Xiao Lu, shouting "Quai Tao!" *Run!*

The next thing Curtiss heard was a sound that would haunt him for the rest of his life: the dull thud of a bullet striking the back of Xiao Lu's head.

She crumpled to the ground like a marionette whose strings had been cut. Curtiss reflexively ducked as several more bullets buzzed by his head and close-range small arms fire echoed off nearby buildings. When he rolled Xiao Lu over, there was no question that she was dead.

Another volley of bullets whizzed by, some skimming and shattered off the pavement near his feet. When two people who were running past him received bullets in their backs, Curtiss's survival instincts took over. Along with countless others, he turned and ran as fast as he could away from Tiananmen Square.

Bright lights atop tanks coming down Chang An Street toward the square scattered Curtiss and the students to the sides of the road, where they hid behind the decorative embankments, fountains, and statues that lined the roadside.

Catching his breath as he watched the tanks roll past, Curtiss noticed that his shoes were wet. Looking down to determine what he might have stepped in in the darkness, he found himself unable to see his feet clearly in the shadows, so stuck his index finger into his shoe and pulled it out: blood. His eyes had adjusted by then, and he noticed small holes in his pants below the knee. Lifting up his pants legs, he discovered both shins were peppered with small, bleeding holes.

The wounds to his legs must have been caused by flying shards of the bullets that had shattered on the pavement around his feet earlier. His coolness vanished for the moment, his heart flopping in his chest as he realized just how close he had come to death that night, but snapped into place again: It wasn't over yet. He needed to get to the airport, and with his legs in this condition, he would need transportation.

A short distance away was a man sitting among a stack of bricks atop his donkey cart, smoking a cigarette and calmly watching the events unfold before him as if he were watching it happen on TV.

"I'll give you five hundred RMB if you take me to the airport," Curtiss said to the man in Mandarin, while waving money in the air.

"Tai Yuan, Le," the man said, refusing. The airport was too far, but he would take Curtiss as far as the Lido Hotel for one thousand in Foreign Exchange Currency. Curtiss agreed, handing the man five hundred FEC and showing him the other five hundred.

While ploddingly tugged along by the scruffy Beijing donkey, as they headed up the Third Ring Road, troop trucks would periodically pass from the opposite direction. To Curtiss's relief, they didn't seem to notice or otherwise have interest in anything but carrying out their deployment orders to the letter.

Strangely, the streets were filling with people, regular folks who emerged from their houses in their pajamas to see what was going on. This was not what he expected a population to do with gunfire and tanks rolling down their street, but nevertheless the donkey cart stopped on numerous occasions when the driver had to shout at people to get out of their way. Consequently, the normally one-hour trip by bicycle to the Lido Hotel took them until dawn.

Curtiss's legs had stiffened up during the ride, but that discomfort was replaced by outright pain when he jumped from the donkey cart to the pavement at the hotel's entrance. He could walk without help, though.

Inside, Curtiss saw that the hotel's octagonal domed reception area resembled a refugee camp of people from all the world's nationalities. An employee of the hotel noticed the blood on Curtiss's pants and came over to him. "Are you injured?"

"A little, but it is not serious. I just need a place to wash up. And some bandages would be nice."

The woman led Curtiss to a corridor where all the hotel room doors were open. Easily a hundred people were milling about the hallway and between the rooms. Curtiss was able to get to a sink where he could properly tend to his wounds. After washing off the dried blood, he could see that while each of his shins had a half-dozen small holes in them, the wounds were only superficial, most bleeding from force of impact rather than from any serious penetration. He set to work gently massaging the few bullet fragments out of his skin.

He returned to the lobby and made himself comfortable with the pillows and blankets that the hotel staff had made available there. He watched as the lobby restaurant's daily-special sign board was pressed into the service by U.S. Embassy personnel, who erased the words: "Western Buffet Breakfast: FEC 88 + 15% Service Charge," and wrote: "American Citizen Collection Point."

"Attention, U.S. Citizens," a U.S. Embassy staffer announced to the crowd. "We cannot confirm the reports that there may still be airplanes at the airport. But we've been informed that our government has leased four jumbo jets to come to Beijing to evacuate its citizens. We are now locating ground transportation and will be taking people to the airport according to number. We ask for your patience and cooperation."

Upon hearing the announcement a sense of joy welled up from deep within Curtiss's chest: a physiological reflex unique to hearing one's mother tongue spoken in ones native accent after not having heard it for a very long time. He flashed his passport to an embassy staffer, who then gave him a slip of paper with the U.S. Embassy seal and a hand-written number on it.

Curtiss returned to his blanket on the lobby floor and looked around. Like in Guangzhou's White Swan Hotel six months earlier, Curtiss was in a hotel surrounded by expat American families. Chances were Curtiss was the only one in the room who was wanted by the Chinese military, who were now in charge of Beijing and its airport—and, for all he knew, the entire country. Having declared marshal law over the city, they were likely keeping an eye out for foreign agents who might have been pro-democracy agitators in Tiananmen Square. No doubt he would have some explaining to do about the blood on his clothes and bullet fragment holes in his shins when passing through security. Guilt by association was the norm in Oceania. If he were identified and arrested on the way to the airport, he couldn't in good conscience endanger these families. Curtiss decided to go to the airport alone.

"Sorry," Curtiss said under his breath as he pulled a bicycle from the employee bike rack behind the hotel, hopped on, and rode off toward the airport road.

There was an eerie silence on the outskirts of Beijing the morning of June fourth 1989, broken only by occasional, distant, staccato-thumping sounds. Perhaps gunfire, but Curtiss couldn't be certain. The one-and-a-half lane Airport Road was empty, save for the occasional passing shuttle bus heading to the airport, the curious faces of expat children and the worried faces of their parents pressed to its windows.

A checkpoint had been set up at a bridge over a river located about halfway between the Lido Hotel and the Beijing Capital Airport. A dozen soldiers with AK-47 assault rifles slung over their shoulders manned the checkpoint and one of them raised his hand to Curtiss, indicating for him to stop. No more than twenty years old, the pimple-faced soldier held out his hand to Curtiss, who responded by handing over his sweat-stained passport. The soldier compared the photo in the passport to Curtiss's face and Curtiss watched helplessly as the soldier's eyes scanned his body down to his bloodstained and torn pant legs. The soldier's eyes snapped back to his and the two men held each other's gaze for a tense moment.

The soldier then looked past Curtiss's shoulder and thrust his chin toward the side, signaling another solider behind him to grab his arm and escort him to a tent that had been set up about ten yards off the road. Curtiss could hear shouting coming from within the tent, which set his heart jumping in his chest again and stiffened his breathing. He would not be allowed to simply ride a bicycle to the airport that morning.

Inside the tent were three young Chinese men with their hands cuffed behind their backs and a noticeable amount of blood on their clothes. Since none showed any apparent injuries, Curtiss deduced that the blood belonged to others. A low-ranking officer was interrogating them, attempting to determine where and how blood had gotten onto their clothes. The three men admitted that they were in Tiananmen Square during the shooting, but vehemently denied that the blood had originated from any attack on soldiers or police. They claimed they had acquired the blood while carrying injured students *and* public security officers to safety.

Curtiss's escort interrupted the officer, who looked surprised by the sight Curtiss's foreign face. He turned from his interrogation of the three men, ordering that they be given a drink of water. Curtiss took this as a good sign, an indication that he did not intend to harm his detainees—at least not for now.

"What country are you from?" the officer asked Curtiss in English. Curtiss saw him glance down at his pant legs.

"United States."

"And what are you doing here in China?" he asked, while calmly looking at Curtiss's passport.

"I'm a tourist."

The officer nodded, then looked straight in Curtiss's eye. "How did you get the blood there?" he asked in Mandarin, pointing to his pant legs.

Though Curtiss understood the officer, he shook his head indicating that he didn't: tourists don't learn Mandarin Chinese for a short visit, but an American spy might.

The officer restated his question in English. Curtiss could sense both intelligence and higher education in this officer, and gambled that being completely honest with him was the best way out of the situation. "I was in Tiananmen Square to see what was happening. Then the shooting started. I ran, but not before I was injured." He pulled up his pant legs to reveal his bandages, some of which had red stains from the deeper wounds that had reopened from the stress of pedaling his stolen bicycle.

"Where are you going now?"

"I am going to the airport. To leave China."

Speaking Mandarin again, the officer asked the escort soldier what

151

Curtiss had with him, and specifically whether or not he had a camera. The soldier replied that he did not, and that he only had the clothes on his back and a bicycle with him. The officer instructed the solder to search him for film and to let him go. After receiving a patdown, Curtiss thanked the officer, returned to his bicycle and rode on to the airport.

As he rode along the airport's perimeter fence, Curtiss was relieved to see several planes bearing the logos of international carriers parked at the terminal, though concerned by the lack of sound and movement within the airport grounds.

His arrival by bicycle without so much as a small backpack drew stares from the soldiers who now surrounded the terminal, but no one attempted to stop him from entering.

The deceptive calm outside gave no hint of the pandemonium that he found inside. He scanned the departure area for any sign of a U.S.-citizen assembly area, but saw none among the abandoned suitcases that were strewn about and the crowd of hundreds of anxious people who were congregated at the doorway that led to the gates. Security officers were barely managing to hold the crowd back and he got close enough to overhear check-in personnel telling security that there were no more seats on any planes. No one was to be allowed through until further notice.

Others heard this as well, as several passengers bolted through one of the doors. When security officers turned to pursue them, the crowed surged forward, sweeping Curtiss through the door with them.

He ran with the herd of desperate passengers who had broken through, and didn't stop running until he'd arrived with them at a gate with an airliner parked at the other end of the gantry. The lone, unarmed security officer manning the gate appeared for a moment determined to keep the mob from pushing their way onto the gantry way, then stepped aside for his own safety.

The gantry swayed as they ran toward the plane's door, which two flight attendants were in the process of closing. Curtiss and the rest fell to their knees as one of the ground crew drove the gantry away from the side of the plane with a sudden jerk. Curtiss was the first to his feet and leapt across the widening gap that had opened between the gantry and the plane, and tumbled through the plane's door.

Several more passengers made it on board before the door was closed and locked.

Standing at the door, he could overhear the captain speaking with the flight attendants, who informed him that they had more passengers onboard than seats. The captain told them that they were not to reopen the door, that they had permission to depart and that the crew needed to find a place for the extra passengers. They were taking off.

*　*　*

Curtiss scanned the faces of his fellow passengers seated with him on the floor atop folded blankets. They were all silent, or spoke only in whispers for the three-hour flight to Hong Kong. Some of their faces were still gripped with the fear born of the horrors they had witnessed and escaped from with their lives. Others were a blank. One had fallen asleep. Curtiss cleaned and re-dressed his wounds with supplies from the plane's first-aid kit.

On the final approach to the Hong Kong airport, the flight crew advised the passengers seated on the floor to lock arms for additional bracing. Some passengers broke into tears when the plane touched down.

Their unscheduled flight had to wait for nearly an hour for deplaning, as the ground crews attempted to cope with a tarmac littered with dozens of aircraft that had either made the one-way emergency trip out of China, or had canceled their flight plans *to* China. Only when the door opened and the passengers began to deplane did the somber group begin to reanimate. Some cheered their salvation, while others quietly smiled and hugged each other for comfort.

Out of danger, Curtiss ran out of adrenalin and collapsed, both physically and emotionally. His hands and the large muscle groups in his arms and legs trembled, and he found himself unable to get up from the floor.

The plane was completely empty when Curtiss at last struggled to his feet and slowly shuffled down the aisle toward the airplane's exit—his open cell door after his six-month term in China. As he walked through the door to freedom, he nearly lost his legs again, staggered by the realization that Xiao Lu had been right: it was her destiny to go to Beijing's Tiananmen Square and be a part of her country's transformation.

CHAPTER 10

The muffled, high-pitched pneumatic scream of the Peninsula Hotel coffee shop's massive brass and stainless steel cappuccino machine put Curtiss on notice that his ordeal was over. Still numb from the previous day's harrowing escape from Beijing, he nursed his hangover—the result of exhaustion, lack of sleep, and an overdose of adrenalin, rather than alcohol—with the first cups of genuine coffee he had enjoyed in six months.

The well-rehearsed choreography of the hotel's waitstaff and its well-to-do guests playing out before him appeared entirely unaffected by the chaos and bloodletting to the north. With a pang of guilt, he realized that life returning to normal for him, after experiencing what would become known as China's June fourth incident, was an option for him to choose.

Xiao Lu had no such option.

As he soaked in the sights, sounds and smells of freedom and safety, he thought about how he would tell Lu the story of Xiao Lu's last hours. As an officer, Curtiss's father surely must have made decisions that resulted in people under his command being killed. How had he handled reporting their deaths to their families? What did he think when he looked at himself in the mirror, knowing that if he had done things differently, they might still be alive?

He dreaded facing Lu. Xiao Lu's parents had only given her permission to go to Beijing because Curtiss had intervened in a family dispute and offered to chaperone her. He should've been more insistent about leaving Beijing when he'd seen things were going

155

wrong. What had been his true motive for going to Beijing, anyway? To help Xiao Lu, or to help himself to an easier exit from China?

Though Lu had taken his regular early morning flight from Taipei, the backlog of flights vying to take off or land on Kai Tak's runway had delayed the flight and he did not arrive at the Peninsula until nearly noon.

Lu's face was pinched with pain as he arrived at his table. Curtiss stood and the men shook hands, Lu clasping his hand with both of his.

"You look thin, Curtiss."

"I don't know why," he said with a strained smile. "Your sister-in-law is an excellent cook."

The men stood for a moment longer, Lu shaking and squeezing his hand tightly. "Are you okay?"

Curtiss could not find words to answer Lu and both men sat down together. Lu ordered them each a glass of bourbon.

Curtiss and Lu spoke until well into the afternoon. Curtiss shared everything about Xiao Lu's recent life and her death. As he described her final moments, the image of her laying dead in the street flashed into his mind with photographic detail: her blood pooled on the ground around her head, the lifelessness of her body as he rolled her over. He felt again his own instincts for survival taking over and pulling him forcefully away from her body.

His sorrow overpowered his composure and he was no longer able to speak.

Lu hung his head, reached over and put his hand on Curtiss's shoulder. "If you did not leave when you did, you would have been dead right alongside her. There was nothing you could have done."

Though Lu's words soothed the pain welling in his heart, they could not erase the guilt he felt over Xiao Lu's death. "She should never have been there in the first place."

*　*　*

Curtiss stood in the shorter of the two lines that stretched around the U.S. Consulate General in Hong Kong: the line for U.S. citizens.

Normally there was no line at all for citizens, just masses of non-U.S. citizen visa-seekers forced to line up under Garden Road's bauhinia tree-covered slopes, which cradled the Consulate. But on June 6, 1989, hundreds of Americans showed up at their Consulate to get a copy of the State Department's travel advisory for China and to seek information about loved ones that were still in China. A Consulate employee walked the length of the U.S. citizen line handing out photocopies of the announcement that designated China as a high risk area and warned American citizens not to travel there until further notice.

"If you haven't registered with the Consulate yet, you should do so now," the Consulate employee announced repeatedly as he walked up and down the line.

Curtiss decided to continue to wait in line so that he could register and wrote the Lee Garden Hotel as his residence on the registration form.

Lu had explained that the nationwide crackdown after the June fourth incident meant that Curtiss was now safe. The White General who had indeed put a contract out on him was going to be completely occupied with the crackdown, or even himself the subject of a possibly wider crackdown on corruption. Either way, the result was that Curtiss's troubles with him were now over. Ng, Lu's former business partner who had set Curtiss up with the White General, was caught red-handed skimming from the partners' profit pool. Lu did not go into detail, but simply explained that he was no longer in the picture and no longer presented a threat. Curtiss was off the hook.

Though this pressure was now off for the first time in six months, it had been replaced with a new and greater weight on his shoulders: Xiao Lu's death. He carried this burden with him down the hill from the Consulate to the Hong Kong Shanghai Bank building to replenish his pocket cash.

The building's street-level escalator plucked him from the heat and commotion of the noisy streets and glided him up into the underbelly of the glass and steel icon of Hong Kong's skyline. It was like an alien abduction, being pulled up on a tractor beam into the cavernous mother ship of some technically advanced race. It was quiet inside, and didn't reek of stale cigarette smoke. Fellow bank customers politely queued in well-formed lines and bank employees greeted him with smiling faces—experiences now alien to him after his long submersion in 1980s China.

From the bank, it was only a short walk to Hong Kong's Lan Kwai Fong bar street. The shop windows along the base of Central's high-rise canyons were filled with everything from Ferraris to jewel-encrusted gold Rolex watches. New York City's yuppies had nothing on the conspicuous consumption of the people of Hong Kong. Living in China had sensitized Curtiss to the stark contrast between China and Hong Kong, and to how truly unlike China Hong Kong really was. Separated only by a common border, they were also separated by a quarter-century of development: Hong Kong enjoying economic growth rates outpacing most any other place on earth, while China stalled at the threshold of the dawn of the twentieth-century.

Curtiss noted the near-ubiquitous presence of cellular phones in the hands of the city's well-dressed businessmen. It seemed that in a matter of only six months they had become as standard a part of Hong Kong businessmen's attire as the necktie. Curtiss came to understand that six months was a long time in this rapidly changing part of the world.

In every Lan Kwai Fong bar he passed, patrons were glued to televisions that carried the latest news about the massacre in Tiananmen Square, and the nationwide crackdown on students and others. Since Curtiss was still re-adjusting to the English-speaking, modern world, he contented himself with overhearing rather than engaging in the conversations around him as he bar hopped up the street. Bellicose Brits openly expressed their I-told-you-so opinions about the goings-on up north and debated why Britain needed to hand over Hong Kong to China at midnight on June thirtieth 1997, when Britain's ninety-nine-year lease expired. "We built the place. Why should we just hand it to them?" one would argue. "The Red Chinese would only destroy the place once they get their hands on it. Look what they are doing to their own capital city!" another would add, and so on. The Hong Kong Chinese standing nearby or working in the bar were silent as they watched the news with a look of grave concern on their faces.

Night had fallen by the time Curtiss had finished drinking at his fourth bar on the street, and the alcohol that had accumulated in his system was having the desired effect. He wobbled as he strained up the steep hill toward the 97 Bar—Hong Kong's trendiest and most exclusive Lan Kwai Fong nightclub.

The tall Chinese woman with hair down to her beltline guarding the entrance to the bar looked Curtiss up and down, from the bare ankles sprouting from his Top-Sider loafers to the wrinkled dress-shirt shirttails that hung over the top of his blue jeans. "Do you have a reservation?" she asked in a perfect British accent.

Curtiss naturally thought of Jacqueline, and smiled, pleased with himself, when he realized that he hadn't thought about her for months. His immune system had covered it, as Gabriel would say: he was finally free from the infection of obsessive love.

"No. I don't," he said to the woman. She looked curiously at Curtiss as he grinned, slid his hands in his back pockets and continued walking up the steep hill, not once looking back.

*   *   *

Though Lu's duty-free business had been severely affected by the post-June fourth crackdown, his other businesses continued unabated. During Curtiss's absence, his export business to Taiwan of special teas and herbal medicines unique to China had grown exponentially. Curtiss found it far less complicated and easier to manage than Lu's duty-free business. It was completely above-board and operated within the international shipping and banking system. He was relieved to no longer be required to carry bags of cash to the bank—and, most important, it kept him out of Mainland China, to which he was not eager to return anytime soon.

After several weeks settling back into Hong Kong and the new business, Curtiss visited Lu at his Yang Ming Shan Taipei home and then took the opportunity to drop in and see Sonya at the Chennault Pub.

"Where have you been, dear?" Sonya asked as she held his head and kissed him on both cheeks. "We thought you'd forgotten about us."

Curtiss was deeply saddened when he saw Sonya, who appeared to have aged years since he'd seen her last. She was drinking tea instead of her usual martini. "Doctor's orders, I'm afraid," she would later explain, sullen about her new restrictions.

Putting on a sanguine front, Curtiss apologetically explained his absence through having been on a six-month assignment in Mainland China. "I would have called, but you know it is impossible to call Taiwan from Mainland China." Sonya replied with an I-told-you-so smile, seeming to have concluded, based on the evidence, that he had decided to give up his life selling junk bonds in New York and embrace the energy and dynamism of the part of the world that she had come to know and love.

When she asked if he had been anywhere near "that nastiness in Tiananmen Square" and he told her that he'd been in the thick of it, she proceeded to draw a detailed debriefing from him, occasionally noting how little things had changed in China since she and Frank had left there forty years earlier. She seemed keenly interested in the army's presence in Beijing in the days leading up to June fourth and pressed for a precise, blow-by-blow description of how they carried out the massacre, and how Curtiss had managed to get out of there.

"A narrow escape for you, Curtiss." Sonya smiled admiringly at him. "Your powers of observation and resourcefulness are serving you well. Who knows? I may need *your* help one day."

They agreed that they would stay better in touch and hereafter would meet for dinner every time she was in Hong Kong and he in Taipei.

Back in Hong Kong, while collecting his mail at the Lee Garden Hotel's front desk, a hand clapped Curtiss's shoulder from behind. The smiling face that greeted him when he turned stunned him for a moment.

"Oh, for the . . . Jimmy!" Curtiss bear-hugged his old U of M classmate. "What are you doing here?"

"That lame letter you sent from Taiwan was frigging useless, Curt. No return address, nothing." Curtiss had written that he was going to be back in New York in a week or two, but after three months had gone by, Jimmy feared he'd gotten into some serious trouble. "So I put in a missing person's report with the State Department . . . "

"My registration at the U.S. Consulate."

"Yep. I got a call a little over a week ago that you'd registered at the Hong Kong Consulate and were staying at this dump. I considered calling, but then just got on a plane as soon as I could break away from work."

"To talk some sense into me, right?"

"Later, Curt." Jimmy appeared not to be in the mood to lecture. "It is so damned good to see you, buddy. Where can we grab a cold one in this sweatbox? It's like a sauna out there."

Curtiss and Jimmy spent the rest of the afternoon and all evening at the Bull & Bear Pub in Central, catching up while feasting on steak and kidney pie and fish and chips as the bartender pulled pints of John Smiths for them from the tap. Jimmy said he was getting signals from the firm about partnership, but the youngest ever partner at the firm was thirty-five, and that was still more than few years away for him. He had received a couple of calls from headhunters about going in-house as a corporate attorney, but was determined to go the partnership route first before considering the in-house counsel track.

At about midnight the two men walked to Queen's Pier to take in the city's lights surrounding Victoria Harbour. "I've got to admit, this is one hell of a city, Curt," Jimmy said as a party-boat Chinese junk disgorged its inebriated passengers onto the pier.

Curtiss agreed that it had its own flavor as they smiled to each other at the sight of three British girls in short skirts and high-heels scream in unison as they stumbled, arm-in-arm, off the junk's weaving gangplank onto the pier. He and Jimmy would always be college buddies when they were together.

"Curt, can you tell me about what happened with Jacqueline? Did you eventually find her?"

Now cured of his Jacqueline pathogen, Curtiss was embarrassed by what he'd allowed it to drive him to over the past year. He saw Jimmy take in his pensive reaction to his questions, and knew that their friendship didn't require detailed answers. Rather, he simply explained that she was determined to go ahead with her marriage and that he wished her well.

Well versed in the code—which called for allowing guys to at least have the appearance of figuring things out on their own—Jimmy responded with the requisite flinty silence.

The next day they quietly took in the view through the window of the Peak Tram as they were hauled up the lush subtropical mountainside to Victoria Peak. After alighting at the top, the two men stood for a moment to consider the Peak Tower building: a 1970s architectural statement meant to express the uniqueness and ingenuity of Hong Kong. The building was a white, oval inverted trapezoidal cone supported by two flat orange-tiled pillars at both ends.

"It isn't pretty, but the beer up there is cold and the view spectacular," Curtiss told Jimmy as they walked to the back of the queue for one of the tower's two tiny elevators.

Seated by the harbor-side window, after clinking their bottles together in a toast to their youth and vigor, Jimmy became serious again. "Curt, have you been keeping up on what's been happening with Drexel Burnham Lambert?"

"Nope. I haven't given them a second thought," Curtiss said, taking a swig from his bottle.

"Well you should. About the time you disappeared last year, the SEC filed suit against them for defrauding clients, bribery, and insider trading, among other things."

"That doesn't surprise me."

"Rudy Giuliani, the U.S. Attorney for the Southern District of New York, indicted your idol, Belkin, just this March. Belkin was forced to leave the firm." He explained that Curtiss's department was completely gone. There was talk of a RICO indictment against other company officers and the firm itself, and that just the threat of RICO had cut off the firm's ability to source funds. Talk on The Street was that it was only a matter of time before they filed Chapter Eleven. "I'd give them another four months—six, tops."

"You know all this through your firm?" Up to now grateful to Jimmy for coming halfway around the world to make sure he was okay, Curtiss now sensed that there was more to his visit than drinking beer and reliving the good ol' days.

"Our firm is doing some of the legal work for the city, but I'm not involved. Curt, this isn't inside information. It's been all over the news for the past year. Don't you watch the news over here?"

"It was a little difficult to get the financial papers in rural Mainland China, Jimmy," Curtiss said with a smile. "Okay, Belkin's gone now. They got their big fish. So it's over, right?" He took another long draw from his sweaty beer bottle.

"That's not what I'm hearing." Jimmy had turned deadly serious. He described how a number of Curtiss's former colleagues were also under indictment or investigation, and that they were getting desperate. A lot of them were negotiating immunity agreements in exchange for testimony. And, guilty or not, Curtiss was especially vulnerable since he was not there to defend himself. "Why not just blame half the stuff on the guy in the department who just up and disappeared one day, right?"

Curtiss could easily see that kind of thing happening with his former Permian-swamp colleagues. The DBL higher-ups had sacrificed Hank Jarvis to save their own skins without a second thought. Why would they hesitate to do the same to him? "Well, there's nothing I can do about it now. Besides, don't they have to serve me process for a summons or something? Will they do that all the way out here?"

Jimmy explained that if they just wanted him as a witness they would probably not pursue it beyond sending a summons to his old address in New York. They had plenty of witnesses for the case, so likely wouldn't need him for that. "But if *you're* the subject of an investigation and they have issued an indictment, then you're on the hook."

Jimmy let that last statement linger for a while, until it morphed into an unasked question about what Curtiss might have done while in Belkin's employ.

"What does the statute of limitations say?" Curtiss asked, with a whiff of desperation. "Couldn't I just wait it out over here?"

Jimmy explained that there are a lot of misconceptions about the statute of limitations. If someone hasn't been charged, then the clock keeps ticking on the statute of limitations. But if they have already been indicted, the statute of limitations is suspended. "And it doesn't apply to fugitives from justice."

Curtiss could see Jimmy struggling to remain professionally dispassionate against his emotions for his old friend.

Jimmy said that most courts agreed that the government must establish intent—that is, that the accused's absence was specifically intended to avoid prosecution. "Unfortunately, the timing of your disappearance this past year looks pretty damning." Remaining out of jurisdiction once he'd learned of the possibility of criminal proceedings was kind of a gray area, Jimmy continued, since it would be difficult to prove what he knew when, and his intent.

"How long would the statute of limitations be?"

Jimmy leaned back in his chair. "Well, that depends on the crime.

Most federal crimes have a five-year statute of limitations. But for some crimes, including fraud against financial institutions and for certain RICO violations, it is up to ten years."

* * *

The high tea served on the Mandarin Oriental Hotel's mezzanine level was the best in Hong Kong and arguably the best in Asia, Curtiss told Jimmy—one final Hong Kong luxury before his flight home the next day. Curtiss ordered them Earl Grey tea and a three-layer high-tea set.

Jimmy turned serious once. "The junk bond market is in free-fall and DBL is at the heart of it—some even say the cause of it," he said. Things were white hot for DBL, and the legal proceedings against the firm and its employees were getting a lot of attention. "This isn't going to just blow over, not anytime soon anyway."

"So what do you think I should do, Jimmy?"

"As your friend and as a lawyer, I advise you to go back and clear your name. First of all, you don't even know if you have been charged with anything yet." Jimmy began building Curtiss's legal strategy: Having been in Red China, where everybody knows there is no information or outside news, his story about not knowing about the possibility of criminal proceedings would hold up well in a hearing. And besides, it was true. That he'd been uncomfortable about the ethics of what the firm was doing and walked away in the spring of 1988 would also count in his favor. Coming back on his own after he emerged from China and learned what was going on with his ex-firm would be a show of good faith.

While he might get tied up in a legal mess for a while, the window of opportunity for offering testimony in exchange for leniency or immunity from prosecution was closing fast. If he didn't take advantage of that now, he would be left holding the dirty end of the stick.

"Curtiss, your future depends on what you do in the next few weeks."

BOOK II: ASCENSION

CHAPTER 11

Belly-up at the bar at the Bull & Bear pub, having had a day to consider Jimmy's advice, Curtiss once again took stock of what he needed to do to return to New York. He had a reasonable stake in the bank and nothing holding him in Hong Kong—except his job with Lu.

Another CBN Financial News report about DBL appeared on the behind-the-bar TV and Curtiss took a deep breath. What would he do after getting himself out of this DBL mess? Perhaps he should go back to Hershey PA to work or teach at the Milton Hershey School. He could even do volunteer work in the community. Coach high school seniors with his hard-won knowledge and wisdom about the way the real world works, and the challenges to their Hershey School virtues that they will face in the outside world. And how those values did mean something out there.

How pathetic was that? From a Wall Street shark on his way to the top to a community volunteer in a single swing of the emotional pendulum. Whatever he did with his life, a tea and herb trader in Hong Kong who couldn't return to his country wasn't going to be it.

Curtiss took a big swig of John Smith's when the news report segued to a related story about the arrest of Bartakamous.

"Yep, it'll be good to leave the 1980s behind, won't it?"

Curtiss briefly glanced at the man who'd spoken from the next stool, nodded affirmatively, and then reaffixed himself to the news report.

"If it were only that easy, you know?" the man said, looking at Curtiss. "To just walk away from your past."

Curtiss felt the pressure of the man's eyes on him and sensed that this person's arrival beside him there at the bar was not accidental.

"I mean, look at these guys at Drexel Burnham Lambert, would you?" the man said, gesturing to the TV. "Those junk bond dealers are all ratting each other out left and right to save their own skins."

Curtiss's gut swam. Would a process server really come all the way to Hong Kong to hand him a summons?

"Those guys all thought they were above the law. Am I right, Curt?"

"All right." Curtiss turned on his bar stool to face the man. He was in his mid-thirties, balding, wearing a three-piece suit. "Who the hell are you?"

The man placed a legal-size manila envelope on top of the bar. "This is a copy of your indictment, Curtiss. It was issued by the grand jury for the Drexel Burnham Lambert case."

"Now there's a good use of public funds: flying process servers halfway around the world."

"Oh, I'm no process server," the man said, handing Curtiss a business card. "I'm with Transnational Trade Services." He allowed Curtiss a moment to peruse the card and to read his name: Ken Wilkenson. "TTS is a front company for your favorite American foreign intelligence service, and I am the Hong Kong Deputy Station Chief."

Curtiss was completely confused. Intelligence agents serving process for U.S. courts overseas? Though the man said he wasn't serving the papers. So what was he doing with them? And what could the CIA possibly want with him?

"We know about your underworld activities over here," the man said, "and your relationship with Big Brother Lu. You lived in China undetected for six months. Congratulations: it's damned hard for a round-eye to hide out in China like that. You know your way around the Hong Kong-China underworld, and speak pretty good Chinese, too. Those are skills that the Agency could use."

Curtiss's mind raced frantically, unable to make any connection that would suggest how a U.S. intelligence agent would know what he had been up to over the past year. "So you're a recruiter?" he said sardonically, doing his best to put up a brave front.

Wilkenson let the comment pass without a response. "China opening its doors to the outside world has created some interesting challenges for our country, Curtiss. Our enemies in Afghanistan are raising cash by exporting opium and some of the trade routes now run through China. Islamic extremists and commies in business together. Go figure." Wilkenson shrugged. He explained that the Agency was convinced that the traffic was funding a new breed of Islamic terrorist on both sides of the Afghan-China border. At the same time, North Korean counterfeit U.S. currency was finding its way through China to Macau's casinos to be laundered. "We have reason to believe that there is a connection there that may be helping the North Koreans to acquire nuclear technology from Pakistan."

Curtiss nodded. "So what does all this have to do with me?"

"Like I said, you have skills that the Agency could use."

"And the DBL . . . situation?"

"We have very high standards at the Agency, Curtiss. We have policies against employing convicted felons or people under criminal indictment," he said, smiling. "So, we intervened with the court on your behalf. We asked them to hold the indictment for national security reasons." Wilkenson placed his hand on the envelope. "This indictment has not been filed or gone on record yet."

Feeling a measure of relief that the clock was still ticking on his statute of limitations, Curtiss knew there was going to be a hefty price to pay for his good fortune.

"So, we thought that you might want to consider working for us." Wilkenson kept his eyes on Curtiss's. "Naturally, if you're not interested in working with us, then we no longer have an interest in the outcome of your criminal charges."

Wilkenson stood, paid his bill and prepared to leave. "Take the envelope and look it over. It's a copy. I keep the original in my top desk drawer. If you want to accept our offer, come see me at this address." Wilkenson handed Curtiss another business card that showed him as the Managing Director of the Fleet Arcade and Director of the Serviceman's Guide Association in Hong Kong. "If not, well, fall is the best season of the year back in New York," he said with a chilly smile. "Oh, and I'm required to advise you to seek legal advice, but it appears that you've already done that."

"Jimmy has nothing to do with this," Curtiss snapped.

"Relax. Your Hong Kong Consulate registration and the State Department? Remember? We just needed to find out who he was and if he was involved somehow."

"He isn't," Curtiss said.

"We know."

* * *

Curtiss's taxi abruptly peeled off from Queensway Road toward Fenwick Pier, then homed in on the American flag waving from a pole in front of the Fleet Arcade, an unimpressive two-story building that would have been better suited to a modest district in Honolulu or a naval base in Guam than to the heart of Hong Kong's high-flying commercial district.

The brass plaque at its entrance informed visitors that the Fleet Arcade was created and funded by the U.S. Navy for sailors whose ships do port of call in Hong Kong. Inside, Curtiss walked past a U.S. post office—complete with the Postal Service bald eagle emblem and a sign which read "We accept American $"—then past shelves filled with hard-to-get American items and Hong Kong tourist trinkets, and finally up diamond-plate steel stairs to the offices.

"Good," Wilkenson said when he saw Curtiss standing outside his office. He then turned to his secretary: "We're leaving. Have the car brought around. Call the The Lowu House and let them know we'll be there in about an hour. I won't be back for the rest of the afternoon."

Wilkenson didn't say another word to Curtiss until they were seated in the car. "We're going to a house that The Company keeps at the border."

As they ploughed through Hong Kong's Harbour Tunnel traffic and meandered through the network of curving roads that carried them to the Hong Kong-China border, Wilkenson explained to Curtiss his induction process. He would start with a month's debriefing and orientation at the British SIS office in the Prince of Wales Building at the Tamar Naval Base on Hong Kong Island, followed by two-months' practical training at a British army base in the New Territories. He would then spend a month each in Okinawa, Singapore and Subic Bay Philippines in a mentor program, shadowing agents and being trained in the Agency's intelligence-gathering techniques and operational protocols. During the entire six-month induction, he would have daily Mandarin language training, focused on the nomenclature, vocabulary and dialogue of the Chinese military and intelligence services, as well as a crash course in East Asian geopolitical history.

Wilkenson parked the car in front of a large house among a row of similar houses along a ridge overlooking the Hong Kong-China Lo Wu border KCR rail station that Curtiss had passed through dozens of times. He noticed that nearly all of the houses flew the Nationalist Flag of the Republic of China.

"A die-hard Nationalist neighborhood, I see," Curtiss said as they exited the car.

"Sometimes the best place to hide is in plain sight."

Inside, Wilkenson pulled a plastic ID badge from his pocket and clipped it to his lapel and Curtiss did the same with the visitor's badge that he was given. As they walked up two flights of stairs, it became apparent to Curtiss that the house was in fact a working office: loaded with several mainframe computers, numerous terminals, and a variety of electronic equipment, all manned by more than a dozen employees.

When they reached the third floor, they walked down a hall and directly into a window-less conference room that had a large wall-to-wall mirror on one side.

"Take a seat," Wilkenson said. "You want coffee?"

"Black with sugar, thanks."

Curtiss noticed that Wilkenson glanced at the mirror as he exited the room.

Wilkenson returned ten minutes later without coffee. "I've got some questions to ask you," he said while taking a seat at the table.

Curtiss took out his wallet, pulled out a slip of wrinkled paper and handed it to Wilkenson. "This is the serial number off a Norden bombsite that was found in plane wreckage on a mountainside near a village in Gui Zhou. I know these things were top secret, and that they were tracked from creation to destruction, so I figured the Air Force might have been looking for this plane."

Wilkenson looked at Curtiss with surprise. "Could you point it out on a map?"

"Yes, if you've got one written in pinyin. I don't read Chinese that well."

"We do." Wilkenson left the room, and returned with a map and another agent. He introduced her to Curtiss as Tracy Clark, an expert in American military hardware—no matter how old—and the one at the East Asia Station who was responsible for tracking it down.

Agent Clark was the statuesque image of a Southern California girl: a tall, fit, strawberry blonde with luminescent blue eyes. "Deputy Director Wilkenson tells me that you've located a Norden bombsite in China, Mr. Bradley," she said. "Quite a find in this day and age, at least as far as our department is concerned."

As she took her seat at the conference table and opened her notebook in preparation for questioning him, Curtiss found himself oddly spooked by her. It had nothing to do with her manner, which was amiable enough. Having been surrounded by petite Chinese women for the last year, it was her physical presence he found slightly intimidating. He shook it off. "People reported that six bodies found in the wreckage were buried in the vicinity," he told her. "I'm sure their families would want to know about that."

"Yes, I'm sure they would. We'll be sure to do that," she said, revealing a warm and perfect smile that wiped away any wariness toward her. Curtiss pointed to the village on the map, gave a good approximation of where the crash site was relative to the village, and provided all the detail about the area as he could recall.

As Wilkenson escorted Agent Clark out of the room when Curtiss was finished, he once again glanced at the mirror, then back to Curtiss. "You want coffee?"

"Black with sugar," Curtiss said with a smile.

Wilkenson returned about ten minutes later, with lukewarm instant coffee in Styrofoam cups and another agent. "Agent Tyler here is going to interview you to get all your details for your induction. You know: blood type, allergies . . . "

CHAPTER 12

Curtiss stood in the third-floor conference room of The Lowu House and, together with two other inductees, held up his right hand and repeated in unison the oath that was read to them by a visiting Deputy Director from CIA Headquarters in Langley, Virginia. He then shook hands with all the other agents in the room, all of who warmly welcomed him to The Company.

It was Friday, a week after Curtiss had completed his induction training and the day before the 1990 Chinese New Year holiday. The new agent swearing-in ceremony was the last official order of business for The Lowu House before the week-long holiday began. Most of the resident staff were busy winding down operations in preparation for the holiday and the expat agents were looking forward to taking their home-leave trips back to the U.S., or to R&R's in locations such as Phuket, Thailand or Bali, Indonesia. Curtiss planned to spend the holiday visiting friends in Taiwan.

After bidding The Lowu House's resident employees a happy new year, Curtiss stood alone on the patio overlooking the border into China. Over the previous six months he had been touted by Wilkenson as the Hong Kong station's new asset for deep infiltration into the Mainland. An American who spoke Chinese and knew China from the inside. Not like the intellectuals or ivory-tower China-philes who came to the Agency fresh from ivy-league schools, armed with only book knowledge, but as a foot soldier with on-the-ground experience and who had faced off with the PLA and survived: something virtually no American had done since the Korean war.

Though uncomfortable with Wilkenson's characterization of his fleeing gunfire in Beijing's Tiananmen Square as "facing-off" with China's People's Liberation Army, he decided not to make an issue of it. For better or worse, he was Wilkenson's new trophy agent.

"I can't imagine that you are in any hurry to get across that border, Curt," Agent Tracy Clark said as she stepped through the patio door.

Curtiss nodded. She was right. He hadn't been back on the other side of the border since his escape with his life, and wasn't anxious to go back anytime soon. Still haunted by the memories of June fourth and the death of Xiao Lu, he wondered if he was really up to the job, let alone to meeting the high expectations that Wilkenson had set for him.

"You have got to watch your back around here," she said, looking over her shoulder. "And I mean Wikenson specifically."

Curtiss thanked her for her concern, and assured her that he had a little experience with watching his back around snaky higher-ups.

Tracy he trusted without hesitation. She had in fact grown up in Southern California, as her physical image all but demanded. Her father was a mathematician at University of Southern California who also did work for the Department of Defense, helping them with formulas for calculating the re-entry trajectories of nuclear warheads from MIRV missiles.

She'd inherited her father's love of military hardware—"Especially the old pre-electronics-age, mechanical stuff," she'd explained. "*Authentic* machinery." She was a full-on geek, chattering on until Curtiss and anyone else in earshot found themselves drawn into passionate conversations about archaic pieces of military hardware she was giddy about: the phallic lines of the Boeing B-29 Superfortress bomber; the simplicity and perfection of the design of the "Yankee Fist", the .45 caliber M1911A1 semi-automatic handgun; the timeless character of her favorite and, according to her, all-time most *authentic* weapon of all: the Thompson submachine gun "tommy gun"—M1921 gangster version, of course.

After a little too much to drink one evening, she'd fallen into giggling fits after Curtiss informed her that he was named after the Curtiss-Wright C-46 Commando. "A Bratwurst with wings, on a grill, about to burst," she said, hooting. "It is *so* not you."

He could be thankful for that much, he supposed.

For Tracy, anything whose purpose did not center upon the direct annihilation of something else simply didn't qualify as serious military. "You are not so much a Curtiss . . . " She cocked her head and squinted at him, then snapped her fingers. "Yeah, that's it: the B-25 Mitchell bomber. The one your dad flew on his raid on Tokyo. It could take a tremendous amount of punishment and keep right on flying. *Now* we're talking. He should have named you Mitch instead."

After he and Tracy had wished each other a happy holiday and parted with a hug, Wilksenson appeared in the patio doorway. "Heading off tomorrow?"

"Yeah, on the China Airlines Dynasty flight."

"Taiwan?" Wilkenson laughed. "Why the hell would you waste a perfectly good vacation in Taiwan? Taipei is a disorganized, polluted pit."

"I have friends there," Curtiss replied, turning his gaze across the border at the horizon.

"I'm taking the wife and kids to Cebu, Philippines. I've got a friend who's not using his timeshare there."

"Sounds great. Have a good time."

"See you bright and early Monday, week after next. We've got some important business to attend to: your first assignment."

*   *   *

"Transnational Trade Services," Sonya read aloud from Curtiss's new business card at her table at the Chennault Pub. "It sounds like a lovely company."

"It's been around for quite a while."

"It's about time this deadbeat got a real job," Wendy said with a good-humored sarcastic smile as she delivered Sonya's tea and Curtiss's beer to their table.

"You know, Wendy," Curtiss returned. "This place is always empty. Think it might have something to do with the friendliness of the service?"

Wendy laughed and went back behind the bar, leaving him alone with Sonya.

"Well," Sonya said, cupping the side of Curtiss's face with a slightly trembling hand, "I hope that this is what you really want, and that you are happy, dear. I'm sure you are doing important work there."

They switched to red wine for dinner—for a special occasion, according to Sonya—and spoke of the many changes happening in Taiwan, in particular about how students were preparing for the Wild Lily pro-democracy demonstration in Taipei's Memorial Square the next month. Sonya explained her view on why democracy would succeed in taking root in Taiwan, then listened intently to Curtiss as he shared his on why the Mainland would not be ready for such change until at least the turn of the next century—and likely a decade or more after that.

Curtiss's meetings with Sonya always fed his soul, and their friendship continued to grow with each subsequent visit. Though he could not share with her his legal predicament, or anything about his new career, he felt as though she somehow understood him. In any event, she always seemed to know what to say to give him the strength to step up to his life's challenges and cope with its disappointments.

Curtiss's affection for Lu approached his feelings for Sonya. Lu had insisted that Curtiss stay at his Yang Ming Mountain house during the holiday. One morning at dawn, while they were enjoying the serenity of Lu's tearoom, Curtiss decided to let Lu know who he now worked for. "Lu, there is something that I need to discuss with you."

Lu smiled. "What, that you are now an American spook?"

Though initially shocked, when he considered how well-connected Lu was, it did not seem so unlikely that he knew what Curtiss had been up to the past six months—since he has respectfully resigned. "I was waiting for the right time to tell you," he said.

"It's okay, Curtiss. I knew you would tell me when the time was right." Lu topped off Curtiss's teacup, then his own. "You'll be good at it. You were a good spy for me, why not for your country?" The men clinked their teacups together to toast their mutual understanding.

"I've been thinking about how we could help each other," Curtiss offered cautiously. "Our two biggest mutual problems are North Korea and their counterfeit U.S. currency, and the drug trade out of

Afghanistan.

"Agreed. Both are bad for business." Lu's gray-market duty-free business had come back with a vengeance since the June fourth crackdown had begun to let up.

Curtiss suggested they exchange information, and explained that his employer's main interest in North Korea was stopping them from acquiring and proliferating nuclear weapons technology. Funds from the Soviet Union were beginning to dry up, and North Korea was getting desperate, buying technology from countries like Pakistan with laundered counterfeit cash and then reselling the technology to generate even more cash.

"And the Afghan opium?"

"We want to cut off funds to our radical Islamic terrorist enemies in Afghanistan." Aside from the Afghan Mujahideen, who had kicked the Soviets out of Afghanistan the previous year, there were many Arab fighters who had joined the fight and stayed there. There were two of particular interest: an Egyptian named Ayman al-Zawahri and a Saudi named Osama bin Laden, who formed a terrorist group named al-Qaeda. "They took the arms and support that we gave to the Afghan resistance against the Soviets, and even before the war was over, started using them against us." The Soviet Union's Najibullah regime was barely holding on to power and a Pashtun political group was gaining footholds across the country. If al-Qaeda succeeded in helping them to power they could become a real threat—not just in that part of the world but everywhere. "What we know is that the opium trade is fueling their machine and that some of it is being smuggled through China, but that is about all we know."

Lu quietly sipped his tea and contemplated what Curtiss had told him. "There is no question that I would like to do anything I can to help you, Curtiss. I'm just trying to think of ways that I can be of help."

Curtiss took Lu's hint. "Our part would be to help choke off North Korea's counterfeit currency, which would help you with your cash businesses. And we would even try to get the hard-core opium black-market smugglers out of your way."

"I really don't know how effective your new employer could be in actually accomplishing those things," Lu said, smiling kindly at him. "As I've always said, terrorism—the actions that governments take to prevent it—is bad for business." Lu pulled on his chin. What he needed most, he said, was information on his rivals, and to know what was happening at the national and diplomatic levels with anything related to the border or cross-border trade. "Even I have blind spots, Curtiss. If you can help me with those, I think we have a good basis for cooperation."

The men spoke for the rest of the morning about how they might cooperate given their respective resources, and shook hands on their new partnership.

* * *

Curtiss was one of the first to arrive at The Lowu House Monday morning, the first day back to work after the New Years Holiday. He made himself a cup of coffee in the kitchen, walked over to the communications room, tore off a page from the telex machine that contained a general memorandum from Langley, and began reading it.

"Our purchase requisition for three fax machines was finally authorized by Langley," Wilkenson said as he entered the communications room. "They should be delivered and installed next week. Of course ours are the encrypting kind, so it isn't as though we could have just picked them up at some electronics store in the Tsim Sha Tsui electronics district. Still, it'll be nice to get rid of this `70s telex junk and take one more step into the second half of the twentieth century, you know?"

Curtiss looked at Wilkenson.

"We're at the ass end of the world out here, Curtiss, as far as the budget wonks at Langley are concerned." Curtiss sensed an unusually vitriolic resentment toward The Company in Wilkenson's voice that morning.

Wilkenson shifted the large sports bag that hung over his shoulder. "Come on. We've got work to do," he said, handing Curtiss a small stack of sequentially numbered briefing books.

When they arrived at the third-floor conference room Wilkenson pulled three blueprint tubes out of the sports bag and laid them on the conference table. "These came in through the diplomatic pouch over the weekend. We have two specialists from Langley who arrived here last night. My car is bringing them now," Wilkenson said as he began placing the briefing books around the table. "Only our guests are authorized to open the tubes."

The specialists arrived, introduced themselves and explained that they were from a division of the Agency that interpreted satellite information. After exchanging pleasantries, they tore open the seals to the tubes, removed large, photographic-quality prints, and spread them over the conference table.

"These satellite photos show what we suspect may be Chinese ICBM silos, here in the Wuyi Mountians in Fujian Province," one of the specialists said, pointing to the photograph.

Wilkenson leaned in tight, examining the photo with a magnifying glass. "Yep," he said, "those look like nuke silos, all right."

The two officers glanced at each other. "Well, that's what we need you to find out."

"Sure. Right. That's what I meant. That's what we have Curtiss here for," Wilkenson said, handing Curtiss the magnifying glass. "Curtiss is the only round-eye agent I know of who was able to hideout in China virtually undetected for six months. He's the right man to get in there and verify your satellite intel."

The briefing lasted the better part of an hour and the specialists explained to Curtiss specifically what to look for on the ground. Wilkenson's part in the entire affair appeared to consist of demonstrating sycophantic behavior toward the specialists that succeeded in making everyone in the room uncomfortable. He invited the specialists to dinner as they departed, but they already had dinner plans and were scheduled to leave for Subic Bay on a Company plane early the next morning.

"I guess the North Koreans and Afghan terrorists will have to wait," Curtiss said after the specialists left the room.

"Let's take a drive."

Wilkenson didn't utter another word until they were tooling their way over New Territory roads that snaked along the border. "Chasing counterfeiters is the Secret Service's job and chasing drug dealers is the DEA's job. Those nuke intel boys never have to fight for resources, I can tell you that. Langley doesn't give a rat's ass about us out here. The Agency's main focus has always been on Russia and Eastern Europe," Wilkenson said with a sniff. "Here?

We're stuck in this backwater chasing criminals. But this? This is the big time, Curtiss. Nukes, and ICBMs no less."

Curtiss decided to hold his tongue and gave Wilkenson the benefit of the doubt.

* * *

"I hate going to China," Wilkenson said as he and Curtiss took their seats on the jet-boat catamaran docked at Hong Kong's Ocean Terminal. "I just hope we aren't delayed this time. The last time, I floated in the middle of the damned river for almost a half hour while they cleared one of the jet intakes. I think it was a body or something that got stuck in there. You'd think those big water jets would just grind up a soft body, wouldn't you?"

Wilkenson was taking Curtiss up the Pearl River to Guangzhou, where he would introduce him to an operative who would take him to Fujian Province and back. Before they left the Lowu House that morning, Wilkenson had given Curtiss a new name, passport and business cards. His cover was a textile machine technician who, accompanied by a translator, was going to a textile mill to troubleshoot and repair their imported equipment.

"All the bathrooms over here are atrocious. I mean, you'd think that with five thousand years of history they would have thought up the plumbing U-bend, so every bathroom doesn't smell like the sewer beneath it."

"Uh huh," Curtiss responded, though focused on deciphering what meaning he could from the Chinese-character captions beneath the pictures in the travel magazine he was thumbing through. When he noticed Wilkenson was staring at him, he said, "Yes, it is strange that it didn't develop during all that time." Curtiss turned the page in his magazine. "You should try a Guizhou public toilet some time," Curtiss said absently.

"Thomas Crapper invented the U-bend in 1880, so it's off patent now. Not that anyone here gives a damn about anyone else's intellectual property." Finally seeming to grasp Curtiss's lack of interest in a bitch session about the discomforts and inconveniences of China, Wilkenson settled back in his seat and left him in peace.

Curtiss's second arrival in Guangzhou, by boat, was a far more comfortable experience than when he swam ashore the first time. Rambo Zhang, the operative who would act as his guide and local dialect translator, met them at the Guangzhou boat terminal. He was a thin young Chinese man with an unruly mop of hair and thick lips that strained to cover his large white teeth. He had a tense and slightly nervous demeanor that appeared to satisfy Wilkenson's requirement that his authority be recognized.

As they taxied from the port to Guangzhou's White Swan Hotel, Curtiss was impressed by the increased activity within the city in only one year's time. But, as he had already learned upon his arrival at the Beijing Rail Station, the south was completely different from the north.

Rambo led them to the lobby coffee shop where the three men went over the mission plan, which Wilkenson and Curtiss explained to Rambo was only a routine infrastructure assessment mission. Rambo presented Curtiss with his round-trip air ticket from Guangzhou to Xiamen, the nearest airport to Yongding County that was accessible to foreigners. They would check into a hotel in Xiamen and arrange for a hotel taxi to drop them at a textile mill owned by a Hong Kong businessman who was friendly to The Company. There, a private car would be waiting for Rambo to drive them the eight hours to Yongding County. They would return to the hotel the same way.

Wilkenson had a ferry ticket for the early evening boat back to Hong Kong. With the hand-off of Curtiss completed, Wilkenson gave Rambo an envelope containing cash and they all walked out to the street to look for transportation. Rambo stood Curtiss and Wilkenson on a street corner to wait while he ran off to find a taxi.

"I'll be glad to get back to Hong Kong tonight," Wilkenson groused as he leaned against the corner of a concrete-walled building.

Curtiss abruptly pulled Wilkenson off the corner of the building. "Don't do that."

Wilkenson yanked his arm from Curtiss's grasp and looked at him incredulously. "Why the hell not?"

"There's a toilet paper shortage in Guangzhou," Curtiss said, then busied himself looking up and down the street for an available taxi or pedicab.

Wilkenson wheeled around to see that the edge of the building was indeed stained from about the waist down. "Oh, you've *got* to be kidding me." He looked at Curtiss, who was doing his best to hold back a smile. "You mean they actually use the corner of the building to wipe their..."

"Who knows what people will do, with all these new, glass-façade buildings they're building these days. The surface of glass is just too smooth to be effective." Curtiss bit his lip to keep from smiling.

Wilkenson closed his eyes and sighed. "I really hate coming to China."

* * *

Though he was skinny, Rambo had an impressive appetite. He grazed at the breakfast buffet non-stop for nearly an hour the next morning.

Curtiss suspected he might be a Taiwan Kuomintang spy, which would reduce the risk of him being a double agent, but his discretion trumped his curiosity on that score and he chose not to pursue the issue. At the same time it dawned on Curtiss that were they caught doing what they were about to do, he'd likely only spend a couple of years in prison before being freed in a spy swap. Rambo's punishment, on the other hand, would be swift and final. Whether a Chinese defector or an embedded Kuomintang spy from Taiwan, he would certainly be executed.

Instead, he asked him why he chose the name Rambo.

"Because Rambo is a hero." He flashed his large white teeth at Curtiss. "A real American hero."

"You know he's just a fictional character, right?"

"Of course. But you have to believe in something, right?" He paused just long enough to tuck in some more fried noodles. "Why not Rambo? He fights for what is right. Isn't that what heroes do? So I took his name to remind me to always do the right thing." The man's obvious sincerity drained his words of all the naiveté Curtiss might've expected them to carry.

As the plane suspended itself just over the Xiamen Airport runway in preparation for touching down, Curtiss was surprised to see that the outer skirt of the entire runway was lined with fighter aircraft covered with green tarps. Wind had broken one of the tarps free, revealing a 1950s-era MiG fighter jet with an empty engine housing and a missing cockpit canopy. There was no telling how many of the planes under the tarps were actually empty shells and how many were fight-ready, but the planes had certainly been placed there to make an impression—most likely on the neighbor who was only a hundred or so miles across the Taiwan Strait. Curtiss made a mental note to include this observation in his report.

The eight-hour drive from the factory to Yongding was a completely miserable experience. The car was an antique Toyota with Asian-sized ergonomics, paper-thin seats, and a worn-out suspension that bottomed out over every bump and pothole in the semi-paved roads.

About halfway through their journey, stacked bails of straw and a hand-painted sign detoured them off the main road onto a one-lane dirt road. When they reached a small wooden bridge that crossed a creek, two scruffy men stopped them and demanded payment for crossing the bridge.

Instantly livid, Rambo bolted from the car and began arguing fervently with the men.

"How much do they want?" Curtiss yelled out the window.

"10 RMB!" Rambo shouted back. "This is highway robbery!"

Impressed as he was with Rambo's knowledge of English colloquialisms, Curtiss wasn't interested in wasting time over a dollar. "Just pay them and let's get the hell out of here."

"No," Rambo replied. "It is the principle. If we give these robbers money now, they will keep doing it to other people."

"What are you going to do, Rambo? Call the police? Hell, they probably *are* the police." And with that Curtiss threw a 10 RMB note out the window and into the muddy track alongside the car. "There's your money," Curtiss said in Mandarin to one of the men. "Now get out of our way."

Rambo was still fuming when he got back into the car. "It's great to stand up for your rights, Rambo," Curtiss said kindly, "but learn to pick your battles."

The bridge incident, as it became known between the two of them, was the topic of conversation for more of their drive than Curtiss cared for, but he decided it was better to let Rambo harmlessly vent now so that they might be more focused on their mission later.

It was sundown by the time they reached Yongding County and stopped at a restaurant for dinner. The waitstaff were fascinated to see a foreigner in their town and, as in Lu's ancestral village, Curtiss once again found himself the zoo animal-like center of attention. The small crowd of onlookers were fascinated that Curtiss was able to speak Mandarin Chinese, and more so the few words of the Minnan dialect he had picked up while in Taiwan. One of them asked Curtiss and Rambo what they were doing in the area. Curtiss gave them their cover story and explained that they were just passing through on their way to a textile mill further on.

"We thought you may have been tourists here to see our Tulou, like the Japanese photographer who was here recently," another of the locals said.

"Tulou?" Curtiss asked.

"Yes, Kejia Tulou. Clan houses of the Hakka people. They are famous in Fujian. And now Japan, too," the man said with pride, handing Curtiss a copy of a Japanese architectural magazine with a cover photo of a cylindrical mud-brick and tile-roofed building. "The photographer was kind enough to send us copies of the magazine after it was published."

Curtiss found the cover story article, accompanied by several pages of photos of circular buildings. He handed the magazine to Rambo and said to the group: "We'd love to see them. Is there a tour guide that can take us there tomorrow morning?" The room erupted with a cacophony of offers to take them on a tour. Curtiss left the selection of the tour guide and bargaining to Rambo, who also arranged a room for them for the night.

The beauty and serenity of morning in the Wuyi Mountains brought back Curtiss's months in Guizhou, fond memories that quickly and inevitably turned melancholy as they led him to recall his motorcycle rides through the countryside with Xiao Lu. He wondered if the burden of her death would ever leave his shoulders.

They drove as far as they could by car, then set off on foot. Ten minutes later, they stood before what looked like the circular fortification of an ancient castle, perched atop a small plateau and seamlessly integrated among the terraced farmland and rolling pine-covered hills around it. Perhaps sixty yards wide and four stories tall, the structure's main door was open to the inside, where Curtiss estimated there were about two-hundred wooden-framed rooms: three levels of cubbyholes lining the inside of the earthen brick outer wall. A tile roof ran along the top of the circular wall with eves that overhung both the inside and outside. Clustered in the center of the circle was a micro-village of one-story, mud brick and thatch roof homes, complete with hanging laundry, running dogs, animal pens and the acrid, musty smoke of low-temperature-burned coal.

The compactness of the way people lived within Tulou in some ways reminded him of George's alley in Taipei. For that matter, the dwellings in the small farming villages dotting the countryside were nearly as tightly packed. This was a stark contrast to the image Curtiss carried of the American heartland, where homesteaders spread out on individual homes plots across the prairie—independent farmers, masters of their own fates. Perhaps the fact that no one in his Taipei alley complained about things like Mr. Ma's funeral going on for three days and nights—even on a street in a modern city like Taipei—could be traced to these rural-cluster cultural roots.

Their tour guide explained that some Tulou could hold fifty or more families—about four-hundred people.

"There are more of these?" Curtiss asked.

"Yes. More than a dozen in Wuyi County alone." And even more in other places, like RuShengLu and HongKeng village, he explained.

After buying a few trinkets and some local handicraft items as a gesture of friendship, they left to explore other Tulou in the area, Curtiss marking their locations on his hand-sketched map.

The following morning at breakfast, Curtiss stared at his map, by now dotted with Tulou sites, and chuckled. "Well, I think we've got what we need on the infrastructure of interest here," he said. "Time to head back."

Rambo beamed with pride when Curtiss acknowledged that their mission was a success and a job well done. "I hope this information makes a real difference."

* * *

"So what do you have for us, Curtiss?" Wilkenson said as he

entered The Lowu House's third-floor conference room with blueprint-tubes in hand and took a seat at the conference table, where Curtiss sat with several other agents.

"The satellite intel is correct. Those mystery silos are for Chinese defense," Curtiss said as he opened a copy of the Japanese architectural magazine to a pre-tagged page and slid it to the center of the table. "Most were built a few hundred years ago by the Hakka minority as defensive fortifications against brigandage."

Wilkenson stared blankly at Curtiss.

"Ken, they're clan lodges, called Kejia Tulou: circular walled buildings that are made from bricks, packed earth and wood."

"Brigandage," Wilkenson repeated in monotone before allowing an awkward silence to engulf the room. Finally he stirred himself. "That's all for the day," he announced. "I'll have my secretary let you all know when our next meeting is, so we can hear the rest of Curtiss's briefing. Thank you, Curtiss."

After the other agents exited the room, Curtiss pulled out his hand-sketched map. "I'm going on memory, but I'm convinced that some of the suspected missile silo sites follow the exact same pattern as what I was able to sketch of the Tulou in Wuyi County," he said, laying the map side-by-side with one of the satellite photos. "Here, look. Even to layman, I think it's obvious that the pattern matches. But I guess we'll need to get an expert to look at it."

Wilkenson put his hand on Curtiss's shoulder. "Let's take a drive."

Wilkenson was particularly aggressive on the road that day, more than once turning wide on left turns and nearly steering into oncoming traffic—a common enough mistake for drivers accustomed to driving left-hand drive vehicles on right-hand side roads, though Wilkenson surely should've adapted by now. Not that Wilkenson had ever exhibited any interest in accommodating himself to the culture around him.

"The winds of change are in the air, Curtiss," Wilkenson finally announced. "The Soviets got their butts kicked in Afghanistan and the Berlin Wall fell just a couple of months ago. Lech Walesa, the Solidarity guy in Poland, is really shaking things up there on their side of the Iron Curtain. Our European stations are calling last year: 'Revolutions of 1989,' and it's shaking the Soviet Union to its core."

"It seems those winds of change aren't blowing to China," Curtiss said. "The Berlin Wall may have fallen, but not the Great Wall."

"Yes. That's right. That's very good, Curtiss. I can use that," Wilkenson said, more to himself than to Curtiss. "Two years ago, Deputy Director Gates made a bet that the Soviets wouldn't leave Afghanistan, and look what happened. Now the odds seem in favor of the Soviet Union losing Eastern Europe, too, and maybe even being taken down itself. And that means budget up for grabs."

Wilkenson paused, either to collect his thoughts or to let his statement sink in with him.

"America needs enemies, Curtiss. Enemies keep us focused and sharp. Well, America need look no further than China. The winds of change blew down the Berlin Wall, but stop at the Great Wall, just like you said. And if the new enemy has nukes, all the better. Bottom line: we need your report to be about ICBM silos, Curtiss."

He'd known something like this was coming, but Curtiss still found himself stunned by the implications of Wilkenson's words. He was being asked to falsify his report. And it appeared that he was considering doing so, which troubled him. Apparently his instincts could keep him cool under fire, but also allowed him to be struck dumb, intimidated by power and position. It had happened with Belkin, and here it was again, with Wilkenson. He could defend his life, but not his integrity—was that it?

"Look, don't worry, Curtiss," Wilkenson said. "Everyone makes mistakes, right? I'll cover for you. I've got your back."

Curtiss fastened his gaze on Wilkenson. "We don't need to do this, Ken. China's had nuclear weapons since the 1960s."

"Right. So it wouldn't be lying, would it?" Wilkenson sounded as though he were speaking to a child.

"Yes, it would be," Curtiss responded, failing to suppress his resentment of Wilkenson's patronizing tone. "We'd be deliberately misreporting the facts. We have evidence that those are not ICBM sites."

"Curtiss," Wilkenson said, stiffening, "we need this. It is right in our back yard. It will put us on the map back at Langley. And we'll get all the funding we'll need for years to come. No questions asked."

Curtiss's silence could have only indicated to Wilkenson that what he had just said had not set well.

"Look, you are a new agent who just completed his East Asian

History 101 classes and his first field assignment." Wilkenson's eyes narrowed. "And I suppose it would not be beyond belief that, after spending six months in China, your judgment and loyalties might be a little . . . clouded?"

Wilkenson's threat boiled in Curtiss's stomach. Whatever the effect on his career, he would not let this self-serving bureaucrat compromise him. "I have no sympathy for the communists across the border," he said, working to control himself. "They killed someone very dear to me right in front of my eyes and one of their rogue mafia-generals was out to kill me, too. I have scars from bullet fragments in my shins from when I *faced off* with the PLA."

Wilkenson tried striking a conciliatory tone: "Curtiss, this is your first mission. I've been with the Agency for fifteen years. If you want to make it here, just follow my lead, okay?"

A Hershey PA chapel service lesson bubbled from deep within Curtiss's subconscious, eliciting a biblical paraphrase in his mind: *Where there is no wise, prudent, sound, and good counsel, for lack of wise guidance nations fall.* "I may be new to the Agency, Ken, but I know that decisions are made based upon what we report back to Langley. What if a war got started on our doctored intelligence?"

"I've got news for you Curtiss: that's a time-honored tradition."

Curtiss took a breath. "It is our job to report the facts, and to report them accurately." Curtiss thought of Rambo when he spoke, so was not embarrassed by his own statement of principle.

"I'm the one who says what our job is," Wilkenson said, struggling to keep his composure. "This is the way things get done here, so just shut up, listen and get in line. I want your corrected report on my desk tomorrow morning, is that clear?"

The next morning, Curtiss dropped one copy of his report at the U.S. consulate for delivery to Langley by diplomatic pouch, and placed the other on Wilkenson's desk. He had made no changes to it.

CHAPTER 13

It had been three years since Curtiss's first mission with The Agency, and it was a cool and sunny late-February Hong Kong morning in 1993, when Curtiss arrived at The Lowu House to find everyone gathered in front of the house's large-screen projection TV. Tracy was there, in tears.

"What's happening?" he asked her.

"There was an explosion in the parking garage underneath the World Trade Center in New York about six hours ago," she said. "I have family who work there." Curtiss put his arm around her shoulders and joined his colleagues at The Lowu House for the rest of the morning, watching the images of smoke and people fleeing the World Trade Center buildings.

Wilkenson had sandwiches brought in for an all-hands briefing that started at noon. "We have confirmation from the ATF and FBI that it was a bomb, and a big one. That's all we have now. We've been tasked with reviewing our records for any pattern in the chatter and to reach out to our informants to see what we can find out. This now takes priority over everything else."

Curtiss could see that Tracy was only going through the motions the rest of the afternoon and he took her to dinner that evening to console her. She had managed to confirm that none of her family or friends were injured in the WTC blast. Nevertheless, she was very close to her large extended family, and although Hong Kong was an exciting and exotic field assignment for her, she was strained by the long family separations. All the more so during this time of crisis back home.

Having grown up an orphan, Curtiss was an expert at coping with life's difficulties in the absence of family. He'd been fortunate to find solace in the kindness and good intentions of the well-meaning people within the cocoon of the Milton Hershey School. That evening at dinner, and for the days that immediately followed, Curtiss made sure that he was that kind of friend for Tracy.

In the ensuing weeks and months they would receive a steady stream of information about the World Trade Center bombing as the case unfolded. A Trade Center Bombing task force room was set up on the second floor of The Lowu House, where the names and faces of the people believed to be connected with the bombing were posted on an organization chart that was drawn on a large whiteboard.

The Hong Kong Station was tasked with focusing on two individuals suspected to be in hiding somewhere in the region: Ramzi Yousef and Khaled Shaikh Mohammed.

Information found in Yousef's apartment confirmed that he was the leader of the terrorist cell behind the bombing. He had fled the United States just hours after the bombing and was thought to have joined his Uncle Khaled Shaikh Mohammed in Pakistan. Both had direct ties to al-Qaeda, with Yousef having actually trained with al-Qaeda in Afghanistan. Khaled Shaikh Mohammed was suspected of being the moneyman, operating with the assistance of al-Qaeda on both sides of the Afghan-Pakistan border. It was the Hong Kong Station's job to follow the money trail back to Pakistan and Afghanistan, and together with other stations in the region, find them and bring them to justice.

* * *

Tropical Storm Ira's winds buffeted China Airlines Dynasty Flight 605 as it made its final approach to Hong Kong's Kai Tak Airport. It was now the first week of November 1993, late in the season for severe tropical storms, and Curtiss and Lu squeezed the armrests of their airplane seats as they neared zero-G on several instances during the airplane's bumpy descent. Through the streams of rainwater wiggling like worms across Curtiss's window, he noticed that the plane seemed unusually high relative to the terminal and appeared to be following an extremely rapid descent.

It was.

It slammed down hard on the runway, only to be blown airborne again. Curtiss assumed that the pilot was doing a missed-approach procedure and was planning to come around again to reattempt the landing, but they came down again and were thrust violently sideways. The plane leaned dramatically to one side—in Curtiss's mind's eye, he saw the tip of the airplane's wing passing within inches of the ground—before dropping down heavily on the remaining landing gear as the pilot managed to right the aircraft.

With all landing gear now on the ground, the 747-400 shuddered, its four engines thrown into full reverse thrust. Curtiss jammed his feet against the seat frame in front of him, expecting to next be pulled forward from the force of the plane's brakes being applied. But, in spite of Curtiss's standing on the brakes, instead they continued rolling at speed until the front of the plane lurched left and its tail swung round like the back end of a rear-wheel drive car on an icy road.

Its passengers shrieking, the plane spun a full one hundred-eighty degrees and was actually traveling backward for a split second before they were jolted by a sudden, violent fall accompanied by an explosive banging sound: they had slid off the end of the runway, tail first, into Victoria Harbour.

The torque on the plane's fuselage popped open overhead luggage bins and sent carry-on luggage and other paraphernalia cascading onto the heads of the now frantic passengers. The cabin lights flickered out and the emergency lights came on.

The flight attendants had flung off their four-point seat belts and leapt to their feet, and were now barking orders in three languages to the stunned and disoriented passengers. Curtiss looked out the window and saw seawater washing over the airplane's wing and splashing up against the side of the plane. The sound of rushing water could be heard coming from the cargo hold beneath his feet and Curtiss's gut detected the exact moment the plane lost buoyancy and begin to sink.

Unless it stopped, he and his fellow passengers would drown at the bottom of Victoria Harbour inside a $135 million tomb.

A seawater and jet fuel cocktail had already begun filling the aft end of the airplane when, to Curtiss's relief, the plane settled on the shallow submerged slope that surrounded the runway. With the aircraft mostly submerged—except for its cockpit, upper deck and vertical stabilizer protruding from the water—Curtiss, Lu, and their fellow passengers had just survived an airplane crash.

Curtiss dropped Lu at the Peninsula, and then returned to his apartment to shower and get into clean clothes. He lathered and rinsed several times and finally had to use shampoo to eliminate the reek of jet fuel that stubbornly clung to his body hair.

Two days later Curtiss dressed down, at Lu's suggestion, since they would be going to Hong Kong's notorious Walled City to meet one of Lu's informants that day.

Curtiss had learned through his British SIS contacts that the vertical stabilizer of Dynasty Flight 605, which still sat pathetically off the end of the runway like some car stuck in a ditch, was interfering with aircraft guidance signals. And since it would take over a week for Asia's largest derrick barge to be towed down from Korea to pluck the airplane from the water, demolition experts were planning to shear off the airplane's vertical stabilizer that morning using shaped charges—an event both men agreed was not to be missed.

Curtiss picked up Lu at the Peninsula and instructed their taxi driver to take them to a hotel in Kwuntong located directly across a narrow waterway from the crash site, where they would have a bird's eye view of the demolition from the hotel's rooftop patio bar. Curtiss had called ahead and arranged for a bottle of champagne to be chilling in an ice bucket on the patio's bar when they arrived.

In position, Curtiss popped the cork, filled two flutes and raised his glass, first to Lu, and then to the airplane in the Harbour. "I had to pull a half a square yard of seat fabric out of my puckered butt cheeks after that one, Lu," he said. The men laughed, clinked glasses, and sipped their champagne.

"There is a reason for everything, Curtiss," Lu assured him. "It just wasn't our time."

As the zodiac boats that surrounded the airplane's vertical stabilizer sped away toward shore, Curtiss turned serious. "I want to thank you, Lu," he said. "You've been a great friend and I know you take a risk every time you help me like this."

"Na Li, Na Li," Lu said with a dismissive wave of his hand. "We who are saved have a responsibility to live a good life, right?"

There was a flash, followed a split second later by a sharp explosion that echoed across Victoria Harbour, and the plane's vertical stabilizer fell leeward. By the time they'd finished their bottle, planes had resumed taking off and landing on the runway at Kai Tak Airport's normal and amazing rate of one plane every minute and a half.

During their short taxi ride to the Walled City, Lu explained what he knew about it to Curtiss. The very first construction occurred during the Song Dynasty a thousand years ago, it was made into a fort during the Qing Dynasty, and has remained beyond the reach of the British after they colonized Hong Kong a hundred years ago— even to this day. "But you won't see a wall there anymore, because during the Second World War the occupying Japanese army had it torn down and its stone used to extend Kai Tak Airport's runway."

The Walled City remained a vestigial microcosm of the gangland-style corruption, decadence and social decay that rotted the Qing Dynasty from its core, Lu explained. Gambling, prostitution and drugs were its main trades now, and it was even possible to find traditional Chinese opium dens there since, run by powerful Triad gangs, the Hong Kong police rarely entered the Walled City, and then only in numbers.

Stubbornly clinging to existence, the enclave had fallen through the cracks during a century of collisions between three great empires: The Imperial Chinese, The British and The Japanese. After the Qing Dynasty fell in 1911, neither the Chinese Nationalists nor later the Communists would avow this illegitimate child. It became an orphaned no-man's land: a 6.5-acre, three hundred-fifty building vertical Petri dish of organic self-governance. But the Walled City wasn't an outsized Kejia Tulou clan lodge lost in some remote mountain range in Mainland China. It was in the heart of one of the most modern twentieth-century cities.

Curtiss and Lu penetrated the darkness of the stifling, six-foot-wide alleyways of the Walled City. Though they tried to give way to the delivery coolies scurrying past, their burdens shouldered on the ends of split bamboo poles, neither could avoid being brushed by a leaking plastic bag full of bloody chickens one coolie was carrying. Lu cursed the man in Cantonese, but the delivery boy ignored him and deftly vanished down one of the narrower, yard-wide alleyways.

Hitting a dead-end, Lu turned around. "Damn, I always get lost in this place," he said to Curtiss. "We are looking for the Yamen. It is the city's central courtyard and it is around here somewhere."

After a couple more dead-ends, they eventually found the Yamen: a tiny courtyard hemmed by a patchwork of disaffected ten-story buildings whose designs blatantly ignored, if not defied, their surroundings. No two buildings shared even the same window or floor height. Exhibiting all the symmetry of stacked shoeboxes held together with bungee cords, the vertical shaft of the courtyard ached for a single straight line among its tangle of wires, hanging laundry, and cock-eyed caged balconies that appeared largely constructed of frayed corrugated fiberglass panels. At ground level at one corner of the Yamen, amongst micro Buddhist and Taoist temples, stood a tiny mosque, and Curtiss and Lu patiently waited outside for the faithful there to complete their prayers.

Lu's informant emerged from the mosque, acknowledged Lu, but did not smile or otherwise show any emotion. He instructed them to follow him to the roof.

As they made their way to the roof along a convoluted, switchbacking path that confounded the logical mind in the vein of an Escher painting, Curtiss got a glimpse into daily life of some of the Walled City's residents. Glancing through caged windows while walking over makeshift pedestrian bridges connecting buildings several stories up across the narrow alleyways, the apartments he could see into were tiny, none, he guessed, more than three hundred square feet.

"You can walk from one end of the Walled City to the other and never touch the ground," Lu explained, ducking beneath one of the overhead cable-stays jutting out from the moldy concrete walls, which carried all manner of cable and leaky pipe.

In some rooms he saw people working, many assembling electrical parts for appliances such as hairdryers and coffee makers, and many others sewing garments. Some rooms were used as dentist offices, acupuncturist clinics, and herbalist shops. It seemed that the Walled City was indeed a largely self-sufficient city in its own right.

Curtiss shielded his eyes from the bright midday sunshine when they finally emerged from the darkness onto the rooftop. They weaved their way through hung laundry, TV antennas, and discarded refrigerators and window air-conditioners to what appeared to be a cluster of abandoned sofas. There they took a seat.

Once comfortable they were alone, Lu's informant reanimated and smiled. He and Lu chatted in Cantonese and laughed while Curtiss watched a 747 fly overhead at what seemed like no more than two hundred feet on its final approach to Kai Tak.

Lu's informant spoke to Curtiss in Pilipino-accented English after the plane had passed. "Is this your first time in the Walled City?"

"Yes it is."

"Well, it will probably be your last time. We are the last holdouts, you see. Next month we are being evicted, and after that the demolition crews move in to tear the entire place down." The man looked around him. "It may not have been beautiful, but it was home to many people."

Curtiss now imagined the Walled City's residents as Neanderthals—not because they were any less than fully human, but because they represented a social evolutionary offshoot that had reached the end of its line. Like Neanderthals, they lived among the competing modern human social order, but withdrawn to dark caverns—those of the Walled City. Its social DNA too different from that of modern society to successfully crossbreed, and surrounded and vastly outnumbered, like Neanderthals', this society's extinction was inevitable.

All at once, Lu's informant threw his arms out as if mimicking an explosion and shouted, "Bojinka!"

"Bojinka?" Curtiss repeated.

"Your man Ramzi Yousef passed through here on his way to the Philippines just a week ago. He was using the name Adam Sali, and was talking about an operation that he was planning called 'Bojinka.'"

"What does it mean? Is it Tagalog? Arabic?"

"I don't know what it means or where it came from, but I do know that it is a code word for something big that he is planning."

"Another target in New York? The West Coast?" Curtiss asked.

"No. It is something over here. Let's just say that it is an interesting coincidence that you two were on Dynasty 605, because it has to do with destroying airplanes and Asian airports."

Curtiss considered this, then chose to prime the discussion about the Afghanistan and Pakistan connection. "We know that Yousef is the nephew of Khalid Shaikh Mohammed, and that he might be getting funding from his uncle."

"Not *might be. Is.* He and Osama bin Laden. If you are interested in the source of money for the Afghan opium trade, you've come to the right place. People not only use opium here in the Walled City, the City's triad drug lords trade it all over the world. Yousef has now set up shop in the Philippines, and when he is not picking up cash while passing through the Walled City, he receives it courtesy of your American Western Union, using Pilipino bar girls to hide his transactions. You should also look into a company in Manila called Konsojaya. He talked about it a lot when he talked about money, so I'd guess that it is being used to launder drug money."

Over the next twenty minutes Lu's informant explained what else he knew about Khalid Shaikh Mohammed and Ramzi Yousef's plan to simultaneously blow up airliners bound for the United States, as well as about their link to al-Qaeda and the Afghan opium trade. They concluded the meeting with a gentlemen's agreement that Lu and Curtiss would never let anyone know who had given them the information. After shaking hands with each of them, Lu's informant turned a stern eye on Curtiss.

"I want you to know that I have no love for your country. The only reason I trust you is because you are Lu's friend. And the only reason I am helping you is because these terrorists are giving all of Islam a bad name. If they succeed, they are going get a lot of Muslims killed when America responds to their terrorist attacks. So you and your friends rub these bastards out for good now, or they will only get stronger. They are dangerous for both our—"

An airplane interrupted him, and the three men paused momentarily to let it pass. But just as the roar of the plane abated, Lu's informant doubled over and rolled off the sofa.

As he hit the floor, Curtiss could hear the too-familiar sound of bullets whizzing by like bees. Lu grabbed Curtiss's shirt, pulled him to his feet and the two of them ran toward the roof exit that they had come up through, dodging and weaving their way through the rooftop debris and flying bullets.

Damn. Shot at and running from people who wanted to kill him . . . *again.*

Curtiss turned just before he and Lu ducked into the stairwell to see a man standing over Lu's informant, executing him with pistol fire.

Two other men with handguns were running toward them.

They wouldn't have the luxury of finding their way to the ground and out of the Walled City in the same, wending, trial-and-error way they'd come in. They had to get it right the first time, or get lucky.

Together they plunged into the fusty darkness of the innards of the Walled City. It took some time for his eyes to adjust to the sudden darkness, but even after Curtiss's pupils dilated he remained locked into tunnel vision by adrenaline, the exertion of running, and the stress of his resurrected fight or flight reflex. Exacerbating it all was the surreality of being swallowed up by the city. While thrashing his way down through its bowels, it was all Curtiss could do to focus on following Lu's back along the narrow, rat-tunnel walkways through and between the buildings.

On some unknown floor, they rounded a corner into an alley barely more than a yard wide and came face-to-face with a half-dozen pig faces—absent their underlying skulls and on their way to a restaurant somewhere—hanging from coarse twine at the end of a bamboo pole being carried by a coolie. Lu used his momentum to shove the coolie to the ground, spilling the pig parts and bloody sack of organs balancing on the other end of the pole, coating the ground behind them with a greasy pool of pigs' blood and slime. Just before Curtiss turned the corner out of the alley, he saw the two men following them slip and fall in the blood.

Serves them right.

Moments later, Lu and Curtiss burst into the light and commotion of a Hong Kong main road. They were out. They ran across three lanes of traffic, jumped the median barrier, then threaded their way through traffic on the other side, announced by blaring car horns. They were getting into a taxi when they saw two shadows hovering just inside the alley they had escaped from, hiding in the safety of darkness at the edge of their world, knowing better than to encroach into the modern world outside of their realm.

"The Peninsula," Lu calmly announced to the driver.

"They will probably dump his body at the bottom of an old well that used to supply water to the city in the old times," Lu explained to Curtiss before taking another sip of cognac in the Peninsula's club lounge. Lu was contemplative. "So he will be buried in his beloved Walled City."

Curtiss said nothing, busy making medicinal use of the cognac to alleviate the worst of his post-crisis stress symptoms. Lu must have noticed him struggling to cover them up.

"Almost killed twice in the same week," Lu said with a smile. "So, what the hell are we going to do for excitement this weekend?"

* * *

Curtiss smiled at Tracy's eye-roll as she exited her meeting with Wilkenson in the The Lowu House's third-floor conference room.

So Wilkenson was in a mood.

It was now Curtiss's turn to update him at the regular Friday one-on-one meetings that he scheduled with his agents. Curtiss gave him a thorough briefing on what he had learned from his Walled City source about Bojinka, and about the murder of the informant.

Wilkenson listened carefully and didn't say a word. When Curtiss finished, Wilkenson looked at his watch and said, "Give me everything you have on this lead. I'll have a look at it over the weekend."

Monday morning, Wilkenson walked into Curtiss's office and said, "Let's take a drive."

Once again, while driving along the New Territories' hilly roads, Wilkenson began with a monologue. "Curtiss, you have done a great job with this Bojinka thing. Really solid work. You are really becoming a valuable asset to the Agency. But the intelligence you acquired from your Walled City source is redundant. There is no need for you to waste any more time cultivating that source. Besides, the Walled City is about to be torn down. It is a dead end."

Curtiss had learned over the past four years working for Wilkenson that it was in his own best interest to quietly listen, and try to decipher what it was that the man was really trying to get at.

"I have more important things for you to work on, Curtiss,"

Wilkenson went on. "I need you refocused on China. Your special knowledge of the Taiwan Strait and China-Taiwan relations is—"

"But that's diplomatic stuff, Ken," he broke in. So much for calm, studied restraint. The fact was, Curtiss didn't always act in his own best interest when it came to Wilkenson, and he couldn't help but interrupt his monologue. "I don't see how I—"

"It also has to do with your special knowledge of . . . Fujian Province missile defenses," Wilkenson said, his cheek twitching. *Ah. There it was.* Curtiss's 1990 report on Kejia Tulou clan lodges—a persistent sore point between the two of them. Not for the first time, Curtiss mentally told himself to keep his mouth shut from now on.

With effort, Wilkenson composed himself. "Well, it may be diplomatic, Curtiss, but it could escalate into something that may soon end up being a full-blown military action. The first direct election of Taiwan's President by popular vote is scheduled for early 1996, and the Commies are all in a twist about it. They don't trust the current President, partly because he served in the Japanese army during the war, but mainly because they suspect that he is secretly a Taiwan independence sympathizer."

"Even though he's in the Kuomintang party that wants reunification with China?"

"I know. It doesn't make a whole lot of sense."

"China won't invade Taiwan over the election; that would be too costly, both diplomatically and militarily."

"Agreed," said Wilkenson. "The problem for the communists is that Lee's opposition is openly pro-independence. The communists are really frustrated by this whole democracy thing."

The men also agreed that if Taiwan got away with both democracy and independence next might be the Uyghur minority in Xinjiang Province, who had recently staged uprisings. Then the Tibetans? "Hell, what's to keep some renegade military general from running off with Guangdong Province? Believe me, I know one of them personally who'd do it in a heartbeat if he had the chance," Curtiss said, with the White General in mind.

"Right. So they'll do anything to keep Taiwan independence from happening."

Wilkenson explained that analysts back at Langley were convinced that there would be some kind of show of force by China leading up to or perhaps during the Taiwan election. A naval blockade of Taiwan wasn't out of the question, though there were doubts that China's navy was up to the job. Were they preparing to make a show of force with the short-range missiles in Fujian Province that they already had pointed toward Taiwan? It was this last question that he wanted Curtiss to answer. "Operation Straits is yours, and I'm assigning you two analysts, full-time."

Curtiss knew to be suspicious when Wilkenson offered him something seemingly of value and treated him with respect. He was surely trying to pull a fast one on him, but there wasn't much Curtiss could do about it. The fact was that Bojinka was out of his hands now, and his boss had given him a new assignment. "We'll get it done, Ken."

This earned him a thin smile. "Curtiss, I can't tell you how important this is to America's interests in the region. I know you are the right man for the job."

*   *   *

"You heard about the bomb?" Curtiss asked Tracy when she appeared in the The Lowu House's kitchen.

"I did. Amazing those pilots managed to land that plane."

It was the day after the December 1994 bombing of Philippine Airlines Flight 434, which managed to land in Tokyo—one passenger killed.

"I don't see Wilkenson here this morning," Tracy said, "so I guess he must be on The Company plane to Washington right about now."

"Oh? What is he up to?"

"He didn't tell you?" she said, looking quizzically at Curtiss.

She explained that Wilkenson had arranged an urgent inter-agency meeting with the FBI about the Philippine Airlines bombing. He thought Ramzi Yousef was involved, and was claiming to have tracked him to the Philippines. He also believes that it was part of some plan Yousef has to blow up airplanes over the Pacific.

Noticing the look of surprise on Curtiss's face, she went on to try to fill the awkward silence—"I guess, since you were no longer involved in that investigation . . . "—but faded off. There was nothing to be said, she knew. She squeezed his forearm, looking sympathetically at him with her big blue eyes, then bit her lip and quietly walked away.

*   *   *

On an early spring morning in March 1995, Curtiss entered the Lowu House to find all manner of workmen swarming throughout the house: carpet layers and electricians, painters and tile layers, all busy sprucing up the interior.

Picking his way through the rubble, Curtiss found Tracy. "What in the name of . . . is going on?"

"You know the Director is coming next week, right? Well, we want to look our best, don't we?" All with her luminescent smile and only the barest hint of sarcasm. "Haven't you ever heard the expression 'The Queen of England believes that the world smells of fresh paint'?"

Curtiss's Operation Straits brief bounced atop his knees, powered by his right foot's impatient twitching. Curtiss, Tracy and several other agents had been sitting on a row of folding chairs in the hallway outside the third-floor conference room for the entire morning awaiting their turns to present their operations to the visiting Director.

Curtiss's brief documented China's deployment of additional M-9 ground-to-ground missiles in Fujian province, within striking distance of Taiwan. It was hard-won intelligence from Rambo and other assets in the vicinity, with Curtiss having personally made several more textile machine repair trips to the area. His analysis convincingly made the case that leading up to and during the upcoming Taiwan election, China's show-of-force of choice would be firing those missiles over the island of Taiwan.

It was nearly noon when Wilkenson emerged from the conference room into the hallway and quickly closed the door behind him. "Look guys, I'm sorry to keep you all waiting like this. We're running way behind. The Director had a change in priorities, so we aren't going to get to you today. But I have each of your executive summaries and will at least brief the Director on your operations before he leaves tonight, I promise. Go on out to lunch, on the house. But be back in time for the Director's briefing at 5:00 pm. Okay?"

Manipulating slippery Southern Chinese cuisine with smooth plastic chopsticks had become second nature to Curtiss over the years, but Tracy had yet to master the art. Watching her stab viciously at her dim sum items, Curtiss gently suggested there was no need to kill her Xia Jiao, as they were already deceased. "A little latent aggression, have we?"

Tracy smiled cynically. "There is nothing latent about it, Curt. Wilkenson is up to something, I just know it." Tracy's mood was about as sour as Curtiss had ever seen it.

"Safe bet," Curtiss said with a shrug.

"I'm serious, Curt. We all have to watch ourselves with Wilkenson, but you in particular—"

"Nothing lasts forever. When the time is right, I'll step away from all this."

Tracy blinked at him, taken aback.

Curtiss had never shared with her the circumstances surrounding his coercion into joining the Agency. Tracy was intensely proud of being an agent, and her family was proud of her, too. She was living her dream and, like Rambo, Curtiss deeply admired and respected her commitment to a cause that she emphatically believed in. It would profoundly embarrass him if she were to find out that his service to his country was only an unplanned detour from his selfish ambitions in the world of Wall Street finance. That he was essentially a fugitive who'd been given a choice between service to his country or possible prosecution, conviction and jail time was not something he was proud of.

Curtiss's comment must have led Tracy to fear her brief flirtation with negativity had adversely affected Curtiss's view of the Agency. "Curt, you can't get discouraged. I've worked in other stations and for some wonderful station chiefs. Wilkenson—" She looked around her, though no one but the waitstaff shared the dining room with them. "Wilkenson is just a bad station chief, that's all. Bad bosses are everywhere: in government, in business."

She pleaded with Curtiss not to quit and instead to focus on the day that either Wilkenson moved on to another station or Langley, or he did. She gripped his wrist. "Curt, you have an exceptional talent as a field agent. Believe me, I've known some very good ones, and you have got what it takes. What you are able to get out of a fortress like China is amazing for a foreigner."

A little embarrassed, Curtiss patted her hand and went back to his dim sum. But he found himself reflecting on his spy career: from spying for Lu in the gray market trade, to his discovery about the Kejia Tulou, his harrowing escape from the Walled City, and now to his intelligence on the M-9 Missiles that the Director wouldn't even see. It was a successful track record, he supposed, but he wasn't at all convinced that he was destined to become a career spy.

As though reading his thoughts, Tracy spoke up again. "Look, I'm sorry you paid such a high price for doing the right thing with the Kejia Tulou. But the Agency needs honest guys like you, Curt. Your country needs you. To hell with Wilkenson."

After their cathartic gripe session, Curtiss and Tracy returned to The Lowu House at 5:00 pm to find the third-floor corridor outside the conference room occupied by the entire Hong Kong Station, all with plastic glasses of red or white wine in their hands. When the door to the conference room finally opened, the Director stood at the entrance and shook everyone's hand as they walked in one by one, introducing themselves. Wilkenson stood beside a podium that had been set up at the far end of the room.

"Is everyone here?" The Director asked Wilkenson when the last hand had been shaken.

Wilkenson nodded.

"Ladies and gentlemen, as you all know, the World Trade Center bomber Ramzi Yousef was arrested in Pakistan last month and, through a well-coordinated inter-agency effort, we've successfully interrupted his and Khalid Sheik Mohammed's so-called 'Bojinka' plot to blow up a dozen U.S. airliners simultaneously while on their way to the States." The Director smiled at the hoots and applause earned by his statement.

"What you may not know is that the intelligence that led to his arrest and the dismantling of his terrorist cell originated from this very office. It is my honor to present Ken Wilkenson with this letter of commendation for actions which led to the prevention of the Bojinka plot and the arrest of Ramzi Yousef." The Director pulled his reading glasses from his suit breast pocket, donned them and began to read from the letter.

A dull echo attended his words in Curtiss's ears. His eyes happened to meet Tracy's from across the room as the Director read, " . . . your identification and cultivation of the Walled City source, acquired at great personal risk . . . ," and he watched Tracy close them tightly, as though shutting herself off from the words.

After the meeting, as people were filing out of the conference room, Wilkenson was at the door to receive congratulatory comments and handshakes.

"Congratulations Ken," Curtiss said when he was face to face with Wilkenson, passing the sternest test ever put before his Hershey PA requirement for politeness.

Wilkenson smiled and grabbed rather than shook Curtiss's hand. "I had to ensure that this one got accurately reported up the chain of command. I'm sure you understand."

When Curtiss stepped out of the conference room, Tracy took his arm and pulled him down the hallway. "Let's go and get a drink. We both need one."

* * *

Curtiss met Lu the next morning for their regular eggs Benedict at the Peninsula Hotel. Lu shared what he knew about the continuing military build-up in Fujian Province and the evolving political situation on both sides of the Taiwan Strait, and then departed for the airport, leaving Curtiss alone at the table.

He'd just finished settling the bill when he saw a female figure walking slowly down the hotel's opulent staircase to the lobby, followed by a skinny older man in an ill-fitting black suit and several bell-hops loaded with a matched set of dark brown luggage with a pink ribbon tied to the handle of each. Her elegance exuded an air of royalty and her presence took the entire hotel lobby back to Hong Kong's Victorian colonial era the moment she set foot in it.

"Hello Sonya," he called as he approached her. "What are you in town for?"

"Why, Curtiss!" Sonya said excitedly, turning to him and clasping his face with her opera-gloved hands. She kissed him on both cheeks.

"What a lovely surprise. Oh, I'm here visiting some old friends."

"I see you brought Kao with you," Curtiss said with a nod to the man. Kao didn't disappoint, puckering his wrinkled face in disapproval.

"Yes, well, traveling does get to be a strain when you get on in years, dear." Curtiss glanced over to the bellmen, who had just finished filling an entire luggage cart with Sonya's matched set of luggage, and smiled to himself. "I just need a little help now and then," she explained.

"You must be on your way to the airport. Do you have time for a quick cof—"

"No," Kao interrupted Curtiss. "We are late. We must go now."

"Nonsense. We have plenty of time," Sonya said to Kao, which sent him off shaking his head and murmuring to himself.

"And how are things with you, dear?" Sonya said as they took a seat by the window.

Curtiss valued his time with Sonya and tried not to waste it by dragging the conversation into a recital of his personal troubles. But Sonya could always sense what Curtiss was feeling and deftly peeled back the layers of his stoic facade. Before he knew it, he had shared as much as he could with her about his sense of helplessness and frustration with his career circumstances.

Sonya advised that he would do well to have a little more patience and to reconsider where he set his expectations of people. Though he risked seeming defensive, Curtiss explained that he felt confident that he could bear most any difficulty, but that once he had lost trust in certain people, he found it nearly impossible to recover it.

Curtiss followed Sonya's eyes outside the restaurant window to Kao, looking impatiently at his watch beside a disinterested Sikh, who was standing beside the open rear door of one of the hotel's green Rolls Royce fleet cars. "I do have to leave now, dear," she said. "We'll have to finish this conversation another time." She slowly rose to her feet, then kissed Curtiss on the cheek. Her parting advice was that if he followed his conscience in all matters, he couldn't go wrong.

CHAPTER 14

Curtiss tugged at his shirt collar and shifted uncomfortably in his tuxedo in the taxi on the way to the Hong Kong Regent Hotel's June 30, 1997, handover party. He'd have to have a word with his dry cleaner about shrinking his shirt and suit, he thought, then recalled that nine years had passed since Sonya had the tuxedo delivered to his presidential suite at George's Palace and decided, with a wry smile, that shrinkage was likely not the issue.

Curtiss had no problem finding Tracy's million-dollar smile as he entered the Regent's grand ballroom. Stunning in her formal dress, she eagerly waved him over to where she stood hemmed in by SIS officers in formal British military dress. She kissed Curtiss on the cheek, handed him a flute of champagne, and took his arm with hers. "I thought you'd never get here to rescue me from our allies."

Curtiss turned to the SIS officers. "Are you guys all packed up there at Prince of Wales Building?"

"We are indeed," one of them said, joining his colleagues in a round of sly smiles. "And there'll be a few surprises for those PLA blokes when they take possession after midnight."

"Oh, let me guess," Curtiss said. "You glued the desk drawers shut? Filed down the office door keys and injected super glue into file cabinet locks?"

"Something like that." They all laughed.

"You know they're never going to do any serious business in that building, knowing that you must have planted a thousand bugs in it before leaving."

"What about you there at The Lowu House?" one of them asked Curtiss.

"Well, we aren't as obvious as you guys in your big white building on a naval base in the middle of the financial district. No, we're the quiet company, so we aren't being evicted," Curtiss said with a smile. "The Lowu House stays, but some of us will be reassigned. Agent Tracy Clark here is on her way back to Washington. She has a cushy assignment at the Pentagon." The group moaned with good-humored envy at the news.

"And what about you, Curt?"

"Me? I move to Beijing next month to set up the China representative office for Transnational Trade Services."

"Beijing?" They all laughed, except Tracy. "Into the belly of the beast, eh Curt? You always seem to get the shite assignments. Has someone got it in for you there at The Company?"

Curtiss just smiled, made as if he'd noticed other people he knew in the crowd and announced that he would mingle for a while. Tracy started to go with him, only to be snagged by a particularly persistent, vertically challenged SIS officer, over whose head she shot Curtiss a beseeching look. Curtiss laughed and moved on, glad enough to be alone for the moment.

The room was filled with second-tier diplomatic types, those of a rank insufficient to receive an invitation to the official handover ceremonies across the harbor in the Convention Center, along with a who's who of Hong Kong's rich and indigenous movie-industry famous. Curtiss picked up a fresh glass of champagne and made his way through them to the three-story-tall window looking out over Hong Kong Harbour.

Taking in the view, it took him much longer than it should have to notice the Chinese woman standing alone at the window not three feet from him.

"Eight years living in Hong Kong and I've never gotten tired of this view," he said.

The woman turned, sweeping her thick, silky black hair over her shoulder, briefly looked at Curtiss, and turned back to the harbor. "I was just wishing that the rest of China will look this way some day."

"Wu Shi Nian Bu Bian," *Fifty years no change in Hong Kong*, Curtiss said, repeating China's public vow not to change Hong Kong after the handover. "But it seems that the opposite is true on the Mainland. Everything is changing there these days."

The woman's smile bloomed in the window's reflection, the lights of the harbor sparkling through the Cheshire-cat-like image of her sparking smile. "That's because China needs to change."

"Chuan Dao Qiao Tou, Zi Ran Zi," Curtiss said, this time reciting a Chinese saying equivalent to, *All things happen in good time.*

She turned to him. Looking him straight in the eye with her big dark browns, she managed to mute her smile, but not the accompanying dimples. Curtiss found them irresistible. "So you know a little bit about China."

A little bit. Curtiss smiled, impressed that she did not reflexively over-compliment his knowledge and understanding of China based on his recitation of one or two simple phrases in Mandarin. "Yes, in fact, the longer I am here, the more I realize just how little I really know," he said, then introducing himself.

She smiled, evidently pleased with his demonstration of the Chinese cultural DNA for humility. "Leah Zhang," she said, taking his proffered hand with a firm grip.

"You're not from Hong Kong."

"No. I am just here for the handover. I was born and raised in Beijing, but spent quite a few years in the States. I did my Masters there. I'm back in Beijing now." Curtiss smiled. Maybe his move to Beijing did have a silver lining after all: at least he'd be sharing the city with this stunning creature.

Curtiss and Leah spent the better part of the next hour cordially exchanging information about themselves, empirically sizing up each other and consulting their intuitions for what it could tell them about one another. Preoccupied with this, they didn't notice the room filling to capacity as they repeatedly exchanged full champagne flutes for empty ones. The crowd surged toward the windows when the fireworks began in Victoria Harbour.

"It's getting a little confining in here," Leah said. "What do you say we experience this thing out from behind the glass?"

Curtiss hesitated. Outside of the Regent Hotel's air-conditioned cocoon of wealth and privilege, he knew the humidity and heat would be rising by the minute in between bouts of torrential rain. The thought of diving into the masses on the street under these conditions dressed in a tuxedo did not immediately appeal to him. But the woman did. "What the hell, a handover like this comes around only once every ninety-nine years, right?"

As they made their way to the hotel's exit, Curtiss's eyes met Tracy's. She stood with a champagne glass in one hand and her late-arrival husband's arm in the other, rescued at last from the diminutive SIS officer.

She'd married John, a Marine guard at the U.S. Consulate in Hong Kong, the previous year. For whatever reason, Tracy and Curtiss hadn't even considered each other romantically, but he had no closer friend in the world, apart from Jimmy. According to Tracy, John was her new favorite all-time most authentic weapon. Curtiss was as genuinely happy for her when she married John as she was for him now, seeing him heading off with the stunning woman. She gave Curtiss a smile and wink so broad he had to laugh.

Within minutes of being outdoors, Curtiss couldn't tell whether it was the intermittent rain or sweat that soaked his clothes to the skin. Either way, his tuxedo's most superfluous accouterments, his tie and cummerbund, now served only to enhance his discomfort and were quickly shed. His jacket would soon follow and later be pressed into gentlemanly duty as a makeshift shawl for Leah's bare, wet shoulders, which glistened with the light of the street lamps and fireworks.

Her wet hair now pulled back, Leah closed her eyes and lifted her face to the rain—a simple gesture of such grace and arresting beauty that Curtiss had to brace himself against a lamp post.

When the fireworks finale completed, and only its echo and smoke trails remained, Leah grabbed Curtiss's hand and pulled him toward the Star Ferry Pier. "Come on," she said with sudden giddiness. "They'll be restarting the ferry in a couple of minutes. Let's get to the Hong Kong side to see if we can watch some of the ceremony from there."

Arriving on Hong Kong Island they flowed with the crowds to Chater Garden, the public park cradled by the Legco Council Chambers, the Hong Kong Shanghai Bank Building and Prince's Building. The park had transformed into an impromptu carnival composed of a collection of sideshows.

American activists—protestors who had flown in for the occasion—were desperately trying to wrap a large yellow ribbon around the Legco building in protest of China's one-child-per-family policy, but couldn't, ironically, since there were simply too many people, their polite pleas of "excuse me" and "pardon me" as they attempted to execute this centerpiece of their protest falling on the disinterested ears of the crowd.

Taiwanese independence activists carrying banners fought for sound bites with the foreign journalists roaming the area in search of a story. Drunken Brits dispersed throughout the crowd, dressed head-to-toe in Union Jack hats, shirts, and pants, sang "Rule, Britannia!" and spilled beer and champagne on themselves and others. And through it all, a loudspeaker volume war was being waged between opportunistic Cantonese pop singer wannabes, pro-democracy demonstrators, pro-China activists, and Pilipino holy rollers calling for repentance before the End of Days.

Back at the harbor Curtiss and Leah could see the royal navy escort ship the *HMS Chatam*, and, just beyond, the Royal Yacht *Britannia* tied up between the East Tamar naval base and the Convention Center. The *Britannia* would carry the Governor and the Prince of Wales away after midnight. The end of the line for Curtiss and Leah was the dock between the bow of the escort ship and the stern of the *Britannia*, with the *Britannia* laying about fifty yards beyond a fifteen-foot fence, which kept them at bay.

At a minute before midnight, the rain stopped and "God Save The Queen" could be heard coming from the temporary stadium where the military handover ceremony was being held. At exactly midnight, China's "March of the Volunteers" national anthem played, after which an eerie silence descended upon the scene.

Time seemed to stand still, as if the people of Hong Kong were holding their collective breath in anticipation of at last receiving the answer to the question they'd never ceased asking in the thirteen years since the Hong Kong Accords: "What will happen to us after the handover?" The engines of the *Chatam* then whined to life and the air was filled with the smell of human sweat, turbine exhaust and even greater anticipation.

Leah tightened her grip on Curtiss's hand, which she hadn't let go of since pulling him down to the harbor. While she scanned the area for the next bit of action, Curtiss studied her just as raptly, utterly bewitched by her and fascinated by her passion.

A motorcade led by the Governor's Daimler rolled down the wet, empty street from the Convention Center to the pier. A small band gathered on the deck of the *Britannia* played "Rule, Britannia!"

Leah took hold of Curtiss's arm and squeezed it tight when the *Chatam* cast off her lines and fell away from the pier. Lining her decks were sailors in their dress whites standing at attention and saluting while a lone bagpiper played taps.

When both ships foamed at the stern and tacked away from the pier Curtiss and Leah subconsciously reached out and pulled themselves close to each other as they watched them steam into the harbor until it was no longer possible to distinguish their running lights from those of the Hong Kong skyline.

"Well, that's that," Leah said, turning her attention to Curtiss. "I thought they'd never leave."

"They haven't been bad tenants, have they?" Curtiss said with a smile as he tightened their embrace.

"Yes, they did a lot for Hong Kong. But it is China's now, back where it belongs."

"So what does one do after a handover?" Curtiss asked, his desire for Leah leaving him slightly short of breath.

Leah put her arms around Curtiss's neck and pulled him even closer. "I don't know. This is all new to me, too."

* * *

Curtiss emerged from his apartment building to find Hong Kong's streets as absent of people as he'd ever seen them. There were no PLA soldiers standing on every street corner or Chinese army tanks rolling down the streets, as the most dire predictions had forecast. The only battle going on in Hong Kong was between gray storm clouds and blue sky for control of July first 1997.

As Curtiss passed a post office on the way to his favorite bakery to collect breakfast for himself and Leah, he noticed a dirt silhouette where the large post office emblem that incorporated the British Royal Coat of Arms had once been. It had been removed over night and would later be replaced with a sign that simply read: *Hong Kong Post*.

Enjoying their breakfast in bed, Leah wiped croissant crumbs from her lips and turned to Curtiss. "You've lived in China and you speak Mandarin, but you still choose to live in Hong Kong. What are you waiting for, Curt?"

"What do you mean, 'waiting for'?"

"Hong Kong is just a city. It is a very special city, but just one city, nonetheless. And it will never be the same after the handover, you know. Not because China now controls it, but because China is changing so quickly that the opportunities are now moving to the Mainland." The Thai economy was looking like it was headed for trouble, she said, and rumors were rife that Thailand would try to float the Baht. If it failed, there could be a confidence crisis in Asian currencies, and Asia's "tiger" economies in general. While Hong Kong was deep into it and so could be severely affected, China was relatively independent from the international monetary system. "If anything, China would benefit."

Reluctant at first to share his plans with Leah, Curtiss's inner voice told him that he could trust her with at least part of the truth. He cautiously explained that he was scheduled to move to Beijing at the end of the month to set up a Rep office for his company, while carefully studying her reaction. She seemed as pleased as he was that they would have the chance to be together again after Hong Kong.

He then shared with her his Tiananmen Square experience, including the death of Xiao Lu, and his ambivalence about returning to the place that had so permanently scarred his psyche.

"Sui Yu Er An," Leah said. When Curtiss looked at her blankly, she translated: "Take the world as it is, Curt."

Like most Chinese of her generation, Leah had grown up amongst the wounded survivors of the injustices and abuses of China's communist revolution: inflicted by the government in the name of fairness, equality and social justice. In the aftermath—impoverished, without recourse and robbed of their trust in their fellow man—the only choice people had was to make peace with their fate. She spent the rest of the morning reaching into Curtiss's heart, working this hard-won salve into his soul.

* * *

"My time here has come to an end," Lu said to Curtiss at their first meeting after the handover. "Everything has become far too black and white now. I no longer have an edge. I've cashed out with my partners and will be dividing my time between Taiwan and the Philippines."

"Come on, you're too young to retire," Curtiss said, though the fact was, Lu suddenly looked twenty years older to him. Curtiss could see that, in his heart, Lu had already moved on.

"I have all the money that I will ever need," he said, sighing from relief rather than sadness. "And I have all the money that my family will ever need, too," he said, laughing to himself. "No, it is time."

Though his dear friend would only be a phone call away, Curtiss felt a sense of loss cave deep inside his chest. "I don't know what I will do without—"

"Curtiss," Lu interrupted. "You don't need me anymore." And in any event, he reasoned, when Curtiss moved to Beijing he would be beyond his reach. He had no connections in Beijing and thus no way to be of assistance to him. "Hell, for all I know they may still want to shoot me for being an army deserter up there!"

"And they'd be right to, because you are," Curtiss said with a subdued smile, eliciting a muted laugh from Lu.

CHAPTER 15

The Beijing Airport expressway looked like any U.S. interstate expressway. As he traveled along it toward the city center, Curtiss could see the tree-lined, one-and-a-half lane old airport road paralleling nearby—his escape route from his near-death experience downtown, eight years earlier.

When the expressway ended at a pile of construction equipment short of the city's Second Ring Road, Curtiss's taxi plunged into the chaotic automobile traffic along narrow side streets that, during his previous visit, had been filled almost exclusively with bicycle traffic. He looked out over fields of bricks, the rubble from Hu Tongs—Beijing's traditional one-story brick houses—that were being torn down to make way for high-rise buildings. People were chipping clinging mortar off the bricks and stacking them on their donkey carts for resale. Stooped over as they were, picking through the barren ruin-scape, they brought to his mind the nineteenth-century peasants in Jean-François Millet's painting "The Gleaners," gleaning a harvested field for stray grains of wheat.

Curtiss arrived at his hotel just blocks from where he'd discovered that his legs had been hit by bullet fragments, prepared for the worst. But he found Chang An Avenue, last seen rife with tanks and gunfire, harmlessly congested with automobile traffic. Pedestrians dressed in the latest western fashions casually strolled sidewalks that had carried panicked, bloodstained students fleeing for their lives. The dread and onslaught of emotions he'd steeled himself against never came. Like him, Beijingers seemed to have chosen the option of life returning to normal after their June fourth incident. The only thing he recognized in the new city before him was Rambo's toothy grin as he greeted him at the hotel's entrance.

"Welcome to Beijing, Curtiss!" Rambo said, pumping his hand. "Sorry I couldn't meet you at the airport, but I was in a queue at the Rep office registration bureau and couldn't lose my place in line. Otherwise we would lose a week—"

"Don't worry about it. You did the right thing, Rambo. It is more important that we stay on schedule."

The men took coffee in the hotel's lobby and Rambo took Curtiss through a stack of documents and registration forms, including the forms Curtiss signed to become Chief Rep of TTS's Beijing office. They would spend the next few days looking at office space and interviewing prospective candidates for the office's six-person staff.

Curtiss took a furnished serviced apartment at Regent Court, a new high-rise apartment building on Chang An Avenue. He chose it because it was just blocks away from the U.S. Embassy—and so, on a clear day, he could see all the way down to Tiananmen Square, should he ever need a reminder of where he was and why he was in Beijing.

* * *

"Well, you called that Asian financial crisis right," Curtiss said to Leah when she answered her telephone. "It's getting bloody down there in Southeast Asia."

From the smile in her voice he could tell that she was happy to hear from him. The month-long separation since their intimate three days together in Hong Kong vanished and they instantly fell back into sync—their conversation spontaneous and genuine, enchanting Curtiss, like when he'd finally gotten jazz right in that grungy Taipei bar. Curtiss missed her and had no qualms about telling her that, trusting her completely as he did. He knew at that moment that Leah was going to change his life.

They spoke for another hour before Leah asked him whether he had plans for the coming weekend. One of her clients was having a barbecue at his house. "I'm welcome to bring a guest."

Leah picked him up by taxi Saturday morning. "Are you familiar with the Shun Yi District? It is an American-style suburb, where most of Beijing's expatriates live. It will make you feel right at home."

She'd just been making conversation, but Leah's suggestion that he would feel at home among a suburban community of expatriates startled him nonetheless. He couldn't quite imagine where would feel like home anymore. He had been living in Taiwan, China, and Hong Kong for nearly a decade, but he was still a foreigner. Having not returned to the United States even once during that time, his image of America was by now only an agglomeration of anecdotes that he had acquired second-hand from colleagues visiting from Langley, plus movie images and cable news bites. He couldn't name a single contemporary American musical group, a baby-boomer was now president, and the kinds of things that he was almost indicted for at DBL had become standard practice on Wall Street. The 1980s America he'd known had long ago slipped away.

After thirty minutes, they arrived at the iron gates of the Beijing Riviera Villas. When security guards stopped their taxi to inquire about the purpose of their visit, Curtiss saw through the gates the greenest landscape he had seen in Beijing—the city's parks included.

The compound appeared to be primarily composed of six-to-eight-thousand square foot houses ensconced within a scene that could have been lifted from any affluent American suburb, but for the sight of a chauffer loading golf clubs into a car's trunk for one of the foreign residents and the presence of Chinese-uniformed security patrolling the neighborhood on rickety, Flying Pigeon-brand bicycles with half-flat tires.

Their destination was the middle of a row of cars that were parked to one side of the street. There was a driver for each car. Some stood beside their employers' cars smoking cigarettes; others had popped open the trunks of their cars to access equipment—long feather dusters, rags hanging from strings strung across the undersides of the trunk lids, and buckets—to wash their employers' cars; a few sat upon folding wooden stools around a shin-high folding table, playing cards. And, like the drivers in Taipei, Taiwan, all of the drivers drank tea from large, reused Nescafé instant coffee glass jars.

As Curtiss and Leah walked up to their host's house, Leah explained that Bill Scripture was an American who had spent the past five years in China for Boeing. As the Scripture's domestic helper escorted them through the cavernous house to the back yard, Curtiss and Leah admired their collection of Asian furniture and artifacts. Two full-sized terracotta soldier replicas manned the entrance inside the foyer whose centerpiece was a nineteenth-century Chinese wedding carrier. The living room was adorned with woodcarvings and furniture from across Southeast Asia and a silk tapestry that Curtiss guessed was from Thailand hung down the entire length of one wall in the great-room. A collection of horse's-hoof-shaped Lotus Shoes on display within a framed glass case caught their attention as the Scripture's domestic helper led them through the sliding glass door to the backyard patio.

"There's my smart cookie," Bill said to Leah as he tugged her to his side with his free arm, the other occupied juggling a scotch on the rocks and barbecue tongs.

"How are you, Bill?"

"A hell of a lot better since you got me out of that Baht-denominated real estate fund. You cut that one a little too close for comfort there, young lady."

"Oh, we had plenty of time, Bill. It only looked close from where you were sitting. Besides, we got an additional five-percent bump the day we pulled out. That's nothing to sneeze at." Curtiss was struck by Leah's ease and self-assuredness as she plied her trade as a personal investment advisor. She inspired confidence in people. She introduced Curtiss.

"Good to meet you, Curt. Welcome. What will you have? Beer? Wine? Scotch? Bourbon?"

"A cold one sounds right about now."

Bill released Leah and dug his hand into an ice chest. Once he'd handed Curtiss his bottle of Budweiser beer, he asked what he was doing in China.

"I run the Beijing office of a U.S. professional services firm. We mainly do advisory work on things like transfer pricing and business modeling for clients who want to enter Asian markets."

"Well, welcome to China. I've been saying for years that if people here ever got their act together, China could become a new economic force in the world," Bill said as he finessed the bratwursts on the grill. Curtiss would later learn that Bill had cases of bratwursts, yellow mustard, American beer and liquor flown in on new Boeing airplanes being delivered to China's airlines. "And now they are well on their way."

Curtiss mentioned that he spent time in China in the late 1980s and agreed that things had come a long way in a short time. "I hardly recognize the place now."

"So you know." Bill nodded approvingly at Curtiss, a fellow traveler on China's often-difficult road toward revolutionary economic transformation—the capitalist kind. "Well, we are easy here," Bill said, gesturing to the buffet table and open bar. "Help yourselves."

Curtiss spent the rest of the afternoon ingratiating himself with Beijing's expatriate community and collected more than a dozen business cards. He also collected invitations for future chats over coffee or lunch. He was already learning that maintaining appearances for the TTS front company would be highly time consuming. Though most of the backroom work was farmed out to the CIA's research group back at Langley, China's notorious lack of accessible and reliable sources of data meant the two CIA analysts who came with him from The Lowu House had to do double duty: analysis for both the CIA and TTS clients. Nevertheless, it was a client-service business and required a great deal of Curtiss's personal time in the form of meet-and-greets, as well as his attendance at client briefings and presentations.

Curtiss couldn't take his eyes off of Leah that afternoon and couldn't help but notice people's reaction to her. Many already knew her and those that didn't made a point of introducing themselves. Most of the conversations she fell into surrounded investing, and she spoke credibly on everything from the impending crash of Shanghai B-Shares, to the dramatic rise forecasted for Beijing and Shanghai's residential real estate values, to the tax opportunities and perils of Americans setting up off-shore accounts.

In demand as she was, Leah was often separated from him at the barbecue that day. Curtiss came not to mind, as scarcely any time would pass before he would find Leah looking at him through the crowd. She had a way of embracing him with her eyes that literally weakened his knees. She was to die for.

* * *

"Dress warm," one of Curtiss's analysts snickered when he announced that he was going to Changchun—the motor city of China—in northeastern China's Jilin Province. He was going for an automotive client who was researching China's car market.

It was bitterly cold there in the best of Januarys, but January 1998 had proven itself exceptional, with temperatures reaching as low as minus twenty degrees in recent days. Curtiss replied to his staff's attempt at humor by inviting them to come along for a little field exposure. There were no takers.

Curtiss was met at the Changchun airport by a man named Shen, who worked for the "Hong Qi," or Red Flag-brand, automobile company and drove him to their factory. Curtiss took copious notes at his discovery meeting with Hong Qi company executives. During a break, when the executives left the room for a smoke, Shen noticed Curtiss admiring the historical photos of their limousines that were proudly displayed on the conference room wall. Many were black-and-white shots, and some showed high-level Communist Party officials waving from their cars to adoring crowds who were all dressed in Mao suits. There was even one of Chairman Mao himself waving to the crowds as he was driven in a convertible past the South Gate of the Forbidden City across from Beijing's Tiananmen Square.

"Hong Qi has been making cars in China since 1958," Shen explained to Curtiss.

"These photos must be thirty or forty years old," Curtiss said. "Those old limos would be collectors' items if they still existed."

Curtiss noticed Shen sizing him up before taking a shot: "I know of one that you can buy, if you are interested."

"Really?"

"Sure. It is in a garage, right here in Changchun. Do you want to see it?"

Early the next morning, they stood in a back-alley garage before a massive black limousine suspended on blocks. Its large whitewall tires had deep treads and were shiny with oil, indicating that, if they were original, the car was not being driven anymore. The chrome hubcaps, bumpers and grill all gleamed, without a hint of rust. There was some slight cracking of the chauffer's leather seats in the front, but behind the glass divider, back in the passenger compartment, the two bench seats—one facing forward and the other facing back—were in good condition. The refreshment bar in the center of the passenger compartment, made of some kind of rich wood, was flawless. Other than the slight fraying of the sliding curtains covering the back windows and the crumbling of the age-hardened rubber door molding, the vehicle was in pristine condition.

"My friend owns it." Curtiss had learned that this was Chinese code for *I don't own it, I don't know who does, but I've got it now and can get it for you.* "It is number sixty-six. That is, it is the sixty-sixth car made at the factory," Shen explained. "It used to be the Jilin Provincial Governor's car."

Curtiss had negotiated many of China's gray areas over the years, including the privatization of State assets. Why not the *privatization* of State automobiles?

In any event, he made it clear to Shen that if he decided to buy the vehicle, he would not pay in full until it was delivered to his home in Beijing, together with the title of ownership having been changed to his name, the vehicle registered in Beijing, and a matching Beijing license plate hanging off the front and rear bumpers. He wanted to buy a car, not a driveway ornament.

Running his hand along the car's body, Curtiss noticed minute, shallow dents along the entire roofline and asked Shen if the vehicle had been caught in a hailstorm.

"They didn't use dies in those days," Shen reported. "The production volume was too low. Everything was hand-made. Those are the original hammer marks of the workers who shaped the panels by hand."

He had to have it. "How much does your friend want for it?"

"RMB 70,000." Curtiss did the mental calculation and determined that they were talking about $8,000 American.

Curtiss shook Shen's hand, and the men returned to Curtiss's hotel to spend the rest of the afternoon discussing other requirements for sale and a process for receiving spare parts or, if they didn't exist anymore, having them made to order in a Hong Qi workshop.

* * *

"Are you still tinkering with that thing, Curtiss?" Leah said as she wrapped her arms around Curtiss's waist as he leaned over the engine of his Hong Qi limousine to tighten a bolt with a torque wrench.

"Hop in the driver's seat and turn her over for me, will you?"

"Okay, but we're going to be late for Bill's tournament if you don't quit working on this beast and wash up right now."

Leah turned the key and Curtiss smiled as *The Beast* coughed itself to life. He found the machine easy to work on. Under the hood, it was little more complex than the iron ox he'd gotten to know so well in China's Southern mountains years earlier. And, since he and Leah had moved into their old Hu Tong house compound, he enjoyed a private courtyard that served as a proper place for him to tinker with it.

Bill Scripture organized one of the best-attended expat golf tournaments in China. Curtiss didn't care much for golf, but that was beside the point. It was Leah's attendance at Bill's spring '98 tournament that was required. Leah's swing was a magnificent thing to watch, one fluid and precise piece of choreography she replicated again and again, without fail. As he joined the appreciative crowd watching her tee off from the first hole, Curtiss was struck again by how much he loved her commitment to mastering whatever she turned her hand to—doing things *right* in all aspects of her life. She was special.

After the tournament, Bill was walking with Curtiss and Leah to the parking lot and barked with laughter at the sight of Curtiss's Hong Qi. "Would you have a look at that tank?"

"It's mine," Curtiss said, proudly leaning against the fender. "I picked it up in Changchun a couple of months ago. I've been restoring it."

"It's his second girlfriend," Leah said, humphing in mock indignation. "He spends more time working on her than me lately."

Bill chuckled absently, running his hand over the car's skin. He was thinking. "Hey Curt, my boss is flying in next week. What do you say you let me pick him up at the airport with your limo? He's an antique car buff and would get a real kick out of it."

"Sure, Bill. But you'd better let me drive. She's real finicky and has to be handled just right—just like my other girlfriend." He accepted Leah's punch in his arm as his due.

"Would you put some communist Chinese flags on the front

bumper too? You know, to make it look more official."

"Sure. What does he drink? I'll make sure there's a bottle of it and some glasses for him in the car's bar."

*　*　*

Knowing that within the half-hour he would be enveloped in Hong Kong's unbearably sticky mid-summer heat, Curtiss consciously drew in deep breaths of the cool, dry airplane air as the flight attendants began preparing the passenger cabin for landing.

He was traveling to a quarterly meeting and went straight from the airport to The Lowu House after landing. It was his fourth trip since he was stationed in Beijing and with each visit he'd noticed that the operations had gotten progressively smaller: one more room closed off, another operation eliminated or relocated to another country.

Curtiss entered the third-floor conference room to find Wilkenson sitting in a chair at the conference room table. Wilkenson stood to shake his hand.

"Where is everyone?" Curtiss asked him.

"Oh, the meeting doesn't start until tomorrow. I wanted you here a day early so we could talk about your new assignment."

Wilkenson's words hung in the air like the first hint of smoke from a house fire. Curtiss parked his suitcase against the wall, took a seat at the conference table with his back to the large wall mirror, folded his hands atop the table, and looked at him.

"Have you heard of the Wakhan corridor?" Wilkenson asked.

"That's at China's border with Afghanistan."

"Yes, that's right. The border is only about fifty miles long, but it's a headache for us right now." Wilkenson explained that al-Qaeda in Afghanistan were recruiting Uyghurs—Turkic Muslims from China's Xinjiang Region—into their jihad against the United States. There were likely a number of them in terrorist training camps in Afghanistan already. And, with the Taliban now in control of Afghanistan, intelligence from the Afghan side of the border was sparse. "So we need someone to get it from the China side. We need to plant someone there, to keep an eye on things for us."

Curtiss sat silently in his chair.

"TTS is branching out, Curtiss. We're now expanding into

contract operations management for our TTS clients. Your cover will be a TTS contract manager for a U.S. venture capital firm that has acquired a joint venture with a local mining company there in Xinjiang. You will be seconded from TTS to the joint venture company to act as its general manager. It's all been arranged. You can finally put some of that business-school knowledge to work."

"What about the Beijing office? I've got a year vested there and my network is just now beginning to produce results."

"Yes, and you've done an excellent job there, we recognize that."

"So who will be taking over the Beijing office?"

Wilkenson shifted in his chair. "Curtiss, since the Hong Kong handover, the center of gravity for this station has shifted into China. The Lowu House is winding down, as you can see."

Curtiss maintained his silence, patiently waiting for an answer to his question.

"I'll be taking over as Station Chief of the Beijing office. I'll be running both China and Hong Kong from the first of next month." Wilkenson didn't give Curtiss a chance to respond. "Look, Curtiss, you are a field guy. You know nothing about running a station office for The Company," Wilkenson said, his tone at once defiant and defensive. "Besides, The Company has already put a rental deposit on my house at the Beijing Riviera Villas. Do you know them?"

Though Curtiss knew that he was once again at a defining moment in his life, he did not need to contemplate his next words. "And if I refuse?"

Wilkenson glanced at the mirror on the wall then grinned spitefully at Curtiss. "Curtiss, I don't need to remind you that I still have something of yours in an envelope sitting in my top desk drawer, do I?"

"Thank you, Ken." Curtiss eased back in his chair. "That's exactly what I needed to know. If the indictment is still in your desk drawer, that means it never got issued, so the statute of limitations has now run out on whatever happened in 1988." He interlaced his fingers and laid his hands across his chest. "It's useless."

Wilkenson's face flushed. He looked at the mirror. "Wait here." He rose and left the room.

Curtiss felt as though a great weight had been lifted off his shoulders. After a decade, he was finally liberated from the consequences of things he'd done so long ago they now honestly seemed as though they'd been the acts of someone else.

Wilkenson returned to the conference room and took his seat. After a long moment gazing across the table at him, he lifted his palms to the air. "Curtiss, you are the best China field agent I've got. Before the handover you were able to get accurate information on PLA troop movements to the Hong Kong border within hours. I had a half-dozen agents on that for weeks and got squat."

Curtiss was unmoved. "I'll stick with you for a month after you move to Beijing, to hand over the office and introduce you around to friends of The Company there. But after that, I'm gone. I'm resigning."

Though thoroughly enjoying his supreme moment with Wilkenson, Curtiss nonetheless nearly choked on his last words. What would he do? Go back to New York and high finance? It was 1998 and the world Curtiss had known there was long gone. He would need to start over among peers ten years his junior—young, single-mindedly ambitious finance majors fresh out of graduate school. And in any event, listing junk bond trading at DBL circa 1988 on his c.v. would hardly be a welcome calling card.

Whatever he did—return to Wall Street, coach Milton Hershey School kids deep in the dairy country of Pennsylvania, or find a job in Beijing and continue living with Leah—he needed to start over. The only thing he knew for certain was that his ten-year sentence under judge and jury Wilkenson was over. And nothing was going to stop him from walking through this open cell door.

Enrobed in his overconfidence, it obviously hadn't occurred to Wilkenson that Curtiss was not only refusing the assignment, but actually intended to leave The Company altogether. For some time he sat across from Curtiss with his mouth slightly ajar, ashen-faced, still as a locked-up computer. Then he flew into motion.

"Now Curtiss, don't be hasty. That is a bad idea. The M-9 missiles flew over Taiwan two weeks before Li Teng-hui's reelection in Taiwan in '96, just as you predicted. President Clinton ordered two aircraft carrier battle groups to steam up the Taiwan Straits as a result. Two entire battle groups changed course on your intel, Curtiss."

Curtiss sat silently watching as Wilkenson, panicked that his heavy-handed tactics had backfired in a way that might leave a mark on his record, struggled to find him a compelling reason for staying. Curtiss had no doubt Wilkenson's career would survive the loss of one effective field agent; he was built to thrive in this environment. The Agency was rewarding people like him with promotions and additional geographies, and if becoming Wilkenson was what it took to be successful at the Agency, then it was not for Curtiss. Even if he were willing to become a Wilkenson, he'd do it on Wall Street, where at least he could get rich in the process. Curtiss toyed with the idea of twisting the blade in Wilkenson by explaining that very thing to him, but his Hershey School-ingrained distain for hubris prevented him from doing so.

"Think about it, Curtiss. You make a difference here."

Wilkenson's Executive Assistant entered the room carrying a note written on a slip of paper. Wilkenson glanced at the note then looked up at the mirror and then at Curtiss. His lips tightened into a furious line; the shrug he attempted came off as a twitch. "Go, then."

* * *

Curtiss smiled as Prince's song "1999" came over the ancient AM radio of his prize Hong Qi convertible limousine two months before the turn of the millennium. With the top down and miniature Chinese red flags flapping from posts affixed to the front bumper, he tipped his baseball cap to Mao's portrait as he drove between the entrance to the Forbidden City's South Gate and Tiananmen Square along Chang An Avenue.

The convertible was the last of his fleet of nine Hong Qi limousines that he would deliver to the Kempenski Hotel. A month earlier, he'd sold the Kempenski Group "Red Flag Over China": his novelty limousine service that shuttled executives from and to the airport, and ferried tourists around Beijing's historical sites on city tours in China's classic cars.

Even before he'd left The Company in 1998, the business had begun growing organically. Bill Scripture's boss had been so impressed by his first ride in The Beast that he'd insisted on being driven around in Curtiss's car every time he came to Beijing. Within a week, word had spread among Beijing's expatriate community and

Curtiss was inundated with requests to shuttle this visiting CEO and that VP of International, and he began charging for the service.

After putting The Company behind him, he turned his attention to accumulating limousines and hiring drivers. After Leah helped Curtiss to create a bilingual website, he got listed on several travel-company websites and immediately had a backlog of bookings that kept his cars on the road day and night. Within a year, Kempenski executives had expressed an interest in buying the business. But it wasn't until he decided to propose marriage to Leah, just two months ago, that he made up his mind to sell.

Curtiss and Leah's Chinese wedding banquet was planned for December twenty-first, an auspicious day, according to the Tung Shing almanac. It would be a lavish affair at the Beijing Hotel, with ten tables and over one hundred and twenty guests. Lu had agreed to fly up from his beachside house in the Philippines and be Curtiss's Ban Lang, or best man. Curtiss would soon have his final fitting for a traditional Chinese silk jacket, made especially for the occasion, and an all-day pre-wedding photo session would follow shortly after that.

These were the things on Curtiss's mind as he drove along Beijing's Third Ring Road toward the Kempenski Hotel. Rolling up to the entrance, though, these happy preoccupations were swept away and Curtiss found himself aching like a child might at his impending separation from a favorite toy.

He laughed at himself, but it was an ache nonetheless.

"You've got to double-clutch her when you go into third gear," Curtiss instructed the parking attendant in Mandarin as he handed him the keys. "And she drinks oil, so you'll have to add about liter a week." The attendant gravely nodded that he understood.

"Huan Yin Ge Wei Lai Bin Lai Dao Zhang Le Ting He Curtiss Bradley De Hun Li," announced the master of ceremonies, welcoming Leah and Curtiss's wedding banquet guests.

Their wedding banquet was the last in a series of elaborate rituals that would complete their Chinese wedding. As the groom, it was Curtiss's duty to pick up his bride at her parents' home that morning and take her to the banquet. The Kempenski Hotel was kind enough to lend Curtiss The Beast for the day. Both bride and groom arrived in traditional Chinese wedding clothing: Curtiss in a black Ma Gua jacket, and Leah in a red dress hand-embroidered with gold and silver thread images of a dragon and a phoenix. They were received at the banquet hall with firecrackers—to ward off any evil spirits that might have wanted to interfere with their wedding.

Halfway through the banquet, Leah disappeared and returned to the banquet hall dressed in a traditional western-style white wedding dress, and the entire room ooohed and aahed its approval. After Leah's third change of clothing, this time into a Chinese Qi Pao, the wedding games began and continued until Curtiss, Leah, and the wedding party had bid farewell to the last of their guests.

"Thank you for enduring all of this for me, Curt," Leah said as he carried her over the threshold into their hotel room.

"Well, the Greeks say that marriage is about willingly sacrificing for the one you love."

"Well then," she said with a wicked smile, "why don't you just go ahead and sacrifice me, then."

CHAPTER 16

Curtiss had a half-day charter booked for early the next morning and *The Beast II*—his charter fishing boat, moored in its berth in Christchurch New Zealand's Lyttelton Harbour Marina—was having engine trouble.

After banging his head on the engine hatch cover for the third time that night, the wrench he was holding slipped out of his hand, then bounced like a pinball—first off the engine's valve covers, then the engine compartment wall, then the engine block, then the engine mounts, before finally landing on top of the boat's inner hull, directly underneath the engine—well out of reach of human hands.

He was cursing the loss of his wrench when breaking news came over the radio: A plane had flown into one of the World Trade Center buildings in New York City.

His mind turned at once to his middle school research project on the B-25 Mitchell bomber Doolittle Raid, done at a time when he was seeking to satisfy his curiosity about his father's war record. In the course of that research he read about a July 1945 accident in which a B-25 crashed into the Empire State Building in thick fog. Hooking up the engine's battery cables, Curtiss shook his head at the idea that that kind of thing could still happen in the age of GPS.

Curtiss and Leah had fallen in love with New Zealand while honeymooning driving around the South Island and decided to settle there. Leah continued to work as an investment advisor via phone, Internet, and periodic trips to Hong Kong, London and New York, and Curtiss invested the proceeds from Red Flag Over China into a charter fishing boat business. These days he divided his time between maintaining his boat, creating deep sea fishing experiences for his clients, and helping Leah raise their six-month old son: Conner.

Curtiss twisted *The Beast II*'s starter-key and the boat's engine roared to life. He took the next few minutes to tune it to perfection before shutting it down for the night. With the engine so hot, he decided to put off the project of collecting his wayward wrench until the morning.

The alarm went off well before Curtiss was ready to wake up, but he needed to be down at the docks well before his clients arrived, with time to pick up bait, ice, and beer. He didn't switch on the radio until after getting coffee brewing, then rushed to the television and sat, stunned by the image of the billowing smoke and dust cloud in lower Manhattan that had once been the World Trade Center.

Jimmy worked nearby. His line was busy.

After the news story had gone full-cycle, Curtiss noticed Leah standing behind him. She was holding their nursing baby in one hand and had her other hand cupped over her mouth.

"I was in the South Tower just last week," she said through tears.

* * *

With the disruption of global air traffic that immediately followed the 9/11 attacks, Curtiss lost all but one charter to cancellations and bided his time tinkering on his boat.

Like so many others in the hours and days following 9/11, he would learn more about the attacks on the World Trade Center and the Pentagon and the heroes of United Airlines Flight 93 who had overpowered the terrorists, only to crash in Shanksville, Pennsylvania. He was among the comparatively select few, however, already sickeningly familiar with many of the names repeated on the news: al-Qaeda, Khalid Sheik Mohammed, the Taliban.

While they were planning their attack on America, Curtiss had gone fishing.

"Three plane changes and twenty hours to get here." Curtiss instantly recognized Wilkenson's voice. "Man, you really picked the ass-end of the world to settle down in."

When he stepped out from the boat's cabin, he found Wilkenson standing on the dock. He had put on a lot of weight and lost most of his hair since Curtiss had last seen him, but the thin-lipped 'gotcha' smile had remained unchanged.

"Hello Ken. The end of the world suits me just fine, thank you." Curtiss manufactured a smile. "Why don't you come aboard for a cup of coffee?"

Struggling to keep his wingtip shoes from slipping on the freshly washed rail and deck, Wilkenson made his way down into the cabin. Before Curtiss had even placed the coffee cup in his hand, he said, "I need you to finish that Wakhan corridor mission there on the China-Afghan border, Curtiss."

He was surprised and relieved that Wilkenson had skipped his usual dramatic wind-up. He studied Wilkenson's eyes and detected something different in them.

"The U.S. will be attacking al-Qaeda and the Taliban in Afghanistan soon and we need people at that China-Afghan border area. We've got a Special Activities Division team assembled in Macau, with two Uyghur operatives, ready to go, and I need my best China field agent to lead them through China to the border." He finally took a sip of his coffee then settled back against the counter behind him. "The mission is to eliminate top al-Qaeda and Taliban who may try to flee Afghanistan through the Wakhan corridor. This is the perfect mission for you, Curtiss. Your face will blend in with the Uyghur locals there, and your language skills will be vital to covering the China side of the border. We need you."

Here Wilkenson exhibited another behavior new to Curtiss: His expression subsided into one of profound sadness. "Curtiss, Tracy Clark was working in the Pentagon on September eleventh. She left behind two children."

Both men sat then, listening to the waves lapping against the side of the boat, each recalling his own, personal images of Agent Tracy Clark. Curtiss's to this point unfocused guilt over his absence from the fight against terrorism boiled into rage when he thought of Tracy's smile and the pain of losing her that her young children would know for the rest of their lives. A pain Curtiss knew only too well.

"I'll have to discuss this with my wife," he said in a muffled voice.

Wilkenson drew a deep breath and stood up. "I'm on tomorrow morning's flight to Sydney, then to Hong Kong and Macau." After setting his unfinished cup of coffee on the table, he paused as if he were going to say something else, but instead just nodded and left.

* * *

Curtiss had never told Leah that he was a spy and dreaded having to reveal that he had kept it from her.

He'd reasoned that they were only dating when he worked for The Company, and after he'd quit and his limo business took off, there was no reason to bring it up. But now she was his wife, and an American citizen, and if he rejoined, even just for one mission, there was no question but that he would have to tell her.

After putting the baby down to sleep for the night, Curtiss sat Leah down and told her everything about his life as a spy.

She listened quietly, intently, until Curtiss was finished.

"I hope you never did anything to hurt my country."

Curtiss explained that The Company had many divisions and that he had served in one that was focused on intelligence gathering. He also shared his feelings about having been on a team that was on the trail of Khalid Sheik Mohammed at one time, and about his contribution to the effort to foil the Bojinka plot and subsequent arrest of Ramzi Yousef.

Leah nodded solemnly. "I realize that you had a job to do and that you were required to keep that from me," she reasoned to herself out loud. "And so I know you didn't deliberately deceive me." She looked at Curtiss dolefully, then took a deep breath, and smiled. "Well, this all makes sense, because I could never figure out how TTS managed to stay afloat the way you ran it."

They shared an exhausted laugh at that, but when Curtiss told her about Tracy Clark's murder at the Pentagon and his intention to exact revenge, her demeanor changed. "If you are going to do this, Curtiss, you must do it for the right reasons. Not for revenge, but to stop anything like 9/11 from ever happening again." She delivered this in an utterly intractable tone. "Only if that is your reason will I support you. And I'll be right here taking care of our son until you get back."

They went to bed that night each quietly imagining their family's future if Curtiss accepted the mission. Long separations. Being out of touch for weeks at a time. Lying to Leah's family and their friends about where he was and what he was doing. Curtiss worried about missing precious weeks and months of their son's life. Leah worried for his safety. And both agonized most over the risk of leaving Conner without a father to help raise him.

At one point during the night, Curtiss woke with a start from a dream that he was once again face-to-face with the White General. This time he was sitting in the dirt, tied to a tent pole inside an army tent. One of the White General's rag-tag squad of renegade soldiers was squatting in front of Curtiss, poking him with a stick to get him to respond to a question that the White General was asking.

He did not tell Leah about his dream the next morning.

Curtiss took a seat beside Wilkenson in the Christchurch airport's business class lounge. "For Tracy."

CHAPTER 17

"There's no way," said Axel, the spotter of the two-man CIA SAD sniper team with whom Curtiss was eating hamburgers and French fries at Macau's Lisboa Hotel. "No way."

Rick, the shooter of the team, just shrugged. "All I can do is tell you."

"There is no way you hit a man-sized target at five hundred meters, off hand, at night, with your legs hanging out the door of an airborne helicopter."

"*Airborne* is the operative word there, Axel."

Axel groaned, and Curtiss laughed. Rick, who was about ten years older than Axel, had already alluded to his years spent in the Army's Rangers Special Operations (Airborne) that morning.

"I'm telling you," Rick said, "you have to time it with the rotor blades so the pressure wave from the downwash doesn't affect your trajectory. The rest is just good shooting." Another shrug. "I'm telling you, that Iraqi soldier came out of his bunker to take a leak in the desert and I hit him dead center—and the range finder was showing five-o-five meters. I got my scope back down on him just in time to see him fold like a jack knife."

"So you gut shot him, then," Axel mocked.

"Bin Laden is six-foot-six. That's our primary target's size. You just concentrate on giving me the right range, elevation, and windage, and we'll see who gets gut-shot."

This was Curtiss's first opportunity to work with SAD, so he listened intently to the tales Rick, the Gulf War veteran, told of his

Desert Storm exploits. Though Curtiss was relieved to have a combat veteran on his team for this, his only military mission with The Company, he suspected he had a better handle on the risks it presented than either of his companions.

The two Uyghurs arrived at their table along with Vincent, their well-dressed, fast-talking Macau-Chinese handler, who seemed more interested in having a good time than getting down to any real business. The Uyghurs, in contrast, remained gloomily serious. Curtiss had seen the occasional Uyghur on the street while living in Beijing, but always at a distance. Close up, he could see that that their faces bore both oriental and European features, no doubt the result of their central-Asian proximity along the Silk Road from Europe to Asia. Their large, Oriental, almond-shaped eyes sat astride European noses, and their faces were accented with Turkish or Persian coloring and characteristics. One of them had green eyes, a trait almost never found in Han Chinese. Curtiss would later learn that their dark, rutted faces would bear a 5 o'clock shadow that would never seemed to go away, no matter how closely they shaved.

After lunch the team went up to a hotel suite, and Curtiss asked Vincent to be back to their room at around 6:30 pm to pick them up for dinner—a hint that he was not invited into the planning session.

The team spent the rest of the afternoon planning their mission. Between a large satellite photo and a topographical map of the Wakhan corridor, the Uyghurs posted ground-level photos they had taken of passes along the border. While Rick and Axel discussed at length the best places to position themselves, Axel labeled waypoints on a mini-laptop device that he carried with him. Navigation and positioning technology had come a long way since Curtiss's induction training a decade earlier. He used the opportunity of this mission-planning session to start training himself up on this latest technology in case, during the course of the mission, he was needed to take over Axel's job for any reason.

Vincent showed up on time, and impeccably dressed. He took them all to the hotel's bar and began talking about their options for restaurants.

"Look," Rick said, interrupting him. "Wherever we go, I want a steak, a good one too. USDA Prime."

"Yeah," Axel affirmed. "This is our last meal before we go in-country, and I'm pretty sure that water buffalo won't measure up to American, corn-fed beef."

Vincent explained that he would take them all to a private, gentlemen's club afterward. Curtiss volunteered to the group that he would pass on the evening's entertainment, but wished them a good time. He then sighed and drained his drink, feeling old—and missing his wife and son.

Their train left Macau for Guangzhou later the next morning, allowing plenty of time for the SAD team to sleep off whatever it was that they had tied on the night before.

Curtiss had stayed behind at the hotel to train his tongue to some basic words and phrases of the predominant Uyghur dialect of the region they were headed to, and to condense their mission plan down to easy-to-memorize bullet-points. It was about 6:30 am when he headed down to the lobby coffee shop for breakfast and to run through his mission plan notes one more time before destroying them.

Curtiss indulged himself with the Chinese food items of the Lisboa's extravagant breakfast buffet. They made him realize just how much he missed authentic Chinese food after the greasy, flaccid spring rolls and doughy sweet 'n sour mystery meat at the all-you-can eat Chinese buffet in Christchurch.

It was then that a familiar, Russian-accented voice reached him from the booth directly behind him. He rose to his feet and stepped over to find Sonya sipping a cup of tea and speaking into her mobile phone.

Sonya appeared just as shocked to find him there. "Gospody! Eto ti?" she blurted out in Russian. *My God! It is you?* She gestured for Curtiss to lean over into the booth so she could kiss him on both cheeks. "What are you doing here in Macau, dear?" she asked after ending her call.

So focused had he been on the mission itself he hadn't given a thought to his cover story. He paused only momentarily, then came out with, "I'm researching a book."

"A book. Well isn't that fascinating. What is it about?"

"Oh, it's a novel . . . What are you doing in Macau?"

"I'm attending a funeral, unfortunately," she said with a sigh. "But that is just a part of life for people at my age." Sonya gestured again for Curtiss to join her at her table. "Come, do you have time to sit?"

They spent the next hour catching up and discussing how much the world had changed. Naturally, the 9/11 attacks were a big part of the discussion, and Sonya pressed for his views on the subject.

He was sad to see that Sonya's general health seemed to be degenerating more rapidly. Though she'd never revealed her age, Curtiss guessed that she was in her early 70s. She took a number of pills with her tea, and a cane waited for her next to her booth. Yet her regal face had hardly changed in the twelve years that he had known her, and her smile was just as warm and generous as it had always been.

"Here, I want you to have this," she said as she reached into her carry-on bag. She handed Curtiss a book: a biography of Russia's Rasputin. "I've just finished reading it. It will help you broaden your mind, dear."

When Curtiss noticed the SAD team and Uyghurs waiting for him by the hotel's main entrance, he excused himself from Sonya and promised to visit her in Taiwan at the first opportunity. She grabbed his hand and held it tight, wincing as she scrutinized his face and, seemingly, his aura, then looked deep into his eyes. Curtiss sat motionless until Sonya relaxed both her grip and her gaze and said to him, "I see that you are going to be all right, Curtiss."

*   *   *

It was late afternoon of September twenty-fourth when the team disembarked at the Guangzhou rail station. The station was as congested as ever, but Curtiss could still easily pick out Rambo's bright grin from within the crowd.

"Hey, Curt, how the hell are you?"

The two men hugged and beat each other on the back. Curtiss had insisted that Rambo be on the team. He'd trusted Rambo with his life on earlier missions and this one was going to be the most dangerous one yet.

"You are a kiwi now, eh?" Rambo said when they pulled apart. "You are getting old, too. I'm seeing a lot of gray hairs up there," he said, studying Curtiss's hairline.

"Thanks. And I see you've finally put on some weight. I always thought you were too skinny to deserve the name Rambo."

After Curtiss made the round of introductions, Rambo informed the team that their next train departed three hours later and that he would take them to a nearby restaurant for dinner. Rambo briefed the team on the logistics of the mission. He handed out individual packets of six train tickets and explained that they would take them only as far as Ürümqi, though thousands of kilometers away, northwest of the Tibetan Plateau. They would provision and overnight there, then take another train journey south, down the western side of the Tibetan Plateau, to the city of Tashkurgan in China's Kashgar Prefecture. From there they would travel by bus to Ke Ke Tu Lu Ke, the closest town to the Afghanistan border. Agents of a cooperative government from one of the "Stan" countries along China's western border would smuggle in their gear and equipment and meet them at a designated GPS waypoint located between Ke Ke Tu Lu Ke and the Afghan border. Ke Ke Tu Lu Ke would serve as the base of operations from which the sniper team would deploy.

"The Gulf, Bosnia, China: all the names of these places sound the same when you don't know the language," Rick observed.

Curtiss listened to Rick and Axel talk about the good time that they had had at the nightclub the night before over the rumbling, thudding and squealing coming from their train car's wheels as it danced its way through the various crisscrossing tracks on its way out of the Guangzhou railway station. The Uyghurs chatted amongst themselves in their native tongue and Curtiss could already pick up a few words here and there. Rambo had already fallen asleep.

A few hours in, Curtiss set down his dry history book about the 1842 massacre of Elphinstone's British and Indian army by Afghan forces and took up the Rasputin biography that Sonya had given him. This was far better travel reading, powered by Rasputin's machinations, his intense, penetrating eyes, and reputed ability to look into others' thoughts and souls. Grinning, Curtiss thought about Sonya's inexplicable power over him, how she would on occasion seem to look at him in the very way Rasputin was said to have done. He toyed with the idea that she was somehow related to him: a long lost White Russian descendent of his, perhaps, whose family had escaped to China?

Over the next two days Curtiss finished the book, the Uyghurs occupied themselves mostly with sleeping, and Rick and Axel found novel ways to work out: doing countless chin-ups from the fold-out upper bunk and inclined push-ups off the lower bunk in their compartment. It felt good to hear and speak mandarin again, and for Curtiss and Rambo to catch up on the years that had gone by. Rambo was now a naturalized U.S. citizen and a full-fledged field agent with The Company, responsible for China's Southeastern region. Curtiss was delighted to learn that he was now married and he and his wife were expecting a child. Rambo had grown into a fine man full of self-confidence, but more importantly he had managed to hold on to both his humility and integrity in the process.

"Is it just me or does every guy in Ürümqi look like Bob Dylan's brother?" Rick asked while looking out the taxicab window on their way from the train station to their hotel.

After checking in, Rambo took them all to a clothing store, where they donned local garb. After three days without a shower or a shave, they blended in well with the locals. They may even have been able to pass at a Dylan family picnic, Curtiss thought.

The train trip to Tashkurgan was uneventful, but the two-day bus ride to Ke Ke Tu Lu Ke was by far the roughest leg of their journey. The ancient, filthy bus belched mostly-combusted black diesel smoke, its shock absorbers had likely passed their intended service lives sometime during the Carter Administration, and its seats had been locally reupholstered using foam so thin that it provided little insulation from the metal frame underneath.

To distract himself from the discomfort of the ride, Curtiss worked at appreciating the rugged beauty of the region. The flora consisted mainly of hearty, spiky-looking trees that clung to life in the rocky soil and between seemingly ubiquitous rockslides. The fauna amounted to domesticated animals, mainly sheep and scruffy-looking Mongolian horses, as well as packs of feral dogs that patrolled the garbage dumps that doubled as bus rest stops along the way. Occasionally he would spot native wildlife such as Marco Polo sheep on the upper hillsides and birds of prey circling in the stark blue sky. The highest peaks of the surrounding mountains were already snow-capped and the meandering rivers had retreated to a mere trickle within their expansive rocky riverbeds in anticipation of the coming winter freeze-over. Slow-moving donkey carts, loaded impossibly high and wide with stacks of hay, blocked the narrower passes on a number of occasions during their journey. Only the heartiest people would be able to live in such a place.

"We need to come back here and go on a sheep hunt one year," Rick said to Curtiss, while scanning the mountaintops. "Marco Polo sheep are on my list."

Rick Nanna was from a frontier family that homesteaded in Alaska at the end of the 19th century. He was five-eighths Native American, raised in Alaska hunting and fishing, and worked as a hunting guide until he was old enough to join the Army. Curtiss had the impression that there wasn't a wilderness in the world that Rick could be dropped into and not feel right at home. "Do you hunt, Curtiss?"

* * *

When they finally reached Ke Ke Tu Lu Ke, the team was thoroughly ground down by their journey. They checked into the guesthouse that would be their base of operations for the next month or so, then all went straight to their rooms without saying a word.

The next morning Axel and Rick busied themselves hooking up a satellite antenna to Axel's laptop device, making a waypoint and sending text messages. The Uyghurs set out to find transportation that could get the team to the border. And Curtiss and Rambo scouted the town for a source of potable water and breakfast.

When Rambo and Curtiss returned toting plastic shopping bags full of bottled water, bread, and over-seasoned grilled lamb on a stick, they found Rick and Axel waiting with important news. "The mission has changed," Rick announced. "We've just received a communication from Langley that fresh intelligence reports now put our primary target much further south, in Tora Bora, down in Nangarhar Province."

"That makes sense," Curtiss said. "That was the Taliban's old hideout during the Soviet occupation."

"Our new mission is to cross the border into Afghanistan before the fighting starts and call in a B-52 Arc Light raid on a terrorist training camp near Badakhshan," Axel said, spinning his laptop device around to show Curtiss and Rambo the location on a satellite map.

"So we'll just have to improvise, adapt and overcome," Rick said.

"Isn't that the Marines?" Curtiss asked, smiling.

"It works for Rangers, too." Rick smiled back. He began envisioning the mechanics of their new mission for the team by walking them through one that he had been on with a Ranger Special Operations team that deployed into Kuwait a week before the commencement of hostilities. They came ashore on a moonless night dressed as Kuwaitis and stole horses from one of the Kuwaiti royal family's stables to speed their deployment to the target areas.

"So this time, instead of riding in on million-dollar thoroughbreds to call in laser-guided smart-bomb air strikes on Iraqi Republican Guard positions in Kuwait, we'll be riding scrawny Mongolian horses to call in an arc-light raid on al-Qaeda terrorist training camps in Afghanistan."

"Sounds great to me," Rambo said.

Though Curtiss didn't share Rambo's eagerness to engage a fanatical enemy in combat, he was again relieved to have a battle-hardened combat veteran on his team. He was also concerned about being the most senior in terms of age. Running a fishing charter business did keep him fitter than sitting in an office chair, but he was in nowhere near the kind of shape as this high-performance SAD pair. And the area they were going to was extremely rugged. Now faced with a much more physical mission than the original, he was determined not slow the team down in any way.

The Uyghurs returned and informed the team that transportation had been arranged: a Chinese four-by-four would be delivered early the next morning. Rambo unfolded a topographical map and showed them the GPS location where they would meet the "Stan" agent on the way to the border to meet up with their gear, equipment and horses.

The next afternoon, after a seven-hour, teeth-jolting journey atop gravel roads, they arrived at the GPS meeting waypoint in the mountain foothills, three-quarters of the way to the Afghanistan border. They found two Stan agents sitting on folding stools, drinking vodka and playing cards under the hooded gaze of their four, monstrously large and heavily-loaded Bactrian camels. The agents spoke remarkably good English and Curtiss's team turned down their offer to join them in finishing off a bottle of premium Russian vodka.

It was too late in the day to go any further. The temperature would begin to plummet the moment the sun fell behind the tops of the surrounding mountains, so they set up camp within a nearby cave where they could build a fire without being detected. Rick and Axel immediately began unloading the camels and taking stock. The Uyghurs remained aloof for the rest of the afternoon and evening, no doubt due to some kind of ancient prejudice that they held against the Stans. The Stans clearly held the Uyghurs in the same regard.

Only after all the gear had been accounted for, the latrine dug, and a hearty meal of mutton and flatbread consumed, did Curtiss, Rambo and the SAD team begin helping the "Stan Brothers"—as Axel had nicknamed them—with some of their vodka.

Over the course of the evening's meal and toasting, it became clear that they would not ride horses of any kind into Afghanistan. A deal was struck that night beside the campfire to trade the U.S. team's vehicle for the Stan Brothers' camels, which could be ridden across the border over a less conspicuous mountain pass. The deal was sealed with handshakes and more vodka, with Curtiss using up a notable portion of his bribery cash to even up the difference in value between one slightly used Chinese four-by-four and four healthy camels.

When they woke just before sun-up the next morning, the Uyghurs, who had set up a separate camp nearby, were gone. Though Curtiss and Rambo knew that this was the end of the Uyghurs' part in the mission—to get them within reach of the border—they thought it strange that they had left without saying goodbye, but ascribed their hasty exit to some quirkiness of the people from the region, or perhaps the friction with the Stans.

"Okay, I was wrong," Rick said as they rode out of camp, leaving the waving Stan Brothers behind. "We don't ride into battle on horses, but on camels instead."

Rambo rallied to their camels' defense. "They will take us all the way to Badakhshan and back on one drink of water, and a couple bales of hay and a few hours of grazing wild."

"Just think of yourself as Lawrence of Arabia," Curtiss suggested to Rick.

The men kept the light-hearted banter circulating—along with gargantuan biting camel flies—as they followed their goat trails deep into the mountains. The camels quickly justified Rambo's glowing reviews, deftly managing the rugged terrain without once losing their footing on the crumbly trails of pumice-like gravel that pulverized into a fine powder under their feet.

It was at a late afternoon rest stop that Axel checked his GPS and announced: "We're in Afghanistan." Using his infrared rifle sight, Rick was able to identify a cave complex that overlooked the headwaters of the Panj River where they would camp for the night.

"According to our maps, we just follow that river below us," Rick said as he poked at the evening's campfire with a brittle stick. "It runs along the Afghanistan-Tajikistan border and it'll take us to within a hundred kilometers of our objective. We'll need to travel fast if we're going to reach the al-Qaeda camp at Badakhshan in time, though. The fastest way would be down the river by boat."

"Wrong season, Rick," Axel said, tucked in over the screen of his laptop device. "It says here that the river runs nearly dry this time of year, when the precipitation in the mountains that feeds the river changes from rain to snow. The inflatable boat is useless."

Rick contemplated this, then said, "Okay, we'll stick with the camels, then. But we'll need to risk traveling the flats alongside the riverbed to make time. And lighten the caravan."

The men spent the rest of the evening going through their provisions and deciding what they would conceal under rocks at the back of the cave and what they would take with them on their mission. The team left behind things like the inflatable boat, excess cases of MREs and chemical weapon protective clothing, in favor of most of the weapons in their possession, all their ammunition, laser targeting equipment, night vision equipment, extra batteries and spare parts for the communications equipment.

After Rambo and Axel had turned in, Curtiss sipped MRE instant coffee while Rick use a borescope to examine the inside of the action and barrel of his primary sniper rifle for any of the fine dust that seemed to get into everything.

"That rifle doesn't look military issue."

"It isn't. And it isn't Company issue, either," Rick said, smiling. "This is The Beast."

Curtiss almost laughed aloud. "Nice name."

"It's a factory-custom .30-378 Weatherby Magnum." Rick pulled out a plump bullet and held it up for Curtiss to see. "A wildcat caliber up until recently. I had the barrel cryogenically stress-relieved down to 300 degrees below zero just last year to further improve accuracy. I've taken Dall Sheep in the Yukon Territory at six hundred and fifty yards on steep slopes with this baby."

Curtiss said nothing, but toasted Rick with a shot of vodka, again reassured by the combat veteran's presence on the mission.

The next morning they brought their caravan down from the hills, kept to the rocky banks of the Panj River, and made much better time than planned. The trade-offs for their improved speed, however, were long days and the inability to make a campfire at night for fear of detection. Their only relief was the ability to bathe in the river, and to heat their MREs and their hands with the flameless radiation heaters that came in each MRE box.

It was October sixth when the team arrived in the hills overlooking Badakhshan, a town perched atop a small plateau countersunk into the mountain range. Axel used his GPS and surveying equipment to identify the terrorist camp, which sat about a kilometer from the edge of town, and to select a spotting location from which the team would position itself when calling in the air strike.

"You want to be positioned perpendicular to the carpet pattern," Axel explained. "You don't want to be at the end in case the bombing run goes a little long." He snickered at the expression on Curtiss's face as he considered a wayward one thousand-pound bomb dropping on their heads.

They stayed out of sight in the hills during the day, and used long-range surveillance equipment to monitor and record activity at the target: a complex of one-story concrete buildings, an athletic track with a soccer field in the middle, an obstacle course, shooting range, and barracks, all contained within in a whitewashed brick perimeter wall. That night, with the aid of their night-vision equipment, they worked their way down to the spotting position at the edge of the plateau, close enough to hear the camp's generator humming through the crisp, dry high-desert air.

The next morning, Axel woke the team with the news that the air strike would happen at 6:30 pm that evening, using B-52 Stratofortresses already fueled and waiting at the U.S. base on Diego Garcia, in the central Indian Ocean. For the rest of that day Rick checked and re-checked his equipment and Axel occasionally talked through the satellite phone while referring to his laptop device. There was little for Curtiss and Rambo to do but wait. After the team finished a late midday meal, Axel returned from his satellite phone, sat down with the rest of the team, joined them for a cup of coffee, and calmly announced that the B-52s were now airborne.

Curtiss's gut twisted. They were now fully committed: within a few hours, they were going to help kill a large number of people. Up to now, Afghanistan had been a quiet and peaceful place, and Curtiss had enjoyed its austere beauty from camelback. But once the bombing began, both that idyll and all diplomacy would be over. Curtiss and the team would be at the tip of the spear leading America's ground war in Afghanistan, the front line in the war on terror. And they would be deep inside enemy territory. Thereafter, how would they know which of the farmers and villagers that they had seen riding donkeys and winnowing wheat in the distance would kill them on sight, no questions asked?

"Axel, you don't think our spotting position is a little too close to the target, do you?" Curtiss asked.

Axel just smiled and sipped his coffee.

It was Rick who responded. "Don't worry. I've been through a couple of these carpet-bombings in Iraq. It's a hell of a lot of ordnance in a very concentrated area, but we'll be good. Just keep your head down and your mouth open, otherwise the pressure wave might burst your ear drums."

Curtiss was glad he'd brought up that point.

With the sun well behind the mountains and the first stars beginning to appear in the darkening sky, the team packed up and hiked down to the spotting position behind a small ridge at the edge the plateau. At half past six, Axel turned off his satellite phone, folded his laptop device and stuffed both into his backpack. He then slid down from the top of the ridge, looked at his watch, and nodded to Rick.

Rick looked at Curtiss and Rambo. "We'll be fine, gentlemen. Everything is all GPS now. Our boys up there got this thing down to the meter. Head down, mouth open."

In the next instant, a bright flash of arc-welding light lit the mountain sides behind them, flashing again and again in rapid succession, like a movie star facing intense paparazzi, until the rolling thunder hit their position. After a ten-second pause, the light and sound show repeated, ending with a single massive explosion, so close that Curtiss felt his teeth rattle in his mouth. Battling his fluttering bowel muscles, he and the rest of the team bounced from the ground as if from a trampoline before coming to rest within the dust cloud that had been thrown up around them.

Holy. Hell.

Over the subsiding echoes of the explosions that reverberated off the surrounding mountains, Curtiss heard Rick say, "You almost soil your shorts the first time you experience one of these at ground level, don't you, Curt?" Even Axel seemed a little overwhelmed by the experience, but Rambo had a huge smile on his face.

Curtiss looked up at the sweeping contrails from the two B-52 airplanes overhead, brightly lit by the final rays of the day's sun as they rounded back toward Diego Garcia. The team then crawled to the top of the ridge and Curtiss stood, dazed and wobbly kneed, beside Rick, and stared into the single massive hole no more than a hundred meters distant.

"Huh, well that one was close," Rick said as he clapped his hand on Curtiss's shoulder. "Oh, yeah, I forgot to mention that there is always one or two drifters that get away from the bunch," he calmly explained. "You got a little bit of a bloody nose going there, Curt. Must be the altitude and dry mountain air."

Rick slung his rifle over his shoulder and drew his sidearm. "Well, looks like The Beast is going to have to sit this one out. It's time to give the ole Yankee Fist a workout." Racking a .45 caliber ACP round into his M1911A1's chamber, he said, "Let's get to work," and began walking with Axel toward ground zero.

The man was absolutely fearless. A five-mile-an-hour wind pushing in the wrong direction on that bomb during its six-mile journey from bomb bay to ground would have had them blown to bits. Had Rick comprehended this risk? Or was he so conditioned to the battlefield that he simply didn't bother to make such calculations anymore? Curtiss wiped his nose on his sleeve and cursed his bad luck for having a battle-hardened combat veteran on his team.

Curtiss had trained on the M-4 carbine like the one he was carrying, and had blown off a thousand or so rounds for fun with Tracy in the hills of Hong Kong, but had never fired a weapon in combat. His hand shook as he thumbed the weapon's safety lever, and he had to visually check the safety—was the up position S or F? Hell. What if he had to shoot somebody?

Rambo, grinning at Curtiss through his meticulously applied face paint, didn't entirely succeed in concealing his struggle against the weight of his flak jacket, rifle, sidearm, backpack and ammunition vest, which he had generously decorated with dangling grenades.

Three hundred meters away from ground zero, the team began stepping through a gruesome debris-field composed of car parts and burning pieces of tires, bricks and weapon parts, whole human limbs and other fragmented, unidentifiable body parts, human and animal.

When they crested the first crater they found it lined with a half-dozen bodies. "You see how the negative pressure sucks them back into the bomb crater?" Rick asked. "After the initial explosion there's a vacuum that sucks them right in. Kind of counter-intuitive, eh? You'd think anything close enough to be sucked in would've been blown to bits and launched hundreds of meters away."

"Yeah, well, there's plenty of that too," Curtiss replied.

As they approached one of several squat, one-story brick buildings that had somehow remained standing, a zombielike man with blood coming from his ears, nose, mouth and eyes emerged, and staggered toward them. His scalp was severely lacerated, peeled back and hanging off the side of his head to reveal the white of his skull—just like the monkey's skull in the Guizhou Healthy Food restaurant. As he attempted to raise a nineteenth-century-looking rifle to his shoulder, Rick walked to within ten feet of him, calmly raised his pistol and shot him in the head. The man dropped dead, to the rubble.

Axel walked over to the body, kicked it off the rifle, picked up the ancient firearm and looked it over from butt to barrel. "Man, a Martini-Enfield," he said, like a kid who'd found his first BB gun under the Christmas tree. "My grandfather has the best World War II small arms collection. His pride and joy is a 4 Mk I British 303 Nazi-killer that he swapped for his M1 Garand with a Brit at the end of the war. He had to pay a fine for doing it, but it was worth it. But he's got nothing like this. This is a museum piece. He's going to love this."

Rambo dropped his backpack, slung his rifle, and ran to each of the remaining buildings in turn, tossing a live grenade in through a window and scurrying away before the explosion's muffled *whump*. Rick gave Rambo a nod of approval when he returned.

Rick climbed atop one of the surviving buildings and surveyed the area in 360 degrees through his rifle's night vision scope. "Call it in, Axel. We're done here. We won't need a second strike." Rick turned to Curtiss. "How much time do you and Rambo need to go through this stuff?"

Curtiss scanned the area through his night vision goggles with his hands on his hips. "Give us the first five hours of daylight in the morning."

"Axel, let them know we'll need extraction around noon tomorrow. We'll set up a defensive position here overnight."

The team took turns sleeping in two-hour shifts until sunrise. In the daylight Curtiss could clearly see that the bodies in the bomb craters looked like half-squeezed tubes of toothpaste: chests and abdomens crushed, innards squeezed out of mouths—and, he presumed, out the back ends, judging by the bulging seats of their pants. The entire area was as quiet as a graveyard and the fetid smell of death had already attracted flies and vultures, some of which had begun feeding on the bodies. The entire team was anxious to leave the scene as soon as possible.

With Rick and The Beast providing cover from the rooftop, Curtiss and Rambo spent the entire morning collecting computer hard drives, floppy disks, CDs, printer and fax machine memory cards, cell phones, paper documents, newspapers, note pads, and any other artifact that might possibly yield information. They also photographed the faces of any of the bodies that looked out of place, such as those wearing Saudi Thobes and two that were dressed in traditional Uyghur attire, and took tissue samples for DNA identification. Over the course of the morning they filled a dozen large collection bags, carefully sealing and labeling each for delivery to analysts back at Langley.

"We got orders to hook up with Army Special Forces," Rick announced. "Air transportation is en route—a Black Hawk and a Chinook helicopter. Curt, Rambo, you two are to return to Ke Ke Tu Lu Ke and await further orders." They'd be splitting up now, with Rick, Axel and the evidence bags in the Black Hawk. "Curt, Rambo, I convinced the Chinook pilot to take you and two of the camels to within a short ride of the Afghan-China border."

Axel began transferring waypoints from his laptop device into a spare GPS unit for Curtiss and Rambo to use to find their way to the mountain pass at the border, where they would meet up with operatives who would take them the rest of the way to Ke Ke Tu Lu Ke.

"Damn," Curtiss said, turning to Rambo. "I was hoping we were headed somewhere where we could get a good steak, a soft bed and a hot shower. We'll get none of that in Ke Ke Tu Lu Ke."

CHAPTER 18

"If those things crap in my bird, I'm tossing them out at sixteen thousand feet," the Chinook pilot shouted over the roar of his aircraft's engines as his crewmen pushed and pulled the surly camels up the rear-loading ramp. "Tie them down good," he ordered. "I don't want two, one-ton animals flopping around my cargo bay."

Curtiss, Rick, Axel, and Rambo stood together beside the Chinook. "Rambo," Rick said, "you chose your name well. You are one hell of a soldier."

Rambo, a little choked up, thanked Rick with a hearty handshake. Curtiss smiled, gladdened that Rambo had received precisely the kind recognition he valued most.

"Damned good mission Curt," Rick said, shaking Curtiss's hand. "If you ever want into SAD, let me know and I'll put in a good word for you."

"No thanks. Just this one mission for me. SAD is a young man's game. My back will never be the same after that camel ride. Besides, I've got a wife and a kid and a charter fishing boat business waiting for me in New Zealand."

Rick appeared a little taken aback. "All due respect sir. New Zealand is a beautiful place, but I can't imagine living anywhere but the U.S.A. I'd rather be dead than call any other place home."

"Food for thought," Curtiss cautiously replied, realizing that he'd crossed an unseen boundary with Rick.

"On second thought, let's do that sheep hunt in America. Alaska. Then see if you want to live anywhere else." Curtiss would later become convinced that right then and there Rick had made it his personal mission to make an intervention regarding his estrangement with his home country.

Curtiss and Rambo sat on the canvas seating along the inner walls of the aircraft while their two camels, latched to cleats in the floor and held fast by cargo nets, voiced their continual displeasure with their travel arrangements.

Once airborne, Curtiss looked out through the gap in the aircraft's loading door at the scorched and cratered moonscape that he, Rambo, and the SAD team had helped make of the al-Qaeda training camp, and whispered the words, "For Tracy."

* * *

"Easy. There you go, boy," Rambo coaxed, gently taking hold of the dangling reins and at last gaining control of his camel as Curtiss and his own recently captured beast watched from a dozen feet away. Curtiss and Rambo had spent nearly an hour chasing down their camels after they'd bolted from the loading ramp of the Chinook and headed straight for the hills.

Curtiss looked up at the mountains before them. "There's no way we're riding these camels through those passes until they are completely settled down."

Rambo agreed, and they picked up their gear and found a spot to camp for the night.

After picking through a case of MREs, Curtiss and Rambo ate dinner together by green light-stick light.

"When I was a teenager and first saw the film 'Rambo: First Blood Part II'—that really changed my life," he said, solemnly, as he dug his spoon into a foil pouch of re-heated beef stew. "Honor, fighting for what is right, and being willing to sacrifice for your fellow soldier . . . " He paused to collect his thoughts. "What we've done together over this past week, Curt—it is living my dream."

"Well, we got a little more action on this trip than we originally planned for, but you handled yourself admirably." Curtiss studied Rambo's pensive expression. "So, are you thinking about applying for a transfer to SAD?"

"Well, you know, with the war in Afghanistan now underway, and the Uyghur involvement in China . . . I was thinking that they might need someone . . . "

Curtiss wondered if Rambo had thought things completely through—like considering that his wife was due to have their baby soon—but held his tongue. "If you are ever looking for a reference, just let me know," he said instead, pulling out a bottle of the Stans' Russian vodka and smiling at him.

Though the camels were still a bit skittish from the previous day's helicopter ride, Curtiss and Rambo's half-day trek through the mountains was uneventful. Their GPS unit emitted a twenty-first century "bling" when they arrived at a narrow pass on the trail. "We're here, right at the border, according to the GPS," Rambo announced.

After dismounting, Curtiss pointed out two horses with riders that had emerged from behind a rock outcropping along the trail. He used his binoculars to get a better look. "It looks like those two Uyghurs," Curtiss said. They waved to the Uyghurs, who waved back. As their horses lumbered over, Rambo broke out a case of MREs to share with them.

The Uyghurs dismounted, carrying AK-47 assault rifles slung over their shoulders—there was a war on, after all—and eagerly accepted the offer of food. They apologized for their sudden departure at their other camp, and called the Stan Brothers former Soviet infidels, confirming Curtiss's suspicion that it had been spurred by their dislike of the Stan Brothers' company. The group ate well and talked about their plan for returning to Ke Ke Tu Lu Ke.

While rifling through the case of MREs for a dessert, Curtiss caught one of the Uyghurs glancing up at the top of a cliff face behind him. When their eyes met, Curtiss and the Uyghur froze in place for a split second. Both Uyghurs then leapt to their feet, pulled up the barrels of their rifles and leveled them at Curtiss and Rambo.

Rambo swallowed hard on a bite of Salisbury steak and appeared to be preparing to reach for his M-4, leaning against the rock he was sitting on, but Curtiss shook his head. He wouldn't make it.

The Uyghurs forced Curtiss and Rambo to lay face down in the dirt and tied their hands and feet. Ten minutes later, they cinched their feet to the backs of their necks so they couldn't see who was approaching from the Afghanistan side of the trail. Curtiss soon heard new voices in a language that sounded different from any that he had heard since being in the region. He only managed to see a pair of sandal-covered feet under what he took to be the bottom end of a Saudi Thobe, just before a burlap sack was pulled over his head.

* * *

"I love you, Curt," Leah whispered, sliding her warm, soft, naked body closer to his in bed. Curtiss breathed deep the smell of Leah's hair and took notice of the sounds of Beijing traffic coming in through the open window of their Hu Tong house. A lock of her hair was tickling his cheek and as he raised his hand to brush it away, he heard her ask, "Curt, where are you?"

He then swatted away what was in actuality a rat's tail that had been lying across his face as it gnawed on the rattan mat that he was using as a pillow.

Now wide awake on the dirt floor, he watched the rat scurry away under the wall of the canvas tent he was lying in. Chained by the ankle to the tent's main pole, exhaustion from lack of food overpowered the adrenalin pumping through his system, and Curtiss escaped back into sleep.

A boot to the ribs the next morning brought him back to the reality that he was being held prisoner somewhere—most likely in Afghanistan. A week had passed since the Uyghers had betrayed them in the mountain pass. Hooded and tied to their camels like baggage, he and Rambo had traveled for two days before arriving at a camp.

Two men dragged Curtiss into a sitting position next to the main tent pole and handcuffed his hands behind his back, around the pole. Sitting cross-legged in the dirt, he watched the tent flap open and a young, bearded, Middle-Eastern or maybe North African man in Afghan clothing enter. He was holding a clipboard in his hand and squatted in front of him. "Wow, that looks pretty uncomfortable," the man said in perfect, American-accented English. "I'd do something to help, but these guys are barbarians, you know?"

Hearing these American-English words from this man, in this place, was surreal. "Where are you from?" Curtiss asked.

"LA. I got my double-E degree from UCLA."

"So what are you doing here?"

The man laughed. "Hey, I'm supposed to be asking you questions. Right?"

"Okay. I'm from Hershey, Pennsylvania, and my buddy and I are on a hunting expedition for Marco Polo sheep. Those two Uyghurs tricked us into believing they were our hunting guides."

The man's smile widened and he shook his head. "Nah. Look. We know from the Uyghurs that you work for the U.S. government—CIA, Army Intelligence, FBI, whatever. And that you did some kind of mission here."

"Well, I've learned not to trust those Uyghurs. But hey, that's just my experience." Curtiss tried and failed to find a more comfortable sitting position. "I hope you didn't give them any money. Hey, since you know those guys so well, could you help us get our $20,000 hunting guide fees and stuff back?"

The young man just shook his head again. "Look, these guys we're with, you know what they're going to do to you, right?"

Curtiss sat silently in the dirt.

"If you tell them what they want to know, then maybe I can help you escape or something."

Curtiss was almost amused at this scruffy frat-boy's pathetic attempt to establish a relationship of trust with him in the hope that he would tell him what they wanted to know. "What about my friend?"

"The Chinese guy?" the man asked rhetorically, while looking down at his feet, grinding his toe in the dirt. "Well, these guys don't care for the Chinese very much. You see, the communists oppressed us Muslims for decades. Destroyed our mosques, tried to rub out our religion in their country."

"He's a U.S. citizen."

"Oh yeah? So am I," the young man said with a sardonic grin. "Chinese communist *and* an American infidel? I wouldn't worry about that guy anymore if I were you. I'd be worried about myself."

Curtiss had a very bad feeling that Rambo, if he was still alive, was far worse off than he was.

"Look. This is really simple. There's only one thing they want to know from you: whether your government thinks they know the whereabouts of Osama bin Laden and Mullah Omar."

"I heard those names on TV after 9/11, but that's all I know about them. I'm telling you, we were on a sheep-hunt. We were in China—check for the visas in our passports—and we met up with those two Uyghurs in Ke Ke Tu Lu Ke, who claimed to be our guides. They led us into Afghanistan, stole our money, hunting permits, ammunition, and rifles—including my factory custom .30-378 Weatherby."

The young man sighed. "Ok. If that's the way you want to do it. Your hunting buddy is talking. But of course that is under much harsher treatment, for sure." The American al-Qaeda stood with hands on hips and contemplated Curtiss for a moment. "I'm telling you, this is going to get real ugly unless you tell us what we need to know." He put his pen back in his clipboard and left.

The American al-Qaeda's clumsy line of questioning reassured Curtiss that Rambo hadn't talked, but he felt sick in the pit of his stomach for what Rambo must have been going through over the past week.

For the entire week to come, the American al-Qaeda came to Curtiss's tent daily and each day he walked away with a clipboard holding blank sheets of paper. During his two weeks of captivity, Curtiss drank muddy river water from an old half-liter plastic water bottle and ate scrapings from the plates of his captors. And there was the occasional beating to contend with. During his first, one of his captors was surprised when he knocked Curtiss's two prosthetic teeth from his mouth and saw them land in the dirt. He reached down for them and smiled at Curtiss, revealing that he was missing a large number of his own teeth, due to decay and likely malnutrition, and mockingly gestured as if he were trying to fit them into his own mouth before tossing them out the tent door.

At the end of the second week, Curtiss was handcuffed to the tent pole as though in preparation for the American al-Queda's daily visit. He waited, slumped over from exhaustion and starvation, but on this day the American al-Queda was joined by a well-dressed Arab wearing a Saudi Thobe under a heavy Versace-labeled overcoat, and these two were then joined in turn by three old weather-beaten Afghan Mujahideen relics from the Soviet occupation era. Curtiss noticed that one of the Mujahideen wore a pistol on his hip in a leather holster with Russian lettering on it and had no doubt that it was a trophy taken off a dead Russian officer. One of the Mujahideen squatted in front of Curtiss and poked him with a stick to get him to pay attention to what the Arab was saying.

The American al-Qaeda translated: "Our exalted leaders are now safe. We have no use for you anymore."

The Arab gestured for the tent door to be opened, revealing an emaciated, battered and bloodstained Rambo, kneeling just outside on a fresh blanket of white snow that covered the landscape. His hands were tied behind his back and two more Mujahideen stood on either side of him. He smiled when he saw Curtiss, revealing that all of his front teeth were missing. The Arab in the tent with Curtiss then took off his overcoat, drew the Yemeni Jambiya dagger from his belt, walked over to Rambo and grabbed a firm handhold of his hair.

The Arab looked at Curtiss then and began speaking in Arabic. The American al-Qaeda: "You Christian infidels at least recognize God. But there is still an even lower form of life than you, and that is the communist atheist." He pulled Rambo's head back and put the tip of the dagger beside Rambo's jugular vein. "I will now show you what we do to the pig-eating pigs: the atheist communist Chinese who dare to deny the existence of Allah." While the Arab waited for the translation, Rambo, whose swollen eyes were transfixed on Curtiss's, managed to get out the words, "Wo Jia," *My family*. The Arab drove the tip of his dagger through Rambo's neck then, slicing its way out, severing Rambo's jugular vein and entire esophagus in the process. Slaughtered like an animal.

The Arab let Rambo's convulsing body fall face first into the blood-spattered snow. Rambo's last thoughts had been of his family; his child would grow up without a father and his wife would be a widow. First Tracy's children, now Rambo's child. Why did this aberrant condition of children losing their parents in early childhood plague Curtiss's life? Would his own death at the hands of these barbarians be his only release from this chronic misfortune?

After he wiped his blade on a fresh cloth handed to him by one of his Mujahideen, the Arab looked at Curtiss and barked out an order in Arabic that the American al-Qaeda did not need to translate.

One Mujahideen undid Curtiss's handcuffs, pulled him to his feet and escorted him outside, while the other drew a Makarov 9mm pistol from his leather holster. Curtiss couldn't bear to look down as he was walked away from the tent past Rambo's body, knowing that the only reason Rambo now laid dead was because Curtiss had insisted that he come on the mission.

Realizing that he was only minutes or even seconds away from his own death, Curtiss's adrenalin kicked in, reviving him, and sharpening his mind and senses. Boiling rage supplanted the hollowness in his gut. Would he really cooperate with his executioners by simply walking to his killing ground? If he gave up now and did nothing to try to stop his own execution, he would be willingly condemning Conner to a family curse of parents dying on their young children.

On their march out of the camp, they passed a man who was struggling to get an iron ox running. Or who *had* been struggling, as he had now resorted to beating it with a stick in frustration and cursing it in Pashto. Curtiss turned and walked over to the iron ox. The Mujahideen shouted, but Curtiss ignored him. Curtiss held his breath as he shoved aside the man with the stick who was beating the machine and heard the sound of the safety being switched off the Makarov pistol right next to his ear. But when he pulled the air filter cover off the iron ox everyone began watching what he was doing. Curtiss repeatedly gestured as if asking for chewing gum until one of the men handed him a stick. He peeled off the foil wrapper, folded it a certain way, and inserted it into the carburetor.

After bleeding the fuel-line, making a few adjustments to the choke and a timing lever, Curtiss gestured to the stick-bearing man to try starting it again. When it came to life with a puff of black smoke, everyone laughed. Lu's nephew had shown Curtiss the foil wrapper trick to get an iron ox running at high altitude during their time together in the mountains of Guizhou.

The three Mujahideen stood dumbfounded for a moment, then talked amongst themselves. They walked over to a convoy of Toyota Land Cruisers that were preparing to leave the camp. The backseat window of one of the vehicles rolled down, revealing the Arab inside. The three Mujahideen spoke with him for several minutes, gesturing toward Curtiss and the iron ox, which was located at the edge of a graveyard of disused rusting farm and military equipment. The Arab seemed to contemplate Curtiss for a moment before he nodded, rolled up the window, and the vehicles left the camp in a cloud of fine snow and dust.

* * *

The smell of a steaming plate of cuscus with bits of meat and warm goat's milk woke Curtiss and enticed him out from under his blanket and off his cot into the cold morning air. Curtiss thanked his guard in Pashto for releasing his handcuffs so he could eat.

After a visit to the latrine under guard, Curtiss walked over to a queue of all manner of Soviet-era tractors, water pumps, and other farming equipment that local people had towed to the camp to be repaired. Like a village doctor, he would do his best to understand their complaints, then give their machines an examination and make a diagnosis. By the time they reached Curtiss, the machines were beyond the simple problems, like sand or water in the fuel lines, using oil of a weight too heavy for the temperature, crusty sparkplugs, or a dirty carburetor. Parts were often needed that did not exist and Curtiss would work with local craftsmen—blacksmiths, tribal jewelers, tinmakers and such—to make parts to order. It was in this way that he survived the month of November 2001 in captivity somewhere in the mountains of northern Afghanistan.

Curtiss did his best to appear unaware of the regular contrail patterns of coalition refueling aircraft and the distant rumbling from the jet engines of fighter-bombers as they made their sorties into Afghanistan from bases in Tajikistan and Kyrgyzstan. He was, however, acutely aware that he was being closely watched, and that his capturers appeared to frequently discuss what was to be done with him.

One morning two guards brought Curtiss at gunpoint to a Russian-made anti-aircraft gun, likely abandoned during the withdrawal of Soviet forces from Afghanistan. One guard dropped Curtiss's bag of tools at his feet and the other gestured with the end of his gun barrel for him to start working on the anti-aircraft gun's rusty mechanisms.

He stood in place and remained expressionless.

One of the guards shouted at him, but he did not move. The other guard jammed the butt of his AK-47 assault rifle into his lower back, knocking him off balance, but still he refused to pick up the tools and work on the gun.

Both guards then leveled their rifles at Curtiss and shouted at him in Pashto. Curtiss held his breath while his captures decided whether to kill him or lock him up again. One guard removed a pair of handcuffs from his belt, closed them tightly around Curtiss's wrists behind his back and pushed him to the tent.

Curtiss did not sleep for the next two days since he had to continuously flex his fingers, hands, and wrists against the icy bite of the tightly closed handcuffs to keep blood flowing into his hands. He wished he could thank Gabriel Zuckerman for showing him this flexing technique for warding off frostbite and gangrene in tightly cuffed hands.

It wasn't until the end of the second day lying in his own filth on the tent's dirt floor that the American al-Qaeda paid him a visit. "You're lucky these mountains are impassable in the winter. Our Arab leader won't be able to return until spring. That means my fellow freedom fighters here won't kill you until spring, when he returns. They wouldn't dare, unless they have orders from him."

Curtiss looked up at him from the dirt. "If your buddies don't loosen these handcuffs right now, I'll likely be dead from gangrene within a week. And that wouldn't please your Arab master."

The American al-Qaeda stared at Curtiss for a moment, then shouted in Arabic for Curtiss's guards to enter and turned back to Curtiss. "Man, you stink," he said, then ordered the guards to remove Curtiss's handcuffs and walk him to a stream to wash up. Though his hands were numb, Curtiss somehow managed to hack a hole in the ice of the frozen stream and one of the guards gave him a sawed-off one-liter Coca-Cola bottle to use to bathe with the ice-cold water.

Over the next three months the camp was broken down and moved several times. The last move happened so quickly that they didn't have time to pack up many of their tents, and they all watched that night from a mountain pass as coalition aircraft destroyed the camp they'd just vacated with cluster bombs.

On the run and short of supplies, everyone suffered from acute deprivation and Curtiss's captors fared little better than their prisoner. By early spring nearly three in ten had died, most from a mysterious respiratory illness that had spread throughout the camp.

He too had developed a persistent cough but, having started the winter more fit than many of his captors, he managed to stay healthier than most others in the camp.

Over time Curtiss became an essential functional part of the camp, whether hacking through the frozen ground to dig latrines and graves, or somehow maintaining seemingly irretrievable 1950s-era machinery and equipment used to support their bare-bones existence. No one ever brought him military equipment to repair again.

Curtiss's knack for quickly picking up languages like Pashto also likely played a role in his survival. He would often participate in conversations with his captors when they talked about their homes and families and of better days. But he was under no illusions. He knew that their apparent compassion was only temporary and that to his captors he was and always would be an infidel, little better than a stray dog that they tolerated.

The mood of the camp as a whole brightened with the arrival of spring, but for Curtiss that meant the possible return of the Arab and his execution order. When the mountain roads became passable, he was back to repairing farm equipment. His hands, damaged by his stint of prolonged handcuffing, gave him considerable trouble. Likely nerve damage made fine work difficult, and general tissue damage from frostbite made the use of tools such as wrenches, and especially hammers, a painful experience.

The spring thaw was just getting underway when a caravan of Mujahideen arrived at camp with supplies and a westerner dressed in rags. Through his open tent flap Curtiss saw that his hands and feet were bound, and he shouted insults and profanities in Australian-accented English when he was thrown off a horse onto the now muddy ground. He was a tall, big-boned man who moved in a way that suggested his frame had once carried a much greater bulk.

"Put this one in the pig pen with the other infidel," Curtiss overheard one of the Mujahideen say in Pashto.

* * *

"Bloody towelies," the Australian man said after the guards dropped him on the dirt floor next to Curtiss and left their tent. "What are you in for, mate?"

"Hunting without a license."

The man laughed heartily. "Good one. You sound like a Yank."

"Yep, American."

"Perth, Australia, myself."

"So what is an Aussie doing in Northern Afghanistan?"

"Same as you, I suspect: Killing al-Qaeda and Taliban," he replied with a smile, revealing missing front teeth.

Curtiss smiled back, revealing his own. "Looks like you've taken a beating or two on this trip," he said.

"Yeah, but I lost my teeth years ago playing Aussie football."

"I lost mine chasing a woman from New York to Taiwan."

The man laughed again. "Seriously, mate—she knocked your teeth out? Sounds like a woman worth chasing."

"I thought she was, anyway. But it was her father's bodyguards who knocked my teeth out."

The big Aussie nodded. "I'm Keith."

"Curt. You'll meet our American al-Qaeda soon, some college kid from LA who joined up with these guys. He's their interrogator, a pretty inept one."

"A traitor, yeah? I wouldn't mind meeting up with that bloke in a dark alley one night," Keith said darkly. "No worries. Already been through about a month of interrogation myself. My two mates didn't survive . . . yeah." Behind his calm grimace, Curtiss could see rage and a thirst for revenge in the man's eyes. The man was like a caged animal that appeared docile behind the bars, but would surely mangle anyone who came within reach.

Initially, both men were obliged to approached each other with caution—not knowing whether or not the other was planted by the enemy to elicit information—but over the course of the next few days Curtiss and Keith got to know and trust each other. Well decorated with tattoos, Keith had once been a semi-pro kick boxer. He had a wife and daughter in Perth and came from a military family: his great-grandfather had been an ANZAC who'd fought in Gallipoli during the First World War, his grandfather had fought the Japanese in the Southwest Pacific during the Second World War, and his father had fought with the Royal Australian Regiment in Vietnam. Curtiss shared with Keith his own family's military history, vis-à-vis his father's World War II exploits. And though they didn't say it out loud, they were both thinking about escape.

"Well, it will be opium poppy-planting season soon," the American al-Qaeda said. "We'll grow it and your people will inject its heroin poison into their veins." He enjoyed trying to goad Curtiss and Keith, as usual this evening handcuffed and laying face down on the floor of their tent, tucked in for the night. "If anything proves the inferiority and barbarism of your western culture, that one fact does. It is just a matter of time before you destroy yourselves."

Getting no reaction from either of them, the American al-Qaeda said, "Spring has sprung, Yankees," and turned to leave. Sliding his clipboard under his arm as he did so, he knocked the Bic ballpoint pen from the clip. It landed directly between Curtiss and Keith, who waited until the tent flap closed after him and then blew dirt over the pen until it was no longer visible.

"A guy like that has got to really tick you off, eh Curt?" Keith murmured. "Yeah. Takes everything your country has offered him, then turns around and betrays you by joining with your worst enemy."

As Curtiss told Keith of the threat embedded in the American al-Qaeda's reference to spring, explaining the impending return of the Arab and all that would entail, the American al-Qaeda suddenly reappeared, throwing open their tent flap and searching the dirt with his flashlight for his missing pen. Muttering under his breath, he finally gave it up and withdrew. Curtiss and Keith smiled to each other, their few remaining teeth a soft glow in the dark, and fell asleep face down in the dirt.

Curtiss woke before Keith early the next morning and worked through his predicament. He regretted having helped the locals with their farm equipment, now realizing that some of it would certainly be used to produce opium and thereby help the enemy's war effort. It was time to make his escape, but Curtiss had no idea where he was and accepted that he would have to trust Keith with his life to do it.

Escape was also on the mind of the big Aussie when he woke up. "We've got to find a way out of here before that Arab comes back, mate." Together they formed their escape plan.

Keith had studied maps of the area as part of his mission and believed that he knew approximately where they were and the way to the Panj River—their only conceivable way out and to coalition forces. That night Keith would feign illness and Curtiss would ask the guard to take Keith to the latrine. When he undid his hands, Keith would disable the guard, release Curtiss, and the two of them would take what they needed and sneak out of camp.

"Let's just hope the guard hasn't seen too many Hollywood movies, because that's a pretty predictable plan," Keith joked.

When the guard released them that morning, Curtiss stumbled as he stood up and snatched the pen from the dirt as he caught himself, and then hid it in his clothes.

Some time after midnight, when the guard made a routine check on their tent, Curtiss told the guard in Pashto that his moaning fellow prisoner was about to stink up the tent and needed to use the latrine. The sleepy guard swung his AK-47 rifle behind his back so he could squat down and free Keith's hands. By the time he had stood up and begun bringing his rifle around, he found Keith standing right in front of him, smiling. Keith's uppercut crackled the man's jawbone like snapped kindling; out on his feet, he was relieved of his rifle by Keith and then allowed to drop face-first to the dirt. Keith then flipped the rifle around and drove the butt into the base of the guard's skull, killing him. They were committed.

After freeing Curtiss, the two men rifled through the guard's pockets for anything useful, stripped him of his coat, boots, and gloves, and dragged his body to the wall of the tent, hiding it under straw mats. They ran from tent to tent until they stood next to the last one, at the camp's edge. Before they could catch their breath, the tent flap was flung open by a man holding a flashlight in one hand and a wad of newspaper strips to be used for toilet paper in the other.

It was the American al-Qaeda.

Startled into incomprehension at finding Curtiss standing before him, he froze in place long enough for Curtiss to draw the Bic pen from his clothing and jam it deep into his eye socket. Before he could shout out, Keith was upon him. One large, meaty hand gripped over the American al-Qaeda's mouth, he pulled him to his chest, lifted him off the ground and wrenched his head around one hundred-eighty degrees. More shattered kindling, this time a violently snapped cervical spine accompanied by a grotesquely dislocated jaw.

"C4 Breath no more," Keith whispered. The American al-Qaeda was dead.

Keith carried him into the tent under his arm like a life-sized rag doll and together they stripped him of his jacket and boots, laid him in his cot, and covered him with a blanket. Keith collected the flashlight and weapons while Curtiss removed a stack of journals that the American al-Qaeda kept in a wooden crate next to a folding table and chair, and stuffed them into a pillowcase.

Twenty minutes later they crested a ridge and took a final look back at the camp to see if they were being followed. They weren't. Keith showed Curtiss how to fashion backpacks out of the extra coats, and they began hiking into the mountains by moonlight.

Keith demonstrated remarkable skill maintaining his bearings through mountains that, after their first day on the run, all looked the same to Curtiss. He kept them to goat trails, veering off them at the first sign of pack-animal dung and frequently stopping to cover their tracks. In ill-fitting boots, sustained only by snowmelt and a few pieces of flat bread that they'd found in the guard's pocket and the American al-Qaeda's tent, they trudged up and down a seemingly endless series of slopes and passes. Though physically depleted, Curtiss was determined to keep up with Keith, who was setting an athlete's pace.

Toward the end of the third day, as the temperature began to drop in preparation for nightfall, Curtiss looked around while pausing to catch his breath. "This pass looks familiar. I'm sure I've been here before."

A short while later they caught sight of the whitewater of a river at the bottom of a valley. "That has got to be the Panj down there," Keith said.

* * *

Curtiss luxuriated in the weight of the beef stew MRE in his stomach and the heat from the fire inside the cave penetrating his entire body. Coffee topped off what was by far the best meal he had ever eaten.

An hour earlier he had led Keith to the cave where he, Rambo, and the SAD team had stashed their excess supplies six months earlier. After eating their fill, the men took antibiotics that they found within a medical kit, cleaned themselves using a dozen packets of pre-moistened disposable wipes, changed into fresh clothing, slid into sleeping bags, and fell asleep.

The next morning over sausage, biscuits, and gravy, they decided to spend at least two days in the cave building up their strength before heading down to the river. During their downtime, Keith explained that he was with Australia's Special Air Service Regiment, deployed to Afghanistan with Operation Slipper to provide intelligence on al-Qaeda and Taliban locations. Their airdrop went awry, and he and his two fellow soldiers got separated from their team.

"Yeah, and the next thing we knew me and my two mates were trapped in a gulley. No way out except up, and those al-Qaeda bastards had the high ground." He described the torture and execution of his two fellow soldiers after they were captured. The anger had gone from Keith's eyes, replaced by grief. "Live by the sword, I guess . . . "

"Well, the power of the pen works all right for me," Curtiss said, risking the joke.

Keith burst out laughing. "Yeah, you sure dotted that al-Qaeda's eye, didn't you, Curt," he said, slapping him on his knee. "I'd bet that you're not regular army. Or special forces, or even military at all." He squinted into Curtiss's eyes. "One of the intelligence services. Yeah. CIA, I'd guess."

"That's right, keep guessing," Curtiss said with a smile. "It's not that complicated, really. We had just called in an air strike on an al-Qaeda camp. There were two of us on our way out of Afghanistan and local guides gave us up to the enemy." Curtiss was not yet ready to talk about what happened to Rambo, and Keith had the good grace not to press for the fate of his companion.

"Special Air Service Regiment," Curtiss said, nodding his head. "So that's where you learned all those survival skills. I thought it might have been . . . you know . . . living with the Australian Aborigines in the outback, or something."

"Every Aussie is Crocodile Dundee to you Yanks."

The men discussed their route home. The river was swollen with snowmelt and so was navigable for the inflatable boat that Curtiss and his team had brought with them. The plan was to simply float down the river until they reached coalition forces, while avoiding locals along the way. They would travel four hours each day: two during the pre-dawn hours, and two during the early evening—river conditions permitting. They would get off the river and stay out of sight the rest of the time.

Curtiss's chronic cough—most likely a symptom of the al-Qaeda camp's mysterious respiratory illness—abated, and the sores that had developed in his mouth began to heal, within two days of starting the antibiotics regime. It took three days for his digestive system to adjust to high-calorie, high-protein food again, and for his urine to return to a healthy color. But the sudden rush of nutrients into his system seemed to make his hands worse, not better, and they began throbbing with pain. He took this as a sign that, with the right nutrients available, his damaged nerves were beginning to regenerate. He knew that Keith was ready to go by the end of the second day, but that Keith was aware that Curtiss was in much worse shape than he was, and never said a word about leaving.

Over dinner on the third day Curtiss said, "If you feel up to it, Keith, we can get started tomorrow."

He looked Curtiss over from head to toe. "Yeah, mate. All right. We'll pack up tonight."

The last thing Curtiss did that night was to stuff the pillowcase holding the journals that he had taken from the American al-Qaeda's tent into a waterproof bag and shove it deep into his backpack.

Two hours before dawn the next morning, they set off down the slopes to the river. The food and rest made Curtiss feel more like his old self and the prospect of getting home soon fired him with renewed energy. Once at the river, they inflated the boat and pushed off from shore, staying close to the banks so as not to get swept into the whitewater in the center. They made good time, then landed just before dawn and concealed the boat and themselves. It was Curtiss's turn to sleep and Keith's to keep watch. In this way, rafting for two hours at a time and taking turns sleeping and standing guard, they made their way down the Panj River.

Just after sunset of their third day on the river, Curtiss and Keith caught sight of a pair of Black Hawk helicopters that appeared to be descending for a landing behind some distant hills. They landed the boat, donned their backpacks and set off on foot through the gathering dark toward the helicopters.

"Damn, it's been two hours now. I'm sure we were headed in the right direction—" Keith was saying just before tracer bullets whizzed by over their heads, sending them diving for cover behind rocks.

Curtiss couldn't make out what was then said over a loudspeaker—garbled Pashto—but he was certain that it was coming from a coalition force translator. "It's the good guys, Keith." Both men stood with their hands up for a good ten minutes until six soldiers wearing night vision equipment emerged from the darkness.

"We're Americans!" Curtiss shouted.

"Speak for yourself, mate," Keith said, and both men began to laugh.

"Drop your weapons. Down on the ground!"

They complied, but continued to laugh uncontrollably.

After another half-hour's hike they arrived at a U.S. base that was no more than a collection of sandbagged bunkers on a ridge. A senior officer confirmed that they were both on MIA lists and Curtiss made a satellite phone call to The Company's emergency number that he had memorized years before.

Within the hour, Curtiss and Keith were airborne on U.S. Army helicopters bound for Bagram Airbase, where Army doctors examined them and recommended that they both be flown to hospitals outside the country. But Keith insisted on immediately rejoining the Australian Defense Forces at Camp Rhino.

"I'm all right," Keith said to Curtiss, who was sitting atop a gurney in a medical tent receiving intravenous therapy. "But you'd better have those hands looked after if you are planning to do any work on that boat of yours. I need to see about getting word back to my two mates' families."

"See if you can't get an air strike on that camp while you're at it," Curtiss said, shaking Keith's hand.

"You can count on it."

CHAPTER 19

"Come on, Curt. Squeeze. Give it all you got."

Curtiss did, and the Guam Naval Hospital physical therapist made a note of the squeeze gauge's reading on his chart. After examining Curtiss's still swollen and discolored fingertips, he informed him that the doctor would be in to see him later that day.

While the therapist was packing up his medical cart, a man and woman entered the room, stood by the doorway without speaking and waited for his therapist to leave.

"Hello Agent Bradley." Curtiss hadn't been called by his agent's title in more than four years. He was surprised by the pleasure he took in hearing the words, like slipping on a pair of blue jeans that he hadn't worn for a long time and discovering that they still fit him. "I'm Agent McPherson and this is Agent Tula. We understand that you have something for us."

Curtiss gestured to the grimy, stained pillowcase on the chair beside his bed. "These are the journals of a Middle-Eastern or maybe North African-American who was at an al-Qaeda camp in Northern Afghanistan." He spent the next hour giving a detailed description of the LA-raised UCLA EE graduate; the Arab, his entourage and the license plate number from one of the Toyota Land Cruisers; Keith's best estimate of the camp's location on the Afghanistan grid the day they escaped; and details of all relevant events that had occurred since October 2001—including the execution of Agent Rambo Zhang.

Early the next morning, a nurse entered his room and announced with a warm smile that he had two visitors. Leah then walked through the doorway holding the hand of their son, who waddled in beside her, taking big, tenuous steps.

"There's your daddy, Conner," Leah said in a sweet tone, her voice hoarse.

Tears flooded Curtiss's eyes at the sight of his wife and son, who was now old enough to walk and talk with his mother. Conner would not know his pain of growing up with out a father.

He swung his legs out of bed, squatted on the floor and opened his arms. Conner toddled doggedly toward him a few steps, then drew up short and began to cry at the sight of his father's broad, toothless grin. Leah cupped her hand over her mouth to hold back a laugh, or perhaps to stifle a sob at the thought of what Curtiss might have gone through. Likely both, he decided.

The family spent the rest of the morning strolling among the tropical flowers and swaying palms of the hospital grounds. The Company had moved Leah and Conner to Hong Kong a week after Curtiss had been reported missing, where she continued to work while her cousin from Beijing helped her look after their boy. Until two days earlier, Leah had not known whether Curtiss was alive or dead. She did not burden him with any of the agony she had endured over the past six months. And he did the same for her.

"The doctors want me to stay here for a full week," Curtiss said as his son slept in his arms. "After that I've been asked to go back to Hong Kong to take care of some unfinished business."

Leah had a talent for articulating through an artful synchrony of silence and body language: an inscrutable look; a flick of her hair; turning her back, then dramatically swinging her body around again. This time, though, she did not require Curtiss to decode her signals. Wearing a look of steely determination as she took their son from his arms, she said, "While you are finishing that up, I can finish up a project for one of my clients and prepare for our move back to Christchurch." She said this resolutely, as if to imply that they were in complete agreement that the family plan was to move back to New Zealand and resume their life there.

* * *

It was Curtiss's turn to carry Conner and pace the airplane floor during their overnight flight from Guam to Hong Kong. Leah tapped away at her laptop while Curtiss once again tongued a new set of prosthetic teeth. The sensation seemed stranger to him than when he had left the Snake Street dentist office in Taiwan with his first set of new front teeth—perhaps since the teeth they replaced were missing for much longer the second time.

Back in Hong Kong the next day, Leah was out shopping and her cousin was napping with Conner in the bedroom when Curtiss stared out the window of their Admiralty serviced apartment. Having escaped from six months' imprisonment in the mountains of Afghanistan, he felt—as he had upon his arrival in Hong Kong from China back in 1989—like a primitive entering a technically advanced alien world.

Wilkenson had briefly spoken with Curtiss by phone while he was in Guam and requested that he come to The Lowu House after he arrived in Hong Kong. He claimed to have something important to discuss with him. Curtiss knew that Wilkenson was far more likely to ask him to permanently rejoin The Company than to shake his hand and wish him well with his charter sport fishing business. But Leah's continued silence on the subject doused any plans he might have entertained beyond collecting his final paycheck at The Lowu House.

The house's exterior had been significantly spruced up and now had a new addition jutting out one side. Several black Mercedes with Chinese flags on posts mounted on their front bumpers filled a new semi-circular driveway. Curtiss did not recognize anyone at The Lowu House, but the place was, unlike in 1998, abuzz with people and activity.

Wilkenson's executive assistant escorted him into his second-floor office.

"Curtiss." Wilkenson jumped to his feet, came out from behind his desk and offered his hand. "You look good," he said, while carefully eying him from top to bottom.

"Hello Ken." Curtiss cringed at hearing himself utter those two words again in The Lowu House. He'd already quit on this boss once. What peculiar fate was it that required him to do it a second time?

They took a seat on the office's sofa and Wilkenson slid back into his old ways. "Curtiss . . . " he announced, pausing momentarily for dramatic effect, "the Station Chief job for Hong Kong and Taiwan is open to you if you want it." Smiling a good deal too happily than the occasion warranted, he added, "You'd report to me just like before."

"Leah and I have discussed it, Ken. We're planning to return to Christchurch at the end of the week."

"You might want to postpone those plans for a little while—at least for yourself. There will be a memorial service for Agent Zhang, at Langley," Wilkenson said, carefully studying Curtiss's expression. "Rambo's wife and daughter now live in Reston, Virginia."

The image of Rambo reaching out to Curtiss in his final moment on earth, with a plea for his family, struck Curtiss in the chest like a sledgehammer. Rambo's wife would still have a husband and their child a father if not for Curtiss.

"The Company jet leaves tomorrow and would have us there in time for the ceremony," Wilkenson said.

"Of course I'll go, Ken."

"Good. Now follow me. I have something to show you," Wilkenson said, as if yanking on a hook that he was convinced he had sunk into Curtiss.

The two men walked to the third floor, stopping short of the familiar conference room door at the end of the hallway. They stepped through another door that took them into an observation room: behind the one-way mirror.

"The Americans are our guys, of course," Wilkenson said, in reference to the people seated at the conference table, facing the mirror. "The ones in Chinese military uniforms are senior officials with one of China's anti-terrorism organizations."

Curtiss felt uneasy to see Chinese military officers in The Lowu House, but the intelligence world had radically changed since 9/11, let alone 1998. "The enemy of my enemy . . ." he said.

"Precisely. Anti-terrorism is just about all we do now at The Lowu House." Wilkenson explained that China had liaisons stationed there on a permanent basis and that what he was seeing was a monthly senior-level meeting, where both sides shared top-level anti-terrorist intelligence. "We give them what they need to know about what's happening outside of China—in places like Afghanistan and Pakistan—and they tell us what is happening with Islamic terrorists within China, mainly with Uyghurs in their Xinjiang Region, but elsewhere, too."

Wilkenson's bookish English-Mandarin translator slipped into the observation room with them about the time the people in the conference room began packing up their briefcases. "Time to introduce you to our new friends, Curtiss," Wilkenson said, as he gestured for his translator to open the door into the conference room for them.

"Gentlemen, this is Agent Curtiss Bradley." Wilkenson's translator quickly followed with a Hong Kong-accented Mandarin translation. "He is the agent that I told you about. The one with first-hand combat experience with al-Qaeda and Uyghurs in Afghanistan." Wilkenson looked smugly at Curtiss, fairly hemorrhaging personal satisfaction at having his trophy agent back on his team.

The highest-ranking Chinese officer was a tall man with stark white hair cropped to a flattop, and they recognized each other the moment Curtiss entered the room: it was the White General. His expression was reminiscent of the one he had worn on the Shenzhen docks nearly a decade and a half ago. Curtiss was surprised that he would remember him—one single victim among many—but then again, how many foreigners had he put a contract out on during his career? Curtiss held his stare, while both men decided how to react to their awkward meeting.

What a crafty one this White General was. Gun- and Afghan opium-running, money laundering, and who knows what else—all while in uniform, no less—and yet here he was in charge of one of China's anti-terrorism intelligence services. Curtiss toyed with the possibility that what they'd both been involved in on that night on the Shenzhen docks was part of what made them effective at their jobs now.

"Ni Hao," Curtiss said, offering the White General his hand.

The White General cracked a wrinkled smile that nearly closed his cataract-fogged eyes. His grip as he shook Curtiss's hand was weak. Though Curtiss was sure that he was still quite lethal, the years had turned the White General into a physically frail old man.

Curtiss and Wilkenson took a seat in the third-floor conference room after everyone else had cleared out. Wilkenson went back to sizing him up. "It is a different world now, Curtiss," he said, "and you have unique skills and abilities that America needs in the war on terror. The Section Chief job will keep you out of the field."

Curtiss sat silently, meditating on his latest fork in the road.

"The plane for Langley leaves at nine tomorrow morning."

* * *

Rambo's wife was dressed in black. She sat together with several other widows in the front row of chairs that were set up in the hall at CIA headquarters, where the memorial wall held anonymous stars commemorating CIA agents who had died in the course of their duties.

The Director personally officiated the ceremony for fallen officers, which consisted of several prepared speeches, followed by blank entries being made in the Book of Honor and concluded with the placement of a star on the wall. Curtiss felt it strange when he heard the Director announce the name Zhang XiaoQi, Rambo's real name. He would always be Rambo to him.

After the ceremony, Rambo's wife walked over to Curtiss. "I recognized you from photographs that XiaoQi had shown me," she said to Curtiss in Mandarin. "He spoke very highly of you and considered you more than a colleague. You were his friend." Curtiss expressed his condolences to Mrs. Zhang and she invited him home for tea.

Their modest home was filled with memorabilia from their lives in China and their new lives as Americans. Both of their U.S. citizenship naturalization certificates were hung prominently on the wall in frames. Curtiss told her about Rambo's acts of heroism, not only in Afghanistan, but on other occasions when they worked together during the early 1990s. And how he died with dignity, engaged in fierce battle with the enemy.

"Your husband was an idealistic man with deep convictions about right and wrong. Everyone admired his sense of personal responsibility for doing the right thing. He had a big influence on me in that way. He died fighting for those beliefs." Curtiss had to stop, choked up as Mrs. Zhang rocked her baby daughter in her arms, quietly shedding tears. "His final thoughts were of you and your daughter."

Curtiss watched from behind the steering wheel of his rental car as

Mrs. Zhang solemnly waved goodbye before closing the front door of her house—one of many American homes where families would have to find a way to go on living without a loved one lost to the war on terror. Would he give cause for Leah and Conner to attend such a ceremony, should he rejoin The Company?

There wasn't a Company jet scheduled to return to East Asia for another week, so Curtiss drove to the airport to board a commercial flight back to Hong Kong. When he saw the exit sign for Washington Dulles International Airport, it occurred to him that it was the first time since 1988 that he had been in the United States. He drove past the airport exit.

He saw the sign for US-15 North: one of the arteries that fed into Harrisburg and, ultimately, Hershey, Pennsylvania. He instinctively veered north, like a salmon heading upriver.

The town of Hershey PA was remarkably unchanged, even after more than fifteen years. He cruised slowly down its main drag and rolled down the windows as he passed the chocolate factory, allowing the heavy, sweet aroma of chocolate to fill the car.

Heading out of town, Curtiss eventually found himself on I-70 west. West—that was all the direction he needed for now.

After nearly two hours on the road, he saw signs for the exit to Shanksville and thought of the thirty-three passengers and seven crew—the heroes of Flight 93—who revolted against their hijackers on 9/11. He thought about the courage of those people, living their everyday lives, then having to suddenly face the horrifying menace of suicidal terrorists with only minutes to make life-and-death decisions. He saw their plane meeting the peaceful, tranquil fields of Pennsylvania at over 550 miles an hour. He'd read in a report that the County Coroner was only able to find a single identifiable body part—five vertebrae—and that less than ten percent of the total body weight of all aboard was ever found.

Knuckles white on the wheel, he took the Shanksville exit.

Curtiss's rage subsided into profound sadness as he stood by his car on a hill overlooking Stoneycreek and the temporary memorial there to Flight 93's victims. He watched people lay flowers and wreaths against the forty-foot chain-link fence, and hang photos of lost family and friends upon it, and light candles. The last of the mourners left just after sunset, the sturdier among them escorting the tearful and overwhelmed to their cars.

It was around 10:00 pm when he stopped for gas and caught himself dozing while the attendant filled his gas tank. Fifteen minutes later, Curtiss collapsed into a motel bed and fell asleep. When he found himself wide awake in the darkness of the motel room, he looked over at the clock radio: 2:00 am. He picked up his cell phone and called Leah.

"Curt, where are you? The East Coast, right? It's got to be two in the morning there now. Still jet lagged?"

"Yeah. I don't know where I am. Somewhere in western Pennsylvania, maybe eastern Ohio."

Silence. Leah of course knew that western Pennsylvania was not on the way home. So what the hell was he doing there?

"I'm going to be a little late getting back."

Leah's continued silence indicated that she was either extremely angry with him, or had intuited the emotions he might be dealing with after attending Rambo's funeral. She chose to share his burden, rather than add to it with the ranting of an outraged spouse. "We'll be here waiting for you."

Curtiss gave up trying to sleep and resumed his journey west. At dawn in the mountains of eastern Ohio, while crossing a high bridge over a river bisecting a gap between two sheer mountain cliffs animated by cascading morning fog, he thought of mornings at Lu's family home in Guizhou. He pressed on until the mountains turned to flat farmland.

When he reached Dayton, Ohio, he saw a sign for the National Museum of the U.S. Air Force. Researching his father's wartime exploits, Curtiss had learned that there was an exhibit and monument to the Doolittle Raiders there, and once again he pulled off the interstate.

At the museum, he marveled at the complete B-25 on display there, amazed that people had done what they'd done in those early 1940s flying machines.

He studied a wall of photos of the Raiders until he found one with his father, together with his fellow airmen, standing on the deck of the USS Hornet in front of their plane. They were young and smiling, apparently eager for their suicide mission to be the first to bomb targets in Japan.

Outside in Memorial Park, Curtiss fingered his father's name where it had been etched into the black stone monument dedicated to the Raiders. Sonya's words to him in the Chennault Pub from so many years ago returned to him: "The world you experienced, Curtiss, is your father's gift to you."

Curtiss never felt more connected to his father than he did at that very moment. But that powerful wave of love he felt reaching across the decades was accompanied by a profoundly unsettling question: What kind of world would he leave to Conner?

Back on the expressway, in the fog of his jet lag's wide-awake exhaustion, Curtiss drove forty-five of the fifty-five miles between Dayton and Cincinnati before he realized that he was on I-75 heading south.

It was early afternoon, when Curtiss finally needed to sleep again, so he decided to keep going to Cincinnati and stay there for the night. He fell asleep immediately after checking in to a hotel, but again found himself suddenly awake in a dark room. He pulled the window curtains aside to discover that this time he had awakened at an even more unreasonable hour than the night before: dusk.

Seeing that the lights were on at Cincinnati's Cinergy Field baseball stadium, and recognizing how dim his prospects for falling back asleep were, he got dressed and walked to the stadium to see the Cincinnati Reds play—the first baseball game he would see live since he and Jimmy Yamandakos had taken in a Yankees home game in 1987.

Curtiss so thoroughly enjoyed every aspect of that evening, from the clean geometry of the game itself to dining on ballpark hotdogs in paper trays and drinking ice-cold semi-flat beer out of large paper cups, that the next day he headed west again on I-70 and was by afternoon asking the clerk at his St. Louis hotel if the Cardinals were playing that night. They could just as easily have been on the road, of course, but he'd somehow known another game would be waiting for him that night.

When Curtiss pulled his compact economy car into an oversized space in the parking lot of Busch Stadium, he found himself flanked by a GMC Suburban SUV and a massive Ford F-350 four-door dual-rear-wheel pick-up truck. He supposed he'd noticed the prevalence of larger vehicles on the road, but here it was hammered home. It seemed to him that three out of four of the vehicles in the lot were either enormous SUVs or trucks of one sort or another. The tailgating experience was similarly super-sized: The food at U of M tailgate parties in the '80s had consisted of hibachi-burned hotdogs, Tupperware pasta salad, and bags of chips, but here he found himself wading through what felt like an endless field of full-scale backyard barbecues, complete with six-burner gas grills loaded with steaks, split chickens, ears of corn and foil-wrapped potatoes. Everything in America seemed bigger in 2002—including the people.

Next morning, Curtiss had breakfast on Styrofoam plates using plastic utensils at one of the new cookie-cutter nationwide hotel chains. While peeling an oversized muffin from its sealed plastic bag, he checked the sports section of the USA Today newspaper to see whether the Kansas City Royals were having a home game that day. They were.

The drive across the wide-open plains to Kansas City's Kauffman Stadium required two tanks of gas and four cups of tepid McDonald's drive-through coffee. The Royals lost the game that day.

The next morning, Curtiss realized that he'd reached the proverbial fork in the road. Should he continue due west to see the Colorado Rockies play, or north to the Minnesota Twins, or south to Houston to see the Astros? He let the nearest one having a home game decide. When he checked the paper he found Houston was.

The long drive to Houston rivaled the drive to Kansas City in degree of difficulty in staying alert and required six cups of coffee to fuel the journey. Curtiss found the oppressive heat and humidity in Houston's Minute Maid Park to be on par with that of Hong Kong summers and hardly noticed the eight large cups of beer going down during the game. The Astros won.

It was near midnight of the following day when Curtiss pulled over on I-10 in the Franklin Mountains overlooking Las Cruces, New Mexico to take in the night sky. The Milky Way was as impossibly clear and bright as it had been in the cold, winter nights at the al-Qaeda camp, and the stars as seemingly close at hand. The lights of Las Cruces flickered in the high-desert air as the rocky, scrub-covered terrain wept heat into the clear night sky. The full moon's rise revealed the Rio Grande river valley cradled below him between crumbly wash-scarred mountains. Just as in Afghanistan, Curtiss came down from the mountains to follow the river to civilization.

The next day, when the check-in clerk at the hotel asked Curtiss what had brought him to Phoenix, he explained to her his ballpark pilgrimage west. "I just wish Phoenix had a team."

The clerk blinked at him. "You're kidding, right?"

"Sorry?"

"Where the heck have you been the last five years? You seriously haven't heard of the Arizona Diamondbacks? They only won the World Series last year!"

They shared a laugh, and that night, Curtiss took in a Diamondbacks win in their massive, domed park in the desert.

Once he got out of the Phoenix area, I-8 stretched ahead of him as empty as the shucked McDonalds coffee cups now rolling around the passenger-side floor of his car. Where had he been the last five years? Indeed, where had he been for the past fifteen?

More importantly, what was he going to do with the next fifteen?

The Padres game was already into its second inning when Curtiss took his seat in San Diego's Qualcomm Stadium next to a group of five U.S. Marines, most likely from nearby Camp Pendleton. He couldn't help but overhear them discussing their deployment to Afghanistan. Curtiss ordered them a round of beer.

"Thank you, sir," one of them said as they all raised their cups to him.

"Were you in the service, sir?" asked another.

"I was a businessman in that part of the world at one time. But I know that you guys are doing one hell of a job over there."

One of the Marines explained that they were all from the same high school, had all enlisted at the same time right after 9/11, and were about to volunteer for a second tour of duty in Afghanistan. "We are good at what we do and like doing what we are good at," one of them explained.

Curtiss nodded. He wanted to say more, but was content to watch them enjoy the game and their camaraderie. He recognized Rambo's passion and commitment in their eyes and spirit.

After the Padres, his only choice was to head to LA to see the Dodgers play. The sight of boats tied up at the Oceanside Harbor

Marina while driving north along I-5 brought to mind his own boat in Lyttelton Harbour Marina on the other side of the Pacific Ocean in New Zealand. Leah had asked a family friend in Christchurch to look after *The Beast II* and his charter fishing business two months after he was reported missing in Afghanistan. Curtiss felt a stab of longing for days spent on the water, and for the quiet comfort of his family's life in Christchurch.

He arrived in Los Angeles several hours early for the game, so drove around the city until game time. Passing by the Beverly Hills Hotel on Sunset Boulevard, Curtiss wondered if he could get an eggs Benedict there that was comparable to the Hong Kong Peninsula Hotel's. He decided to find out and made a U-turn. He discovered that the Polo Lounge's eggs Benedict was indeed very good, but he thought that the Peninsula's was better. That evening Curtiss didn't notice whether the Dodgers had won or not.

Next: The Giants. He took Highways 101 and 1 to San Francisco, where he discovered he'd need to wait two days for a game. Walking the city, the smell of Chinese food drew him into Chinatown, and to one particular Cantonese restaurant packed with Asians. Surely he could get an authentic dim sum there. He ordered his favorite items and slowly ate while reading an article in the *San Francisco Chronicle* sports section critical of the season the Giants were having.

When Curtiss looked up to acknowledge a server topping off his teacup, he saw a college-aged Asian woman with long dark hair and black-rimmed reading glasses having dim sum together with a pile of books. She smiled shyly when she noticed Curtiss watching her subconsciously whirling and flipping her pen as she read.

CHAPTER 20

Curtiss's key card no longer worked in the lock of his family's Hong Kong Admiralty serviced apartment, so he knocked on the door. Leah's cousin answered, her face opening up in surprise at finding her cousin's wayward husband standing there. Leah was out with a client, and Conner was taking a nap. Curtiss showered, then lay down with his son and stroked his hair while watching him sleep before falling asleep himself.

It was 9:30 pm when he awoke in his son's bed, just in time to commence another three-to-four-day jet-lag regimen. Leah's cousin was already asleep in the guest bedroom. Curtiss went to the kitchenette to boil water for a cup of tea. He heard the apartment's door lock bleep and Leah walked in. After a moment of stunned disbelief at finding him there, she threw herself into his arms.

"I'm sorry I wasn't here when you got home, Curt. I had a client dinner and—"

"It's okay. I didn't let you know when I was coming back. *I* didn't know when I was coming back. Besides, your work's important. It's what's keeping us going. We need you." Curtiss pulled back and looked deeply into her eyes. "*I* need you."

He made them both tea and they sat together on the living room sofa. After a disoriented silence, Leah traced her fingertips along one of his forearms. "Look at that tan," she said with a smile. "You spent that whole two weeks at the beach, didn't you?"

He smiled, then described for Leah what he had witnessed at Langley, what was said in Rambo's home, and what he had experienced on his drive across America. He spoke of his conviction that there were young people, some not even out of their teens, who should be cruising the main drags of their hometowns all across America and listening to their equivalents to the Beach Boys during their endless summers, the way he had. But they weren't. They were facing death at the hands of a fanatical enemy and under horrible conditions. And they volunteered for it.

He owed it to them, he said—owed it to them, and to Rambo, and to his father—to do what he could to stop the terrorists he knew were determined to strike again. And he owed it to Conner to help create a world that he could happily, safely grow up in.

"I have skills that can make a difference, Leah. I can't just sit on the sidelines. I have to put them to use," Curtiss said. "I've been asked to rejoin The Company, based in Hong Kong, as Section Chief for Hong Kong and Taiwan."

After a long, silent moment simply looking at him, his wife's beautiful, clear eyes pooled with tears. "Curt," Leah said in a broken voice, "I don't want our family to go though what we've been through this past year, ever again." She lifted her head and forced back tears, then sighed. She slid closer to him and took his hand in hers. "I've told you before, I'll support you if you are doing it for the right reasons. And what I'm hearing from you now are the right reasons, Curt."

She smiled a pained smile. "I love Christchurch, but I can work from anywhere and Hong Kong would be a far more convenient place, frankly. And having my cousin with us here in Hong Kong, and visiting my family in Beijing these past months, has shown me that Conner will need to be with the only extended family he has."

Curtiss understood how important extended family was for Chinese. And knew that Leah understood how important it was to him that Conner grew up with family, having never grown up with one himself.

Leah looked sternly at him and made him promise it would only be a desk job. "No more missions, or fieldwork, or whatever you call it." Then she heaved another sigh and smiled, looking relieved. "Besides, if I have choke down one more meal at that all-you-can-eat Chinese buffet à la New Zealand, I'll go mad."

*   *   *

When Curtiss arrived at The Lowu House third-floor conference room for their meeting, he found Wilkenson sitting with two copies of an employment contract and a confidentiality agreement laid neatly before him on the conference table.

"Welcome back, Curtiss," Wilkenson said, smiling smugly.

Curtiss steeled himself for Wilkenson's obligatory preamble.

"We are what we are, Curtiss," he said on cue, flicking the pen in his hand. "People can't escape their destiny—"

"I've always believed that we make our own destiny, Ken," Curtiss interrupted. He went on to explain his reasons for deciding to rejoin The Company, concluding with, "I'm here because my country needs me."

The observation-room mirror on the wall behind Wilkenson suddenly flexed and vibrated as if someone had opened the door to the observation room behind it. Wilkenson, who'd been glaring at Curtiss, visibly displeased at having his prepared remarks obviated, noticed the shift in his gaze. He looked back over his shoulder at the mirror, then turned back with a new, tense expression.

A moment later the conference room door opened and Sonya walked in, with an aide's assistance.

"Now you are starting to sound like your father," Sonya said to Curtiss, through her warm smile.

Wilkenson shot to his feet and pulled out a chair for Sonya, who slowly eased into it. She thanked him.

Sonya? Ken? My father? Curtiss was dumbfounded by this collision of three of his seemingly unrelated worlds. Sonya smiled again, seeming to enjoying his astonishment.

"I suppose you are wondering what I am doing here?" She made a gesture to her aide as though lifting a cup to her lips, and he rushed off to fetch her tea. Then Sonya smiled at Curtiss again. "I am the Agency's Asia Region Chief emeritus."

Here Sonya painted her story in only the broadest of strokes, but later Curtiss would learn that she was regarded as the covert Grand Dame of the spy business in the Asia region. She had made one of the early contacts with Communist China on behalf of the United States at the end of the 1960s, accompanied Secretary of State

Kissinger to China for his secret talks there in 1971, and advised on the drafting of the Shanghai Communiqué issued during President Nixon's much-publicized 1972 China trip. After the U.S. and China normalized relations in 1979, she was the top covert agent in the region. She became influential with a number of senators and congressmen, and continued to counsel the Senate Committee on Foreign Relations and various national security committees. Her emeritus status actually afforded her more prominence in Washington, since—untethered by the executive entanglements of budgets, acquiring resources and such—her opinions were viewed as being free from bureaucratic self-interest and the influence of Washington politics. Senators and Congressmen knew that they could count on getting the straight story from Sonya.

"You see," Sonya said, "Frank was an Air Force pilot for most of the war, but was recruited into the U.S. Military Intelligence Service as a G2 officer before the war ended. Knowing all his contacts socially, when he passed away, I simply picked up where he left off—but working for the CIA. And after that, with the help of some friends in Washington . . . " Sonya concluded with a nonchalant shrug.

"You knew my father?"

"I knew him well, Curtiss." She expressed her shock when Curtiss had stumbled into her Taipei headquarters at the General Chennault Pub—after their chance encounter at the airport—and happened to announce that his father was William Bradley, who'd flown on the Doolittle Raid. She wasn't 100% convinced at first, not until after she had gotten his passport number from Taiwan Immigration and checked on him back in Washington.

After arriving in Kunming following the Doolittle Raid, his father became part of Sonya's gang of Flying Tigers. "Your father Will was dear friend and a wonderful man. And he fit right in with us misfits there in Kunming." She paused to sip her tea and to allow Curtiss time to grasp what she was telling him. "You are just like him, you know."

Sonya's words filled Curtiss with an overwhelming sense of gratification and absolution.

"Ken may be right about destiny," Sonya said with a smile. "And we take care of our own in the services. So there was Will Bradley's kid, dragging himself through the gutter in Taipei. Well, I couldn't just let you stay there." She explained that she had asked Lu to pull him out, to take him under his wing and familiarize him with the way things worked in that part of the world. "To see if you were made from the same cloth as your father."

So it was Lu who had arranged for the Mystery Caller to call him those evenings in George's presidential suite, gain his trust and talk him into going to Lu's Yang Ming Shan Taipei house that first time. "So . . . Lu is with The Company?"

"Not exactly." When he escaped to Hong Kong during China's Cultural Revolution, Lu was recruited out of Rennie's Mill by the Taiwan intelligence services, which regularly collaborated with The Agency. He operated under deep cover as a gray-market smuggler, which gave him access to both sides of the border. "But it was bad luck that you got mixed up with the White General the way that you did. I was ready to pull you out right then and there, but Lu thought that living in China's countryside in Guizhou would be a good experience for you."

"What about Gabriel Zuckerman there in Guizhou? Is he—"

"Oh, no. He's the genuine article. We have been keeping an eye on him, but he is harmless. He's a draft dodger, but worse for him is that he hasn't filed a tax return since 1965 and so can't return to the U.S. without being arrested for tax evasion. And you know how vicious the IRS can be with tax dodgers," Sonya said with a sardonic smile. "Lu kept tabs on your development while you were in Guizhou. We thought we'd lost you there in Beijing in Tiananmen Square in '89, but then you turned up at the Consulate in Hong Kong. It was then that I decided to have Ken bring you in."

All at once, Curtiss recognized Sonya's hand in his life from the moment he'd arrived in Asia. It was she who'd been pulling his strings from behind the one-way mirror all along. She'd used her influence to have prosecutors hold his indictment in New York. And she'd always been there for him: rescuing him from Taiwan customs, soothing his disappointments over breakfast at the Hong Kong Peninsula Hotel, or kissing his cheek for good luck in the restaurant of the Macau Lisboa Hotel before he took the SAD team into China and Afghanistan.

"I was preparing for my complete retirement at the end of 2001, but 9/11 put those plans on hold." It was her health. She was not well and medical complications were making it difficult for her to travel and do the other things that she used to do.

It was her opinion that he now knew the field as well as any career field agent. He had first-hand experience on the ground in China and with the Agency's new priority threat: Islamic terrorists in Afghanistan and around the region. In her view, the Agency had enough Ivy League-pedigreed armchair bureaucrats making life and death decisions for their people.

"The intelligence services were born in the field, Curtiss. After the Second World War there was hardly an agent who didn't have field experience." Sonya paused again to sip her tea, then went on.

She was convinced that the spy business is a people business and his compassion and empathy for people were essential elements to success. "By volunteering to go back into the service of your country—for all the right reasons—you've convinced me that your heart is now in it and that you are the right man for a bigger role than Station Chief for Hong Kong and Taiwan."

Throughout Sonya's monologue, Wilkenson had remained rigidly watchful. Now, however, he could hold himself still no longer: his cheek began twitching and he fidgeted with his pen.

"And I will be making just that case in Langley when I am there next week. I'll be suggesting to my friends in Washington that you replace the current East Asia Region Head when he rotates back to Langley the beginning of next year."

Sonya turned to Wilkenson, whose pen got away from him, tumbling to the floor. She paused as if to wait for him to pick it up. He didn't. "Ken, as the Greater China Region Station Chief, if you are comfortable reporting to Curtiss, that's fine. However, if you would prefer a transfer elsewhere, I understand. And I can be of assistance to you with that."

Wilkenson had nothing to say.

CHAPTER 21

January 2006 was an exceptionally cold month in St. Petersburg. Though Curtiss was wearing warm gloves, the Russian winter bothered his hands nevertheless. Standing in the Russian Orthodox cemetery for Sonya's funeral, he managed to discreetly exercise and massage his hands the way the physical therapist in Guam had taught him too.

Sonya's casket was draped in three flags: the United States', the Russian Federation's, and one bearing the coat of arms of one of the branches of the Romanov family. A representative from the Russian Federation's diplomatic corps read aloud an official government statement apologizing for injustices carried out against her family during the Russian revolution, and the Deputy Director of the CIA Bart Winston gave the eulogy to the somber crowd of mostly elderly people. This was followed by a Russian Orthodox ceremony officiated by black-robed, white-bearded priests wearing stovepipe hats. The funeral concluded with a rifle salute given by a U.S. Marine rifle party that had been flown in from the American embassy in Moscow for the occasion.

Sonya's casket was lowered into her grave among the other members of her extended family, whose bodies had also been brought back to be buried together in the St. Petersburg cemetery for former Russian aristocracy. Sonya's family had been scattered across the globe by the hardships of twentieth-century Russian life, only to be reunited in death in the twenty-first.

The next day Curtiss and Deputy Director Winston used the

opportunity of being in the same city to hold a briefing on East Asian developments, but spent most of their time together talking about the profound influence that Sonya had had on their lives. On their way to the airport together, Curtiss learned that she had recruited him into The Company, too, though not surreptitiously.

"She changed the direction of my career and my life," Deputy Director Winston said in wonderment. "It was at a diplomatic ball and she convinced me on the spot that my military career meant that I would always be preparing for something—the possibility of war—but that in the CIA I would actually be doing something every day." He smiled, a reverent expression on his face.

"Yes, she was a very persuasive woman. A visionary."

"She had a gift for reading people," Winston said while staring out the window.

Curtiss had heard through the grapevine that Bart Winston was one of those who would be considered for promotion to Director of the CIA, should a President decide to promote from within. In which case Curtiss could add one more qualification to Sonya's known repertoire: kingmaker.

He flew west, back to Washington, and Curtiss flew east, back to Hong Kong.

Among Sonya's many gifts to him, there was none he was more grateful for than introducing him to his father. As Curtiss watched in heated comfort the snow-covered Himalayan peaks crawling beneath the wing of his airplane, he conjured up images of his father and his compatriots flying the *Aluminum Trail* below him—so called because 700 planes were lost flying the Hump during the war. Young men, in their early twenties, dressed in thick sheep's wool and leather clothing inside their C-46 Curtiss Commando as it lumbered over and between the peaks at a mere two hundred miles per hour. The hardships of the Doolittle Raid and being on the run in China would have toughened his father for flying the *Skyway to Hell*. Still, having experienced battle himself, Curtiss understood that fear and apprehension would have been his father's constant companion onboard.

If he were still alive, his father would have been only a few years older than Sonya.

* * *

"Welcome home, Mr. Bradley," his driver said as he took Curtiss's bag from his hand and led him to his car at the Hong Kong airport pick-up area.

In the car, the driver smiled at him in the rearview mirror and brought him up to date: Conner had attended his first day of elementary school the day before, and had seemed to like it; their housekeeper had returned to the Philippines while he was gone, so he and Leah would be interviewing replacement candidates in the morning; and Leah had a special family dinner planned for that evening. "Oh, and she asked me to remind you not to make plans for tomorrow night: you will attend that Save The Children event."

Curtiss nodded his thanks for the update, then shook his head at his hand-held device as it began downloading the dozens of messages that had accumulated over his twelve-hour flight—a good many of them flagged urgent. It didn't stop downloading until his car cleared the Tsing Ma Bridge. He closed his eyes to the little screen, then raised them to once again appreciate Hong Kong's nighttime skyline glistening off the choppy waters of the harbor before he was drawn down from the bridge and into the evening traffic.

BOOK III: REVOLUTION

"I would remind you, that extremism in the defense of liberty is no vice...that moderation in the pursuit of justice is no virtue."—Barry Goldwater

CHAPTER 22

Each of the three volleys fired by the three-man rifle party tolled Curtiss's central nervous system like struck tubular bells. He took the rolled-up funeral notice from his suit jacket pocket, and unfurled and reread it: Rick Nanna. Born: May 19, 1972. Died: May 22, 2020.

The Fort Yukon Police Officer who discovered Rick's partially eaten body on the porch of his house perched atop a cliff overlooking the Yukon River was also an ex-Army Ranger and decided to rule his death accidental—the result of an animal attack. But the words of Rick's suicide note were embossed on Curtiss's mind:

"Thirty years ago we fought to bring freedom to Kuwait. Twenty years ago we fought to keep our country free from foreign terrorists. But for the last ten years I've been unable to ensure freedom endured in my own country.

I don't know this country. No elections. The Constitution doesn't matter anymore. This is not the United States of America. It is a strange and hostile land where the people in charge have contempt for people like me, and the things I believe in. I don't want to live anywhere but in the America I once knew and loved. It is time for my story to come to an end."

It pained Curtiss to recollect how dejected Rick was two months earlier when bureaucrats in Washington D.C. decreed that his family's property deed would become a five-year government lease. Rick's house and the surrounding acreage had been in his family for three generations. "They have finally taken everything that matters from me," he said in a candid moment as the two of them sat on Rick's porch, drinking coffee and watching the early spring sunrise.

Curtiss and Rick had become good friends after Afghanistan and they met every year they could for a hunt here, or a hunt there: mostly Alaska and the Yukon, but also the occasional trip to places like Africa and even China. They did finally manage a hunt in western China for Marco Polo sheep. Over the years Curtiss learned from Rick how to move while blending in to the terrain, and hunt and shoot, and shoot well. And Curtiss always struggled to keep up with Rick, who, though younger than he, still never seemed to age.

Curtiss tried to do something for Rick at the Agency, but Rick only withdrew into his solitary lifestyle preferring to live, hunt, and fish in Alaska to living with people in the lower forty-eight who seemed hell-bent on fundamentally transforming America—even eventually his beloved Alaska. Curtiss supposed it was post-traumatic stress disorder at the beginning, but later, after Curtiss had returned to live in the United States in 2016, he too recognized the dramatically changed America that Rick lamented about. Things went from bad to worse for Rick with the U.S. Federal Government's legal seizure of his property after the United States signed on to the United Nations-sponsored environmental protection law that extended the Antarctic Treaty to the Arctic. The treaty meant that all lands and seas north of the Arctic Circle, which included vast tracts of land in the northern parts of Alaska, Canada, Scandinavia, and Russia, would, like the Antarctic, be used only for scientific research and as a wildlife sanctuary. Barring any unforeseen acceleration of the seizure process, his property lease would expire upon his death and the land be declared Arctic Wilderness under no national sovereignty. That he would be allowed to live on his land to the end of his days, but having had to auction off his prized Iditarod trail sled dog team and equipment to pay the first five-year lease and maintenance fee for the privilege proved the last straw for Rick.

The Antarctic-Arctic Treaty forbade Rick's body being buried in Alaska and his house had likely already been razed—wiping any trace of his existence there. At Curtiss's request Rick's body was being buried at a Revolutionary War-era military cemetery in the Blue Ridge Mountains.

Curtiss looked up from the funeral notice and around at the forlorn faces of the funeral party: excluding a small group of Rick's extended family, it was composed exclusively of people from the Agency. It tore at Curtiss to realize that they were a collection of colleagues who had been ostracized and forced into early retirement, and Curtiss stood together with them sharing their grief at watching one of their own being buried. Only Jake, the CIA shooting range Range Master and Curtiss were still employed at the Agency.

Director Winston was the last to speak at Rick's funeral service, and he and Curtiss were the only ones who knew that his death was by suicide. The once Deputy Director Bart Winston, when Curtiss had met him while attending Sonya's St. Petersburg funeral, had become Director Winston after having served as the head of the Agency from 2012 to 2016. He was fit, straight, and cleaver-jawed as ever, despite being in his sixties, and standing there in his Army military uniform he brought to mind the image of a portrait that Curtiss had once seen of General Pershing mounted on horseback: rugged, stalwart, and a pillar of strength.

When the funeral service ended Director Winston called Curtiss and their Agency colleagues together to invite everyone to his hunting lodge estate in Kentucky for an upland bird hunt.

* * *

The day after Rick's funeral Curtiss was due at a morning reading of Rick's last will and testament at a D.C. law office. As he pulled out of his driveway he realized the drive to the cemetery had drained his gas tank. There was just enough time to fill up and grab a quick bite to eat.

The gas pump handle clicked off at 18.2 gallons and $17.76. Inside the gas station's retro-1950s diner Curtiss wolfed down a donut in four bites, then dropped three quarters on the dining counter: one for the donut, one for the carryout coffee, and one for a tip. The waitress, dressed in a period white soda-shop uniform that had been worn too long and washed too many times, smiled gratefully at Curtiss when she picked up her tip.

The law firm was one of those owned by the Federal Government. Its lavish D.C. head office bore all the hallmarks of the wealth and power that government-owned enterprises enjoyed in the now fundamentally transformed America: oriental rugs in the reception area, and in the conference room, oak paneling, plush leather chairs plugged in around a massive wood conference table, and pictures of old English hunting scenes with inaccurate depictions of a horse's true gait.

Curtiss had met most of the members of Rick's family who were seated around the conference table: a brother who lived in Phoenix who had joined them on hunts before, his elderly mother who lived in Fairbanks, and a gathering of assorted cousins, all of whom Curtiss shared his condolences with there in the law office conference room.

After explaining the legalities of Rick's Alaska Yukon homestead being ceded under the Antarctic-Arctic Treaty, the lawyer reading the will went through the list of Rick's assets. Rick had amassed a respectable amount of physical gold holdings. But the 2018 law forbidding the hoarding of gold within the United States, which criminalized the use and transfer of monetary gold, meant that Rick's gold assets would be transferred to the Federal Reserve and exchanged for U.S. dollars at the government rate of $20.67 an ounce. He willed to his mother an acre vacant lot in a Dallas, Texas suburb that was left to him by an uncle: "Uncle Alan's Dallas land should have gone to you in the first place. I never had any use for it," he wrote in his will. The day before his suicide, Rick had sent a box containing his service medals, memorabilia, photos, and his Iditarod trophies to his mother. Rick's other possessions were auctioned off in Fort Yukon, a town upriver from Rick's house, and the proceeds equitably distributed amongst his family.

Rick had ordered that one of his possessions not be sold at auction: his Weatherby .30-378 rifle. Curtiss was bathed in kind looks from all eyes in the room as the lawyer read: "And to my dear friend Curtiss Bradley, I leave you The Beast. Curt: I've just had her rebarreled and cryo'd, and she's broken in. May it help you bring down the biggest and most dangerous game."

CHAPTER 23

Curtiss steadied himself on the railing to keep his thick wool socks from slipping on the polished wood stairs as he descended to the first floor of his five-bedroom Reston, Virginia house. The frostbite he'd suffered in Afghanistan bothered him more at night and he took to wearing wool socks to bed, and around the house. It seemed to help. He opened the door to the closet under the stairs, scanned his finger on his safe's Biometric lock, put his home defense pistol away, exchanging it for his carry pistol, and thirty-five dollars in cash in denominations of one and five dollar bills—enough carrying around cash for most of the week. He pulled his robe tight across his waist as he sat at his kitchen dining table to drink coffee and browse the morning's streaming video news clips on his tablet. A USN D.C. Update report about rumors of an upcoming leadership change at the CIA took Curtiss back to the day that Director Winston asked him to move to Langley.

"I need people around me I can trust," Director Winston said on their personal IP video call. "You haven't been contaminated by the D.C. mindset that has made its way into the Agency these days," he shared, while shaking his head in disgust. He went on about being pressured by the D.C. power structure to turn the Agency into a domestic spying machine: to spy on the American people. He bemoaned the younger generation's being in lockstep with it all. "They've been convinced that it's what's good for the country. But they don't know any better. I need your voice here because you of all people—with your years in China—know what can happen. I need someone around me who understands and who will help me resist the tide. We can't let the politicians turn the Agency into the KGB."

While running Asia for the Agency Curtiss had only periodically visited the U.S. in the course of his work and a couple of vacations, and hadn't really lived there since the 1980s. So when Curtiss and his family landed back in the U.S. in 2016, once the flurry of finding and moving into their new house and getting Conner settled in high school was over, after a short while he felt like an actor on stage where everyone but he had read the script. Leah found work right away with a D.C. private wealth management firm, one that served the rich and powerful political class there; wealth having dried up in the usual places like Wall Street, the industrial Midwest, and Silicon Valley.

It was only a matter of months before Curtiss, like Rick, concluded that he had arrived in a strange country. The American popular culture that had evolved while Curtiss was away for those thirty years was a powerful distraction that wasted the minds of a generation, maybe two, filling them with hollow entertainment rather than facts and information. Grievous ignorance about the ways of the world seemed to rule the day—even celebrated as a kind of 'new enlightenment' by the media, public school system, and the entertainment industry. It was no longer what or how much you knew, but the political correctness of one's opinion that was important. Whereas in China forty years earlier, when Deng Xiaoping's axiom that it *didn't matter what color the cat was as long as it caught mice* launched reformations that put China on a long road of economic and political liberalization, in 2016 America, the political color of the cat had become more important than its ability to catch mice.

When Director Winston was succeeded by a D.C. political operative shortly after Curtiss's repatriation the last of any kind of resistance to politicians' usurping the Agency fell away. A kind of political mania overtook the CIA that culminated in mass firings the day after the 2018 mid-term elections were postponed. The D.C. political elite swept out the dinosaurs, as they were called, and budget cuts to the CIA all but eliminated divisions like SAD. Remaining funds and resources were rolled up into domestic spying programs and Director Winston's worst nightmare for the Agency became a reality. Its focus shifted to the threat that Americans might pose to their government and it began keeping dossiers on citizens, so-called American malcontents who challenged the postponement of national elections and those who made constitutional legal challenges to sweeping legislation that dramatically increased the reach of the Federal Government bureaucracy. "This place is becoming more like China used to be every day," Curtiss would sometimes mutter under his breath after concluding another frustrating day at the office.

Dissident efforts failed, one after another, to reign in the Federal Government as its coils steadily grew and tightened around every aspect of American life. Curtiss was kept in a benign hold-for-retirement position owing to his age and seniority, but mostly to the personal intervention of Director Winston, who still held a little sway even after his retirement. But Curtiss had little to look forward to at the Agency. After the global economic crash of 2016 even government pensions were only promising to be paid out at twenty cents on the dollar.

Learning to cope with the fundamental transformations of American life, Sonya's teachings were never far from Curtiss's mind. There wasn't a day that went by that he wasn't recalling one of them or another. When many Americans eventually lost their sense of solidarity after 9/11, he was too far away to have noticed the queer dependency relationship that began to develop between large segments of American society and their Federal Government. At the time Curtiss gave insufficient credence to Sonya's prognostications, based on her life experience, of how this would become a threat to the country in time. But before she left the world she recognized what were, to her, early signs of division within the country: divisions between the producers and the growing social acceptance of those who did not produce or contribute more than they consumed. "If more and more people keep taking and taking, and putting nothing back . . . " Sonya said to Curtiss one evening over red wine and pasta in the General Chennault Pub, " . . . in the end we'll have nothing," she continued, wagging her finger at him while Wendy nodded her head in agreement from behind the bar. Though she died in 2006, through the prism of her life experience *and* her top-level D.C. connections she could already see the 2008 debt crisis on the horizon, and the subsequent doubling down on all its causes resulting in later economic collapse. Why not? She'd lived it all before in more than one place on the Eurasian continent. Did she really need to stretch her imagination to foresee eventual economic ruin from the government borrowing a third of every dollar it spent? After all, mathematically, what other possible outcome could there be but insolvency?

While visiting her one foggy day at Matilda Hospital hidden atop the lush hills of Hong Kong Island during one of her last days on earth she shared: "Your father's generation created such equity in our country. But now the numbers just don't add up, Curtiss. There just isn't enough money in the world all of a sudden to buy all these things. You can't borrow a lifestyle," she warned. "Some day you will have to pay the bill. And the things you once thought held value one day will be worthless the next."

First it was the 2008 global financial crisis; then, after eight more years of debt-driven economics, the Crash of 2016 and the ensuing Great Depression of the Twenty-Teens. The Crash realized the worst nightmares of the earlier global financial crisis: collapse and default of the worldwide financial industry. Like falling dominos, a financial tsunami followed the sun around the world: first Hong Kong, then London and the European bourses, and finally New York and Chicago. Trillions of dollars in pension funds, 401k assets, and precious metals mutual funds evaporated—along with the hundred-year-old financial institutions that managed them. People by the tens of millions descended on their investment firms hoping to retrieve at least some of their lifetime investments. Pathetically banging on their door, last 401k statements in hand, their run was for naught. The signs on doors told the story: "Out of Business." The things that people thought held value one day became worthless the next.

The subsequent run on banks also collapsed the banking system, but the Federal Government made good on all FDIC-covered deposits at fifty-one cents on the dollar, lest there be a revolution. Credit cards had become a thing of the past but government-issued debit cards survived: to continue distributing wealth transfer benefits.

In the lead-up to the crash skeptic economists had everyone focused on the lessons of Germany's Weimar Republic of the 1920s, which saw hyperinflation as the government printed more and more cash. But hyperinflation never came in America. Deflation did. For what the economists failed to grasp was that in the twenty-first century the United States and the Federal Reserve 'printed' its money in the form of zeros on computerized spreadsheets. Quantitative easing simply created electronic money that, after the financial services industry imploded, left nothing: the zeros simply disappeared off everyone's computer screens. People only had what they had in their pockets, and for those lucky few who saved cash: their FDIC checks to deposit when banks reopened under their new Federal Government ownership. The aftermath of the 2016 Crash was more like the 1929 crash: suddenly cash was king, but there was precious little of it around. Prices collapsed overnight as all economic activity waned. Gas stations would only accept cash and so freeways were empty. Price wars raged at the pumps and Curtiss would see prices like he hadn't seen since he was a boy in the 1970s: a bittersweet nostalgia.

The official word on unemployment was that it stabilized at twenty percent, after hitting a peak of forty-five percent. But like in every authoritarian state everyone knew the statistics were untrue: there was no recovery. Tens of millions were unable to make payments on properties that were selling for a fifth of their outstanding mortgage value—if they could find a buyer. But with the Federal Government having taken over the banks, it effectively held the mortgages of the vast majority of American homes. So, rather than see millions of American families on the streets outside vacant houses, Americans went from being homeowners to renters from the Federal Government.

While the traditional bastions of wealth toppled across the country, Wall Street fell the farthest of all: who needed stock markets and financial markets when most corporations that still existed were crippled, operating under bankruptcy, or owned by or on permanent life support from the Federal Government? Lower Manhattan became a wasteland, where people began living in the abandoned office buildings. Though most economic power went to D.C., some of it remained in the Midwest where the bases of the value chain such as food production, mining, and transcontinental rail transportation—necessities—became the new things that held the most value.

No matter how much the government intervened in the collapsing economy, and the more they took for redistribution to more people, the less everyone had. When D.C. bureaucrats mandated wage levels and prices, businesses that had managed to survive the initial blows finally went bankrupt, one after another. And this crisis, the government viewed, was its mandate for taking over the railroads, airports, other transportation systems, and key industries from cars to steel: "To ensure people have the ability to go to work to rebuild our country." And for every bankruptcy that the U.S. government took over, any land involved would automatically be ceded to the Federal Government as compensation. Thus by 2020, combining its ownership of residential and commercial properties, the U.S. government ended up owning over sixty-seven percent of the land in the United States. Step by step, takeover by takeover, the Federal Government controlled nearly seventy-five percent of all U.S. economic activity and wealth.

Within months of the crash desperation and fear gripped the country, and the new The 99% Party won the Presidency and majorities in both houses of Congress in 2016 on the platform of making things better by taking idle wealth from the rich and giving it to the poor. A chill went up Curtiss's spine that election night, when Sonya's voice once again played in his mind: "When governments cloak themselves in the mantle of social equalizer they begin by redistributing the income. Then, when the income runs out, the redistribution of wealth. Then, when the wealth runs out, the redistribution of scarcity." But voters didn't know Sonya, nor did most of them care to remember the outcome of the very same redistribution philosophy of twentieth century experiments in communism. "Equality is insatiable," the Sonya-ism rang in Curtiss's ears. "Fairness a weapon of social warfare. And governments that impose them won't stop until they've equally impoverished everyone but themselves."

Almost immediately after the 2016 election, strategically placed rumors began conditioning the population to the notion that the 2018 mid-term elections may need to be postponed until the crisis abated. "The country can't afford to change horses mid-stream during a crisis of this magnitude," it was heard said around D.C. and through virtually all media. "Our leaders need to focus on fixing the nation's problems, not on special interests and lobbyists so they can get reelected." So when the time came for the mid-term elections to be held, and they weren't, people hardly noticed. Their only concern was whether they would continue to receive their government debit cards on time and getting a good place in line at the new Redistribution Centers: to get their fair share and maybe a little more.

There were legal challenges to the election postponement by the few who cared enough to protest, one that even rose to the Supreme Court. But they came and went. In the end, it was declared constitutional as long as it was a temporary suspension: " . . . for the duration of the crisis," so said the ruling.

It was also declared constitutional to tax religious organizations, temporarily of course, to unlock the idle wealth being hoarded by religious groups across the nation, to: "Do their part to help the government solve the crisis." Concurrently, a National Interfaith Ministry was created to protect the people from "exclusionary discrimination that is inherent in all religions." Susan Dalworthy was appointed as the National Interfaith Administrator, and in addition to officiating at all D.C. public events she was in charge of regulating, directing, approving, and, of course, taxing the activities of all religious institutions in the United States.

But Curtiss was most alarmed at the under twenty-five generation. Cold-hearted and mercenary, their mindset was the culmination of nearly two decades of systematic demonization of financially successful people—at least those with the incorrect political orientation. And the dehumanization of the better off in society was most insidious in schools. The wealthy were regularly caricatured and humiliated in a standardized way, almost as if it were formally part of the D.C.-dictated public school curriculum. Elementary school children were encouraged to beat piñatas of supposedly wealthy people, to destroy them, then grab the candy that poured out from within their empty shells. Curtiss was aghast at the theme of one of Conner's school plays where the story involved a mob of youth marching handcuffed rich people through the streets to meet their social justice jurors. All that was missing for it to be a revival of China's Cultural Revolution, Curtiss thought, was for the dialogue to be in Mandarin Chinese and the kids to be wearing Mao suits and Red Guard armbands.

Curtiss did what he could to offer his son an alternative to all the messaging—to try to teach him the values of self-reliance, enterprise, and small government—but it was hopeless. He could not match the glitzy campaigns by his schoolteachers, peers, and the media and info-entertainment industry to denigrate the well-to-do. By the time Conner was old enough to understand his teaching him the adage *when you steal from Peter to give to Paul, you can always count on the support of Paul,* it fell on deaf ears. "Dad, you are such a capitalist," he would reply, unflatteringly, whenever Curtiss offered him the counter culture point of view. Conner's teenage rebellion ensured he would neither recognize nor accept the America Curtiss knew when he was growing up, nor heed his lessons learned from his years in China.

But Curtiss recognized the ragged remnants of the American ideals of his youth wherever he found them. When making his commute into D.C. he would make a point of noticing the small, pathetic protests of diehard liberty advocates. Some were simply patriotic individuals, others members of loosely associated grass roots liberty organizations, and all would maintain vigil in front of D.C. government buildings. Some wore frayed and faded tri-corner hats, others woefully homemade Uncle Sam outfits. They tended to be elderly and always seemed to be crumpled, half asleep in folding chairs, and appeared as threadbare as the American and yellow Gadsden "Don't Tread On Me" flags that had their flagpoles zip-tied to the frames of bent and rusty shopping carts. And they carried out their protest not only in D.C., but also in front of government office 'oases,' as they had become known, in cities across the country.

Government offices had indeed become economic oases: the only bright spots within the sprawling landscape of urban blight that had become most American cities. D.C. acquired the best buildings through bankruptcy confiscation, meeting the rapidly expanding space needs of the burgeoning federal government after the crash. The streets in the vicinity of those buildings were maintained by federal government road crews, regularly cleaned by federal government sanitation workers, prettified with small parks built in empty lots and maintained by the National Park Service. And buzzing around them were the businesses that served the D.C. employee gentry class: restaurants and shops, salons and spas, with taxis queued up each afternoon to shuttle the ruling class to fashionable society affairs.

Conner would also never recognize the United States Federal Government that Curtiss once knew: the mostly benign entity that was always in the background of American daily life and that wore the innocuous faces of National Park rangers and U.S. Postal Service postmen. Or the reverent faces of young military personnel who would accompany old veterans on Fourth of July parades through Hershey PA and the crew-cut NASA scientists and administration personnel that one would see interviewed on television and who presented as highly competent professionals focused on achieving their mission. Or the faces of the U.S. Customs and Immigration Service that would greet one upon entering the United States—not always wearing pleasant expressions, and often standing around in larger-than-seemed-necessary groups where one might automatically wave you through while not breaking stride with the personal conversation they were having with their colleagues.

No. In Conner's world, to be a D.C. government employee made one one of the new 'have' class, and like Europe of old, government oases became their castles among the poor feudal masses. As the new gentry class entered and exited their buildings, they would smugly walk past the disheveled liberty advocates protesting on the sidewalks just outside their castle walls. They would poke fun at them, mock them, and make them the butt of their jokes, fully confident that their hopeless calls for the reinstatement of elections—to hold the D.C. government and, by extension, the aristocracy themselves accountable—were going absolutely nowhere.

As for the rest of the masses within D.C.'s serfdom, they were simply focused on their daily lives, dealing with what they had in front of them at the moment, and always scheming for ways not to have it taken away from them. They too did not hear the liberty advocates' weak voices making grand statements about freedom and self-reliance as their words were lost to the wind, blowing through downtown canyons together with scraps of paper, plastic bags, and Styrofoam cups. Liberty and freedom were just two more throwaways in the now fundamentally transformed America.

Though Conner didn't know any better, such scenes boiled Curtiss's gut since Conner was unknowingly denied his American birthright and even convinced that he should celebrate it. Rick was right. The America they knew was long gone. And it wasn't coming back. Not without a fight.

* * *

Curtiss's coffee had gone cold while retracing the steps that brought both he and his nation to the point where he now loathed to open the monthly bank statement that lay atop the pile of unopened mail before him on the kitchen table. It was about this time the previous year that his statement showed a twenty percent-of-balance withdrawal line item labeled: "Internal Revenue Service – Economic Justice Contribution." Directed by an asterisk to the fine print on the back of the statement, Curtiss read: "With the authority of the 2018 Economic Justice Act, under the auspices of the U.S. Equality Board, the Economic Justice Department's annual means test assessment and computation has concluded that this amount of idle funds would be redistributed to a family in need. You may request your contribution's computation details by visiting our website at . . . "

The Supreme Court had already dealt with the legal challenge that appropriation of bank deposits based on a means test violated the Fourth Amendment's unreasonable search and seizure provision. It upheld the Economic Justice Department's actions and its ruling's opinion included the language: " . . . to save our democracy from the injustice of wealth hoarding . . . right the wrongs of the past . . . " and " . . . create an equal and just society as the Founding Fathers intended." The crux of the ruling was the rationale that people like Curtiss, who'd acquired, accumulated, and managed to save wealth, were only able to do so with the help of infrastructure such as roads, bridges, police, and fire, etc.—and other supports such as the U.S. Customs and Immigration Service, FBI, the Courts, and so on that had been provided by the government. That as such: " . . . the Federal Government's appropriation of private assets constitutes a retroactive tax and is therefore constitutional under the government's power to levy taxes," explaining that it had the right to appropriate private assets same as any outstanding taxes owed. That higher income people like Curtiss had paid hundreds of thousands of dollars in taxes over the years for those services was conveniently never mentioned.

Senator Tarleton, the head of the so-called Gang of Five Senators who created the 2018 Economic Justice Act, took a victory lap upon the ruling's promulgation: "Today's ruling is a victory for the people. Let this be a warning to those selfish rich in our society: your greed will not be tolerated. Whatever you have, you didn't build that. The government helped you build it. So you cannot hoard it for yourselves any longer. It is the property of the people and it is high time you gratefully paid the people back for your success."

Curtiss expected that the only thing different with his bank statement this year, given the Supreme Court's ruling, was that his annual bank account line item withdrawal would be re-named, no longer using the word 'contribution,' but something along the lines of: Internal Revenue Service – Economic Justice Tax.

Curtiss was distracted from his distressing musings about his monthly bank statement by a USN interview with Secretary-General of the United Nations Morgan Père that began streaming through his tablet. He was being interviewed by well-known news presenter James Benedict, who had become a household name when he teared up with joy on air while announcing the passage of the Economic Justice Bill. He finished his famous commentary with the oft-quoted wrap-up: "And now, as I close this broadcast, after two hundred-forty-four years of class struggle in America, we will now truly have equal justice for all." Since that career-defining moment Benedict rose from obscurity to the very top of the info-entertainment industry, commanding a huge following, not only across the United States but around the world.

Benedict's guest, Père, was born in South Africa and was a recipient of the Nobel Prize and Time Web's Person of the Year. The interview caught Curtiss's attention when Benedict asked Père about his long-frustrated initiative to disarm the American people. "America was one of the last countries in the world to ban slavery," began his response. "So it is consistent with America's behavior that it is now the last to allow people the barbaric practice of killing their fellow citizens at the drop of a hat." He put Americans on notice that the rest of the world cannot fathom how America continues to allow individuals the right to play God: to have the power of life and death in their hands by allowing them to possess guns. That the U.N. membership has done its part by applying significant pressure—even the threat of worldwide sanctions—to force Americans to get rid of their Second Amendment. He boasted that he was now working hand-in-hand with Senator Tarleton and the U.S. president to bypass the State ratification requirement for constitutional amendment. "Ultimately, we will not allow a few backward American States to hold the world hostage." Benedict nodded approvingly of Père's statement, then closed the Secretary General's comments by reminding viewers that The 99% Party, at the federal level, had overwhelmingly passed a bill that repealed the Second Amendment immediately after their rise to power, but that ratification was stalled in most States.

Benedict then moved to another Père favored topic of the day: global equality. Père smiled greedily in his close-up, gloating about how he and Senator Tarleton and the Gang of Five Senators were working together to bring about global equality. "If it is correct for Americans to tax their wealthy to bring about equality on an American scale, then it is obligated to do so on a global scale." Benedict used Père's comment to segue into a welcome-to-the-show introduction for Senator Tarleton; the camera pulling back from Père revealing Tarleton now sitting across the news desk. Père and Tarleton reached out and held a photo-op style handshake, spurring resounding applause from the audience.

A founding member of The 99% Party, Tarleton was the unofficial Chairman of the Senate and House of Representatives' inner circle: the Gang of Five, which constituted the new dominant power structure in D.C. Together, they divided the country into five regions: Northeast, Southeast, Central, Northwest, and Southwest. Each Gang of Five member was responsible for garnering support from the States within their regions. At first there was some resistance, but the successful postponement of the 2018 mid-term elections released an endogenous greed for power that quickly metastasized throughout D.C.'s senators and congressmen when they realized that they would not face reelection. The five-region structure—with the Gang of Five sitting at the top—quickly solidified.

Benedict asked a question that teed up a platform for Tarleton to make a speech. Speaking directly to the cameras:

"The U.S. is into its fifth year of recovery from The Great Depression of the Twenty-Teens. After the 2016 Crash the

American people lost everything, the result in part from predatory capitalist countries like China stealing Americans' wealth and jobs for decades—to make themselves the preeminent economic power in the world. People's wealth disappeared in gambling casinos called stock markets. But your Federal Government was there for you when you needed us and together we began the arduous journey to rebuild from the ashes of capitalism. The residual predatory capitalist forces, the forces of greed and self-interest that still stain this country to this day, have prevented the full economic recovery that you deserve. Capitalism is what brought us here, folks. And it will never bring us out. It will only bring more misery. When Americans stood to lose their homes by the tens of millions, it was your government that stepped in to help homeowners stay in them—granting them a favorable lease. That act alone prevented tens of millions of American families from becoming homeless. When America's financial services industry collapsed, your government was there with Social Security and FDIC. And for those in need of everything from food to furniture, we built the Redistribution Center system for you. And now, thanks to the Economic Justice Act, a few wealthy Americans will no longer hoard *your* wealth while you go without. Listen to us, America. We are your government. We have your back, folks."

With James Benedict displaying the appropriate level of reverent admiration and awe, Tarleton went on to praise the work of the Economic Justice Department and used the opportunity to introduce the Department's head, Mr. Jon VanJones, who was sitting at his right elbow. VanJones began his career in the mid-1970s as a domestic American terrorist. Curtiss was old enough at the time to now remember seeing his face on the news—a mug shot—during the national manhunt for him. He was the leader of the Chicago Underground: a small band of violent anarchists who were jailed for committing several bank robberies and a number of home invasions—one that led to a notorious murder of one of the who's who of Chicago. Curtiss also remembered seeing news coverage of their sensational trial. VanJones and his cohorts—many of whom now held tenured positions at the nation's top universities—

screamed "death to the pigs" into the TV cameras as they were led out of the courtroom after receiving their sentences. More recently, VanJones's triple life term prison sentence was commuted to time served through a presidential pardon shortly after The 99% Party took the reigns of power. The media celebrated his pardon, twisting the release of a convicted murderer and terrorist and his ascent to head of the Economic Justice Department as a victory for freedom and, though long delayed, justice. No mention was made of the murders, of course. For all younger Americans knew, Jon VanJones and the Chicago Underground were American freedom fighters who helped protect the American people from capitalists.

VanJones picked up where Tarleton left off with an even more vitriolic tirade filled with rewarmed twentieth-century collectivist platitudes such as: " . . . pry the country's idle wealth from the hands of the rich and greedy." And, " . . . bringing down capitalism for good," and in doing so " . . . bringing about social and economic justice for all." And of course a repeat of the line he had become famous for: "They may have the wealth, but we have the hands. There is nothing stopping us from just taking it."

Tarleton concluded with praise for VanJones:

"I've known Jon since the beginning. He is an honorable man with the most honorable of intentions. He has the discipline, dedication, and integrity to do what is necessary to bring about real equality in America. He is our tip of the spear for redistributing the hoarded wealth of this country from the few, for the benefit of the many."

Curtiss's gut always twisted when hearing how elected leaders and bureaucrats of the new, fundamentally transformed America were now speaking. The language of any of the men's diatribes could have been direct translations of routine government pronouncements of the former Communist China. Did they know they were repeating nearly verbatim the words and ideas of last century's communism? Did they care, as long as it brought and kept them in power? Did the American people really understand what they were getting themselves into as they waged their class warfare? Curtiss knew that they didn't. The new enlightenment of grievous ignorance and dependency on the government ensured that they didn't. They hadn't heard about what Curtiss had seen in China: the damage done to an entire society from perpetual class warfare. The broken lives and scarred people: China's walking wounded who managed to survive their Cultural Revolution. The unspeakable injustices as people were moved and sacrificed like chess pawns often to settle personal power squabbles like the ones now happening inside the D.C. beltway.

For the general population there was no escaping the steady stream of class-warfare propaganda. The United States News network or anywhere else Curtiss went on his tablet broadcast essentially the same message. After the 2016 election Community Advisory Boards funded by the Federal Government began targeting television and radio stations across the country, harassing stations that broadcast dissenting talk radio programs, and their sponsors, with a parade of punitive lawsuits and IRS audits. Then after the suspension of elections, the government simply shut down opposing media outlets, claiming they were protecting citizens from stations that were promoting mob rule and so threatening the success of the National Recovery. The more control D.C. took over the lives of the people on the receiving end of redistribution, the more it seemed they wanted things done for themselves. And like their other rights, the First Amendment slipped away from them like a majestic ship that suddenly lost buoyancy and, almost unnoticed, quietly slid beneath the waves in the middle of the night.

Once Curtiss had had enough of the official news he went to his pantry, opened a large breadbox, and removed an antique 1960s era shortwave radio that he'd acquired years earlier. Jake the Range Master was a spy device aficionado and antique spy equipment collector, and kept Curtiss in vacuum tubes. It was already tuned to Radio Free America: the bootleg radio station that broadcast from aboard a ship that remained in international waters—the only dissenting mass-media voice that remained for Americans.

" . . . and, as many predicted, with the disbanding of the U.N. Security Council in 2018, banana republics, countries within the Islamic Caliphate that stretches from Morocco to Indonesia, and tin horn dictators everywhere are now jockeying for position to take away pieces of America's remaining wealth for themselves. Like a ripe watermelon, Secretary General Père plans to cut us into pieces and share the spoils: a tax here, a fine there, arrests and trials of past senior officials who had participated in military actions in the war on terror, and multibillion-dollar compensatory damages for past conflicts. If there was ever proof needed of their intentions, the ceding of the top half of Alaska to some nonsense global sovereignty experiment is it."

The talk radio show host concluded his brief dirge about America's loss of her republic and liberties, and then moved on to the news.

"And now the international news. China, the world's dominant economic power and second most populous democracy, called for the United States to reinstitute elections at the earliest practical opportunity or face the risk of economic sanctions. Having become a multiparty republic in 2016, China has quickly become the preeminent voice in the world promoting economic and political freedom. Here with analysis is China expert . . . "

∗　∗　∗

Leah's high heels chopping their way across the foyer's hardwood floor caused Curtiss to remember forgetting to change the front door lock code. In the remaining moment he had before facing whatever ire she held for him that day, he recalled their conversation over dinner at a pricy D.C. restaurant while celebrating their seventeenth wedding anniversary. The topic was, the money having run out in the private sector, how Leah was now prospering in service of her new client base: the *nouveau riche* D.C. Aristocracy. After the 2016 Crash and The 99% Party's rise to power, personal wealth empires sprouted up within the D.C. beltway. Skilled as she was, it was a seamless transition for her. "Governments are where the wealth is today, Curtiss." She was proud that she was able to rebuild her career in D.C. so quickly after their move there.

Curtiss realized that their marriage's tipping point had been reached when Leah announced at their anniversary dinner: "It isn't about 'other people's money' like it was before with the private sector. Now it is about The People's money," she said with a derisive laugh. "I've seen this movie before, Curtiss. We both have, in China. So I know where things are going and how to keep ahead of the curve. My job has always been to help the rich get richer. I haven't changed," she said with her trademark self-confidence before sipping her wine. "It's the new American way, right?" Curtiss's initial assessment of Leah back when they were dating in Beijing was still correct: she was committed to mastering whatever she turned her hand to—doing things *right* in all aspects of her life. But now he understood that that included doing the *wrong* things right.

Tipping point led to breaking point for the tension that had been building between them when Curtiss held his ground on the principles that he still believed in: free markets, private enterprise, self-reliance, limited government, and service to country. The old American way. "We are supposed to serve our country, Leah. Not serve it up on a platter to looters," he concluded. Curtiss was indifferent about Leah taking his comment personally. They were silent for the rest of the dinner. And for the drive home. And as they prepared for bed, where they would sleep facing away from each other at opposite ends thereafter.

From that evening on they could get nothing right together. Most contentious was Conner's schooling. They fought bitterly over whether or not to put him in a prestigious Washington school for incubating future D.C. aristocrats. Curtiss's objections to the school were, of course, easily countered by Leah: "Don't you want what's best for Conner? Be realistic. This will prepare him for the future."

At the school Conner would be trained for life inside the D.C. beltway, which had become an American Versailles in the tenor of its worse excesses of absolutism, ostentatiousness, and self-aggrandizement that put Curtiss's 1980s era of conspicuous consumption to shame. In 2020 Mr. Smith came to Washington and stayed. His wife became a lobbyist, his children followed in his footsteps and family dynasties were created within the massive Federal Government bureaucracy—with the Gang of Five families playing the role of royalty. And after the elections were postponed family members assumed their peerages, engaging in the occasional battle with America's other dukes, marquis, and viscounts—like the corrupt and vile intrigues of the aristocratic Europe of old—all of course at the people's expense. Was this Conner's future? It ravaged Curtiss that Leah might be right. Was his clinging to an America that no longer existed hurting his son's future prospects?

Curtiss and Leah jointly filed for divorce not five months after their seventeenth anniversary. Leah moved with Conner into a D.C. townhouse that was within walking distance to K Street, and his elite school. Eventually the overwhelming pressure on Conner's worldview—with help from his mother, his school, and the info-entertainment culture that he was immersed in—thoroughly poisoned him against Curtiss. Conner drifted away from him. Their weekend visits were frequently postponed and when they did happen it was clear that Conner was only going through the motions.

Leah appeared in the kitchen doorway. When she saw the pile of unopened mail in front of Curtiss on the kitchen table, she put her fists on her hips and scowled at him.

"What the hell is your problem?" She said through a fatigued exhale. "I received a call from my friends at the Economic Justice Department. We both need to sign the Department's college declaration form for Conner. It will reduce our annual economic justice tax."

She gave up trying to talk to Curtiss and began flipping through the pile of mail on the kitchen table. When she found the document she pulled it from the envelope and pushed it in front of Curtiss. Curtiss blithely made his signature in a space marked by a yellow arrow sticker beside Leah's.

"I saw your boyfriend James Benedict on video this morning," Curtiss said with a wry smile.

"Yes. James and I are planning a much needed vacation in fact. Washington is crazy these days with all the good work being done there," she said sarcastically, clearly meant as a dig to Curtiss. "We are going to Aruba for a few days. Conner will fly in from university and join us. He is really looking forward to it."

"It's been a year or so for you two now, hasn't it? Aren't you ever going to get married?"

"Marriage!" She laughed. "That's the trouble with you, Curtiss. You are so stuck in the twentieth century. Don't you know that marriage is completely passé? Unless you are gay, of course. And believe me, honey. I am not gay. Even after being married to you for seventeen years."

Curtiss pushed the paper back to Leah. "I can understand why you and Benedict enjoy screwing each other, but why do you and he have to screw everyone else in the country with your so-called good work?"

"You are such a bore, Curtiss," Leah said, scooping up the paperwork as she turned to leave the house, brushing off Curtiss's comment with the impassivity of someone who genuinely doesn't care.

CHAPTER 24

When Curtiss arrived at CIA Headquarters he found that someone had parked in his parking space. He drove on to the far end of the parking lot where the unreserved spaces were. There was to be a briefing to senior Agency officials that day: Director Winston's successor, a The 99% Party political appointee, would announce his retirement and his replacement. No longer welcome in anyone's inner circle at the Agency, all Curtiss knew was that the Director's successor was rumored to be a career-CIA insider. Curtiss sat at the center of the small auditorium and busied himself watching next-generation officers filling the auditorium, gravitating and buzzing in and between cliques until the event began.

The outgoing Director brought order to the room with a prattling speech about his many challenges—bravely faced—and supplanting unworthy prior Agency missions with the nation's new mission: to bring about equality, fairness, and economic justice. Towing the party line he repeated well-worn talking points about the greatest threat facing the country being the continuing failure of the National Recovery, and how it was their mission to protect the American people from those preventing its success. Most of the audience fiddled with handheld devices, read briefs, cleaned fingernails, and otherwise distracted themselves from yet another self-serving political lecture from the Director; they'd had four years of it after all. But when he moved to announcing his replacement he caught the audience's attention. With the briefest of preambles he raised his right hand to his side and Ken Wilkenson walked in from house left, waving to the crowd as he crossed the stage to shake the outgoing Director's hand and pose for photos. Curtiss stood and left the auditorium.

* * *

With only his empty, lonely house awaiting him Curtiss decided to drop in on Rambo's wife on the way home from the office. Their daughter was doing her university studies in Beijing at the University of International Business and Economics, UIBE, which had surpassed the likes of Harvard, Wharton, and IMD as the world's top business university. Those once great institutions of learning had become more like political asylums: where both professors and students, having gone mad over bizarre theoretical reinventions of the constructs of human society, spent their time debating tired old twentieth century collectivist political and economic philosophy as if they were something new. Anything and everything but private enterprise and free market economics. Institutions like UIBE, on the other hand, were producing future global business leaders. Curtiss was pleased that Rambo's daughter was headed in the right direction. He had discussed with Conner the possibility of completing his university education in China, but Conner was dedicated to a career in American government that had so thoroughly ensnared him and his vision for his life. He was still young, Curtiss, hopefully, reminded himself.

Rambo's wife lived alone with her memories in her meticulously tended empty nest. Having sprung from big-city life where she was constantly surrounded by people, she now coped well with her quiet existence and her long, lonely journeys of isolation between her daughter's homecomings, chatting with neighbors at her mailbox, and Curtiss's occasional visits.

She was always delighted to see Curtiss and warmly welcomed him into her home, but clearly bore an aching pain and anxiety that was lying just beneath the surface. Each time he visited, after initial courtesies, it eventually came pouring out of her like the tea from the spout of the teapot she used to fill their teacups.

Curtiss helped her understand the complex regulations in unintelligible legalese of government letters that the American people

316

now regularly received from D.C. Last time it was a reduction in Rambo's pension and Social Security survivor's benefits. "How can they do that? Rambo gave his life for his country," she told Curtiss after he explained what it was that they were doing. He could only reply that the government is broke.

This time she handed Curtiss her bank statement and asked him about the Internal Revenue Service – Economic Justice Tax line item. "America is like China used to be," she said, sorrowfully shaking her dainty head, the wrinkles born of years of despair and worry creasing her face. "I can't understand why America is following the same path that China followed in the 1950s and '60s."

Curtiss sat patiently as she rifled through the familiar list of observations about America's growing dystopia and its parallels with communist China. The parallels were, of course, frighteningly accurate. "The world is upside down, Curtiss. China is now a democracy and capitalist, but we are going in the opposite direction. America is now a dictatorship," she said, clearly struggling to hold back tears. "The American people don't know yet: those people in government are never going to restart elections. Our democracy is gone. Don't people understand that?" she pleaded to Curtiss. "They just gave it all away . . . their democracy, their freedom . . . that is what Rambo fought and died for." She began to cry.

She was right. When Curtiss walked through dilapidated public spaces in America's cities he was reminded of the train station in Beijing in 1989 just before the Tiananmen Square incident. Like the people he saw there, large swaths of the American people had now become gray and downtrodden, sad and colorless. In his mind Curtiss would be haunted by his own words: "Tiananmen Square will never happen in America," he would conclude whenever people asked him about his June 4, 1989 Tiananmen Square experience. "The American people would shoot back," he'd say with pride. But the reality was that the vast majority of Americans were not interested in shooting anything. To Curtiss's understanding, they'd become content with being like caged animals in a zoo, biding their time with their particular self-indulgences, waiting for their D.C. zookeepers to feed them.

As tears streamed down her face she concluded: "I am just glad that Rambo never lived to see this day. It would have broken his heart." Curtiss expected his usual punch in the gut whenever guilt about Rambo's death gushed into his abdominal cavity. But this time, the usual hollowness was filled with rage.

He drove home to his own cocoon of quiet desperation.

* * *

When Curtiss returned to the office the following Monday he found the same car parked in his parking spot. He jotted down the license plate number and handed it to the building security officer sitting at the reception desk, who was new and didn't know Curtiss. The security officer looked up the license plate number on his computer, raised an eyebrow, and informed Curtiss that his parking spot had been reassigned. Curtiss said nothing as he passed through the X-ray security check—at least his electronic security badge still worked.

Laying his briefcase down on his desk Curtiss noticed a Post-It note stuck to his computer screen: See Wilkenson. As he walked down the hallway to Wilkenson's new office, he noticed a number of empty offices that were occupied not too long ago. Curtiss was numb to it. He found Wilkenson's executive assistant sitting just outside his office, who reflexively gave him a warm smile, but then bit her lip and winced slightly. They pleasantly chatted about the weather and traffic until Wilkenson emerged from his office.

"Bradley. You are here." Wilkenson focused his eyes in near space as if he were sorting through something in his mind. "Now is as good a time as any, I suppose," he said under his breath. "Come in," he said as he turned his back and reentered his office as if not giving a second thought that Curtiss would be right behind him.

"Right to the point: I need to count on my team to toe the line, whatever that line may be. You are unreliable, Curt. There is no place for you in the CIA that I am building."

Curtiss nodded and smiled. It was payback time. He was pleased, though, that either the weight of his new responsibility, or time and experience, had liberated Wilkenson from his compulsion for tiresome preambles. "I agree."

Wilkenson flipped open a file that he had sitting on his desk and began to read. "You are three years shy of the fifty-nine retirement age," Wilkenson nodded and pursed his lips, before flipping a page and reading more. "In view of your years of service . . . blah, blah, blah . . . you will be given a lump-sum payout equivalent to your current pay through your fifty-ninth birthday and receive full retirement benefits. Whatever that is this week," he said, while furrowing his brow.

To Curtiss, Wilkenson seemed disappointed at the generosity of the terms of his early retirement package that the Human Resources Department had prepared. Curtiss couldn't help but smile at the irony of Wilkenson, who was once so determined to bring him into The Company, being so eager now to fire him.

No doubt noticing his smile, Wilkenson's face twitched with frustration. "It's okay," he said with a dirty smile. "It's okay." He handed Curtiss his termination letter. "With income tax rates where they are, and the Economic Justice Department's retroactive taxes, you'll be giving it all back to the people before too long."

Curtiss continued smiling and recited a Chinese saying: Si Zhu Bu Pa, Kai Shui Tang. "The dead pig does not feel the burning water," he translated.

Wilkenson shrugged and shot him a muzzy stare.

"When you are slaughtering a pig, after you kill it you pour boiling water on the skin to blanch it, so you can scrape the hair off more easily." Wilkenson tilted his head in befuddlement and shifted nervously in his chair. "I'm dead already, Ken. There is nothing more that you can do to hurt me."

* * *

Curtiss's alarm went off as usual the day after his firing, but for the first time since volunteering to rejoin The Company back in 2002, he simply turned off his alarm and remained in bed. He thought to drive to Penn State University and drop in on Conner. But Conner had already told him that he didn't appreciate visits since they disrupted his schedule. Curtiss picked up a book about battles of the American Revolution from his nightstand, turned to the pages holding the bookmark that he had inserted the night before and began to read.

Sometime mid-morning a banging at the front door forced him to rise from bed and get dressed. There were four late teens standing on his porch, each wearing YEAC—Youth Equality Activist Corps—uniforms. Three of them were young men ages around eighteen or nineteen years old who looked witless while they awkwardly shifted on their feet, looking around in all directions. The girl of the group, who couldn't have been any older than sixteen, stood with her feet firmly planted and her fists propped on her hips. Her military-style YEAC uniform was studded with achievement badges, campaign buttons, and other insignia. The two long braids that emerged from beneath her YEAC beret-style cap descended down behind her ears and slightly past the top of her shoulders. Except for her blond hair and blue eyes, standing there, she was to Curtiss all the image of one of Chairman Mao's Red Guards. Xiao Lu immediately appeared in his mind and he flinched when the dull thud of the bullet striking the back of her head haunted his ears. Curtiss opened the door. "Good morning, sir," the girl said pleasantly through the storm door. "We are interning with the Social Justice Department and we have an order to inspect and appraise the contents and condition of your house," she said pertly, as if she were selling Girl Scout cookies.

As the American Red Guards awaited his response, Curtiss was flooded with rage at the specter of American kids being used by D.C. in the same fashion as Mao squandering the lives of an entire generation of Chinese youth to serve his selfish political purposes. He was frozen momentarily—half from indignation and half from the crushing weight of his disappointment. Curtiss's hesitation drew an angry look from the girl, whose demeanor now turned severe as she pointed her finger at him and squawked: "This can go easy or hard for you. We can always ask the police to get a search warrant." Curtiss looked at the boys sternly in the eye, one by one, all of whom appeared too embarrassed or intimidated to challenge him. But the teenage girl had the vindictive look of a true believer in her eye.

Curtiss tightened his grip on the doorknob and slowly closed the door.

Having not bothered to set his alarm the night before, the next morning Curtiss woke to the familiar suburban sound of lawnmowers in the distance and the sweet smell of cut grass coming through his open bedroom windows. Together they brought him back to the rolling green hills of Hershey, Pennsylvania and his youth—so filled with confidence and promise of opportunity.

Hearing voices outside Curtiss pulled his window curtains aside to watch the YEAC patrol dutifully working his neighbor's house. These children are victims. Their youth, innocence, and country stolen from them. Curtiss pitied them their denial of what America once was and despised his generation for having spent their lives enjoying the promises that America offered, but consuming them until there was nothing left—for their own children. They certainly understood what they were now doing with America's youth: using them as pawns in their ongoing social warfare campaign. But he was convinced that the youth did not understand what was happening to them.

The burden of what he witnessed weighed heavily on him as he went through the motions of his morning's grooming and nutrition routine. With nowhere to go and nothing to do, he opened his gun safe then took out Rick's rifle, spotting scope, and ammunition; loaded them into his car; and began driving to The Company shooting range for a little practice. On the radio Senator Tarleton was speaking to a group of The 99% Party supporters outside the gates of a factory in California.

"We brought down the economic tyrants on Wall Street, and together we are going to bring down the economic tyrants on Main Street," he said to cheering crowds. "And after we take down these criminal companies, next is the wealthy individuals, the economic criminals who hoard *your* wealth and keep it from you, the people. It is they who caused this Great Depression and now prevent the National Recovery. They are responsible for your misery and they must be made to pay."

A radio host concluded the segment by announcing that Senator Tarleton would be leading a rally at a two hundred-year-old Saratoga, New York tableware factory in one week's time. The turnout was expected to be in the thousands.

At the next intersection Curtiss saw a man, his face shaded by a hood, on a street corner holding a sign: "War On Terror Vet, Will Work For Food." Curtiss turned off the radio and drove the rest of the way in silence.

Walking up to the CIA's long-distance shooting range Curtiss found Jake; the range master's portly frame dolloped onto a plastic folding chair alongside empty three hundred-yard shooting benches. Curtiss smiled when he noticed that a breeze had set askew Jake's combover atop his perfectly round head and that his silhouette somewhat resembled Georges Remi's cartoon character Tintin—from the neck up anyway. Jake, a fellow fifty-something, was a career agent and one of the best shooting hardware and performance guys in the business: he taught the best to be the best. Curtiss had never seen the range completely empty as it was that day.

"Hey Jake. Am I early? Are you closed? Where is everybody?"

Jake sat up in his chair, turned and pulled back wrinkles born of decades of heavy smoking, slowly like curtains on a stage being drawn open, to reveal his smile. His hound-dog eyes reconfigured from whatever unpleasant thought he had been deeply into, now looking genuinely pleased to see him.

"Nobody sees much point in coming here now." He gave Curtiss a questioning look. "You do know that Director Wilkenson has ordered long-distance shooting ranges closed by the end of the month, don't you? Only the tactical ranges are needed now: to train cadets on how to breach the front doors of people's homes and collect for the IRS," he said bitterly, losing the smile from his face. "Nope. No need for long-distance shooting in the cyber century," he said within a sigh. "Drones are supposed to do all the long-distance work now. Take aim with joysticks and fire with buttons from thousands of miles away is what it is these days."

Curtiss could see that the range closure was a blow that Jake was struggling to withstand with dignity. The long-distance range was his, in the best sense-of-ownership meaning, and its closing meant the end of his career. For Curtiss, it was just another piece of his world that was being taken away. Curtiss attempted to cheer Jake up with an injection of old-time optimism by delivering in mock TV documentary voice: "Since man invented the first sling to throw his rocks faster and further, it has been all about improving accuracy and hitting at further and further distances." Curtiss shrugged. "So now it isn't a thousand yards with a rifle, it is ten thousand miles with a drone."

It worked. Jake laughed as he stood, grabbed Curtiss's hand, put his arm around his shoulder, and walked him to one of the shooting benches. He pulled down a stool that was resting inverted atop the shooting bench, replaced it with a couple of sandbags, then patted Curtiss on the shoulder. Curtiss opened his rifle case and slid the bolt through the rifle's receiver bridge.

"Stretching the legs of Rick's .30-378 today, huh?" Jake's comment was followed by a moment of silence before he walked down to the range master's station and switched the *range is cold* green lights off and *range is hot* red lights on.

Rick's rifle was printing groupings within an inch and a half on the target, and about six inches high at three hundred yards, which, true to form, meant Rick intended to be dead on at four hundred yards. Jake ambled over to Curtiss's bench with two coffees in hand as he was packing the rifle into its case.

"You know, Curt, our generation used to brag that we were inspired by JFK's 'Ask not what your country can do for you, but what you can do for your country.' But these days it seems that we've inspired a generation with 'Ask my country what it can do for me and don't ask me for jack squat.'" Curtiss got the message: Jake needed a cathartic venting session. He was happy to oblige since such a session might also be a good emotional purgative for him.

While Jake and Curtiss sipped their coffees together among the empty shooting benches they reflected on their lives. Neither of them could understand what appeal fundamentally transforming America had for people. Their earliest common memory was of America's moon landings, about how Apollo had unified the country in a way not seen since World War II; and though they were too young to remember the height of the Civil Rights Movement, how Jake was an unwitting part of it. "I was one of those kids who got bussed . . . you know, the desegregation bussing?" Jake volunteered. "I remember being scared at the time and devastated that I couldn't go to school with my friends anymore. But my parents told me that this is what the country wanted us to do. So I did it. Yeah, I was pushed around a couple of times and the school was so lousy that my parents had to pay for a tutor and send me to summer school for a couple of years, but it was an experience that helped make me the man I am today."

They bemoaned having to endure throughout their teens a decade of self-loathing and rampant skepticism of the country and its core values as the nation's popular culture became unduly obsessed with the imbrues of the Vietnam War. But Curtiss reminded Jake that they also had the privilege of watching the country rally back to greatness during the 1980s, rediscovering the principles that made the country great. And as their generation began taking up the reigns of power in the 1990s, their parents' generation gave them a parting gift, the result of decades of disciplined vigilance, the outcome of their standing up to the oppression of global communism: victory in the Cold War. Their generation's coronation? Witnessing the joy of freedom spreading to hundreds of millions who were finally released from behind the Iron and Bamboo Curtains, watching free people cloak themselves in the same principles and ideas enumerated in the U.S. Constitution.

"Yeah, there were problems. But between the golden rule and respect for the law people were generally decent to each other in those days. They respected each other's privacy—and rights. Especially each other's right to hold their own opinions. What's that we used to say? 'I don't agree with what you say, but I will fight and die to defend your right to say it?'"

So it pained them to now witness so many Americans accepting fashion and politicians' chicanery as fact: disparaging the Constitution as being a negative document and faulting it for not going far enough to grant government powers. That the constraints that were placed on government by the Founding Fathers were somehow negative liberties: that the Constitution shouldn't say what government can't do, but what it *should* do.

How it would have broken Sonya's heart to see Americans with their eyes wide open line up to meekly hand their liberties over to tyrants such as those in Russia who disintegrated her family and set her on the course of being a lifelong refugee. A life of staying just ahead of the oppression, anguish, and missed opportunities that the social cancer of communism had imposed upon hundreds of millions of her people for most of the last century.

"Maybe we are just a couple of grouchy old guys who imagine that things were better in the past and are unable to accept the future?" Jake said, looking broken and nearly defeated.

Curtiss shared what he had learned in China about the worst kind of catastrophe a country could experience: a society set against itself. Lincoln and the Bible's house divided. Haves versus have-nots, educated versus uneducated, and even children against their own parents. Americans did not have the benefit of hearing firsthand about China's tearing its society to shreds in the name of equality and social justice. About how those goals, without the protections *and limitations* of the U.S. Constitution, were perverted by human nature, greed, and lust for power. And how Americans were now speeding toward that same kind of social catastrophe. With no view on history, or inkling of how bad things could get, the darkness of oppression crept over them unnoticed—willfully accepting their insidious loss of freedom. But Curtiss knew all too well the eventual outcome of the class warfare that the D.C. aristocracy now inflamed at each and every opportunity.

"No, Jake. This time the problem isn't us. It *is* all going horribly wrong. And it *can* get much worse unless it is somehow stopped." They sat in silence for some time, listening to the eternal wind through the trees gently remind them of the fleeting nature of the machinations of humankind. And their own insignificance.

"What happened to us, Curt?" Jake said, slumping back in his folding chair again.

"We walked down that pathway to hell that was paved with good intentions."

* * *

The day's mail contained a letter from the Economic Justice Department. Curtiss tossed it atop the other unopened mail piled on his kitchen table and consciously ignored it each time he passed by while frittering the late afternoon and evening away—just going through the motions before going to bed.

He couldn't sleep without knowing. He rose, walked downstairs, sat at his kitchen table, and opened the letter from the Economic Justice Department. It read:

> "In view of your empty nest, with the divorce from your wife, and your son attending university it has been deemed by the Economic Justice Department that the five bedroom, four thousand square foot home that you now solely occupy, constitutes idle wealth. In the interest of equality, fairness, and social justice, and in support of the National Recovery, it will

be made available to a larger family in need. This is your ninety-day notice that you must vacate the house with all your possessions. Your government will provide you a twelve hundred square foot, two bedroom apartment in the city's central district for your convenience with using public transportation. A donation of your vehicle to the government for use in wealth redistribution efforts would be creditable at its original purchase price value against future annual Internal Revenue Service – Social Justice Tax assessments. The vehicle donation credit may be carried forward for up to five tax years. Please see enclosed IRS instruction for applying . . . ''

Asleep that night Curtiss's subconscious emotions were stoked by an agglomeration of memories and imaginations that amounted to a visitation of blood lust. The way thick red blood dripped in a steady stream from a cow's hanging carcass and the way it slithered across the tile floor and down the drain: an elementary-school memory acquired while helping butcher a cow on a Hershey PA farm. Flickering oversaturated, scratchy Technicolor images of Ohio state patrolmen pulling bloody and broken bodies from crumpled `57 Chevys and Ford Thunderbirds: his recollection of *Mechanized Death*, a 16mm driver's safety film shown to him in high school. The way bright red blood beaded on the thick cream and tan coat surrounding the hole that Curtiss's bullet had made through the chest of an Alaskan caribou. The five-foot by three-foot picture of a motorcycle traffic accident that hung on the Taipei city government office wall where Curtiss got his Taiwan motorcycle operator's license. The picture served as a graphic safety warning to those acquiring their licenses there. The image was of a young man lying in the gutter, several feet from his crumpled motor scooter. Everything perfectly in place: his shoes, his pant legs, the pager intact on his belt and the watch on his wrist, only where his head used to be there was a two-foot diameter red and black patch on the pavement studded with white bits of skull with scalp and black hair still attached. A five-foot line of bloody slime streaked away from the body, terminating where his entire brain—brainstem clearly visible—lay in the middle of one of the adjacent traffic lanes.

Curtiss briefly regained consciousness from a hypnic jerk: his leg had kicked backward in bed while in his subconscious he was reflexively pulling away from the monkey's desperate grasping of his pant leg below the table at the Healthy Food Restaurant as blood squirted in pulses from its fast-vacating brainpan. But after submerging again back down into deep sleep, he was back at the intersection where the man holding the War on Terror Vet sign pulled back his hood, revealing himself to be Rick with a bullet hole through his head. He walked over to Curtiss's car and began telling him how, before the start of the Gulf War, Israeli psy ops officers— veterans of numerous Israeli conflicts with its neighbors—briefed their team. They explained that whenever possible they should shoot the enemy in the face, or better yet blow out the face with a shot to the back of the head to exploit the jihadist's belief that Allah would not recognize them when they got to heaven to collect their virgins. This would exacerbate their fear and break their lines: they would scatter or retreat.

Curtiss was then sitting in Jimmy Yamandakos' U of M dormitory room listening to a recording of a speech given by Ronald Reagan: an assignment from their political science elective course.

"Freedom is never more than one generation away from extinction. We didn't pass it on to our children in the bloodstream. It must be fought for, protected, and handed on for them to do the same, or one day we will spend our sunset years telling our children and our children's children what it was once like in the United States where men were free."

*   *   *

He didn't know what time it was when he rose, packed a suitcase with hunting clothing and gear, and loaded it and Rick's .30-378 into his car. He then disabled the vehicle's navigation device and its locator transponder, pulled a wad of cash from his safe and drove off into the night.

Curtiss rang Jake's doorbell until he answered the door. "Curtiss? It's the middle of the night. What are you . . . are you all right?"

"I need to borrow that handheld HERF you told me you keep around here. Do you still have it?"

"What? Yeah. What the hell do you need . . . "

"I'll return it. I just need to borrow it for a couple of days."

327

Jake paused for a moment to study Curtiss standing at his doorstep, then swung the door open, turned to walk back into the house, and down into his basement.

Jake was a widower. His foyer and living room were full of five-by-seven and eight-by-ten photos of his and his wife's thirty-two years together. There was also one of Jake and Rick on a bird hunt that looked like it might have happened in Mexico.

He returned with a rifle case in hand. "I hope you aren't going to zap your neighbor's dog for barking or anything like that," Jake said. "Just be sure to keep it pointed below the horizon. You don't want to shake up any passing airplanes with that thing."

"Are the batteries charged?"

"Yeah. And I threw in a couple of spares just in case." Jake looked as though he wanted to say more, but he let Curtiss off with only a thank you, before he loaded the HERF into his car next to Rick's rifle, and continued on his way.

Alone with his thoughts heading north on the virtually empty expressway, while passing the I-270 interchange, which would have linked him to US-15 and back again to his Hershey PA spawning grounds, Curtiss realized that the compelling instinct that took him back in 2002 was long gone. No matter, his spawning grounds were now owned by COFCO: a global Chinese food and beverage conglomerate.

As Curtiss tossed an empty fast food coffee cup onto the passenger side floor he recalled how he and Jimmy would snicker at the Soviet Union making up economic figures year after year: a bumper crop of something this year, or a record-setting something else the next. Yet there were always shortages and lines for everything—just like in 2020 America. Jimmy lost everything in the crash, though his firm survived and even prospered by doing legal work for companies that were taken over by D.C. Jimmy wasn't laughing when he talked to Curtiss about his firm and becoming a legal rubber stamp, vouching for the financial reports of government companies. He saw no humor abetting—like the Soviet Union they once snickered at—the D.C.-owned auto companies, airlines, railroads, and agro industries that would somehow always achieve record levels of production and sales, yet always needed billions in bailouts year after year.

His firm also began taking on civil cases on behalf of D.C., which used the law to persecute anti-government voices and whistleblowers. Deemed dangerous to society for deviating from the D.C.-prescribed track for the National Recovery, the most prominent resisters were committed to rehabilitation facilities. And in the name of equality, fairness, and social justice, one could be certain that this was a humane gesture since polished advertisements were run to that effect: complete with video ads featuring Hollywood celebrities endorsing the program and testimonials from those who had personally "recovered from the grip of greed."

It was then that Jimmy decided to leave the firm and law altogether. Though he had numerous offers—as always—he refused them since they were all offers to join the vastly expanded tentacles of the Economic Justice Department in one form or another, whether directly or by way of a proxy firm. Jimmy went back to Detroit to help his brothers run his father's Greek Town restaurant. Nevertheless, he couldn't avoid serving D.C.: downtown Detroit hosted the largest detention and reeducation complex in the country. Ironically, his family's business thrived off serving breakfasts, lunches, and dinners to prison guards and rehabilitation officers.

After the perversion of Conner's worldview, Jimmy's fate presented the saddest spectacle for Curtiss. Attending a Christmas dinner at his Detroit area home one year Curtiss found him a deflated man, and like himself, just going through the motions of the remainder of his life. Hollowness, like a crushing vacuum that threatened to implode his torso, opened in Curtiss's chest when he recalled Jimmy's strained smile while saying grace before the meal.

Later, while passing the turn off that would take him to Princeton University, Curtiss pondered a particularly contentious lecture that he'd once given there. As they'd been taught to do since primary school, the Q&A session began with the students approaching the country's founding as being fatally flawed and its principles irrelevant owing to the Founding Fathers' status of being dead, their skin color, and gender. "I disapprove of what you say, but I will defend to the death your right to say it . . . Voltaire," Curtiss countered, but it was clear that his intended irony about Voltaire's being dead, European, and a man went unappreciated.

"Why on earth would anyone want to fundamentally transform

America?" Curtiss provoked his audience, drawing boos and catcalls. He reminded them that the Constitution could be revised and updated at any time through the amendment process. But this too was dismissed by the students, who were convinced that the Constitution couldn't possibly be of any value because it was produced by slaveholding self-deluded religious zealots. And predictably the argument of the document's age, and therefore irrelevancy for modern times, was the next point raised in defense of its abolition. Curtiss drew on what he had absorbed somewhere along the way in China: a thinking process derived from pragmatism and considering history in terms of centuries, even millennia, instead of years; or, as it seemed lately, months. "If you want true objectivity, only trust history that is written more than one hundred years after the event," he proposed to his youthful audience. Curtiss then teased their minds with the proposition that the document's age actually worked in its favor. That precisely *because* it was nearly two hundred-fifty years old, that, like history books, time gave it credibility: a buffer against scoundrels in government acting in their own self-interest and favoring the special interests of the present day.

And as he came to do with all such speaking engagements, Curtiss would pass on an amalgamation of Sonya thought—distillates from lectures he'd received over the years while sipping wine with her in the General Chennault Pub or having eggs Benedict at the Peninsula Hotel in Hong Kong:

Life in 1870 BC and life in 1870 AD were essentially the same. Romans had plumbing, the Chinese invented gunpowder, and trains came around the 1700s, but nearly all of humanity still lived hand to mouth, on someone else's land, raising food with basic implements, and saw at night by burning animal fats or kerosene. That for thousands of years nothing had fundamentally changed for the vast majority of humanity.

There have always been brilliant, ambitious, and creative people, but throughout history they served at the discretion of aristocrats: whether patron of the sciences or arts. And if something didn't serve the interests of the aristocratic classes, or worse, benefited the servant classes in ways that empowered them, it wasn't pursued—and may even have been deliberately suppressed if it endangered the social power structure. But one hundred-fifty years ago something changed: the U.S. Constitution, newly emancipated from its own shackles of human slavery, appeared on the world scene.

The best of humanity, the ambitious and passionate about improving themselves and their lives chose to leave the oppression that held them back in their homeland; whether the aristocrats of Europe, imperial rule of China, or India's caste system. Within the crucible of constitutional freedoms and with the riches of the North American continent these Americans *made* fortunes—not by inheriting or seizing them from others, but by *empowering* the masses by providing them things like electricity, transportation, telephones, appliances, petroleum products—not by withholding it from them. Together they pushed humanity into its next eon by bringing these innovations to the masses at an affordable price, for profit: Tesla, Ford, Edison and Westinghouse, Bell, Gustave Whitehead and the Wrights, Ron Popeil, what have you.

And true to form Americans didn't keep it for themselves either. During the American century the nation led the replacement of a world order founded upon unequal treatment under centuries of European colonialism with free and fair trade that brought prosperity to hundreds of millions, if not a billion or more human beings. Living on the North American continent, under the U.S. Constitution, freed the human spirit. And under these conditions it wasn't one hundred years— within the span of a single human lifetime—that they led humankind from horseback to the moon.

At this point, when he had most minds in the audience thinking rather than preparing to blurt out rote-learned protestations to politically incorrect thought, he would come full circle with: "And, why on earth would anyone want to fundamentally transform that?" He then broke the silence with: "Government imposed equality, fairness, and social justice seem to be all the rage on your campuses these days. But consider that Karl Marx arrived on the scene with the exact same idea at about the time of America's emancipation from slavery. But whereas the American constitutional path lifted the human spirit, Marx's path quashed it and led to untold human suffering . . . " Curtiss paused as the image of the tears of pain welling up in the village elder's eyes flashed through his mind: a boy's dream of soaring with the Flying Tigers stolen from him, one of hundreds of millions of lives crushed by a lifetime of brutal and unjust social experiments that sought to impose equality through government-instigated class struggle. " . . . That in one way or another destroyed the lives of as many people during the twentieth century as that century's horrific wars."

He switched on his clip-on microphone and stepped out from behind the podium to better connect with his audience. He drew a long breath: "A wise woman once told me that equality is insatiable; fairness a weapon of social warfare—and governments that impose them won't stop until they've equally impoverished everyone but themselves," he said to a completely silent auditorium. "And the worst of it isn't the impoverishment of the pocket, but the impoverishment of the human spirit. Government-imposed equality, fairness, and social justice aren't the pathway to the future, ladies and gentlemen, they are a pathway back to stagnation—back to the way things were for millennia."

His lectures increasingly drew the ire of the university establishment who clucked their tongues at their inconsistency with the prevailing values and philosophy of their institution or society at large. It wasn't long before they stopped asking him to speak altogether. But while it lasted, Curtiss could always count on reaching a few students—those who would approach the podium to thank him and to shake his hand after his lectures. And as he fielded their questions he would think of Conner, praying that he was having similar exposure at Penn State. Wondering whether there was another person like him who spoke of the country, its history, and its values the way he did. And precisely because it wouldn't be Curtiss, his father, he would listen to that person and begin to unravel the cocoon of cynicism about the country that enveloped him; rescuing him from the lifelong barrage of D.C. propaganda, its public school curriculum, and the complicit info-entertainment media that preyed on his generation's minds. The very same onslaught that had so irretrievably contaminated his entire generation that they now passively watched their constitutional protections being taken away, one by one, by the scoundrels in D.C.

Strangely, though, one constitutional right endured: the Second Amendment. Though restricted, and continually under assault, D.C. was never completely effective with infringing on the people's right to keep and bear arms.

Dawn broke just as Curtiss pulled into the Saratoga no-tell motel parking lot.

CHAPTER 25

It was 3:00 am when a secret serviceman who was patrolling the woods surrounding the park where Tarleton would speak later in the day quickly scanned the trees with an infrared device. Hugging the tree trunk while wearing heat signature concealing camouflage the way Rick had taught him must have worked: the secret serviceman did not seem to detect Curtiss's presence in the tree fifty feet from the ground. The floodlights shining on the stage that was receiving its finishing touches enabled Curtiss to confirm through Rick's riflescope that he had line of sight on the podium where Tarleton would be standing. By the time dawn broke his fifty-something joints and muscles were screaming to him that he was too old for this. He methodically unknotted each cramped muscle with long, slow yoga-like stretches.

By 10:00 am, when a crowd had gathered in the park, he was physically depleted and running on adrenalin and sheer determination. Local police lightly patrolled the area and, like the deer he once hunted, never thought to look up into the trees for trouble.

The stage's backdrop was a billboard-sized photo of Senator Tarleton's face. He arrived on stage at 10:06 am, together with Jon VanJones, his Economic Justice Department henchman. Today was Curtiss's lucky day.

As Senator Tarleton's rally got under way with him repeating what he had said on the radio about it being time to take down the economic criminals on Main Street, Curtiss caught sight of the eye-in-the-sky surveillance drone that appeared from behind the top of one of the buildings surrounding the park's square. It was making a long slow arc around the event. He raised the HERF to his shoulder and put the circling drone into the center of the HERF's holo sights and zapped it. When the drone's circling arc abruptly straightened out and it flew off at an oblique angle Curtiss knew that its autopilot had taken over after he'd momentarily scrambled its electronics.

After the drone had disappeared behind the roof of a building, Curtiss hung the HERF on the stump of a branch that he'd cut earlier in the morning for that purpose. He took Rick's rifle in hand and put the cross hairs of its scope on Tarleton, who had just turned to welcome a guest to the podium. His range finder flashed the red digital number '432 m' through the ocular lens.

Curtiss didn't need to worry too much about windage: it was a breezeless morning, evidenced by the still trees around him and the bushes down in the park that he could see through the riflescope. He would only have to worry about compensating for angle of elevation. As he placed his finger on the trigger Curtiss whispered within a breath-controlling, deep exhale: "If you want social warfare, let it begin here." He became conscious of his heartbeat as time slowed and silent tunnel vision encroached until all of existence minimized to the image that met his eye through the riflescope. The finely tuned trigger of Rick's .30-378 seemed to respond to his thought as it broke back from the weight of his index finger. He did not feel the substantial kick in response to his 130 grain, .30 caliber bullet leaving the end of the barrel at over four thousand feet per second. Curtiss managed to get the scope back down onto Tarleton by the time the bullet pierced the back of his head. The hydro shock blew out his face and frontal lobes, the spatter spreading well across Tarleton's massive face on his stage's backdrop portrait. His body fell vertically in place—the strings of his marionette cut just like Xiao Lu's on the street near Beijing's Tiananmen Square. Senator Tarleton was dead.

Startled by the explosion of Tarleton's head next to him, before Jon VanJones could react, Curtiss was on him with the crosshairs. Justice delayed? Justice delivered, Curtiss thought as his second shot executed VanJones, dropping him right next to Tarleton. James Benedict, who was seated on stage with other VIPs, received his fair share of both Tarleton's and VanJones's blood and brain matter, covering his shirt with colorful bits like the splattering turtle did to Curtiss's on Taipei's Snake Street.

When the scene broke into chaos Curtiss slipped the rifle into its scabbard, karabiner-clipped the HERF, rifle, and knapsack to a tether and quickly dropped them to the ground. He descended down the same line seconds later, but not before posting a message on the tree trunk that read: "The tree of liberty must be refreshed from time to time with the blood of patriots and tyrants—Thomas Jefferson." He had signed the note: Timothy Murphy.

* * *

Curtiss was calm as he replayed the shoot and escape in his head while driving along I-90 toward Syracuse and New York's Finger Lakes Region beyond. Domestic terrorism now being the exclusive domain of the new CIA, Curtiss wondered whether Wilkenson's investigative team would suspect that it was an inside job after receiving the report about the drone's scrambling. Would they be able to tell the difference between a malfunction and him deliberately disabling the aircraft? Certainly they wouldn't trust a malfunction mere moments before an assassination. Far too coincidental. It would be for Curtiss anyway.

Alone on the road he amused himself imagining a couple of twenty-something Agency case investigators examining his note at Langley Headquarters:

Agent 1: "Timothy Murphy can't be the shooter's real name. No one would be dumb enough to do that, would they? To use their own name?"

Agent 2: "I don't know. We'll need to run down the name in any event. So how many Timothy Murphys do you suppose there are in the world?"

And when they made their report to Wilkenson, surely his face would twitch uncontrollably as he would say: "Didn't the Thomas Jefferson quote give you two a clue?" The agents would then give him their best dumfounded look as he'd explain to them that Timothy Murphy was an American Revolutionary War figure. Curtiss issued a crooked smile when he imagined Wilkenson shaking his head in disgust at the product of the generation that was not taught about the accomplishments of their nation's founders and Revolutionary War heroes because of their status of being dead, their skin color, and their gender.

Hours later Curtiss drove through a small artist community nestled on Lake Cayuga, between Lakes Cayuga and Seneca, before pulling up to a turn-of-the-twentieth-century mansion on a retired orchard located along the shore about three miles outside of town. He smiled when he saw a portly older man with a long white ponytail hanging down below his beltline flanked by two slender Asian women who together were repairing a snow fence. Curtiss stood for a moment, staring at his back, then smiled before saying: "Well, if it isn't the old commie millionaire come home to upstate New York to roost."

The man stiffened, no doubt confounded by the voice that he seemed to recognize, but couldn't place for lack of context. He turned and looked at Curtiss through rose-colored Englishman workman glasses. He didn't recognize him; it had been thirty years and Curtiss's arrival at his estate was most certainly a complete surprise.

"I ended up giving that motorcycle of yours to a young man in Guizhou. He deserved it more than me."

Gabriel's face broke into a smile signaling that his brain finally received the context that it was searching for. "Curtiss!" He shouted as he stumbled across the ruts left by his four-by-four. Gabriel was at least fifteen years Curtiss's senior and in spite of his new heft seemed in good shape for his age. Their hearty bear hug affirmed it.

"What the hell . . . how did you know I was back? How did you know how to find me?"

Settled on the porch in homemade rocking chairs, Gabriel pulled a meerschaum pipe from his pocket and stuffed a large marijuana bud into its bowl. "You want a hit?" he said, turning the pipe stem toward Curtiss. "It's cool. It is legal now, you know."

"Naw. I never cared for it. It was alcohol for me, when I used to drink. Shame I lost interest, really. There is a lot more to drink about these days."

"So how the hell did you find me?"

Curtiss confessed that he was with the CIA and ran the Asia

region for over a decade.

"I never took you for a spook. Just a lovelorn, misguided kid."

"I wasn't in the Agency when we knew each other. I was a gray market smuggler, remember? That was for real. That wasn't a cover, or anything like that."

"Yeah? Well half the economy here is gray market now. Maybe you should put those skills to use."

Curtiss smiled. "I did get roped into the Agency right after Tiananmen Square though."

"Yeah, it was a shame about that girl you were with being killed."

Gabriel no doubt saw Curtiss shiver at the pang of guilt that instantly materialized in his gut when he heard the dull thud of the bullet striking the back of Xiao Lu's head replay in his mind. Both men sat together in silence for a moment: Gabriel rubbing the scars around his wrists and Curtiss retracing his steps in Tiananmen Square, both of them pausing to refile their most unpleasant memories of their life in China.

After they'd returned to the present, Curtiss told Gabriel about the CIA's file on him and that it dated back to 1966, when he left for China. "Yeah, I kept an eye on you. It was my job. But also just to check in on you from time to time to see how you were doing. To make sure you didn't get yourself thrown into prison again, or something."

"Wow. I guess the old saying is true: just because you're not paranoid doesn't mean that they aren't out to get you."

A Chinese woman who looked to be in her late forties placed a tray with Chinese tea on the Biedermeier style tea table that stood between their rocking chairs. Curtiss studied her face as she poured tea into their cups. A glint of a grin emerged, before she turned to look at him with a broad, pleasant smile. She was the young lady who'd tended to him at Gabriel's Guizhou compound when he was ill. Curtiss smiled back, nodded, and said: "Xie, Xie."

"I'm surprised you didn't bring your Guizhou children back with you too."

"Naw, they're all grown up now and don't need me anymore. Besides, they'll never want for anything: they're in the new land of opportunity." Curtiss could tell by the way Gabriel spoke about them that he missed the village children as if they were his own. And, that he missed being needed. "They are certainly better off there than here. Not a day goes by that some ex-stock broker, or PhD in economics doesn't come knocking at my door looking for a meal in exchange for handyman work around the estate. I mean . . . what is this, Curt? *The Grapes of Wrath*, or something? What the hell happened here while we were away?" he said, while shaking his head in disgust.

"Well, you finally got what you wanted," Curtiss said with a kind, joking smile. "Communism in America. A government that takes care of its people cradle to grave and protects them from the evils of capitalism." Curtiss paused to melodramatically stretch his legs, one after the other. "We know this, of course, because they tell us that every day."

A look of disgust came over Gabriel's face. "This isn't what I wanted, you know that. The looting bastards and outright crooks in our government are making all the same mistakes that the Chinese made seventy years ago. Problem is, people are so willfully ignorant they don't even know they are repeating history." Gabriel then looked deeply troubled as he explained: "If I knew that the price of coming home was going to be the IRS taking everything except this house from me, I would have stayed in Guizhou."

Surely Gabriel knew that it was only a matter of time before the Economic Justice Department took his house too. Curtiss thought to inject wry humor along the lines of: 'Well, what did you expect? You are a draft dodger and tax cheat, and you haven't filed so much as a change of address with the IRS since 1966,' but decided that it wouldn't help Gabriel's state of mind. "So, are you still a believer in the cause?"

Gabriel started to say something, then stopped himself and only sighed. Instead they spoke about social warfare in America following the same bizarre social aberrations that had plagued China during its communist phase: the government's classifying of people by what property and wealth they held, then looting and forcibly impoverishing them to feed their insatiable bureaucracy. But they agreed that the worst parallel was happening with schools, government propaganda, and the pop culture, which all worked to desensitize the country's youth: America's lost generation. They felt nothing wrong with inflicting acts of cruelty on their discredited and demonized neighbors in the name of equality and fairness: so much social justice. They discussed one recent news report that hailed neighborhood teens who ransacked an elderly man's house and found the cash he'd hidden in his home as heroes. Their story received a standing ovation when it was told before a session of congress by one of the Gang of Five: lauded for wrenching from his hands idle wealth and unselfishly redistributing it to their neighbors. That the old man committed suicide a day later on his porch—for all his neighbors to see—was mentioned in subsequent news reports, but in a way that one would announce the execution of a criminal who got his just deserts.

"Fact is, nobody got it right, Curtiss. Not the Chinese, not the Russians, not even Castro. And certainly not us Americans now," he said while staring at the waves on Lake Cayuga—a languorous look on his face. He shook his head as if he had reached a long-sought conclusion right then and there: "Not on this planet, not with human beings."

"Equality is insatiable; fairness a weapon of social warfare, and governments that impose them won't stop until they've equally impoverished everyone but themselves," Curtiss recited.

"Yeah. Tell me about it, man."

*   *   *

When Curtiss passed his home bar cart that held various bottles of alcohol left over from the days when he and Leah entertained he thought to have a drink. But he knew that he did stupid and impulsive things when he drank—more stupid and impulsive than assassinating a U.S. senator and federal government department director? But that wasn't who those people were. No elections means no republic. No Constitution means no United States of America. They were domestic enemies, tyrants who had usurped the country and they reaped what they had sown on the social warfare battlefield.

"They were the shots heard round the world . . . " the Radio Free America announcer erupted, Ed Herlihy style over Curtiss's shortwave.

" . . . That executed Tarleton the Tyrant and his head henchman, the Economic Justice Department's Jon VanJones. Their faces shot out by someone who was clearly a master of the shooting arts. Who is this mystery patriot who liberated Americans from these two enemies of freedom? Sources tell us that the patriot, whomever he or she is, left a message, a quote in fact, of Thomas Jefferson: 'The tree of liberty must be refreshed from time to time with the blood of patriots and tyrants.' And best of all, folks, the patriot takes the name of our Revolutionary War hero Timothy Murphy. For those of you who don't know, Sergeant Murphy was a Morgan's Rifle Corp. rifleman who was particularly skilled at picking off British officers at great distances from up in trees. He is credited with killing British General Simon Fraser at the unbelievable-for-its-time distance of three hundred yards during the Battle of Bemis Heights in Saratoga, New York. Murphy and his fellow Kentucky riflemen's sniper tactics—targeting British Army officers—cut the head off the snake, stopping British advancements in their tracks on that fateful day. The British Army retreated and surrendered ten days later on October 17, 1777."

* * *

Director Winston's upland bird hunt had arrived and Curtiss had an eight-hour drive to his Kentucky estate to listen to news radio sensationalize the story about the domestic terrorist who'd killed Senator Tarleton and Jon VanJones. An interview with a criminal psychologist who theorized about the shooter's profile brought a smile to Curtiss's face: " . . . narcissistic . . . delusions of grandeur . . . acting out an Odeipus Complex born of a deep-seated hatred for his father . . . a mind twisted by a lifetime of religious cultism: a derivation of the Christian faith, most likely . . . " There was no mention of Curtiss's note quoting Thomas Jefferson in any of the reports.

He arrived at Director Winston's massive log-home hunting lodge when his guests were already well into an evening of heavier-than-usual drinking. The men and two women, almost all former SAD, were collected in his great room under its floor-to-ceiling river-rock fireplace that, alongside soaring naked log posts, imbedded itself into the latticework of interlocking crossbeams that rivaled Taipei's

National Theater in its complexity and beauty. The room was festooned with taxidermy of every conceivable game animal from five continents and all exquisite: from antler and shoulder mounts to full-body, life-size action scenes.

There, within Director Winston's rustic American outdoorsman cathedral, the conversation eddied around Curtiss free-form on topics ranging from anecdotes about individual war experiences or on the hunt with Rick Nanna, to their respective government property seizures and, of course, the assassinations of Tarleton and VanJones. The shooter's pseudonym seemed to be of particular interest. They all knew of Timothy Murphy, whose exploits were taught as part of sniper training—at least in their day. Curtiss sat quietly and sipped his coffee, listening to them speculate about the shooter.

"Well, one thing's for sure, the guy is definitely ex-military," one said. "I see Army Ranger all over it," another piped up. "Yeah, but this guy was making a point. Normally you'd go for body, center mass, right? But the headshots mean this shooter had psy ops training, for sure. Gulf War vet, I'd bet." Still another challenged: "But that doesn't necessarily make him Army." One of them even joked that it was a Company job: that the shooter was SAD. When laughter erupted among the group, Curtiss and Director Winston made eye contact. Neither of them was laughing. Curtiss satisfied his urge to shrug.

Curtiss woke in one of the bunks in Director Winston's lodge. He was quite used to the absolute silence of his home and couldn't get back to sleep through the snoring and wheezing of his quadragenarian and quinquagenarian bunkmates. He discovered Director Winston standing beside the fireplace, smoking a cigar, brandy in hand, while teasing the logs with a fire poker. Curtiss contemplated Director Winston for a moment, who wore the look of discontentment that they all wore, but also a steely look of determination born of dignity that had already been beaten out of most men. He walked up beside him to help stare into the flames.

"Bart, there is something I need to discuss with you."

* * *

Curtiss woke the next morning to the smell of bacon and the

rustling of middle-aged men stretching sore backs and cracking stiff joints. He smiled and shook his head, watching from his bunk as they donned tri-focal glasses, gobbled medications, used nasal sprays, and rubbed pain-relieving ointment on their sore joints and muscles. After breakfast the entire hunting party filed out the door into crisp dawn air, shotguns in hand, and spent the best part of the morning following the half-dozen or so hunting dogs who expertly scared up game birds for them.

Director Winston put together a first-rate hunt. The dogs were superbly trained. It was put-and-take and so everyone was going home with a bird; not the ones they shot, but ones that were shot on earlier hunts—defeathered, frozen, and tagged and ready to go into insulated bags for the trip home. At midday they arrived at a clearing where there was a wooden Conestoga-style western chuck wagon parked together with two circa World War Two Willys-Overland Jeeps and a vintage International Harvester Scout. Together they had a hot meal in the field: a pleasure that many of the men hadn't enjoyed in some time. They scattered themselves among the waving grasses, stretched out and leaned on elbows to talk, or laid back to stare at the near cloudless sky to digest their midday meal. Director Winston sent the cooks on an errand back to the lodge in the Scout, then sent Curtiss a nod.

Curtiss stepped to the centroid of the group. "It's great to be back in the field with you guys . . . " He paused to allow his preamble to draw their attention and create one final moment for him to contemplate his taking another step past the point of no return. He imagined his father having the same feeling in his gut when his B-25 cleared the end of the USS Hornet's flight deck, on his way to his suicide mission.

There under the watchful gaze of the surrounding mature trees, their creaking against the breezes whispering a promise to keep his secret, Curtiss spoke with complete trust and honesty, totally unrestrained and from the heart as he'd never been able to before. "I killed Tarleton. And VanJones."

The group began rising to their feet, just a few at first, but the rest quickly followed in unison.

"And if I could have, I'd have killed all the other D.C. tyrants who destroyed our republic and our Constitution." The zealousness with which he spoke drew intense stares that connected them all, like the spokes of a wagon wheel with Curtiss at its hub. "The Supreme Court justices who threw out the Constitution. And the Hollywood moguls and media talking heads who lied and told the people it was all right. And all the other elected officials who watched it all happen and did nothing because it meant job security to them—glad they would no longer be held accountable. If it would have stopped them from destroying our country, I would have shot them all." Curtiss's profound disgruntlement and inner rage welled up from his chest and coalesced in his throat, causing him to lose his breath for a moment.

As his audience silently drank in his words, quenching their powerful thirst for new hope, Director Winston set down his coffee cup, stepped up beside Curtiss, and put his arm around his shoulder. "It is time for America's second revolution against tyranny," Director Winston announced. "We have a duty to stop those D.C. looters who now fleece the American people like sheep. The D.C. aristocracy is our enemy, ladies and gentlemen: the domestic one that our Founding Fathers wrote about and that we all swore an oath to protect and defend our Constitution and republic against. The D.C. tyranny has destroyed our republic and now directly threatens our lives and our families. And it is to their destruction that I now pledge my life, my fortune, and my sacred honor. If I can take out three or four, or more of those looters in D.C. and die bleeding on the flag, well . . . then my life will have had a purpose." The men and women broke their silence to respond to Director Winston with a cheer, the expression of the dignity of free people having returned to their faces.

Curtiss's voice returned: "Equality is insatiable; fairness a weapon of social warfare . . . " Director Winston looked over at Curtiss, smiled, then finished: " . . . and governments that impose them won't stop until they've equally impoverished everyone but themselves."

"Let's put some warfare in their social warfare!" Curtiss shouted, raising his shotgun above his head and stoking more cheering from the group.

"I am looking for volunteers to reform Morgan's Riflemen. Anyone around here interested in signing up?" Director Winston announced to a roar of affirmation.

CHAPTER 26

Curtiss pulled the Monte Carlo comb atop the stock of Rick's .30-378 against his cheek as he replayed in his mind the news broadcast two months earlier showing Senator Kent—the Gang of Five senator who took the mantle of Chairmanship after Tarleton—on the steps of the D.C. Capitol Building with the remaining Gang of Five the day after Tarleton's assassination. There, they joined arms with Senate and House colleagues, and other D.C. aristocracy who gathered to make tribute speeches to Tarleton and to show their solidarity. Kent spoke of carrying on his predecessor's work and he and the others delivered predictable sound bites: " . . . will not be terrorized . . . continue to fight for the people . . . equality, fairness and economic justice for all . . . " Kent announced that Tarleton's body would lie in state at the Capitol to the end of the legislative session, after which they would go home to their respective districts. Kent would accompany Tarleton's casket to his hometown for burial before returning to his own home district.

Curtiss matched his mental image of Kent on the Capitol steps with the image of him within his riflescope as he gave Tarleton's graveside eulogy. *That's him.* Curtiss was tempted to look up to check for the surveillance drone that should be buzzing the cemetery where Tarleton's casket was being laid. But he put that out of his mind to concentrate on the task at hand; trusting that Director Winston had been successful with having a software virus inserted into the Company's surveillance center computers and that the three-hour national drone blackout had begun.

Ken Wilkenson was seated directly behind Kent and Curtiss was confident that he could take him out with a quick second shot like he did Jon VanJones. But he put that out of his mind too. What he was about to do to another human being was about refreshing the tree of liberty with the blood of tyrants, not saving his own ego. Given the closer range Curtiss was unable to get the scope back onto Kent before his bullet had shattered his head. When the image of Kent reappeared in his riflescope, his lifeless body was lying in Wilkenson's lap and the funeral party had just begun to scatter in panic.

Positioned among a pile of logs at the edge of an adjacent tree line, Curtiss threw off his camouflage covering to begin making his escape. He slid the rifle into its scabbard, stuffed the camo suit into a bag, and shoved both into the burial tube that lay at the bottom of the shallow trench that he had dug earlier. He lifted one end of a tarp that slid enough dirt into the trench to cover the tube then used his hands to brush leaves and other ground cover over the bare dirt to conceal the burial. He would come back for Rick's rifle later.

In street clothes with nothing but his keys and wallet on him, Curtiss took a deep calming breath and turned to begin walking through the woods toward his car. His heart jumped into his throat when he locked eyes with a soldier who had been quietly watching him conceal his tracks. The pounding in Curtiss's chest and additional rush of adrenalin left him dizzy and the moment slipped into the surreal. Seconds seemed to stretch to hours as the soldier, wearing the New York State National Guard shoulder sleeve insignia—a scarlet sword atop a yellow seven-point crown representing the Statue of Liberty as a symbol of freedom from tyranny—and cradle-carrying his M-4 rifle made no attempt to bring its muzzle around onto Curtiss. Rather, he stood there quietly and appeared to be contemplating him.

Curtiss slowly reached into his shirt pocket and pulled out a playing card bearing the symbol of the Gadsden Flag and placed it on top of the log pile. He and the soldier continued to hold each other's stare until the soldier made a marching maneuver style ninety-degree pivot and began to slowly walk away as if he were simply on patrol.

* * *

The Riflemen joined Curtiss and Director Winston in the great room of his lodge, where Curtiss learned the details of the Riflemen's Day of Reckoning activities while listening to them give Director Winston their individual field reports:

The remaining three Gang of Five were killed virtually simultaneously by three Riflemen. The Southwest Sector Senator was shot and killed with a rifle bullet through the kitchen window of his San Diego home as he was preparing breakfast just before dawn. Moments later, the Southeast Sector Senator was shot through the chest on the doorstep of his Weston Florida home from four hundred-twenty yards. Up in Chicago, the Central Sector Senator was arriving at a meet-n-greet photo op at a popular café when his Riflemen walked up behind him wearing a motorcycle helmet, pulled a Yankee Fist from his jacket, and shot him in the back of the head. The Rifleman instantly turned the gun on his bodyguard before he could draw his weapon. He took the bodyguard's weapons from him before having him lie face down on the sidewalk and zip-tying his feet together, and hands behind his back. The Rifleman dropped a Gadsden Flag playing card, and then put two more rounds into the Senator as he began walking to an alley to make his getaway on a motorcycle.

In the same hour, the Chief Justice of the Supreme Court, who declared the National Equality Law constitutional based on his rewording 'confiscation' to 'retro-active tax,' was walking across the grounds of a university to give a speech on the antiquation of the U.S. Constitution. He was with a well-known university law professor who frequently appeared as an expert commentator on government news broadcasts and who was consistent in stating that the U.S. Constitution is an inherently unfair document and should be tossed out. Both the Chief Justice and the university law professor were shot dead with well-placed rifle bullets. During the planning of the Day of Reckoning, the law professor was designated a target of opportunity and the Rifleman who killed him expressed his gratefulness that he could take them both in a single shooting.

On a prestigious Massachusetts golf course reserved for the Washington, D.C. aristocratic elite, a simpatico Supreme Court Justice was crumpled on the fifth-hole green from the sudden appearance of a fist-sized hole in his chest. His Rifleman reported that he had passed a .50 caliber bullet through the Justice with a twelve hundred-yard shot. His fellow Riflemen moaned to express their dubiousness about the actual distance he was reporting with a shot made from a traditional rifle. Moaning turned to laughter when he said: "Hey, I made a hole in one . . . and on a thousand-yard hole, too!"

The third Supreme Court Justice on their target list was walking down D.C.'s K Street, when her head was shredded from the impact of a single shotgun blast from a passing car. Looters stole her wallet and belongings and it would take days to identify her. In the meantime, government news reports simply listed her as a Jane Doe and speculated that her murder was likely related to the other assassinations that happened during the same three-hour period.

Meanwhile, on the West Coast, in Los Angeles, news and entertainment mogul Winnie Bhindi was in a Beverly Hills spa where she was getting a massage and facial. Her female Rifleman, dressed as a masseuse, walked into her private massage room, pulled a suppressed .380 pistol from the stack of towels she was carrying, put the end of the barrel to the back of Bhindi's head as she lay face down on the massage table. She pulled the trigger twice. Another Gadsden Flag card left behind.

Climate change magnate Bibi Clark, a D.C. Aristocrat who'd siphoned billions from taxpayer-funded clean energy boondoggles that never came to fruition—deemed the greatest legal theft in American history—was shot by a Rifleman from a position on the bluffs overlooking the Carmel, California beach that he regularly jogged along at sunrise. A rip current took his body out to sea. It was found two days later by beachcombers.

Morbidly obese and famously hedonistic Hollywood film director Alan Monty was waddling his sizable mass away from his limo parked curbside toward the entrance of a Beverly Hills law office. Monty was best known for directing pseudo-documentary films that stirred up racial and class hatred, and government news agencies declared him man of the year for doing the most to " . . . put a stake through the heart of capitalism in America." His films depicted capitalists as greedy, evil exploiters of the people and made it his life's work to personally demonize the highly successful. This included, most recently, a film about Jack Mack, the super wealthy software and cellphone network hardware magnate who was subsequently having his tech empire dismantled through government confiscation, in part in populist response to Monty's film. Before he could reach the building door Monty was enticed over to a limo by a raunchily clad woman who was seductively leaning out the window. When he arrived at the limo the woman's head was replaced with a shotgun barrel and Monty received a charge of OO buck into his massive gut before falling backward and landing on the sidewalk like a jellyfish. His woman Rifleman emerged from the car as some passersby began to flee the scene, while others stayed to watch. She surmised that they thought the scene might be a Hollywood film shoot. The onlookers watched as Monty's assassin stood over him. Under his own bulk he could do little but flail his hands and pathetically kick his legs like an infant in a crib, she reported. His mouth moved but he was unable to speak. The excited onlookers reeled in horror when the stiletto-heeled, fishnet stocking, and leather corset-donned Rifleman pulled strands of her billowy pink wig past her sunglasses then blew Monty's head apart with a point-blank shot. She recalled there being total silence as she walked back to the limo before speeding off.

Hollywood movie mogul Janssen Quint had just left Duke's Malibu restaurant and taken his seat behind the wheel of his vintage Maserati Quattroporte parked out front when his Rifleman put the crosshairs on him from the scrub-covered hills across the Pacific Coast Highway. Quint was the king of Hollywood's gratuitous violence genre, which, in service to his D.C. comrades, always depicted D.C. aristocrats as heroes and those calling for the reinstatement of elections and America's return to its founding principles as the bad guys. The Rifleman put a glass-penetrator bullet through his driver's side window and his head.

Jerry Danke, whose Internet social networking service made him a billionaire by the age of twenty-two, was on the treadmill of his Tucson, Arizona in-home fitness center when the Rifleman assigned to him arrived. Danke's social media empire was so instrumental in leading The 99% Party's pervasive disinformation campaign that he later bragged in a news interview that he was at the center of influencing the outcome of the 2016 elections. Working hand-in-hand with the traditional info-entertainment media complex his staff bloggers would propagate mythology around favored candidates and vilify those not in favor: attributing to them acts of sexual depravity with minors, starting chat rooms about candidates' criminal backgrounds that did not exist and quoting vile statements that they never made. News agencies would then pick up the story and report it as fact throughout the wider info-entertainment echo chamber. At the same time, opposition candidates who would attempt to use his social media tools for their campaigns would be blocked, or if not, it was later discovered, their pages and chat rooms deliberately tampered with by his staffers. Danke's social media empire was now as much responsible for promulgating D.C. economic justice propaganda as any of the official government media outlets—most effectively among the nation's youth. The presence of Danke's bodyguards compelled the Rifleman to take his shot through thick two-story-tall glass. Prepared for this contingency, he assembled his compact single-shot shotgun, placed a FRAG-12 high explosive fragmentation shell into a slot in a handheld device, programmed the shell to detonate two meters beyond the impact point with the glass, and fired it at Danke. Through his spotting scope he saw that the glass had shattered in a radial spider web pattern around the half-inch hole his smart projectile had made through it—blocking his line of sight on Danke. But the large amount of blood spatter that was visible across the inside of the window and on a nearby wall confirmed that the target was dead.

Back on the other side of the continent the National Interfaith Administrator Susan Dalworthy was leaving her mistress's NYC townhome. According to her public schedule, she was on her way to be keynote speaker at a mass wedding of YEAC volunteers at the National Cathedral. Texting at the top of the stairs of the brownstone's entrance while waiting for the doorman to have her car brought around, her well-dressed Rifleman trotted up the steps beside her like a resident who was simply entering the building. But instead of entering through the door he turned and shot her point blank with a round to the back of her head. She fell forward, her lifeless body fluidly sliding down the steps until coming to a rest in a grotesque twisted heap on the sidewalk.

Three blocks down, as police cars on their way to Dalworthy's assassination scene whizzed by, sirens blaring, two USN reporters who had made their bones artfully reporting D.C. propaganda as fact, slandering anyone who supported the Restart The Elections movement or otherwise interfered with The 99% Party's transformation of the country, were having breakfast with who they thought were two informants about to give them a tip on who shot Tarleton. They told them that it was Timothy Murphy, their fellow Rifleman, who had killed Tarleton just before unloading their entire ten-round magazines of hollow-point 10mm bullets into each of the reporters. One of their fellow Riflemen who was listening to their field report to Director Winston pointed out that they had broken the law: "Ten-round magazines are illegal in New York City."

Within the quarter-hour the reporter's USN Chief Editor Jackie Strawn was shot while getting into her car in the driveway of her Connecticut home. She was distracted with starting her car, speaking on her cell phone, and attempting to put her seat belt on after putting her coffee into its cup holder. Her assassin, parked two blocks away, rolled down his window, laid a Remington XP-100 bolt action pistol atop his car's driver side-view mirror and passed a .221 fireball round through her head before she'd managed to close the car door. He drove away with her collapsed halfway in and out of her car, her shoulder resting on the driveway pavement.

Comprehensive Electric Chairman and CEO, D.C.'s largest corporate welfare recipient and anointed monopolist, was cruising Miami's Intercoastal Waterway in his powerboat the morning of The Day of Reckoning. From two-thirds of a mile away, and aboard a boat himself, his Rifleman used his precision-guided rifle to tag and lock onto the CE CEO after he'd slowed to five mph to pilot his boat through a no wake zone near his Miami house. No one thought the lesser of the Rifleman who confessed that he broke down and acquired a precision-guided rifle a few years earlier, when his shooting accuracy began to deteriorate with his increasing age. The Rifleman watched through his scope the CE CEO's pilotless boat crash into a stone retaining wall then sink.

Forest Glendale, octogenarian investment billionaire who quickly bought up agricultural land and railroads that had not yet been confiscated just after the crash, then retained his fortune by selling or leasing them to the D.C. government, was enjoying breakfast tea at the kitchen table of his Springfield, Missouri home that he had lived in since childhood. He didn't believe in security and often joked about it in news interviews: that with all the good work that he and his partners in The 99% Party government had done together for the people over the years "who would want to bother a gentle old man like me?" When his Rifleman arrived he looked up from his teacup into the face of his assassin, stood up, and allowed him to take his life without protest.

Five hundred miles to the northeast, Chicago's multibillionaire Mayor Anthony del Gatto, a former investment banker who used his fortune to buy his way into Chicago politics just before the crash, was riding a horse at his personal stables he had located in Olive Park just aside Lake Michigan. Del Gatto ran the city like it was his own personal fiefdom: food from America's Midwest breadbasket; fuel from the Dakotas; anything on a truck, train, or boat, or in a pipeline passing near or through Chicago, he personally received a cut. In a few short years he earned billions more from what amounted to abject extortion, including squeezing massive subsidies from taxpayers vis-à-vis sweet deals with the D.C. government. An estimated nine hundred-thirty-yard shot from a .50 caliber rifle rolled him backward off his horse.

Morgan Père, the General Secretary of the U.N., was leaving his brownstone for the U.N. building to lead a conference entitled "War Reparations: Atoning for the American War of Northern Aggression." When amnesty was granted to illegal aliens in 2016, the United States added thirty-two million voting citizens overnight: seventeen million illegal immigrants and another fifteen million through chain migration. Predominantly of Mexican origin, and the largest unified voting block in the country, demands began with Hispanic-American activists and community organizers calling for war reparations from the D.C. government for the suffering caused to the ancestors of Mexican Americans. D.C. complied and once the money began to flow Père saw opportunity for the U.N. He organized a declaration from diplomats of mostly despotic nations to deem the Mexican American War, the American War of Northern Aggression and to nullify the annexation of Texas, declaring it an illegal action. And, that the later Mexican Cession should also be nullified and that all lands be returned to Mexico together with reparations that would be administered through the U.N. The Rifleman fired on him as he waited for his limousine to arrive. But

Père was lucky: he turned and took a step toward the doorman just as the assassin's bullet whizzed by his head, missing him by millimeters. Before the Rifleman could work his rifle's bolt and get back on target, Père realized what had happened and took cover behind a large concrete flowerpot. The Père assassination was aborted.

The Rifleman would learn through news reports that the Chairman of the Federal Reserve—the FED, having been acquired by the D.C. Government's Treasury Department years earlier—was shot to death with a pistol while ascending the steps of the U.S. Treasury Building. The Rifleman who'd assassinated him was cornered by building and grounds security. It was reported that he pulled a Gadsden Flag card from his pocket and let the wind take it before putting the pistol to his own head and pulling the trigger.

The Day of Reckoning closed with the only assassination abroad. No one knew the true extent of the wealth of Alois Anagnos, a European aristocrat who was lionized by the American media and who exploited D.C. corruption to such an extent that he ended up pulling many strings within The 99% Party, that he helped fund into power. The plan was for a Rifleman's bullet to take his life while having his daily high tea on his home's patio overlooking Lake Genève. A coded posting on a pre-designated blog confirmed that Anagnos was dead.

LAWRENCE L. ALLEN

CHAPTER 27

Curtiss adjusted his headphones while a Radio Free America assistant leveled a microphone on a swing-arm near his mouth. Clearing his mind in preparation for his interview Curtiss noticed that vibrations from the ship's engines caused a continuous circular ripple in his coffee cup, but that the radio broadcast studio was insulated well enough such that none of the ship's noises were audible. Curtiss's interview was scheduled to follow the news.

" . . . And finally, there was another violent clash yesterday between citizens and aliens in California's southern Central Valley. Mostly in their late-twenties and early thirties the Americans were fighting with seasonal workers from south of the border who were there for day work. Representing his small band of Americans, their impromptu spokesman had this to say." The news presenter flipped a switch to play a recording. "We have a right to be here and I don't care what the U.N. or anybody else has to say about it." Cheering voices rose in the background. "We are all college graduates, we even have PhDs here. And we are all citizens. We have a right to be here." Cheers again. "We have a right to pick the tomatoes in this field for two bucks an hour today." Curtiss shook his head in disgust at what he was hearing. Long gone were the days when graduates like him daydreamed from taxicabs careening down New York City avenues imagining that it would only be a matter of time before they would occupy the top floor of one of the buildings parading past their taxicab window. Curtiss looked over at Director Winston who was standing outside the booth on the other side of a pane of privacy

357

glass, and who gave him a stalwart nod of confidence. Using his network and influence, Director Winston had arranged for Curtiss's debut on Radio Free America.

"And now a man who we'll only identify as Timothy Murphy, the revolutionary war sniper, his namesake," the news presenter-turned-interviewer announced to his audience, turning to Curtiss with a smile. "Your actions and those of your fellow Riflemen have ignited a second American revolution across the country. A revolt. And it all began with your assassinations of Senator Tarleton and Jon VanJones. Please tell our listeners why you did it."

"Well, these D.C. aristocrats have been running plays from Chairman Mao Tse Tung's class warfare handbook. And Mao is known for saying that political power grows out of the barrel of a gun. So, we just thought that it was high time to put some warfare in their class warfare."

"So, are you seeking political power?"

Curtiss smiled at the question. "We are simply Americans who refuse to be led like sheep by an illegitimate government. The report you made just before we started this interview is a good example of how desperate things are in the nation that only fifty years ago took humankind from horseback to the moon in the span of a single human lifetime. But now Americans are fighting migrant workers for day work? And lining up at redistribution centers for handouts? Are the Riflemen seeking political power?" Curtiss said with deadly seriousness: "We are soldiers in a war against the D.C. tyrants, our domestic enemies. But folks can consider us the loyal opposition if they wish."

"The D.C. government says you are a rogue military unit that is planning a coup, to take over the government and impose a military dictatorship."

"All of the Riflemen have sworn an oath to protect and defend the Constitution from all enemies foreign and domestic at some point in their lives. But no, none are active duty military personnel, if that helps you. Look: the D.C. tyrants and aristocratic elites have taken our country. They aren't accountable to the people through elections and they do not follow the U.S. Constitution. We aren't a bunch of crazed gunmen assassinating duly elected representatives of the United States of America. We are enforcers, shooting looters who've stolen the country. You know, like the sign says during natural disasters, 'Looters will be shot'? Well this is a national disaster, but our signs are the same: Looters will be shot."

Closing the interview: "Do you have any other message for the D.C. government?"

"Yeah. But first a message for the American people: Equality is insatiable; fairness a weapon of social warfare. And governments that impose them won't stop until they've equally impoverished everyone but themselves. And, to the tyrants in D.C.: If your voting record shows that you were against the abandonment of the U.S. Constitution, the suspension of elections, the seizure of private property, destruction of the free press, then you are not in the sights of the Rifleman. But if it is . . . well, you should have disarmed us first."

The tape-delayed broadcast of Curtiss's Radio Free America interview echoed off the concrete walls of the underground minuteman missile complex media room beneath the North Dakota prairie. The Riflemen looked at Curtiss and smiled when they heard his final remark before the presenter concluded with: "This is our final broadcast from this ship. But we will be back soon, broadcasting to you from another location. This is Radio Free America signing off."

When the station's dead air turned to atmospheric noise the Riflemen who had placed the shaped charges on the inside of the bottom of the ship's hull announced that they must have gone off as planned. He then shared his hope that the military's rapid response team—that was surely sent out to the ship to capture or kill Timothy Murphy—arrived at its last location after the ship had sunk. He then looked around at the group and shrugged: "Hey, I used to be one of those guys."

The radio was switched off, the television switched on, and together the Riflemen watched the president who was making a speech from the White House press room. It was in response to the riots and looting that had begun at Wealth Redistribution Centers across the country. The sudden removal of the Gang of Five and nineteen celebrity Nobles of the aristocracy left a power vacuum, and the public's anxiety about what would happen next was palpable. Chaos reigned in the Senate and House as politicians jockeyed for position. There was even a murder in one of the bathrooms of the D.C. Capitol Complex. Though it was likely the result of politicians eliminating a rival, false reports that the Riflemen had breached the D.C. Capitol Building stirred the sense of panic that was spreading across the country to a head.

The president was struggling to fill the void left by the Gang of Five, but weak, vacillating, devoid of personal charisma, and having been thoroughly outmaneuvered by the Gang of Five for years, it was beyond his capabilities. According to Director Winston's sources, he was reading a speech prepared by some of the more influential members of congress.

"These terrorists jeopardize the National Recovery," began the president with as much conviction as he could muster. Appearing old and frail, Curtiss thought he still lacked the requisite sense of authority. "They are looters and criminals who are fighting against the economic justice laws: the laws that ensure government can continue keeping a roof over your head, clothing on your back, healthcare at no cost to you, and yes, even food in your belly. If these terrorists succeed, they will take all of that away from you and you . . . " he paused for dramatic effect. "You will be on your own. Alone, to fend for yourselves. I beseech you: turn in these so-called 'Riflemen' terrorists for your own good. The life you will be saving will be your own," he concluded, his thin, colorless lips quivering on his pasty, cadaverous face.

But the president's scare tactics combined with the sudden parade of unfamiliar faces from D.C. in the news and public commentary in the days that followed the Day of Reckoning, only exacerbated the public's consternation and caused them to lose faith in the government's ability to protect and provide. One individual or D.C. faction would manage to maneuver the public mouthpieces and attempt to seize their moment with a promise of a return to stability and order under their leadership, only to be smeared, discredited, and brought down in the public eye by a rival faction mere days later. After several of these volleys, the public wasn't listening to anyone from D.C. anymore—especially the president. Consequently people began taking matters into their own hands.

Day of Reckoning copycat incidents erupted across the country. In Hollywood, eight of the best known politically active movie stars and film producers—The 99% Party propagandists—were hunted down by roving mobs with the same pit bulls used to immobilize feral hogs for sticking, and murdered in their Beverly Hills homes in the same way.

In States across the country there were attacks on federal and state senators, congressmen, and judges—those who supported the D.C. tyranny. An easy and popular intimidation tactic that spread across the country like wildfire was using high-powered rifles at distance to take out windows in their State Capitol building offices, and their cars and homes. A mob savaged the Colorado State Capitol building, looting it and setting fires in the offices, while in Minnesota the governor's office was occupied, and the governor and a dozen of his supporters were tarred and feathered and marched through the streets riding backward on donkeys.

The spreading violence caused four Southeast Sector D.C. senators to cut their Boca Raton, Florida golf game short to rush back to the relative safety of D.C. It wasn't until they had boarded their jet at a private airfield that they found it occupied by an angry group of citizens who were waiting on board to end their lives. They were found in their seats stuck like pigs.

The leadership of the nation's largest unions were holding a strategy session on how to get in front of the people's anger and make the growing rebellion against the D.C. government a union-led issue when a local militia group burst into their conference room and gunned them down before setting the building ablaze.

And in Chicago, notoriously corrupt figures, members of del Gatto's political and extortion machines, had their hands and necks immobilized in makeshift stocks hung on the enclosure fence of del Gatto's Olive Park riding stables. Citizens were lining up to throw horse manure, rotten kitchen waste, and epitaphs at them. It was reported that some of them had died of exposure—if not the public humiliation—after several days in the stocks.

The NSA's Utah Data Center was evacuated by a bomb scare, then set ablaze and destroyed by strategically placed fertilizer-fuel bombs by a well-organized group with military precision. The bombs were placed in critical locations that would disable the facility's information systems and networks and destroy records, indicating that at least in part it was an inside job.

In an attempt to bring order the president called on the National Guard to protect those who would be the object of the people's ire, authorizing the Guard to go door-to-door if need be to apprehend violent perpetrators. But the increasingly balkanized Guard—friendly to other State Guards but leery of D.C. authority—seemed to always be at the wrong place at the wrong time, and unfailingly too late.

Ever-increasing in ferocity, as these acts spread America's elites and aristocrats fled *en masse* the country's heartland and hinterlands, escaping their increasingly hostile districts and hometowns for the relative security within the beltway of the District of Columbia. Media images of the renamed Tarleton National Airport, Dulles, and Baltimore Washington airports strewn with chartered commercial aircraft and private business jets of every make and model that had made the urgent one-way trip to D.C. at the behest of the nation's ruling-class families, brought vividly to mind Curtiss's memory of Hong Kong's Kai Tak Airport after the June 1989 Tiananmen Square incident. But what was happening in America was antipodal to China's Tiananmen Square incident: The ruling class was fleeing the American people by escaping *to* the capital, rather than the Chinese people fleeing the ruling class by escaping *from* the capital.

D.C. hotels quickly filled to overflowing as aristocrat refugees poured into the beltway. Almost immediately the government began displacing D.C. residents; ordering a reluctant military to seize properties and evict their residents to make room for the politically well-connected VIPs. The Riflemen cheered the day Director Winston stood before them and announced that his sources had informed him that the Army Corps of Engineers were erecting a concrete wall around D.C., following the outside edge of the I-495 interstate highway. It was being called the Beltway Wall and it was built so the Riflemen *and* the people would no longer be able to reach them.

So D.C. would become their prison. Curtiss smiled at the thought.

*   *   *

As Minuteman missile facilities go the one that the Riflemen now called home was considered large. In addition to the underground launch control center for the ten ICBM silos spread across miles of the surrounding countryside it had other facilities including a media room, should it need to serve as an alternate command post, and an older missile silo annex left over from an early phase of the Minuteman program. Though the annex was long mothballed it was not destroyed with the implementation of the START agreements, but rather left intact for purposes of historical preservation. The primary complex in its entirety was designed to accommodate about an eight-person missile combat crew and occasional overnight stays by maintenance and service contractors. So for the twenty-five men and women who comprised the Riflemen it made for very tight quarters—even with the missile and much of the equipment removed.

Enclosed in greenish-gray painted steel and concrete walls, and floored in diamond plate metal or worn commercial carpet, life in the complex was akin to living in a submarine: complete with submarine-style breech doors, but for protection from nuclear blast and fallout. And the comparisons with submarines were not too far off in other ways: launch control centers are cylindrical in shape and hemispherical at both ends, and theirs patrolled one hundred feet beneath the waving sea of the North Dakota grasslands above.

Ambling through the facility would take one along a maze of metal mesh staircases and platforms and past crawlspaces strewn with folding cots that would need to be stepped over in order to pass. And it was a struggle not to trip over debris: a blue and white Maxwell House coffee can that had once doubled as an ash tray, an extension cord powering a stained circa 1980s Mr. Coffee automatic drip coffeemaker that still worked, and shoes that tripped one up as reliably as the devil's club undergrowth that plagued Curtiss and Rick on their Alaskan hunts.

Though the facility was not destroyed by START it was completely dead nevertheless. At times at night, between rustling of Riflemen, there was absolute silence and his close proximity to the errant Badakhshan B-52 Arc Light raid bomb, countless gunshots over the years and over-amplified musical jam sessions in his youth would all come back to haunt him with an indistinctive ringing in his ears; his mild tinnitus filling dead silence.

How this place must have thrummed in its day, Curtiss thought one evening. He imagined the symphony of sounds that accompanied lonely missileers on mind-numbing duty: clicks and whirrs from the equipment, the hum from vacuum and cathode ray tubes. Also long gone was the agricultural chemical reek of the solid rocket fuel in the silo and the dry purified air in the crew area: specially filtered from below-ground systems that were reportedly so effective that it would be safe to breathe even after a nearby nuclear strike. But those were gone now, replaced by a simple forced-air fan system that struggled to deal with the overpopulated complex where everything from breathing and showering to heating MREs and laundry done by hand made the air sticky and musty like a gymnasium locker room.

A lucky Rifleman might have a bunk tucked into the gaps between ancient floor-to-ceiling electronic consoles whose black plastic maintenance grab handles now served as coat hangers and ties for clotheslines that would need to be ducked under. With only a makeshift curtain for privacy, decoration amounted to multicolor cable bundles, stretched over lengths of musty foam-backed Naugahyde sound-deadening insulation that flowed out of and back into crevices. Flickering fluorescent lighting along the narrow corridors completed the 1970s nuclear missile bunker décor.

"Woah! India Allen, playmate of the year 1988," a Riflemen exclaimed in wonderment one evening from behind his curtain, bringing Curtiss into the know about the stack of *Playboy* magazines that were discovered in a closet and that were making their rounds among the Riflemen. "And she's posing with a Lamborghini Countach. Man, just look at the lines on that car!" Curtiss was amused at how declining testosterone levels might have contributed to the over-the-hill Rifleman even noticing the car. He thought to stop and explain that the word countach is Piedmontese . . . but he decided to leave well enough alone.

All cell phones were locked up, and landline telephone and Internet communications were not permitted so as to make them electronically invisible to those who might be looking for them. So that they weren't completely cut off from the outside world, and for security, they returned to the practice of hand-carried dispatch letters for outside communications. One could count on seeing a pensive Director Winston in the missile silo annex sitting, writing dispatches at one of the two launch control desks beneath control panels studded with manual dials, rows of toggle switches protected by red plastic flip-up covers, and color-coded coaxial cables that spurted out of one panel and dove back into another. And, of course, the padlocked red metal box that used to contain one of the two launch keys: to be turned simultaneously together with a second missileer who would be at a duplicate desk a prescribed number of feet away. Somehow, Director Winston looked right at home among the Panaplex numeric display, olive green oscilloscope screen, and Western Electric circa 1960s-style phone handset's thick coil cord and rotary dial mechanism. They were, after all, hallmarks of his era.

Riflemen were only permitted to exit the facility two at a time on a rotational basis, for fear that more might be detected and interpreted as enhanced activity by a passing drone or satellite. When it was Curtiss's turn to stretch his legs on the surface and bask in a rainbow-esque sunset one evening he promenaded around disheveled surface buildings and across a parking lot shattered to near rubble by decades of freezing and thawing, all enclosed within a razor wire-topped rusty hurricane fence. He thought how the entire scene resembled for all the world a long-abandoned drive-in movie theater. The unsuspecting could not imagine that technology once decades ahead of its time was lying just thirty or so yards beneath their feet. That under the *wrong* conditions one hundred ton blast doors would be blown open and around the three hundred-sixty degrees horizon ten intercontinental ballistic missiles would explode from beneath the ground atop pyroclastic-flow like waves of smoke and fire. And that they would then fly thousands of miles, over the North Pole and precisely cast off their payload to detonate within a football field's distance of their target—replicating for a brief instant on earth conditions hotter than the sun.

For Curtiss who grew up during the early nuclear age, the existence of these weapons of horror dangling overhead were a reluctantly accepted part of life. He even wrote a Hershey School term paper defending Mutually Assured Destruction. But this was 2020 and the enemy was not thousands of miles away, but in D.C., and with world civilization receding from its high watermark during the debt decades of the 1990s and early 2000s it now all seemed like a colossal waste of resources and effort. It was as much a relic of a clash between lost empires as Hadrian's Wall that Curtiss, Leah, and Conner had visited on a driving vacation through the U.K.'s

Northumberland region during their family's better days.

* * *

During the recent social breakdown, roving gangs of looters were known to murder entire families in their homes then claim they were empty and that they had been squatting there for some time. Curtiss worried about Conner's safety: he kept things at the house and returned from university from time to time to pick them up and drop them off. He knew how to shoot, but had no interest in guns, and certainly didn't carry one. What if he returned home and came face-to-face with squatters? These were dangerous times for politicians and citizens alike. This is what was on Curtiss's mind as he slid a bookmark into the copy of Leo Tolstoy's *War and Peace* that he'd found in the Minuteman facility's modest library when Director Winston had him called from his bunk to the media room.

Upon entering Curtiss was startled to see Director Winston sitting with Jack Mack: Mr. software and cellphone network. The scene didn't compute for Curtiss. Mack was an ardent and very public advocate for The 99% Party in its early days. Director Winston gave Curtiss a reassuring tilt of the head, indicating that he should sit and listen before passing judgment.

After making introductions, Director Winston explained, "This launch control center and missile silo, and the surrounding thousand or so acres, are owned by Jack."

Mack smiled with the insincerity of one who was attempting to remain humble, but just beneath the surface was gloating about his self-perceived superiority. His over-exercised, zero-body fat physical persona, while great for television, made him look gaunt and dried out in person. He spoke through florescent light-like bleached white teeth: "I pay a hefty tax to D.C. for the privilege of owning this land, and several other mothballed ICBM missile complexes across the Dakotas and Montana," he said while dusting off his sleeves. "The silos are decommissioned and the land largely unproductive, so rather than bear the expense of confiscating them from me, D.C. lets me keep them because the fees and taxes I pay are just another way of confiscating my wealth." Curtiss thought to ask him why he bought them in the first place, but his curiosity didn't trump his caution about Mack. "It is the same as them taking your little house . . . but only on a bigger scale," Mack added.

Director Winston shook his head in the negative, as he no doubt noticed Curtiss's face flush at Mack's last, condescending statement. True to his public image it was always and only about money with Mack. He was indeed the greedy, arrogant egotist that the late Alan Monty's film made him out to be. Nevertheless Curtiss swallowed hard and decided not to look this gift horse in the mouth. Director Winston had arranged the meeting and so he was, if for no other reason, deserving of Curtiss's courtesy.

"So, when my dear friend Bart here told me about your mission, and your need for . . . let's say, a hideout, I was more than happy to oblige. And, when he told me that you Riflemen were going to do Monty, well, I just had to do what I could to help," he said with a vindictive, satisfied smile. "I understand that you personally did Tarleton and VanJones and got this whole thing started, Mr. Bradley," Mack puckered his lips and nodded approvingly. "Consider this facility your Rifleman's sanctuary," he said, opening his arms in a welcoming gesture.

* * *

When Curtiss was again summoned from his bunk he was told that the national Emergency Alert System had been activated and that the president was underway with making an address. "It's the president and that U.N. Père," said the Rifleman who came to collect Curtiss as they walked to the media room. Père and his family had taken up residence in D.C. after his Day of Reckoning assassination attempt and he was now standing at his own podium bearing the U.N. emblem, beside the president's podium on stage at the White House press room.

"And to better execute my sworn duty to ensure domestic tranquility and to protect and defend the American people from the Riflemen terrorists and the ensuing chaos that they've caused, by the power vested in me, I hereby declare civilian law suspended and that martial law will take immediate effect, under my direction—until such time that peace and good order has been restored."

Brief, halfhearted applause could be heard from the White House

Press Corps audience, but they quickly dropped off. The press room became eerily silent and one could feel through the open microphones the sudden consternation over the uncertainties of what they'd just heard griping the audience.

"Well, that gutless coward picked a fine time to grow a spine . . . " Director Winston said with contempt, before stopping himself to hear what would come next after the television camera zoomed out to include both the president and Père.

"And Secretary General Morgan Père has assured me that I will receive the full cooperation and support from the United Nations during our time of need." The president looked down to read from a prepared speech. "Nobody knows peacekeeping better than the U.N. They are experts at managing civil unrest and so Morgan and I will be joined at the hip as, together, we bring America back to stability and greatness. U.N. peacekeepers will begin deployment to urban centers across the country, coordinating the valuable tasks of protecting our food convoys and the rights of all Americans to access their redistribution centers in a safe and orderly fashion—wherever help is needed."

The president looked up and paused for expected applause that never came. The press room remained deadly silent: not an artificial camera click could be heard, nor a photo flash seen through the historic moment. People were genuinely made speechless by what they were hearing.

Over the years Curtiss had seen Director Winston frustrated, perturbed, and even angry, but never blind with fury. "Why that pusillanimous unprincipled scumbag . . . " All eyes in the control center media room turned to Director Winston as he strained, red faced and with flames in his eyes, to restrain himself.

Père cleared his throat and spoke. "The great and generous nation of the United States has given so much to the world. And the world owes you-all a great debt of gratitude. And it is for this reason that I reassure you today, the American people, that I—in concert with your president—will do everything within my power to carry on Senator Tarleton's work." His words also met a silent press room. "Together we will make it our mission to not only finish the work of Tarleton's Economic Justice Department in America, but to roll it out to the rest of the world; to create equality, fairness, and social

368

justice on a global scale. To unlock the great wealth that America's greedy capitalists now hold for the benefit of all humankind." The president remained silent at Père's side, unflinching, in tacit approval.

"Sniveling . . . traitorous . . . looking for legitimacy . . . selling us down the river!" Director Winston stopped making sense as he swung his boot against the television, folding it in the middle, before sending it crashing to the ground. "That sneaky son of a bitch! This is his end-around the Congress? Pawning off his powers as commander in chief to that U.N. looter?"

Curtiss looked over at the media room entrance to see Mack leaning against the doorjamb, arms and feet crossed wearing a smug smile on his face as he watched Director Winston's rage send everyone in the room back on their heels. Mack calmly unfolded his arms, nodded, and slowly walked away.

Within hours of the president and Père's broadcast, news agencies were running a breaking story of a lone gunman making sport of shooting out U.N. Building windows one by one. And the window-plinking wasn't the only threat to U.N. foreign nationals and personnel that exploded after the president and Père's broadcast. Other spontaneous incidents began accumulating, including mobs turning over the Mexican and South African ambassadors' cars while the ambassadors were still in them. Those episodes triggered an evacuation of all U.N. foreign nationals to D.C. under threat from what was being described as a coordinated attack by "American Riflemen insurgent terrorists." Though the U.N. exodus was carried out and protected by military convoy, the U.N. building was left vulnerable. The building's fire control system was disabled by rioters and the building set ablaze. It burned uncontrollably—destroying any future usability.

* * *

Curtiss became convinced that historians would write that it was the president's order for martial law that was the trigger event for the secessionist movement that spread across all fifty States. Up to the president's declaration of martial law, forty-six State legislatures had already passed non-binding resolutions for secession at one time or another—to show their dissatisfaction with the suspension of national elections and the abandonment of the U.S. Constitution. Their basis for secession was universal: that for these two reasons the legal entity that they had been in union with—the United States of America—no longer existed. But the efforts stopped short of actual secession in deference to people's faith that God still blessed America, that elections would one day be restored, and that they would have the chance to vote for representatives who would once again live by the U.S. Constitution. But for many those hopes were dashed when D.C. fell into chaos after the Day of Reckoning, and the ruling class families descended deeper into the worst old world, European court-style subterfuges—squabbling for dominion over the rights, fortunes, and lives of the American people. The declaration of martial law, with the U.N. interference, was the last straw.

Secession began with the southwestern States that were claimed by Mexico—a claim that Père gave voice to in the U.N. The governors of the States of California, Arizona, New Mexico, Nevada, Utah, and Colorado banded together the week that they each signed their respective legislature's secession declarations into law and jointly made the announcement: "The people of our States are not chattel to be traded or fought over. Given the choice between our citizens being servants to the D.C. tyranny or being usurped into the nation of Mexico, we the people of the southwestern States have decided on a third path: independence." Within the following week, which became known as secession week, all fifty States had formally and legally declared independence.

The Riflemen watched with trepidation the streaming video that was projected to the media room's screen as the president declared the secession movement illegal and announced the formation of a constitutional commission that would develop a new United States Constitution, "A modern constitution, one that would be a positive document, that would clearly enumerate the obligations of the government to serve the people. And a new bill of rights—rights granted and guaranteed by your government: the right to food, the right to a home, the right to medical care, the right to . . . "

Director Winston had been away during secession week and all eyes in the media room locked onto him as he entered with a sense of purpose in his step. He took the podium and calmly asked that the president's broadcast be switched off. He looked exhausted and road-worn, but smiled contentedly. He paused to take a deep breath, appearing humbled in appreciation of the grandeur and importance of the moment. "There will be a constitutional convention held in Philadelphia in two weeks' time," he said with a broad smile. "Each of our fifty States are now selecting two delegates to attend the convention where they will declare Philadelphia the new capital of the United States." The room erupted into cheers.

While Director Winston waited for the applause to die down, he looked at Curtiss with an expression of deep concern. After his speech, in a private moment, he would confide in Curtiss his apprehension about where the U.S. military stood within the nation's authoritative ambiguity. Though Director Winston was able to speak with state governors and representatives, all of whom expressed their personal commitment to participate in the reformation of the United States in Philadelphia, he was unable to reach the Joint Chiefs who were inaccessible to him at the Pentagon—behind the Beltway Wall. While he was convinced that their hearts would be with the *rebels*, smiling at his use of the dysphemism, he was not certain about where their heads would be with regard to where they thought their duty lie. These were dangerous times and nothing could be taken for granted.

Director Winston refocused on the men and women who were waiting on his next word. "Prepare for a road trip, ladies and gentlemen. We are headed to Philadelphia," he shouted as the Riflemen rose to their feet in unison with a spirit resembling the hat toss at an Annapolis graduation ceremony.

CHAPTER 28

The routine of exercise, personal grooming, washing one's clothes by hand, and passing around scuffed and dog-eared pre-1990s books had the Riflemen becoming stir-crazy. The prospect of a near two thousand-mile road trip through America's heartland and the anticipation of eating something other than MREs had everyone around Curtiss in the media room, turned makeshift daily cafeteria, smiling.

"Equality is insatiable . . . I should have known it was you." The words came from over Curtiss's shoulder in a distantly familiar voice that sent a shockwave through his body. He quickly turned to see a well-dressed elderly man wearing a bow tie with a carnation in his suit coat breast pocket standing behind him. "I knew it was you when I received transcripts from your Radio Free America broadcast. What other American freedom fighter would have quoted Sonya?"

Easily in his mid-seventies, it was his old teacher, confidant, and friend Lu. Though Curtiss kept tabs on him from afar, they hadn't spoken since he'd moved back to the U.S. Senator Lu was China's representative from the province of Taiwan and a prominent national defense committee member in the government of the new democratic and reunified China.

Lu's presence out of context momentarily discombobulated Curtiss, who became overwhelmed with an amalgam of long unpracticed emotions that suddenly welled up: paramount among them a foreboding sense of loss. Lu meant many things to Curtiss, among them a father figure, but also a very different time in his life—

and in the world. Together, Sonya and Lu had reshaped the theme and direction of his life. Though he and Lu had defied death together on occasion, more important was that they had always embraced life when they were together. And though Curtiss bore many burdens throughout his life, after his Hershey School childhood, the years that he and Lu were together were the most free and easy of them. Curtiss was now estranged from who he was then, during his early years in Asia, wrapped up as he was in the monumentality of the disintegration of his family, the degradation of his country, and his recent embedment with the Riflemen and their mission. Curtiss was too choked up to say anything, so he simply stood, grabbed Lu's hand for a handshake, then pulled him in for an embrace.

Walking alone among the abandoned buildings on the surface together Curtiss and Lu caught up on each other's lives. Curtiss observed that only in the land of opportunity, China, could a half-starved kid who'd once floated down a river to freedom clinging to a basketball become a national senator representing a province of twenty-five million people. Lu chuckled at Curtiss's remark, offering only a slightly embarrassed smile through a thousand-yard stare as a response.

Lu expressed sadness at learning about his and Leah's failed marriage. "Though it is called social warfare, people always seem to focus on the financial and material costs. They never talk about the personal losses and social destruction." He was also disheartened to watch Americans make the same mistake with stateism as the Chinese did seventy years earlier. "But at the time we were so poor, and you Americans were so rich. It just goes to show that these things happening isn't about impoverishment of the pocket, but an impoverishment of the human spirit." Curtiss smiled, pleased that one of his favorite lines from his university lecture quiver had unknowingly come from Lu somewhere along the way.

Eventually Lu explained that he was on a secret diplomatic mission and was authorized to offer the *rebels* military, intelligence, and financial assistance for their fight for liberation from the D.C. tyranny. "Consider it a gift from the people of China to thank the American people for their efforts promoting democracy and freedom in China forty years ago. I have discussed our offer with Mr. Winston," Lu said, smiling broadly. "But he told me that he would let it be your decision. You are his Asia expert and he trusts your judgment. So it is your decision whether to accept help from China, or not."

Their time on the surface was up and Curtiss began walking Lu back to the elevator. "Let me think about it overnight," he said, putting his arm around Lu's shoulder. "Let me buy dinner tonight. The MREs are on me."

Back on the surface the next morning to see Lu off Curtiss thanked him for his people's offer of help, but respectfully declined.

"I will inform my government," Lu said with a gracious bow. "If I can't help your people's struggle on behalf of my country, let me help you personally as a friend who has seen just a few things in his life." Lu paused to take a deep breath and collect his thoughts. "That statement: equality is insatiable . . . it cuts many ways, Curtiss." Lu placed his ageing hand, fingers slightly twisted with arthritis, on Curtiss's shoulders. "You know, the old Chinese saying 'Give a man a fish, feed him for a day. Give a man a fishing rod, feed him for life'?" Curtiss nodded that he had. "That is only one side of the story. Another side, the one you don't often hear about, is: Give a man a fishing rod, feed him for life. Give a man a fish, and he will beat the life out of you once you aren't giving him fish fast enough."

* * *

Lying in his bunk atop a steel maintenance platform that extended midway into the annex's missile silo Curtiss listened to the peculiar way the eighty-foot deep, twelve-foot diameter silo and rocket exhaust vents at the bottom corralled and twisted the sound of dripping water into a bizarre echo. As his mind wound down and began preparing for sleep he imagined there being similar sound in the caves of Afghanistan. His semiconscious mind pondered the irony that, like the al-Qaeda terrorist enemy that he had once fought, that hid in caves in places like Tora Bora, that he now was the one taking refuge underground—albeit in manmade caves.

And what of Lu's advice? He had lived through some of the toughest and most chaotic times for human beings: China's communist era. He knew exactly how desperate people become when a society had been deliberately pitted against itself. Would the riflemen be welcomed as heroes or villains? Were they seen as an anachronism like their enamel-coated, analog Minuteman facility? A throwback to another era in the country's history that few knew about and even fewer seemed to appreciate? Did the majority of Americans value freedom and self-reliance anymore? Or do they now fear it?

How would people react to the Riflemen threatening their barely adequate but steady flow of fish from the D.C. regime?

Townspeople began arriving at the launch control complex's crumbled parking lot in the early, pre-dawn morning. By 7:00 am the lot was half full with aging but able pick-up trucks, a small moving van from a bankrupted nation rental center, and a vintage yellow school bus: the Riflemen's transportation. From a nearby town of one hundred-twenty souls, it seemed as if they'd all shown up to see the Riflemen off. Prairie breezes fanned the surrounding grassland as families and friends spoke in hushed voices, seemingly in deference to the somber historic moment.

As the Riflemen loaded their gear, while milling about the crowd, Curtiss came upon Director Winston speaking with a woman—her pre-teen children clinging to her side. Her weathered-beyond-her-years face bore the same distraught expression of the 1930s depression-era mother escaping the dust bowl that Curtiss had once seen in an American history textbook photo. "Please get our country back," he heard her say to Director Winston. "You go and put those bandits who stole our country from us in their place."

Before Director Winston could respond, the voice of the town's mayor through a police cruiser's loudspeaker interrupted. But Director Winston's taking of her hands in his and giving her a reassuring smile said enough to bring a hopeful smile to her face.

"We want to thank the Riflemen for their courage in standing up to D.C. and to let them know that it has been our privilege to have helped provide them sanctuary here," the mayor began. The townspeople's applause was nearly blotted up by North Dakota's wide-open spaces. "This land is *our* land. It is for you and me, not those scoundrels in D.C. . . . . "

The Mayor was himself then interrupted as a man began leading the townspeople in a spontaneous recital:

This land is your land, this land is my land
From California to the New York Island
From the Redwood Forest to the gulf stream waters
This land was made for you and me

As I was walking that ribbon of highway
I saw above me that endless skyway
I saw below me that golden valley
This land was made for you and me

I've roamed and rambled and I followed my footsteps
To the sparkling sands of her diamond deserts
And all around me a voice was sounding
This land was made for you and me

There was a big high wall there that tried to stop me
Sign was painted, it said "No Trespassing"
But on the back side it didn't say nothing
This land was made for you and me

In the squares of the city, in the shadow of the steeple
By the relief office I seen my people
As they stood there hungry, I stood there asking
Is this land made for you and me?

When the sun came shining, and I was strolling
And the wheat fields waving and the dust clouds rolling
As the fog was lifting a voice was chanting
This land was made for you and me!

Nobody living can ever stop me
As I go walking that freedom highway
Nobody living can ever make me turn back
This land was made for you and me.

By the final verse the townspeople had come close enough
together that the mayor dropped the radio handset onto the seat of

the police cruiser and walked up to join them. "Today . . . " pausing as a preacher does when drawing the attention of his flock " . . . we are gathered here to send these brave men and women off on their perilous journey to help bring our land back to us." He seemed to want to say more, but simply ended with: "Godspeed, Riflemen."

* * *

"Radio check," Director Winston said into the vintage 1980s Cobra CB radio handset. The others in the convoy acknowledge 10-2. "We're going to need a pit stop soon."

This was it: their Riflemen rebels' first stop. Irrespective of the state of elections or D.C.'s adherence to the U.S. Constitution, they had directly attacked the leadership of the country—and then some. They were the enemy and they were now exposing themselves to the general population for the first time since the Day of Reckoning. And having seen firsthand in Afghanistan what happens to enemies of the U.S. government when they came out of their caves and exposed themselves, Curtiss considered for the first time that they may never make it to Philadelphia.

Avoiding stopping in larger cities, Director Winston led the Riflemen off I-94 to fill up in the small town of Barnesville, Minnesota, about thirty miles past Fargo, North Dakota. Curtiss's leg jackhammered the passenger side floor of their pickup while he watched their vehicles fill up two at a time. Though they were doing so as orderly and efficiently as Curtiss had seen jet aircraft fill up at airborne KC-135 Stratotankers, they couldn't do it fast enough for his liking.

Curtiss choked up when he saw an eight-vehicle column of Minnesota National Guard coming their way from down the road; though he rationalized that there was nothing inherently suspicious about a cluster of twenty-five or so men and women gathered to fill up a hodgepodge of aged vehicles at a two-pump gas station. Watching the column pass in the side mirror of their truck, his gut twisted when the convoy's brake lights came on, they pulled to the side of the road in unison and the lead Humvee made a U-turn for the gas station. Through the windshield Curtiss could see Director Winston standing by the edge of the road, calmly with hands on his hips, watching the proceedings. He looked over and with a head gesture requested Curtiss to join him.

After the Humvee arrived, to the drum roll of Curtiss's heart kicking inside his chest, a senior officer exited the vehicle and walked up to them. He smiled and saluted Director Winston. "We've never met, sir, but I served under you in Operation Desert Storm."

Curtiss resumed breathing normally while he listened to the two men cordially exchanged information about commands, campaigns, and battles.

"We have orders to keep an eye out for those Riflemen wanted by D.C.," the officer said while looking over the Riflemen's convoy with a somewhat star-struck expression. "You wouldn't happen to know anything about that, would you, sir?"

"Well, we'll be sure to let you know if we can be of any assistance," Director Winston replied through a half-cocked smile.

The officer nodded. "Good hunting, gentlemen," he said after saluting Director Winston and shaking Curtiss's hand, before reentering his vehicle and continuing down the road with his column.

After starting their truck, Director Winston glanced over a crooked smile. Curtiss was certain that his exasperation about their encounter with the Minnesota National Guard, and his frustration with Director Winston's not letting him know about the arrangements he'd made with them, was clearly visible on his face.

"Let's just hope the Wisconsin, Indiana, Ohio, and Pennsylvania Guards are equally collaborative," Director Winston said as he put the truck in gear. "Illinois? Their Guard no longer exists. And, with Mayor del Gatto gone, they are completely dependent on D.C. now. I've heard it is chaos there. That hundred-mile stretch along I-90 between South Beloit and Calumet Park on the lake could be a problem—Chicago especially," he portended.

Saluting Wisconsin National Guardsmen standing beside two Humvees greeted them at the I-94 exit for their next gas stop at the town of Eau Claire. The gas station attendants seemed to have been anticipating their arrival and they eagerly helped fill their gas tanks—turning the pedestrian gas station into the first service-with-a-smile, full service station Curtiss had been to since he could remember. Nevertheless, having been molded in the ways of the Quiet Professionals, Curtiss was unsettled by watching the gas station attendants attempt to shake hands with every Rifleman they could during the fill-up.

Any stealth they might have had on their journey to Philadelphia was completely lost by the time they'd reached Edgerton, Wisconsin: their last fill-up before possibly running a gauntlet through Chicago. Their convoy was met with hand-made *Welcome Riflemen* banners held by people who waved to them from the side of the road; welcoming the Riflemen like some liberating army. When they finally rolled to a stop at a gas station they were surrounded by folks who loaded them up with bottled water and sandwiches, home-baked pies and cookies, and the like.

"Which one is Timothy Murphy?" Curtiss heard one overzealous, budding teen ask. The Rifleman going about their business around him ignored his repeatedly asking the question of anyone nearby. "We don't identify individuals," one Rifleman finally said, kindly, as a father to his son. "People have families to worry about, son. Besides, you aren't even supposed to know we are here. Keep it quiet on your social network until we get to where we are going, okay?" Though clearly disappointed, the youngster nodded compliantly.

Rolling across the Illinois border it was easily apparent that the first State to declare bankruptcy after the 2016 Crash was well along with its social entropy. The Riflemen's first piece of evidence was a vacant and vandalized I-90 toll station. Brigands had made Illinois' toll booths far too dangerous to man and drivers not paying their automated toll bills received in the mail meant there was no practical means of collection. Without money for road maintenance, potholes grew prodigiously and the Rifleman's convoy had to routinely swerve around shards of truck tire, rotting deer carcasses, and chunks of fallen concrete from neglected overpasses. But the human cost of Illinois' deterioration revealed itself as their convoy approached the outskirts of Chicago: settlements on the grassy medians between the interstate roadways.

Chi-Towns, as they were called, were a modern take on 1930s Hoovervilles, where motorhomes and RVs replaced corrugated metal and plywood shacks as makeshift homes and ties for hanging laundry. Though similar shantytowns could be found across the hardest hit parts of the country, they began in Chicago and so the name stuck. They were configured like circled wagons: bulwark against marauders.

"I imagine that it was for times like these that China's Hakka minority built their Kejia Tulou," Curtiss noted to Director Winston, before telling him of his adventures in Fujian—and with Ken Wilkenson.

The thousand-yard stare of a woman sitting on the shaded side of her camper in one Chi-Town, her children gleefully playing around her and unaware of their poverty and dire circumstances, hauled up into Curtiss's consciousness more black-and-white images of desperation and futility on the faces of folks living out of Model Ts and in Hoovervilles. The look on their faces were the same. And the look on the faces of the men on the motorhome rooftops, sitting in lawn chairs under frayed patio umbrellas and holding rifles at the ready told everyone who passed to just keep on rolling.

"There's our welcoming committee," Director Winston said as they looked up through their windshield from the I-90 President Barrack H. Obama Expressway at an overpass, upon which several men were standing—one speaking into a walkie-talkie.

"They'll have the high ground," Curtiss said as a pang of doom appeared in his gut, same as when the two Uyghurs trapped him and Rambo at the bottom of the narrow pass on the trail out of Afghanistan.

The two men scrutinized each oncoming bridge until they approached the I-290 Ernesto Che Guevara Expressway's westbound overpass. "Here we go. Prepare to engage," Director Winston said into his CB radio handset when they saw fifty or so people poised at the overpass guardrail.

It began with a few pings on their truck's fenders: poorly placed gunfire, most likely from pocket pistols. Riflemen reaching out through the windows of their bus responded with automatic gunfire, raking the overpass's crumbling concrete guardrail with suppression fire. Curtiss felt relieved after passing through the cascade of concrete chips coming off the bridge: they'd made it.

The bus was still passing under the westbound overpass while Curtiss and Director Winston approached the eastbound overpass and so they would momentarily lose the benefit of suppression fire. Director Winston hit the gas and swerved to make them a more difficult target for the refrigerators, window air conditioners, various other debris and Molotov cocktails that were dumped on them from the overpass. Curtiss was nearly seesawed into the interior roof of the pickup when a full-size refrigerator clipped the left rear truck bed wall. A few more pings could be heard in the truck bed before they got out of effective range.

When they could see in their mirrors that all their vehicles had made it through Director Winston called for a casualty and damage assessment. One Rifleman was dead: he took a bowling ball directly to the chest while sitting in the front passenger seat. The shattered windshield made the vehicle unusable, and another was leaking gas, most likely from a bullet hole through the gas tank, and also needed to be abandoned. All other vehicles sustained some damage, but were working well enough to continue. They stopped only long enough to move gear from the two disabled vehicles and the body of the Rifleman to the bus. The dead Rifleman was from Toledo, Ohio and Director Winston decided that they would bring his body home to his family when passing through.

"We've picked up an eye in the sky: a helo off our starboard. Can't make out the ensign. It's keeping its distance," one of the Riflemen announced over the CB radio after they had passed the last exit for South Bend, Indiana. Curtiss glanced over his right shoulder and saw a helicopter paralleling them at some distance.

During the drive Director Winston had made Curtiss aware that the president's enlisting U.N. Secretary General Père to co-lead his so-called American peacekeeping mission inspired a National Guard moratorium on executing any orders from D.C. to engage civilian targets. However, it was not known how regular forces of the U.S. military would behave. Their top command still remained inaccessible behind the Beltway Wall. But Curtiss had already resigned himself to not knowing what hit him should he and the Riflemen be unexpectedly obliterated by a deluge of 30mm high explosive incendiary rounds from an A-10 Warthog's Gatling gun. So he simply looked over at Director Winston with his best battle face and nodded.

"Pit stop in Fremont," Director Winston announced over the CB after checking his hand-written mission plan in a small notebook that he slipped back into his shirt's breast pocket.

Curtiss kept his eye on the helicopter as their convoy wound around the exit ramps at the I-69 interchange. While Director Winston began searching the mostly rural landscape for their designated gas station Curtiss studied the half dozen motels along the way: half of them were boarded up and having been on the road for nineteen hours straight, the ones that were still open looked extremely inviting.

While filling up the Riflemen looked for Director Winston's signal to arm and prepare to engage the helicopter that had finally approached them and was setting down in a plowed field beside the gas station. It was a South Bend news station helicopter. Curtiss stood watching a reporter, cameraman, and soundman stumble with their equipment over the ruts in the field as they made their way to the gas station. Director Winston emerged from the truck wearing a cap and sunglasses and joined Curtiss where he was standing.

"Are you the infamous Riflemen?" the reporter said slightly out of breath, in an all-business manner just before putting a microphone under Director Winston's chin. She was an attractive, well-kept woman who modeled an athletic posture and, like Director Winston, was exceptionally fit for her age—which Curtiss put at early fifties. She appeared more youthful, though, as she struggled to tame her wind-blown hair by repeatedly pinning it behind her ears. Director Winston glanced over at Curtiss and cracked a cheeky grin; another expression Curtiss had never seen in all the years he'd known him.

He turned back to the reporter. "If you turn off your camera I'll talk to you." The reporter requited with a sparking smile, paused for a moment, then asked her team to wait at the helicopter.

As the three of them walked over to a next-door family restaurant Director Winston gestured to the Riflemen that they should find a meal and that they had thirty minutes to do so.

"Your news organization is part of the D.C. regime," Director Winston said after the waitress brought weak coffee to their booth and took their order. "Now why would we tell you anything?"

"Some of us feel that we are as much a prisoner of D.C. as those people up in the Detroit reeducation camps," she said with distain, draping a pall over the moment. "I studied journalism to be a journalist, not a mouthpiece for D.C." Director Winston considered her for a moment then took off his hat and sunglasses. Her eyes scanned his face and her smile quickly returned. "You're CIA

Director Bart Winston."

"Yes, but that has nothing to do with . . . "

"Yeah. No, I get it," she said with an adorable, almost giddy excitement. "The secession movement. The Constitutional Convention in Philadelphia. The Riflemen . . . it's you guys."

"We are a small part of it." Director Winston carefully considered his next words. "The Riflemen are only a catalyst for the nation rejecting D.C.'s rule. But we aren't running the show by any means. The States are leading it."

Director Winston's lack of hubris appeared to impress the reporter. "It is nice to meet a man of integrity for a change. There aren't many of you around anymore." She blushed like a schoolgirl when she caught herself admiring Director Winston like a freshmen co-ed with a crush on her professor.

When the waitress returned Curtiss looked at Director Winston and the reporter, then asked the waitress for his meal to go. "My turn to watch the vehicles while the guys eat," he announced, smiling.

Forty-five minutes later Curtiss glanced through their truck's open driver-side window at Director Winston and the reporter shaking hands: she was holding his hand with both of hers. "If you promise to keep us off the radar until we reach our destination there is an exclusive interview waiting for you after we complete our mission," he overheard Director Winston say to her.

"I'll see you in Philadelphia then, Bart," said the reporter, still embracing Director Winston's hand.

Aside from the occasional hunt Curtiss and Bart Winston had never been close in their private lives. What he knew about his family situation was that he had four grown children scattered across the globe and that he became a widower the year Curtiss and his family moved back to the United States. The next, mundane sixty miles of I-80 couldn't wipe the endeared smile from Director Winston's face. He said nothing, while appearing to be absorbed in thought.

"So you have a date in Philly, huh?"

"She knew too much already," Director Winston blurted out, not allowing a split second to pass before issuing what seemed to be a prepared answer. He straightened up in his seat and inhaled sharply through his nose: "Better to keep your enemies close."

Curtiss smiled, looked up through the windshield mockingly

searching for the helicopter and nodded to let the tension build for a moment. "Yeah, and *this* enemy even closer."

The route to the dead Rifleman's family home took them off the I-80 interstate and eventually onto North Summit Street through what was once the heart of Toledo, Ohio. "You could have a shotgun fight here downtown and nobody would get hurt," Director Winston said while scanning the ghost town straddling the Maumee River. Curtiss studied the eclecticism of the city's structures—remnants of Art Deco besieged by blatant glass and steel insults from the modernist movement, plastered with postmodernist grafts that failed to sustain the dying patient—and speculated that the city might inspire an archaeologist a millennium later to deduce that the society there had a golden age and series of renaissances before its inexplicable demise.

They pulled to the edge of a vast expanse of overgrown concrete pavement and rubble that used to be a parking lot and entrance to the Willys-Overland Jeep plant. Once one of America's iconic arsenals of democracy it produced the country's most recognizable automotive export: the Willys-Overland Jeep. While parking in the shadow of its sole remaining structure—a smoke stack adorned with the name Overland—a photograph of Curtiss's father came to mind: one of he and his fellow crewmen posing in and around a Jeep parked on a dirt airfield in front of a Curtiss-Wright C-46 airplane. Though the plant produced the humble Jeep rather than the glamorous B-25 Mitchell that he flew over Tokyo, its celebrity in the war made Curtiss feel connected with his father nevertheless: another intersection of the trajectories of their lives, peripheral as this one was. But his recollection was appropriate in other ways since the memory of his father's generation and their accomplishments and sacrifices were now as abandoned and in ruins as the Willys plant in the now fundamentally transformed America. Schoolchildren were taught that their era was a dark age, one of war and oppression, led by America, before the current regime had liberated the country from its war-lording past. Curtiss hoped that he and the Riflemen's fight for freedom and a restoration of the republic would eventually lead to a resurrection and rehabilitation of his father's generation and their achievements.

The two who knew the dead Riflemen best, with Director Winston acting the senior officer, left to bring the body of the fallen Riflemen to his family. The remaining Riflemen seized the moment to stretch stiff backs and exercise long-ago injured knees and other joints from the ossifying effects of their road trip. The parking lot promenade morphed into an impromptu minute of silence for the lost Riflemen. The unscripted milling around that followed allowed the overwhelming sense of entrapment from antagonism, atrophy, and death, the likes of which Curtiss hadn't felt since his days held captive in the camp in Afghanistan, to overrun his emotional defenses and flood his consciousness. What twisted the blade in him was that this was all happening in the heartland of America.

"Hold up. Let's see if these people need our help," Director Winston announced as they passed a cul-de-sac on the road that was taking them back to I-80 east. Smoke was rising from a cluster of burned-out cars at the cul-de-sac's center and a front-end loader was placing the final concrete median barriers forming a rampart blocking entry from the street. All work stopped as the new exurban citadel's residents, each carrying a rifle slung over their shoulder, turned their attention to the Riflemen pulling to the side of the road. Something needed to happen fast, or it looked to Curtiss as though shooting might break out at any moment. Director Winston spoke into the CB handset: "Stay in your vehicles." He looked over at Curtiss as he exited their truck and tugged him along with his glance and a tilt of his head.

Five men and one woman met them at the gateway of the cul-de-sac's new defensive wall. Wearing knit caps and dressed in camouflage overalls and rubberized neoprene waterproof boots they looked ready for a hunt more than anything else.

"This is none of your business," one of them stated through a cold, determined look. "You need to keep going."

"We thought we might be able to help," Director Winston replied, turning on his air of irreproachable command authority that served him well in battlefields in Iraq as well as political ones inside the D.C. beltway.

"We don't need any help. We can take care of ourselves," the youngest member of the group defended as he gestured to the four smoking cars in the center of the cul-de-sac. A woman was using a garden hose to douse the last remaining flames in one of the cars while a man wearing yellow household gloves, white disposable painting overalls, a paper mask, and dust goggles had just pulled a body out of another car and was dragging it over to join eight more laying under a blue plastic tarp.

A broad smile spread across the face of the woman. "Stan," she said to the apparent leader of the cul-de-sac defenders, "I think they're those Riflemen." She turned to them and asked: "You're the Riflemen aren't you? We heard on the shortwave that you might be passing this way."

"We are, ma'am," Director Winston said without hesitation.

The small posse instantly broke into smiles and handshakes. Husky, bearded, in his early fifties, and wearing wire-rim glasses that belonged on an accountant, "Stan" announced their arrival into his camo-decorated walkie-talkie: "Stand down. They're friendlies. It's those Riflemen."

The posse-turned-welcoming-committee virtually dragged them into the cul-de-sac while the woman waved the rest of the Riflemen over after Director Winston hand signaled them the all clear. Within minutes an impromptu block party sprung up on the front lawn of one of the houses and the road-weary Riflemen found themselves queued up with plastic plates at folding tables loaded with venison sausage, pasties and chili, and a host of home-baked breads and desserts.

"I worked at Tony Packo's for ten years," a woman said as she placed a chili dog on Curtiss's plate. "These are the best you are ever going to eat."

While the Riflemen stretched out on the cul-de-sac's manicured lawns to nap and digest as youngsters hovered around them in hopes of eliciting a war story, Curtiss and Stan watched as his neighbor looped a chain attached to the bucket of the front-end loader around the roof panel of one of the burned out cars in preparation for its removal. Meanwhile a breeze had blown back a corner of the blue plastic tarp revealing two of the bodies.

"You know, I've shot deer through the heart that ran two hundred yards afterwards, but boy a .30-06 round with hunting bullets sure does make a mess of a man at close range, doesn't it?" Stan observed, as the two men surveyed the wounds on the bodies. "They were looters, or worse," he said as he sucked air through his teeth and tugged his pants higher on his protruding midsection. "I guess they thought that they could roam around, terrorize neighborhoods, invade people's homes, steal, rape. But they made the mistake of coming here to our cul-de-sac," he said, before taking a sip of coffee from a thermos flask cap. "Yep. A bunch of punks with 9mm pistols were no match for deer hunters with rifles. They drove into this cul-de-sac, you know, doing donuts, shooting in the air and such. Guess they through they'd scare us into submission." Stan nodded and took another sip of coffee. "There is a deer hunter in every house here," he said waving his cup around the cul-de-sac. "When they started to get out of their cars they got one hell of a crossfire laid down on them. Nearly three hundred-sixty degrees."

"Looks like you've taken neighborhood watch to an all new level, Stan," Curtiss said, with a smile. Stan smiled back.

"What do you want me to do with the bodies?" the front-end loader driver said while walking up to Stan.

"Take a few pictures first. We'll post them on the Internet. You know, give it the title 'Suburbia Welcomes Looters,'" Stan said, punching out the headline in the air with his hand. "Like Timothy Murphy said that one time on Radio Free America: Looters will be shot. Maybe that's a better title, come to think of it." Stan glanced at Curtiss, most certainly not knowing that he was quoting him, but rather attributing the quote to the Riflemen in general. "Then throw them into the front-end loader's bucket, drive them over to that field two blocks down, dig a hole, and bury them," Stan ordered.

"Saddle up!" Director Winston bawled to his Riflemen.

Stan reached out to shake Curtiss's hand: "We'll take care of the looters here on Main Street. You take care of them there in D.C."

Director Winston smiled at Curtiss as they rolled back on to the road to the expressway: "Looks like those folks don't need anybody's help."

* * *

The Riflemen were surrounded by semi-trailer trucks that came up to speed from where they were waiting along the shoulder of I-80, southeast of Toledo. They were greeted with honking horns, blinking lights and waving hands. "Break-19. Big trucks have got your convoy's back all the way to Philly," one of them announced over the CB. Evidently their cross-country journey had been quietly monitored by the trucking community.

Director Winston seemed to take this development in stride and Curtiss thought to ask him if he had made the arrangements, but decided simply to enjoy this turn of good fortune without question. Rather, Director Winston glanced over at Curtiss then quickly refocused on the road ahead. "Curt, I think it's time to bring you up to speed on the *Philadelphia Plan*."

CHAPTER 29

"We are here in Philadelphia for the same reason our Founding Fathers were here in the summer of 1776: to declare independence from tyranny," the foreman began to the State delegates convened in the assembly room of Independence Hall as Curtiss, Director Winston, the Riflemen, and others, and a small section of the world's media looked on. "When our sixteenth President, Abraham Lincoln, was facing a disintegrating union he resolved that the government of the people, by the people, for the people shall not perish from the earth. And that is also our purpose here today." The foreman paused to allow his words to receive a standing ovation.

"Benjamin Franklin described the 1787 Philadelphia Convention, and by extension the Constitution it produced, as being so close to perfection as to be astonishing. Therefore, the first vote before this 2020 Philadelphia Convention will be on the motion from the delegate from the great State of Virginia: that this body reinstate the supremacy of the U.S. Constitution—as it had been amended and existed in 2018 prior to the suspension of national elections. We will then, in due course, entertain motions for establishing a provisional government until which time national elections can be held . . . "

They were witnessing history in the making. Curtiss and Director Winston smiled to each other with great satisfaction during one of the early procedural votes passing a declaration that Philadelphia become the capital of the United States of America, and territory and authorities within the Beltway Wall of the District of Columbia a hostile foreign state. The Beltway Wall would demarcate a permanent national border. Like Hong Kong's Walled City, D.C. had become America's Walled City: where a malignant vestige of twentieth-century variety archaic despotism, excised from its host organism, would be isolated to decompose to its eventual extinction.

The participants and witnesses to the 2020 Philadelphia Convention mingled during recesses atop the narrow brick-cobbled streets and sidewalks surrounding Independence Hall. Roads leading to the building were closed from three blocks away, allowing no motorized traffic, and the sight and smell of policemen on horseback inspired Curtiss to muse over what people were thinking on the very spot he was standing back in the latter 1700s. The uncertainty. The leap of faith they were making. Bucking the most powerful empire the world had known.

Two policemen zipping by on Segways and the squawk from their police radios brought Curtiss back to the twenty-first century and the realization that they had it so much easier than the founders did. They knew what an independent and successful America looked like. The Founding Fathers didn't. They had no bloody Revolutionary War to contend with. And they . . .

"We're moving. To Washington Square Park. Now," Director Winston said as he walked past; the sense of purpose and determination in the stride of the Riflemen who followed him drawing Curtiss along with them. Before leaving the immediate grounds Curtiss spied the South Bend reporter and her crew standing in the Independence Hall green—her eyes riveted on Director Winston, an admiring smile of astonishment on her face.

Underneath a mighty oak at the center of Washington Square Park the Riflemen formed around Director Winston, splayed out like orderly iron filings around a magnet. "It's time to saddle up again. This time we are headed into the belly of the beast: D.C. We have cut the head off the snake, but a severed snakehead is still dangerous and must be defanged and buried to be made safe. The statesmen are busy with the burying: reforming the government here in Philly, establishing diplomatic relations with countries around the world, drafting treaties, connecting with the World Bank, and the like. But the defanging? That's our job. Transport will be waiting at Penn's Landing pier, about five blocks east of here. Tomorrow, 18:00 hours. Details will be briefed en route." Director Winston glanced at his watch. "You have twenty-seven hours to yourselves. Make them count."

"Your friend from South Bend is looking for you," Curtiss said to Director Winston after the Riflemen broke up and the two of them began making their way along South Sixth Street back to Independence Hall.

"She is waiting for both of us," Director Winston smiled. Curtiss had become comfortable with Director Winston always being one step ahead of him.

When Curtiss saw her again, and that her crew had set up at a park bench along the circular path that surrounded the center of the Independence Hall green, his apprehension about a public interview began to build. It wasn't his quiet-profession modesty, this time. What would he say? Would he proudly tell the world about assassinating people?

"Gentlemen," the reporter said first shaking Curtiss's hand, then embracing Director Winston's. "Thank you, Bart."

She directed them to the park bench, where her cameraman checked the light and attached microphones to their lapels. "This interview will be seen by over half the world before it is all said and done. And will be on record, for posterity."

Pangs of anxiety now rose from Curtiss's gut, gripping him deep in his chest. Not quite one hundred years earlier Governor Franklin Roosevelt dedicated a marker for Timothy Murphy at the Saratoga Battlefield where he shot General Simon Fraser off his horse. Would he be treated as kindly by history as Murphy was? Murphy killed British officers under orders while wearing the rank of sergeant within the legitimacy of a declared war. Would historians a hundred or two hundred years hence understand the nature of the social warfare that gripped Curtiss's era? Certainly Curtiss, by his own measure, was himself too close to the events to be objective. Would their hindsight from the history that followed allow them to interpret the circumstances and stakes to have been just as dire for the American people as the causes of the Revolutionary War, as Curtiss had? Or would he simply be lumped together with other terrorists of his era—even the ones he spent the latter part of his life fighting against—held up as a manifestation of a violent era of American history.

* * *

The sun had just set when the Riflemen's three motor coaches arrived at where the Baltimore-Washington Parkway dead-ended at the bottom of the recently completed thirty-five-foot tall D.C. Beltway Wall. Klieg lights atop the wall lit the scene, their intense white light punctuated by bluish, strobe-like flashes from welding torches making finishing touches to the steelwork creating a surreal night scene reminiscent of a taxi ride through late 1980s Shenzhen China.

Though the concrete at the center of the thickest parts of the wall was probably still setting, extensive graffiti had already made its appearance on its façade. Knowing full well that their work had a likelihood of being recorded and broadcast through some kind of unofficial media, revolutionary graffitists had painted images from the American Revolution: a reproduction of Benjamin Franklin's *Join, or die* woodcut print but showing the snake cut into fiftieths rather than eighths as it wound down the length of the wall, a Gadsden flag of course, and in traditional serif typeface the words *Live free or die*, and *Liberty or death*, among others. There were even impressive interpretations—spray paint on concrete—of Emanuel Leutz's painting *Washington crossing the Delaware* and Archibald Willard's *The Spirit of `76,* but holding a computer tablet and modern scoped bolt-action rifle, rather than fife and drum.

Spotlights from along the rim of the wall honed in on the front of their lead motor coach; white flags zip-tied to the side mirrors in clear view. Director Winston calmly rose to his feet and stepped through the door of the bus, disappearing into the bright light. He reappeared moments later at the bottom of a construction elevator's mast tower that was pinned up the side of the wall.

While they watched the hoist car slowly glide down to ground level to meet him, Curtiss recognized the scene as being similar to Napoleon Bonaparte's return from exile on Elba. He imagined that Director Winston, flanked by his Riflemen as Napoleon was flanked by his personal guard, was reenacting Napoleon's first meeting Bourbon king Louis XVIII's Fifth's Regiment on his march back to Paris—a regiment that was sent to destroy him. Could Director

Winston be as persuasive as Napoleon in convincing the regular army troops they now faced at the Beltway Wall to march under the banner of the United States of America: the one with its capital in Philadelphia? Or like Napoleon, would this be the beginning of their Hundred Days and result in the Riflemen's second and permanent exile—or utter destruction?

The door to the hoist car opened and a half-dozen men emerged, coming face-to-face with Director Winston. Having attended his meeting with the heads of the National Guard in a Philadelphia hotel ball room the night before, Curtiss knew that he was now attempting to convince them to escort his contingent to the Pentagon under a white flag, and there, to meet with the Joint Chiefs of Staff.

"Now we wait for their answer," Director Winston said through a heavy breath, after returning and taking his seat.

The excruciating hour-long wait in silence that followed ended with an officer and two armed escorts arriving at their motor coach's door.

"Follow us."

Curtiss and the other riflemen steadied themselves with the grab handles on the seat backs as their caravan picked its way along a rutty dirt construction road that ran parallel to the Beltway Wall. Curtiss watched through his window as people harvested wall construction jetsam: concrete forms and scrap rebar and empty wooden cable rolls and the like. American gleaners.

Piles of luxury cars strewn on either side of the road composed a corridor that led them to a gate in the wall. Once though the wall and out from under the I-495 overpass just behind, more luxury cars abandoned by the side of the road, some overturned and bearing scars from being shoved aside by heavy equipment spoke of panic during the American aristocracy's exodus to D.C. Roads jammed, they had no choice but to abandoned their cars and walk the rest of the way into their promised land.

As their procession cleared the Good Luck Road overpass Curtiss got a glancing look at some of the refugees in their new habitat. The lush forest in the immediate area alongside the road was clear-cut and a tent city built there. It resembled a military base: orderly and lit with portable electric light towers, and studded with rows of portable toilets. As they passed, Curtiss was just able to make out a line of people stretching from a large oval tent that he took to be the canteen.

When the Humvees ahead of them later stopped to clear a checkpoint beside the L'Enfant Plaza refugee camp, Curtiss got a closer look at the people there. He could see them milling around and queued up at tables filling out forms and carrying MREs stacked in their arms. Against the chill of the night air some gentlemen wore their cashmere overcoat lapels up around their necks, and ladies wore their furs; fur having made a big comeback with the rise of the D.C. Aristocracy. Still others wore ski outfits that were last year's fashion on the slopes of Aspen and Switzerland's St Moritz. But though the digs at the camp were far better than any Chi-Town, the body language of the people there spoke the same: desperation, fear, and disquietude.

The entrance to the Pentagon was fortified in a way that Curtiss had not seen since visiting Washington, D.C. to attend the ceremony placing Rambo's star on CIA Headquarters' memorial wall in 2002.

"Three personnel. That's it," the lead escort officer said to Director Winston when they met at the motor coach door. "Your other men will have to wait here."

Director Winston selected Curtiss and the former head of the SAD who once served as the Agency's Pentagon liaison officer, and who had impeccable military service credentials. Under armed escort they were led into the Pentagon, along its hallways and through a conference room door located in the bowels of the complex. Seated at one end of a conference table was the Chairman of the Joint Chiefs of Staff General Scott Mclelland, flanked by the Vice Chairman of the Joint Chiefs of Staff and Chiefs of the Army, Air Force, Navy, and Marine Corps. Absent of course was the Chief of the National Guard Bureau, Major General Michael Siena, who Curtiss had first met the evening before in Philadelphia.

"So how's Siena doing, Bart?" the Chairman asked Director Winston as the three of them took a seat at the other end of the conference table. "We don't see him around these parts much anymore," the Chairman continued, his drawl divulging his Texan roots.

"He's pretty busy these days, Scott."

The Chairman tilted his head, leaned forward, laid his interlaced hands on the table, and nodded. "As you know, this body now has direct operational command authority over the Armed Forces and serves at the discretion of the commander in chief, who has issued specific orders for the elimination of you and your Riflemen." He looked over his bifocals at Director Winston. "So how can we help you?"

"We are here to help *you*, sir." Director Winston's statement met absolute silence. "Your chain of command has been broken since the day the politicians suspended the elections and the SCOTUS suspended the Constitution." General Mclelland held a steely look on Director Winston, while the other Chiefs' inscrutable expressions suggested a willingness to listen. "We've all sworn an oath to support and defend the Constitution of the United States. Well, the living Constitution and the Capital of the United States no longer exists inside the Beltway Wall. They now reside in Philadelphia." Leaning back in his chair, crossing his leg and laying his hands in his lap: "So, we've come to offer our assistance with moving your command operations there."

Any humor in the proposition that Director Winston's band of riflemen who had arrived in borrowed motor coaches and under white flag should offer assistance to the Joint Chiefs of the Armed Forces, was trumped by the question of at whose discretion the Joint Chiefs now really served. Though it was Director Winston's good manners and discernment that he chose to not mention the president's power-sharing arrangement with U.N. Secretary General Père, it became that much more powerful as an unasked question that burned on everyone in the room like a blowtorch.

Director Winston went on with the most eloquent, deft, and skillful confabulation that Curtiss had ever personally witnessed from him—and few others for that matter. He led them though in intricate detail the *Philadelphia Plan* and enumerated the verdicts of plebiscites of the ongoing 2020 Constitutional Convention. What happened next would determine whether Director Winston was indeed Napoleon's compeer in the art of persuasion.

General Mclelland listening intently to Director Winston for the better part of an hour and a half, managing to interrupt him only several times with questions before looking over at the Chiefs for their affirmation that they were ready to conference.

"Have you and your men eaten?" General Mclelland asked, before directing his staff officer to see them and the Riflemen in the motor coaches to a twenty-four-hour cafeteria down the hall.

Rumors that had made their rounds weeks earlier about secret summary executions of counter-plutocracy incorrigibles were likely on everyone's mind as the Riflemen dined in silence while the Joint Chiefs deliberated. If this was to be their last meal Curtiss would have insisted on better. Though flying in a Hong Kong Peninsula Hotel chef at public expense to whip up an eggs Benedict would not have been considered extraordinary for your average D.C. aristocrat, it would likely have been out of the question for a death-row candidate in these austere times.

Curtiss's culinary musings were interrupted by General Mclelland's staff officer who announced: "The Joint Chiefs will see you now . . . all of you."

The Riflemen were welcomed back into the conference room with salutes from the two security officers that flanked the Joint Chiefs' end of the conference table, while the Riflemen's end overfilled to standing room only.

"We have only one question for you and your team: we need to know if there is any interference from outsiders. Are foreign government in any way involved in the Philadelphia Plan?"

Director Winston explained that with one exception the only contacts that have been made with foreign governments involved efforts to lay the groundwork for diplomatic recognition from long-time allies. He looked over at Curtiss, giving him his cue.

"China sent an emissary who offered assistance. We declined their offer." Though Curtiss had been front and center for the miraculous things that had unfolded since his assassination of Tarleton, it wasn't until making this statement that he actually felt part of the history being made around him.

General Mclelland drew a long breath, nodded, then looked at the Chief of the Army, General William McFarland, and in a calm voice said: "Bill, please instruct your men on the Beltway Wall that their mission has changed. They are to now consider the wall a national border. And their immediate mission is to assist military command personnel, selected American citizens, and their families within the beltway to make an orderly safe-haven repatriation from hostile foreign soil. Their long-term, primary mission will be to guard the nation's new national border with D.C."

He looked over at his staff officer. "Get the DOD Military Planning and Policy wonks out of bed and working on adapting the Emergency Relocation Group evacuation protocols from the Continuity of Operations plan. We need a re-draft converting from Civilian Government evacuation of Washington, D.C. to all willing Department of Defense personnel and military family members currently residing within the Beltway Wall. The evacuation plan should call for complete evacuation within seventy-two hours. On my desk tomorrow oh nine hundred." General Mclelland's Staff Officer sat with his mouth slightly agape, momentarily stunned by what he was hearing, then suddenly began feverishly taking notes.

"Have them work with Director Winston here who has the list of alternate facilities around the Philadelphia area where they're to be temporarily relocated," he concluded, shooting a look over at Director Winston who closed his eyes and nodded that that would work well for him.

He then turned to the Chief of the Marine Corps. "We need the Marines to get us on the other side of that wall. Transport and security is yours. We don't want to be shooting our way out of D.C."

"We need you and your top officers at Cheyenne Mountain," he next said to the Chief of the Air Force. "So what do you think? Can you keep everything grounded for the next seventy-two hours to be on the safe side?" The Air Force Chief nodded that he did and that he would.

The Chief of the Navy piped up: "We'll keep the Navy at sea and out of the way for the meantime, but we need to tell them what the hell is going on, Scott. Quick." All of the other Chiefs looked up in agreement and turned to General Mclelland for his response.

"Our Riflemen friends here and their fellow patriots in Philadelphia have taken care of ECG." General Mclelland's staff officer looked up from his rapidly filling yellow legal pad revealing a slight panic in his eye. "Enduring Constitutional Government," he explained with a smile of genuine appreciation to Director Winston and the Riflemen.

"The provisional government in Philadelphia and the collective

National Guard are working on a communiqué specifically for the armed forces as we speak. We think it best that communication happen through your individual chains of command," Director Winston said, his comment acting like a release valve, instantly lowering the pressure in the room.

General Mclelland finally turned to the Vice Chairman: "You play golf with Perry Lubbock over there at Secret Service, don't you?" he asked rhetorically. "Please ask Perry to get the damned nuclear football away from the president and bring it here directly." General Mclelland seemed to be prepared to move on to his next order of business, but then turned back to the Vice Chairman and said in an aggrieved tone of voice: "Oh, and if that SOB Père is anywhere near the football, you have my orders to shoot him on sight." Quiet laughter surged and retreated in the conference room like a wave on a beach. "Let's get moving gentlemen, we are out of D.C. in seventy-two hours."

* * *

It was late evening when the final convoy leaving D.C.—lightly armored and carrying General Mclelland, top military officers and specialists, and a good many of the Riflemen—rolled on to the 14th Street Bridge over the Potomac River. Curtiss and Director Winston looked back from one of the lead passenger vehicles at the flames from the Pentagon licking at the damp, thick cool night air. High explosive detonations could be heard destroying the building's computer and data centers, and communications facilities—shaped charges strobing the scene as they cut down satellite dishes, communication towers and the like.

"It looks like that Atlanta burning scene from *Gone With The Wind*," Director Winston said, looking over his shoulder.

"We never forgave you Yankees for that," General Mclelland said from the front passenger seat—his staff officer snickering behind the driver's wheel.

Upriver, an eerie pulsating orange light emanating from below the horizon about ten miles distant signaled that CIA Headquarters in Langley was ablaze. Director Winston held the Book of Honor on his lap.

The lead vehicle, a diesel smoke-spitting MRAP Buffalo, used its plow attachment to smash through a cluster of abandoned cars, clearing the way for their motorcade to head down Constitution Avenue and to come to a halt in front of the National Archives building.

General Mclelland checked to make sure a round was racked into the Yankee Fist he kept in his chest holster, then asked he and Director Winston: "Are you coming in?"

When Curtiss exited the vehicle it seemed as if he'd stepped into a hole: the protective service detachment that General Mclelland had hand picked for this assignment towered around him. They were some of the largest human beings Curtiss had ever seen off a football field. They wore extensive body armor, carried ballistic riot shields and were armed with AA-12s, and formed and moved in unison in a half-moon Spartan phalanx formation behind which the General, Director Winston, and Curtiss approached the building's main entrance.

The detail reformed behind them as General Mclelland banged on the brass-plated main door. After a third round of knocking a flashlight beam could be seen darting around the atrium within. They calmly watched as an old man in a security guard uniform struggled to not drop his flashlight while he flipped through a handful of electronic key cards. When the security lock turned green the detail burst into the quiet atrium like a dam had broken.

"We are here for the Constitution and the Declaration of Independence." General Mclelland's voice echoed through the atrium while the frail security guard looked around in amazement at the massive wall of soldiers surrounding him.

"I'm only the night watchman," he said shivering like it was ten degrees below zero. "I don't know what the code is. Only the Chief Archivist knows the . . . "

"We have the code," the general said while putting a slip of paper into the guard's shaking hand. "Please bring it up for us, now." He said in a softer tone. "We are in a bit of a hurry."

It took about ten minutes for the automated system to cycle and raise the documents to atrium level, and once the old man had relaxed he began filling the time with non-stop chatter. "So you boys are taking the Constitution and the Declaration of Independence," he chuckled. "Nobody comes here anymore to see those documents. Those government scoundrels sure don't use them anymore these days." Curtiss tried not to smile too much when it finally dawned on him that the old man looked and behaved for all the world like a Walter Brennan late-career character. "Heck, I don't think anyone in D.C. is even going to miss 'em." He quickly endeared himself to everyone around him.

"I've spent the last twenty-five years looking after these documents," he announced to the soldiers of the detachment who were using battery-powered drills to screw together a wooden crate around the glass and metal cases that held the documents. "Say, where are you boys going? I've got nothing holding me here in D.C. I'm a widower and all my children and grandchildren are out west. What do you say you take me along with you?"

General Mclelland broke a warmhearted smile. "Wherever these documents go this man goes," he announced as if he were giving an official order. Wrapping his arm around the old man's shoulder: "You can look after them for another twenty-five. How do you like Philly?"

"Oh, that's fine. That'll be just fine."

Heading up the Baltimore-Washington Parkway they found the truck columns that had stretched from the Potomac to the Beltway Wall over the past three days were gone. They had the expressway to themselves. Marine detachments blocked traffic from entering the expressway at all ten or so entrance and exit ramps along the final stretch to the wall. As was done with any VIP motorcade that rolls through town, just after it passed, the exits were reopened. But in the case of the Marines and the evacuation of D.C. they would pull up stakes, then fall in behind the motorcade on their way out of D.C.

Curtiss only peripherally noticed that General Mclelland had received a call on his satellite phone. He was therefore surprised a moment later to find the general looking at him from over the back of the front seat, extending his phone to him: "It's your wife."

Curtiss was taken aback by the sudden interjection of his former family life into a moment that could not have been more out of context. There was a rare panic in Leah's voice that Curtiss had heard from her only once or twice during their entire marriage. She explained that her car was blocked at one of the entrance ramps to the Baltimore-Washington Parkway and had just seen their motorcade pass by on the expressway. "Curt. You can't leave me behind here. It isn't right for Conner to have his mother locked away in some . . . prison," she found the word difficult to say. "Please, if our marriage meant anything to you," she corrected herself, " . . . if our son means anything to you help me get out of here, tonight."

Curtiss knew that Conner would never forgive him if he found out that he could have helped his mother, but didn't. He was about to tell her to sit tight and that he would work through diplomatic channels to get her out later, but she had already handed the phone to a Marine. "We are just about to move out, sir. Shall we bring her party with us?"

Curtiss could see the lights from the Beltway Wall fast approaching through their vehicle's windshield. "Yeah, okay, let her through."

*   *   *

Owing to utter exhaustion Curtiss slept through the morning, without dreaming—his consciousness seeming to have left the world entirely and entered a void. He woke refreshed, relaxed and at peace. He took a long, hot shower then began sorting through the toiletries and new clothing that had been prepared for him and that were placed on the second of the two hotel room beds.

Behind a pair of suitcases that he had last seen in North Dakota was the hard case for Rick's .30-378. He placed it on the bed, opened it, slid the bolt through the receiver bridge, shouldered the rifle, and quickly cycled the bolt a couple of times. It was all like a dream to him now: the revolution. That is what it was after all, a revolt. The people rising up to pry the fingers of usurpers from the throat of the country. And it was a relatively bloodless revolution, too. Better the blood of only a handful of tyrannical aristocrats and scoundrels refreshing the tree of liberty than them hiding behind the deaths of tens of thousands of innocents in a long, bloody war.

Curtiss racked the bolt again, slowly this time. Rick would have been pleased that his rifle had helped take down the most dangerous game that their generation would ever face. Rick Nanna would always be that confident image of courage that Curtiss saw standing on that berm at Badakhshan and so he still couldn't reconcile Rick' taking his own life when he could have stuck around and changed things—at worst, dying while fighting in a cause that he believed in. Dying in a cause that made a real difference and rescued the America he so loved. Then again, Rick had walked through the valley of death so many times; perhaps he didn't fear it like most people do. Perhaps it was just time for his story to come to an end.

The doorbell chimed and Curtiss found a young Marine in dress uniform standing at his door. "Sir, we wanted to let you know that your wife and her friend, Mr. Benedict, got through okay last night."

Benedict? How the hell did he get through? Then he recalled the Marine on the satellite phone asking him if he should let *her party* through. He had set Benedict free.

"Thank you, son," Curtiss said to the Marine who looked pleased to have successfully completed his assignment.

CHAPTER 30

Watching the mind-numbing parliamentary procedure of the provisional government as it worked through the mechanics in minutiae of the special elections to be held in three-month's time was the limit for Curtiss. He rose and left Independence Hall to stretch and stroll in the fresh air of the green.

The revolution was over. It was time for him to go home. He would bid his farewells in Philadelphia and leave for his house in Reston, Virginia the next day. He thought to drive to Penn State to see Conner, but decided not to. Would Conner hate him for his part in destroying his future as a D.C. aristocrat? Personally killing the principle architect of the world that he had spent years preparing for? What would he be in the eyes of his son, now? His father? A hero? Or, an assassin and terrorist? The destroyer of worlds. He would use the drive time on his way home to think about what he would say to him.

Curtiss looked up from his feet to spy the South Bend reporter and Director Winston completing an embrace, just before he opened the television van door for her and gently guided her in with his hand. Director Winston watched the van until it disappeared around a corner. He then turned around revealing the smile on his face and caught sight of Curtiss watching him. Director Winston approached on foot unsuccessfully reigning in the hint of swagger in his gait.

"She finally got her exclusive from you, huh?"

"A gentleman never tells," he said as he clapped his hand on Curtiss's shoulder and continued to Independence Hall without stopping.

"Is he the only one giving an exclusive today?" he heard spoken in a female British-accented voice.

Jacqueline.

Every disappointment and every sorrow, every disillusionment and every frustration, and every ache and every pain that he had experienced over the past thirty-two years left him at that moment. It was 1988 again, and he was young and in love. He turned to see her sitting on a nearby bench looking even more captivating than when he first saw her in the Chinatown restaurant.

"The whole world is watching, Curtiss," she said as he slowly stepped toward her. "I jumped on a plane as soon as I saw your interview with that reporter." She stood to receive his embrace.

The clock read 3:00 am. A gap in his hotel room curtains laid a ribbon of city light across Jacqueline's face on the pillow as Curtiss watched her sleep. Her scent, her touch, her voice, her passion overwhelmed his immune system triggering a relapse from the virulent pathogen of obsessive love that had laid dormant somewhere deep in his being. He wondered what had happened to the Tiffany's necklace that he had tried to give her the last time they'd lain together. Like their romance, it was lost somewhere in the years and among the many currents that carried them to different places. And that those currents eventually brought them together again now was kismet.

Then again, she could have found him anytime over the years. She needed only to keyword search his name on the Internet to find university websites referencing his speaking engagements—let alone the link to his bio on the CIA website. He knew of course that she was now there beside him because she was attracted to power and money, and notoriety. But he didn't care. That she was there with him was all that mattered. At his stage in life he didn't have the luxury to concern himself with making moral stands about why.

During an interlude in their lovemaking the night before she talked about her life with an openness and candor that he'd longed for from her when they were together in New York. Her father's passing away and her conflicting feelings about it. The new attitudes and mores in Taiwan that set her free from the imposition of the more archaic traditions. Her divorce, followed by *her* lost years, then dedicating herself to altruistic pursuits rather than solely self-indulgent ones. He pitied her not having children. She would have made beautiful children; *they* would have made beautiful children together. She shrugged it off as a choice that she made and didn't regret. He didn't believe her.

When room service knocked at their door at 7:00 am with their breakfast Curtiss went for the door while Jacqueline shot out of bed for the bathroom—giddy with laughter and wrapped only in the top sheet.

"Hey, you're one of the Riflemen," the room service attendant said as he rolled their room service cart into their room. "We were told that some of you were staying at our hotel." The attendant had a look of utter fascination on his face. Polite and respectful, he explained to Curtiss that he had been following them since they first became news. He asked Curtiss for career advice about joining the military now that it was part of the United States again. He refused the tip: "Thanks but no. Just meeting you is enough. And getting your advice."

The room door closed and Jacqueline swung open the bathroom door revealing her slender, fit mature body barely wrapped in a plush hotel towel. She leaning against the doorjamb with one luscious shoulder, pursed her lips, and nodded as she looked Curtiss up and down. He was certain that she was sizing him up for how comfortably he wore his newfound fame. She walked over, put her arms around his neck, and pulled him into the shower.

"Breakfast can wait."

Standing at the hotel's valet parking for their respective rides—Jacqueline's taxi to the airport and Curtiss's rental car for his drive back to Reston—he loathed parting with Jacqueline again, even if it were only for a short while. But Curtiss had to go to his house to see what was left of it. And, more important, he needed to reconnect with Conner, who he hadn't spoken with since before the day of reckoning. Jacqueline would go to her family's house on Maui where the two of them would be together again as soon as Curtiss could get there. He trusted Jacqueline, in spite of all that had happened, because there was nothing at stake for either of them now, being lovers. But he couldn't help but feel the same dread as when they last parted at the Brother Hotel entrance in Taipei. Same as it was then, as she looked at him through the taxi window while it drove away, it was as if a rope that had tethered their lives together had been severed—again.

* * *

It was dusk when Curtiss pulled into his driveway, where he could already tell that his house had been invaded. His lawn was long and scraggly and garbage—some in bags and some not—littered the landscaping around the front of the house. There was a plywood panel over one of the windows that he supposed was smashed to gain initial entry. Who put up the plywood? His feet crunched on a used syringe as he stepped into the foyer and saw the fist-sized holes in the wall leading up the staircase. Books were strewn across the library and shelves emptied, indicating that the looters had looked for a safe. He went to his gun safe under the stairs: it was scratched and the manual lock drilled, but it hadn't been opened. He scanned his index finger on the Biometric lock. It still worked.

Curtiss was putting Rick's rifle away when he heard footsteps above his head. He grabbed his home-defense pistol and cautiously made his way to where he was still under cover, but could put his sights on whoever was descending his stairs. His heart pounded in his ears as the shadowed image came into the light. It was Conner.

Conner stopped and turned, startled by the sound of Curtiss de-cocking his pistol. "Dad?"

The two of them spent the next two days cleaning up and making urgent repairs to the house. The looters had also squatted for a while and it seemed that there wasn't a part of the house that they'd left untouched. Everything seemed either damaged or soiled. At the beginning neither of them quite knew what to say to the other. Long stretches of silence were punctuated only by functional conversation: I'll order the pizza. Help me carry this down, will you? And, I'll get the dishes this time. It wasn't until the second evening over dinner that they began a conversation.

Conner had never had much interest in what Curtiss did for a living, but now asked about his time in Afghanistan. He told him about his exploits with the Agency, Keith the big Aussie, and Rick. And Rambo. But Curtiss was careful not to unduly glorify his brief war experience. Rather, he tried to impress upon Conner the character of the people who fought to preserve the way of life that Curtiss and they believed in. To recognize the sacrifices they had made and why.

The subject moved to his half-year in Guizhou: "That part of China in 1989 was a totally different time and place from what you're used to when you visit your mom's family in Beijing." He shared his adventures and his fears while a fugitive, and his thoughts about the serendipity of likely escaping on the very same roads that his father had taken forty-five years before. Conner's eyes lit up when he talked about his paternal grandfather and Curtiss could see that he was eager to learn more.

"I never really knew your grandfather. I was too young when he died to remember much." Talking about his father was the toughest conversation Curtiss would have with Conner. Curtiss was well able to deal with his own emotions, but he felt a responsibility to present his grandfather to him in a way that was both accurate and meaningful. So, though he enumerated the things his grandfather did during his life, his accomplishments and the history he was part of, he described *who* he was as a person through talking about Sonya. Curtiss could only smile when he realized that even now she was still helping him with the most important things in his life.

As their discussion went on well into the evening they launched into debating their points of view and life philosophies, sharing in a way that the two of them hadn't for as long as Curtiss could remember—maybe for the first time ever. They still didn't agree on everything, indeed Curtiss hoped Conner would always have his own views and opinions. But they now listened and began to understand each other. And nothing in Curtiss's life was more fulfilling.

Late the next afternoon Conner needed to leave, to head back to university to take exams. When he went out the back door to retrieve his motorcycle Curtiss went to his safe and retrieved a legal-sized envelope. He met Conner on the driveway and held it up in front of him to show that it was from the U.S. Military Intelligence Corps and had a typewriter-typed mailing label that was addressed to Curtiss at his former Milton Hershey School student home.

"This is the official report about the circumstances surrounding your grandfather's death," Curtiss shouted over the hum of the motorcycle. "I never worked up the courage to open it myself." Curtiss unzipped Conner's backpack and slid it in. "Maybe it will help you get to know your grandfather a little better."

Curtiss recognized his little boy again in Conner's eyes that were tearing up within his helmet's visor. When Curtiss stepped back to allow him to roll onto the street and watched him get on his way he realized that he had succeeded: he did not condemn Conner to a family curse of parents dying on their young children. Conner was a young man and he was now certain that he was on the right track.

* * *

Curtiss was alone again. The echoes from the whirlwind that was his recent life tapered off and the silence of his empty house returned. As did the loneliness. Asleep in his living room recliner chair he woke from the whirring of the electronic front door lock. Someone walked in. It was dark outside. What time was it? Did Conner forget something? He dropped the leg rest, stood and was met by a flash from the dark foyer, accompanied by a punch in the gut that took his legs out, the wind completely out of him, as a hot metal bullet burned in his liver.

Lying flat on his back, James Benedict's face appeared in Curtiss's tunneling field of vision. "Let this be the last shot of your revolution," he said as he trained his pistol's muzzle on Curtiss's head and returned him to the void.

ABOUT THE AUTHOR

Lawrence Allen lived in Greater China for 20 years. While at university his parents made an early, pioneering trip to China in 1980. Intrigued by their photos and tales from a newly emerging China, Lawrence linked his interest in international business with his fascination for China. He launched his career serving various executive roles with multinational companies in Taipei, Taiwan in 1989, followed by postings in Hong Kong, Shanghai, and Beijing.

In 2010 Lawrence published *Chocolate Fortunes: The Battle for the Hearts, Minds, and Wallets of China's Consumers* (AMACOM 2010), a China business book that chronicles the quarter-century battle between the world's chocolate companies for the hearts, minds, and taste buds of China's emerging chocolate consumers. Chinese language edition:

巧克力之战
世界五大巧可力巨头的中国竞争战略
［美］劳伦斯。艾伦（Lawrence L. Allen）著
冷迪 译
中国人民大学出版社
China Renmin University Press